MW01119940

The Crying Orchid

(A fictional novel about a young woman's challenging life experiences of her near death experience, love, betrayal, sexual abuse and domestic violence as well as her humanity, strength and resiliency in being able to leave the abusive relationship and start her life over with a young child. The suspenseful novel captures the impact of trauma that stems from child abuse, early warning signs and patterns of abusive relationships and the cycle of domestic violence while the readers follow the intertwined lives of the main characters from an eastern European environment in the 1980s.)

By

GABRIELA ELIAS

abbott press®
A DIVISION OF WRITER'S DIGEST

Abbott Press books may be ordered through booksellers or by contacting:

Abbott Press
1663 Liberty Drive
Bloomington, IN 47403
www.abbottpress.com
Phone: 1-866-697-5310

Because of the dynamic nature of the Internet, any web addresses or links contained in this book may have changed since publication and may no longer be valid. The views expressed in this work are solely those of the author and do not necessarily reflect the views of the publisher, and the publisher hereby disclaims any responsibility for them.

Any people depicted in stock imagery provided by Thinkstock are models, and such images are being used for illustrative purposes only.
Certain stock imagery © Thinkstock.

ISBN: 978-1-4582-1429-4 (sc)
ISBN: 978-1-4582-1431-7 (hc)
ISBN: 978-1-4582-1430-0 (e)

Library of Congress Control Number: 2014902608

Printed in the United States of America.

Abbott Press rev. date: 03/24/2014

Author's Note

ONE IN EVERY THREE WOMEN around the world has been beaten, forced into sex or has been otherwise abused during her life.[1] Domestic violence is prevalent in 324,000 pregnant women each year perpetrated by an intimate partner.[2] Women are more likely to be injured during a domestic violence dispute than men.[3]

The statistical numbers are even higher as these domestic violence incidents are often unreported. Although emotional/mental abuse is often more damaging to a person as it is more difficult to recover from because the emotional wounds are much deeper and it is more challenging to leave such a relationship as the woman often questions whether there is real abuse happening in the first place or wonders whether it simply was a common argument that she experienced with her partner. When does it cross the line? On the other hand, the physical abuse is generally easier to recover from because the bruises and broken bones, as painful as they can be, eventually heal faster than the emotional wounds and the woman is more likely to leave the physically abusive relationship sooner; however, it can be sometimes deadly. More often, there is a combination of the different types of abuse including emotional/verbal abuse, physical and yes, sometimes even sexual abuse (even if it is from the husband/partner that the woman is normally intimate with).

There is no excuse for abuse, yet women often stay in abusive relationships for years and they cannot leave for various reasons. There is this well known phenomenon of emotional paralysis that has been well researched in women experiencing domestic violence. People who do not understand and/or have not experienced domestic violence often question – "Why doesn't she just leave him?" But if you are in this situation, you know very well why. You know it is not that easy. There are many barriers whether it is financial, lack of supports, emotional attachment to the abusive partner, believing that it is best for the children to try to make it work, or simply not believing in yourself that you can have or deserve better. These are just few of the examples of why women stay or have such difficulties leaving in the first place. It is harder for women to leave when they go through the full cycle of domestic violence going from a "critical violent incident" to what we call a "honeymoon period" where the man apologizes, sometimes buys flowers and other gifts and says nice and loving things to his female partner often asking for forgiveness and promising he will not do it again, promising he will change because he loves her. This is often what keeps women in violent relationships for many years because it gives them hope albeit false and they feel that this is the only person that will ever want them and love them because they often suffer from a very low self-esteem and self-worth. The cycle becomes shorter, going through it faster, experiencing more frequent abusive incidents which are often more intense and dangerous. The "honeymoon period" usually does not last very long and soon the woman starts to feel the tension in her home building up before another violent event follows. And so the cycle continues. In many cases the "honeymoon period" is either non-existent, or it eventually disappears. The cycle then continues with "tension building" to a "critical incident".

There is also often a generational cycle that might have contributed to the fact that if you are a woman who has witnessed domestic violence as a child, you will likely chose an abusive partner. If you are a man who has witnessed domestic violence as a child and although you might have been quite protective of your mother in your childhood, as an adult or even as a teenager you are likely to display abusive behaviours to your wife, common law-partner or a girlfriend because that what was modeled for you. If you are in an abusive relationship, think about what your children are seeing and learning and how it will impact them in their life.

Working as a Child and Family Therapist in a therapeutic setting with trauma resulting from issues of domestic violence impacting abused women as well as their children, I wanted to bring awareness to domestic violence and other types of abuse, such sexual abuse to women across the world in a new and creative way, by writing this fictional novel that captures the red flags of an abusive relationship, the cycle of violence and the difficulties of leaving an abusive relationship. Although it is a suspenseful story with fictional characters and imagined events, I tried to use typical abusive signs before and during the domestic violence. Such signs often include, but are not limited to isolation, violent temper, hitting/punching/throwing things, yelling, blaming his abusive behavior on his partner and many other abusive signs, such as restricting her from working, controlling her financially or preventing her from having other friendly relationships.

In this book, I have also used typical behaviours of men that perpetrate domestic violence to capture the cycle of abuse and the difficulty for a woman to leave such a relationship. I have also included the faulty thinking that women often experience which makes it difficult for them to leave. A woman in an abusive relationship tends to leave on average about seven different times before she definitely leaves as she keeps returning for various reasons. This story also portrays humanity, hope, strength and resiliency.

Although I am aware that domestic violence also happens to men, elderly people (both male and female) and same gender couples; this book is focusing on typical domestic violence perpetrated by a man towards a woman as it is more common. Domestic violence happens in every culture, in every part of the world although it appears to be more tolerated in some cultures and/or some countries. In Slovakia and Czech Republic (previously called Czechoslovakia) before the separation in 1993, the term 'Domestic Violence' was not commonly used and to this day it still does not have the same meaning as for example in North America.

When I visited Slovakia in 2006 I had difficulties explaining what I do for living when I tried to clarify that I help treat women recovering from trauma and issues of domestic violence and work with perpetrators of domestic violence to recover from their own trauma and acknowledge and change their abusive behaviours. It can be translated as violence but it is often used in the context of sexual violence often understood as rape usually perpetrated by strangers. Some cultures have predominant beliefs that the 'Man' is the head of the household and therefore can treat his wife/partner whichever way he pleases. Slapping on occasion is often tolerated and it is not considered abusive in some cultures. Not to overstep on any cultural and/or religious beliefs, personally I do believe that whether it is an occasional slap, name calling, yelling, demeaning behaviour or whether it is sexual or physical violence, it is all abuse and women do not need to tolerate it, or anyone for that matter.

A woman who has just left an abusive relationship is usually at a highest risk as she is trying to get power and control back into her life. In turn, the male perpetrator of domestic violence is losing the power and control and has the need to get it back sometimes at a very high cost. There is a right and a wrong way to leave an abusive relationship. Often women feel 'safer' while they stay in the relationship because they usually know what to expect even when it is abusive. Please make sure that you have the supports and stay safe especially when you decide to leave an abusive partner. There is help out there. If you or someone you know is experiencing domestic violence you can call 'The National Domestic Violence Hotline' at 1800-799-SAFE (7233) or call your local women's shelter in your area.

If you are a man reading this book and you find yourself in some of these characters perpetrating domestic violence or sexual abuse towards your loved one, please know that I do not think you are an evil person or that this cannot change for you. I have worked with mandated men that perpetrated domestic violence and I am amazed at how much pain and suffering these men have endured through their own traumatic/abusive experiences often from their own childhood. It is no excuse for abuse, but I understand it changed who you are or who you could be.

There is help available to heal from your own trauma and to understand your own abusive behavioural patterns and how to change them. You are not the monster that people might believe you to be, but you are wounded soul that needs to heal the inner child within you. Nobody is born bad; nobody was born to become an abuser. Something changed you along the way. Hopefully, this book will help you stop making excuses and blaming others for your abusive behaviours and you need to be honest with yourself. You will be a lot happier man. Do it for yourself and if you have children, do it for your children because they suffer the most as they have no other choice and are often caught in the middle. You know who you are and be honest with yourself first. You can call the 'National Resource Center on Domestic Violence' at 1800-537-2238 to seek help and to heal from your own trauma or call a counseling agency in your area. There is no shame in that. It takes a courageous and a big man to do that. Admitting your mistakes is 50% of work done towards recovery.

Whether you are a woman living in an abusive relationship or a man that has been abusive with his partner at any point in time, you can change your life around and live happier lives. Your children will thank you for that. Do not let them continue in the same troubled path; in the same generational cycle of abuse. Break the cycle of domestic violence now.

Prologue

1988

MICHAELA WAS PACING BACK AND forth in the two bedroom apartment after she tucked her little girl into bed. She did not know when her husband, Eddy would be home or what she could expect from him each night. But she knew this waiting game way too well; this feeling of anticipation, unpredictability and fear. It was like walking on egg shells before another big blow up. Sometimes things were just fine and her husband was very loving and attentive to her. She did love that part of him so much and did not want to give up on their love. But when he was drinking, he became a different person. He became a monster that she feared. She knew that he often drank to a point that the next morning he would be oblivious to what he has done the previous night and blamed her for any damage, often denying that he played any role in it. She feared every pay day as that was the likely time that her husband went out drinking with his buddies and spent majority of their money. This would not be the first time that they would not have money for rent or for food. This would not be the first time that Michaela would have to ask her mother for financial help just to make it to the next pay day.

Michaela's anxiety was building up even though she made sure that everything was perfect before Eddy came home. The supper was ready on the stove, the table was set for supper even though it was getting late, the apartment was neat and clean and their daughter, Orchid was sound asleep for the night. They chose this unusual name because it means a fragrant flower symbolizing love, beauty and sophistication. And little

Orchid had all those qualities even at age three. What she did not have was a peaceful home, despite her mother's attempts to calm things down in her relationship. Michaela loved her daughter with all her heart and would do anything for her. Even when it meant putting up with Eddy's violent temper when he was drinking because she knew that he loved his daughter too and Orchid deserved a whole family. Michaela knew how difficult it was for her mother as a single parent when their father left them when she was only couple years older than Orchid. Eddy could be such a loving and caring father; nothing like her absent father that was never there for her. And little Orchid adored her daddy when he played with her and bought her dolls. She wanted her to be happy, playful, untroubled little girl that she deserved to be. She has to make it work; she can't give up on their love; on their marriage. That's the easy way out, she thought. Isn't it? She didn't want her daughter to come from a broken home like she lived in as a little girl. She knew too well how terrible that felt to her growing up not even remembering her own father.

Eddy did love his little girl, but at times he also made her feel scared and often made her cry, just like he made mommy cry. Little Orchid tried to stifle her cries the best that she could because even at a young age she already knew that Daddy did not like when she cried and it made him very angry, but sometimes she could not help it. Nevertheless he would never hurt his little girl. She was his little flower; his little princess that he adored.

Michaela tried to distract herself by watching TV while waiting for her husband. She tugged her legs under her, covering herself with a brown blanket that provided her with some warmth as she felt the chills go down her back when she thought of the worst possible situation. She was flipping channels mindlessly as nothing caught her attention; her mind wondering somewhere else. The long wait made her dose off waking up to a loud banging on the door and yelling. She quickly checked her watch; it was 12:37 a.m. and she immediately knew that it would be a tough night. She ran to open the door for Eddy before he woke little Orchid up as he was getting lauder, trying to get in. Michaela knew from being married to Eddy for four years that when he was drunk, it was best to be just quiet and hope she would not do anything to provoke him and that he would just go to bed to sleep it off and tomorrow would be a new day; different Eddy. But she knew that Eddy never went to bed right away when he was drunk. In fact he would become aggressive, even violent and not remember anything the next day.

"Where the fuck are you?" Eddy yelled at her after she opened the door. He tumbled into the kitchen adjacent to Orchid's room and yelled at her.

"Woman, where is my fuckin' dinner?" Before Michaela had a chance to respond or give him a plate with his food, Eddy started pulling all the plates down from the cupboards starting with the bottom one, breaking everything he touched and making horrendous noise.

"No, not again. STOP, please, Eddy, stop, you'll wake Orchid up ….wait I'll give you your supper". It was too late; she quickly realized that mentioning their daughter's name at this point was a big mistake as he headed towards Orchid's room.

"Kid…..Kid!" He sometimes called his daughter 'Kid' for short as a derivative from her name, which Michaela despised but at the moment that was least of her worries.

"Where are you my little flower? Come to me. Daddy is home." Eddy was slurring his words and stumbling into his daughter's room. She needed to stop him before he opened the door and woke the little girl up. Although he never hurt Orchid, there was volatility of what he would do in his drunken state which he would normally not do when he was sober. Michaela instinctively and without lucidity grabbed an empty cooking pan that was sitting on the nearby stove and hit him over the head with it; not to hurt him but to stop him….she had to stop him for the sake of their daughter.

Much to her surprise, Eddy did not fall to the ground after the impact. He shook his head briefly and turned his two hundred pounds body towards her physically unaffected by the impact but a lot angrier he lashed out for Michaela. She tried to run out of his way as he reached for her, but it was too late. He grabbed her by her long brown hair and dragged her towards the balcony. The cool November night sent chills down her spine as did Eddy's unpredictable reactions. Michaela was crying in pain, pleading for him to stop.

"I'm sorry, Eddy, please don't hurt me, please stop…." but Michaela's pleas were futile.

Instinctively she grabbed the curtain to hold on to as he dragged her over the threshold of the balcony grabbing her by her neck trying to push her over the fence. Luckily the metal curtain rod did not give in. Michaela's back was pressed against the railing. Half of her body was leaning over the balcony, her feet losing the ground from under her as Eddy was pressing her hard against the railing. She briefly looked down from the ten story building down to the concrete ground realizing her life hung on a thin line. Hanging with her head upside down she was sure if she fell there would be only a bloody mess left of her. She realized that the curtain that she was still clutching in her hands was her only chance of survival or maybe not. All of a sudden Michaela heard screams from her three year old daughter that distracted her father.

"Mommy………MOMMY!!!!! Orchid was screeching, terror in her face, big brown eyes staring in fear. Michaela was sure he would have throttled her to death if it was not for the sudden scream from the kitchen that quickly caught his attention. Eddy suddenly dropped Michaela down on the balcony floor like a little rag doll. Michaela holding her sore neck from the pressure of his fingers, trying to catch her breath and get to her feet, while Eddy turned his drunken awareness to their daughter walking back into the kitchen where Orchid was standing and crying uncontrollably. Wearing her pink pajamas with flowers in the middle of her top, she clutched her teddy bear to her chest, her little body shaking with fear. Even in her young age, she knew something was wrong. With her big brown eyes that she inherited after her father, she was watching his every move, mortified with fear as her father was fuming and walking towards her, bumping into the table and chairs. Eddy grabbed his daughter's small body with a force as she was screaming and in an instant Michaela realized that her worst nightmare has only begun.

Chapter 1

1984

"I DON'T WANT TO GO on vacation with my family", Nikole complained to her friend, Michaela.

"Are you kidding Niki", you don't know what you're missing. Going to Bulgaria to the Black Sea…I would go in an instant", Michaela said wistfully.

"You don't understand, Mika", that's what her friend called her for short, "we are going by a van, packed up for a month with camping supplies on a three or four day road trip through three countries all the way to the Turkish border before we pitch a tent. Then we sleep in the tent on the floor for a whole month. Yeah, sure, the beach and the sea will be nice but listening to my parents' bickering in a small space, nowhere to escape is not my idea of a fun."

"Don't worry Niki, you'll be just fine. I'm sure it's worth it." Michaela tried to reassure her friend, but Niki complained further.

"Did I mention that my annoying brother is tagging along with us and I have to share the back seat with him smelling his sticky feet?" They both laughed.

"Give it a break, Nikolas is quite cute."

"Are you kidding me? He is a little brat."

"He is nineteen." Michaela pointed out.

"He may be sixteen months older than me, but his brain is that of a thirteen year old annoying brat that does what he wants. I'm really not looking to this long boring trip. I wish you could come with us at least. Then it will be fun."

"And where would you guys pack me up? On top of your minivan?" They both laughed again.

"But seriously, would your mom let you go with us if my parents were ok with it?"

The same evening Niki pleaded with her parents to take her best friend to the Bulgarian Black Sea coast so she would not "die from boredom" as she put it. While Niki was persuading her parents, Michaela was working on her mother to let her go until she finally agreed although with a great hesitation and great worry about all the dangers that might be "out there" waiting for Michaela.

The two girls were friends since kindergarten and their mothers were good friends too, so for Klaudia Martenz it was not that she did not trust the Senko family with her only daughter, but not having any control over what happens. She trusted the family and trusted Michaela that she would follow all the "rules" and not get involved with anyone, not separate herself from the family alone and will not go into the deep water especially since Michaela did not know how to swim. Michaela gladly agreed to all her mother's conditions just so she would let her go.

It worked itself out when the two mothers discussed it over coffee the next day. Klaudia Martenz was beside herself with worry about her daughter going without her for such a long time to a foreign country, in fact through several countries.

"Not to mention the dangers of the sea and young boys preying on young beautiful girls like Michaela", said Ms. Martenz to her friend, Maria. Maria Senko has reassured her that Michaela will be safe and they will take a good care of her.

"You know I will take care of Michaela as good as my own daughter. I understand that you're worried, but don't forget, we will be there at all times and will watch over her. Both of our kids are going, so don't worry; I'll watch them as hawks. The tent is big enough and the girls will have their privacy on one of the separate sides of the tent. It's a great opportunity to go to the sea."

"I don't doubt that, but how can I compensate for what you're doing for her?"

"Trust me; you will be doing me a favour when you let Michaela go. She is a good girl and I'm worried if she doesn't come, Niki will pull out her defiant attitude and will refuse to go. And I can't leave her here alone for a month. She'll set the house upside down. She already has been giving me grief about this long trip, but if she has her best friend with her....well, both girls will have so much more fun together this summer", concluded Mrs. Senko.

Klaudia Martenz had to admit to herself that as a single parent she would never be able to afford any kind of vacation by the sea. She did not even have a car, so giving Michaela such a great opportunity to see the ocean was something she could only dream about. Of course, she was nervous and went on a long preaching about all the things that Michaela is not allowed to do and specific instructions to follow, such as not going anywhere with anyone and not going too deep into the ocean. Michaela embraced her mother with excitement realizing her mother telling her all these rules about what she should and should not be doing means a positive answer for her to go on this amazing vacation with the Senko family. Michaela was very excited about this trip because she did not go anywhere her whole life even though her mom worked two jobs, but money was always tight. She never knew her father, even though from pictures she knew who he was, but he never bothered to visit her or even send her a birthday card. She knew her mom would never be able to afford much along a car; not to mention a vacation by the sea.

In four days the Senko family along with Michaela set out for the long camping trip to the Bulgarian coast by the Black Sea in Varna. They knew that it was a long trip, especially with one driver, Nikole's father, it would take them at least three or four days, but it was affordable rather than going by the plane which was only a dream that was not realistic for the Senko family even though they considered themselves to be a middle class family. They were going to take advantage to look at and enjoy some tourist attractions along the way. The two places they wanted to visit on their trip was the Miskolc Tapolca Thermal Spas in Hungary and in Romania they were planning on visiting the Bran village that surrounded the Transylvania Castle of the famous Wallachian prince, Vlad Tepes; known as the Draculas's Castle although it is only a common myth that he was the one who built it.

Nikolas who recently got his driver's license at the age 18 as in Czechoslovakia a person had to be eighteen years to receive a driver's license after an extensive testing and CPR course, he was hoping to get finally his turn in driving the family car although his father was hesitant about that.

Packed up all the way to the roof, the minivan was sitting low and the drive seemed long and slow, especially after the Hungarian border, for the longest time, there was only one lane each way. And although drivers could pass it, they had to of course give the right of way and the traffic was quite busy. To pass several cars in the row, took quite a bit of risk going into the upcoming traffic and since Mr. Senko was a very safe driver, the first day on their venture seemed extremely long. They took their small breaks at the local park stops to stretch their legs from sitting for hours, despite the spacious minivan, but the large tent and many other things they needed for a month of camping took a lot of space and they had bags even beside their feet.

Nikolas did not have to say much but it was obvious that he was quite happy about his sister's friend coming with them because he always had a secret crush on her and was quite excited about this vacation. He often threw a glance in Michaela's direction who was sitting with Nikole in the very back seat. He often turned to them and tried to entertain the girls with his jokes or clever remarks.

Although Miskolc was not too far from Kosice, their home town in Czechoslovakia, with a snail pace that Mr. Senko was driving it took them a while to arrive at Tapolca Thermal Spas despite leaving early in the morning. Certainly it was worth the wait. As they walked towards the main building of the thermal cave baths of Miskolc-Tapolca luxurious spas and saunas, they saw people walking in their bathing suits in an out of the building; some enjoying the summer day on the patio, eating and drinking under large red umbrellas. In front of the building to the left side was a gorgeous white statue of a naked woman with a small fountain in front of her. Michaela admired the view and even the building with its large semi-circle windows that surrounded each side of the main entrance. She was quite excited to see what awaited them inside. She often heard about the magical caves and the healing powers of the thermal baths that were in these caves.

After they changed into their bathing suits they met at the pool of the cave bath. Tipping her toes first to test the water for temperature, Michaela felt nice warm water washing over her left foot. It was pleasant and she did not hesitate any longer and went into the heavenly blue waters. Nikole and the rest of the family followed, sitting in the water on the edges around the cave bath, looking at the marvelous natural designs of the cave. Michaela closed her eyes relaxing in this warm healing water, thinking that this is what a good life feels like; going places enjoying yourself; not worrying about the cost of it. Nikolas interrupted her train of thoughts.

"Do you want to see the rest of the cave?"

"Yes, I do." Michaela agreed with enthusiasm. Nikole joined them on their venture, while Mr. and Mrs. Senko had a moment alone for themselves, sitting and enjoying the healing powers of the thermal water.

Nikolas took every opportunity to hold Michaela's hand as in helping her walk through the shallow water that reached only up to Michaela's chest. At one point they had to get out of the waters walking through a small staircase overlooking the shapes and arches of the natural caves where the waters were from the natural stones giving it a healing power. Here the waters were bluish green.

"This is a deeper end of the pools where we can swim right under the arches of the caves." Nikolas explained and held out his hand to Michaela once again.

"Come." Nikole, who was a good swimmer, did not hesitate and submerged herself in the deep water that was slightly cooler but felt good on her warm skin; she was swimming with enjoyment.

"Come on guys, the water is exquisite." She exclaimed.

Michaela hesitated and finally said.

"I can't.....Nik, I can't swim. I can't go into the deep end."

"Don't worry, Mika, you're with me. Nothing is going to happen to you. Don't be scared. Climb onto my back once we're in the water and we'll swim together. You just hold on to me and I promise, I will not let you go." When he saw her debating with herself whether she should stay where she was or go on this new venture with Nikolas he wanted to reassure her and repeated.

"Promise, I'll never let you go." He licked his two fingers and held them up in a pledge manner. After a short hesitancy looking forward seeing more of the cave's picturesque site, she agreed.

"Ok, let's do it. I trust you, Nik."

She held on to Nikolas' strong back, wrapping her arms around his neck, as they submerged themselves into the deep end of the cooler water. Nikolas was a great swimmer; he even volunteered as a life-guard throughout the year at the indoor local pool in Kosice. Now his confidence and great swimming skills came in handy and he was swimming slowly making sure Michaela did not slip off his back. He liked the feel of her body wrapped around his back and her arms holding from behind around his neck. Michaela thought one moment he sneaked a small kiss on one of her arms that was holding tight onto him as he was swimming but perhaps that was just the water washing over her arms as she was distracted with the beautiful arcades of the cave. He reassured her when he felt her body tensing.

"Just relax and enjoy the view. I got you."

She smiled to herself and definitely was enjoying herself. They swam around a curve of the cave going then back to the shallow end of the other pool back into the warmer water. The thermal waters temperature was at least 30 degrees warm and it was a pleasant change from the cooler pool in the cave.

Michaela thanked Nikolas for swimming with her and showing her the deeper and mysterious side of the cave.

"This is amazing. All of it; I have never seen anything like that." She had a bright smile on her face as all three of them tried the thermal whirlpool where the water was even hotter.

"Now lets the vacation begin." Nikole said with enthusiasm and she was glad after all that she came with her family, even though it might not sound 'cool' to go at 17 with your parents, but she no longer cared; she had her friend with her and she was having fun. Even her brother, Nikolas did not annoy her as much as she thought he would, unless he was teasing her about something or splashing her with water.

Michaela was sad having to leave the magical caves and wonderful healing waters. She could have stayed here whole summer vacation, but it was time to move forward. She did not know what else awaited them and what she would have missed out on.

After a great relaxing afternoon at Tapolca, the Senko family and Michaela headed on their way to their destination. They decided to sleep in Hungary close to the Romanian border as they believed it to be cheaper than in Romania and as the night was setting in. They picked a cheap motel in Debrecen and took two rooms. Nikole and Michaela shared the motel room and Nikolas was in the same room sleeping on a cot with his parents just so they would save up on the overnight accommodation.

In the morning, right after breakfast they were again on the road. Once they crossed the Romanian boarder, they stopped in a local small store to get some drinks. Michaela walked into the store shocked what she has seen. Coming from a small town in Slovakia under the Communist era, growing in a single parent household was difficult and she was not accustomed to any luxuries, but nothing has prepared her for what she saw in this small Romanian town. Walking into the small store she was shocked to see a huge dice of soap that was to be cut for the customers and some cans and nothing else. A young woman grabbed Nikole by her arm and started to pull on her jean jacket showing her a bunch of their money indicating she wanted to buy it. Nikole shook her head no, but there were many others that started to approach the tourists and were talking to them in Romanian wanting to buy their things; whatever it was.

Maria coming from a Hungarian background herself spoke well Hungarian. She spoke to one of the local Hungarian man who explained that a small percentage of Hungarians lived in this region and spoke usually both Hungarian and Romanian. The old man also explained that people generally have their money, but they don't have what to buy and whenever people see tourists, who are packed up going on vacation to the sea, they know they have lot of things with them and hope to buy anything; clothes, shoes, food.

Michaela exchanged glances with her friend. Despite living from her mother's pay check to pay they were never rich, but they never starved, no matter how difficult times they experienced. It was truly a sad picture seeing little kids running towards them barefoot grabbing onto their clothes and pointing to their shoes. They just wanted to leave from this power stricken town as quickly as possible. First time Michaela saw what real poverty was like and thought that nobody should live like that. She hoped for a better life for herself when she was older.

Mrs. Senko noticed several cars with CS signs on their cars indicating that they come from Czechoslovakia. Maria Senko was a social butterfly and easily engaged in conversations with others she just met, finding out about their destinations as it was obvious they were tourists just as the Senko's.

Mr. Simon Senko was a polar opposite of his wife. He was getting tired already from all the driving and was frowning, totally disengaged from others. Although he was a good hearted man and dearly cared about his family, his facial expression would put off many people that have just met him. He stretched his body before he had to go back into the van and drive, when Maria enthusiastically told him that there are four different families from their country and one Hungarian family heading to the Transylvanian Alps where they wanted to visit "Dracula's Castle" or other surrounding areas. Maria excitedly continued.

"You know, Simon, it is so much safer to follow up in a group, especially when we have to sleep somewhere in the middle of the mountains".

"Yes, and Dracula will come and bite you at night," he mocked his wife who was not laughing at his unsuccessful joke.

"I'm not worried about Dracula but about Gypsies or other gangs that might attack us at night for a piece of bread. Look at how poor these people are. I wouldn't be surprised if some made it their living by stealing from tourists. They would take the clothes from your back. And besides," she went on, "it is too much to drive through Romania and Bulgaria in one shot. I'm sure you don't want to drive all day and night."

"Well, it's not like you're driving. But you're right, darling." His voice softening as it always did when he talked to his wife whom he adored for over twenty years.

"I don't want to drive throughout the night. I need my beauty sleep." He attempted another joke that he laughed at lightheartedly. It made Maria smile although she did not always find his jokes as amusing as he did, but she adored his sense of humour. After a short while she continued with excitement.

"All the other families agreed to stay together at least until we arrive at the Transylvanian Alps and we would go our separate ways throughout the day and sleep in a designated area, in a group at night to stay safe." All the families when Mrs. Senko spoke to them were in agreement about why waste more money on hotels if they can sleep in tents or cars.

Mr. Senko agreed with his wife who so eloquently made all the arrangements acknowledging that she had some valid arguments.

"All right, we'll stay with the group for now", Simon agreed.

Chapter 2

THEY ARRIVED AT TRANSYLVANIAN ALPS before noon. They found a designated area at a large parking lot where six families, including Senko's family agreed to meet at around eight o'clock in the evening. The families then scattered in different directions; some went into the nearby villages or towns, some went hiking, while others drove up to the Bran Castle to admire the historical fortress with all its treasures. Mr. and Mrs. Senko thought that this is what they should have done after they experienced their short-lived hiking adventure realizing that it was no longer for them.

They all enthusiastically started their early afternoon hike from Transylvania on the main route through the Bran Mountain pass. Nikolas holding a tourist map in his hand was in the lead along with Michaela who was in a good shape thanks to her regular jogging, while Nikole did not seem to enjoy the hiking adventure after about the first kilometer and was tagging slowly behind them along with her parents who could not keep up with the two enthusiasts. They saw more frequent sites of carts with horses on their way. Nikole with her parents soon gave up the hike and settled in for lunch that they brought in their backpacks in the middle of a meadow on a large rock overseeing the picturesque view of the pastoral landscapes where the shepherds tended to their flocks.

"Well, what about you? Do you want to continue on this hike with me?" Nikolas asked Michaela mysteriously.

"Of course, I'd love that." Michaela answered excitedly and was eager to move forward on their journey admiring the wonderful landscape.

"I had enough." Nikole complained and sat down on another rock beside her mother. "I don't think I'll go all the way."

"Join the club." Mrs. Senko said out of breath and was glad to be sitting on the rock even though not very comfortably.

"It will take you at least another three or four hours to go up and come back down." Mr. Senko pointed out looking at a tourist guide and was handing it to Nikolas.

"I know you always wanted to see the Bran Castle Nik and had your heart set on this wonderful hiking tour, but make sure you're back before dark. It gets darker in the mountains faster. We'll go back to the car and just drive around to the Castle that will be easier for us. How about we meet you in front of the Castle by seven thirty and then we go meet with the other families like we promised?"

"Sounds good to me, dad. And don't worry; we will not get stuck in the mountains in the dark."

He turned to Michaela and asked again.

"Are you up for an adventure?"

"Absolutely."

"Nikolas, you take good care of her as if it was your own sister." His mother warned him. Although Nikolas never looked at Michaela as his sister as he liked her for a long time and was excited to spend some alone time with her, he quickly reassured his mother.

"Don't worry mom, she is in good hands." Michaela smiled and nodded her agreement.

"I have no doubt."

"Take lots of pictures on your way, Nik. Alright?" Nikole reminded her brother.

"Do you want to take an extra bottle of water?" His mother queried.

"Don't worry guys. I have everything under control." Rummaging through his backpack to make sure he had everything they needed before they continued further on their mysterious hiking adventure, he double checked his things.

"Camera - check, bottles of water - check, warm clothing - check, sandwiches - check, tourist guide and map - check, flash lights – check, compass and watch – check, hat and sunglasses attached, head on my shoulders – check, toilet paper – check, Michaela - check." He looked up and gave her a quick wink and a bright smile. He was so happy she was coming with him.

"I think now I have everything." He added.

"Now, you're set for sure." Nikole laughed at his last few inventories.

"I have extra things like that too, so I'm sure we will be just fine." Michaela added to reassure his parents. She was wearing her comfortable hiking shoes as was Nikolas and she was ecstatic to go on this adventure. She has never been in Romania; not along to see the legendary Castle of Vlad Dracula.

Michaela and Nikolas continued on their several hours journey overseeing the breathtaking wild Carpathian Mountains in the Transylvanian Alps. As they were moving away from the rest of the troops, Michaela joked.

"Hmm, interesting how you stack the order of importance," referring to his little "checking" joke he had made back in the valley. They both laughed again although she was not very fast with come backs.

"You're always my number one." He said it more seriously and touched her cheek gently. Michaela blushed and put her head down shyly moving quickly ahead of him on the path. He caught up with her with ease.

"I'm glad you came with me because you're the only one that can keep up with me on this hike." He teased her trying to make her more comfortable and joking often worked great between them. To prove his point, he ran ahead of her few meters calling to her to hurry up holding out his hand to her to help her. She caught up with him and they ran a short distance together hand in hand their backpacks jumping on their backs resembling from the distance two silly little kids skipping together on their venture.

"Look. Look this way." He pointed to the side of the path overseeing the meadow below through the trees a picturesque view of different shades of green. She saw yellow and purple flowers from far away. She saw little white houses with red brick roofs in the distance that looked like a miniature world out of a story book that gave this place its mysterious feel.

"That must be the Bran village ahead of us." She exclaimed excitedly. And that tall peak in the distance.....that is the castle, right?" Michaela caught her breath, looked with more focus at the beauty around her. The small village was surrounded with forest from both sides giving the place a magical touch.

"Yes, you're right." Nikolas agreed standing beside her. This alone was worth the hike and they were just about half way through.

"It's breathtaking." She said with wide blue-green eyes that sparkled with joy, feeling content and happy. She turned to Nikolas with a big smile on her face, showing her perfect white teeth.

"Yes, breathtaking." He repeated, smiling back, but he was not looking at the beautiful view anymore, but at her.

They have always gotten along well even as little kids, but they bonded even more over this experience. They could always talk about anything. Conversation with Nikolas was effortless and natural; it was never forced. They talked about the view, the hike, the birds, the forest and flowers, the castle, the history of this fascinating country and how much fun they had together. She felt comfortable with their conversations they had and she also felt comfortable with him walking in silence at times, just taking deep breaths of the fresh mountain air. It was always like that with them since they were little kids. It made Nikole sometimes jealous of her brother considering how close in age they were and she always felt that he was taking her friend away from her whenever Michaela visited them.

They walked through wooded valleys and alpine meadows. They had their picnic in the midst of the beauty of their surroundings and ate hungrily their cheese and Hungarian salami sandwiches with green peppers on the side that his mother has prepared for them for the trip. Mrs. Senko always bought Hungarian salami whenever they visited Hungary and yesterday was not an exception. They drank from the same bottles of water, sharing it along the way, without hesitation as if they have always done so.

Chilly breeze surrounded them as they were approaching the castle as if it was the ghost of this legendary Impaler.

"Here, put on my sweatshirt. It's getting cooler in the mountains and we still have to get closer to the castle; into the Bran village. It might be cool inside the castle too." Michaela thanked Nikolas for his consideration and pulled on his oversized gray sweatshirt that warmed her up almost immediately.

Nikolas again held out his hand to Michaela especially during the steep parts of the mountain hike. They continued on this intriguing journey until they finally reached the spectacular Bran, the little town that holds the mysterious castle of Dracula. It looked far from menacing with its captivating reddish towers and whitewashed walls. The 13th century hilltop fortress looked enchanting resembling a fairytale castle; it looked exactly as the castle of a vampire should look like. The legend-filled fortress was spectacular. Unlike anything that Michaela had ever seen. The castle was well preserved from the medieval times. It certainly was worth the effort to climb up all the way to see that and she expressed that to Nikolas with joy in her voice.

"Wait until you see it on the inside." He said enthusiastically seeing her wide eyes looking at the magical castle.

The fascinating fortress was perched atop 60 meters high in the middle of the Bran village. Since the castle is situated on a cliff it appears as if it is rising from top of the trees giving it a dramatic and ominous appearance. They arrived at the cliff within a narrow rocky passageway. They could see some taxis and busses that were bringing new tourists to see the magnificent castle but from there it was still about fifty meters climb to the front entrance. Looking at the castle from a close up was even more mesmerizing.

They have not seen Nikole and her parents who gave up on their hike before they barely started it, missing all the spectacular view from the mountain top; but the Castle was enormous and Michaela could only imagine that one could easily get lost in there.

"Let's go in." Nikolas urged Michaela to proceed. Since they did not have a personal tour guide with them, Nikolas relied on his tour guide booklet and his knowledge from the book he purchased back home about Romania, its history and about the Bran Castle. He has read it prior to going on this vacation to assure that he had enough knowledge and he tried explaining to Michaela about the palace as best as he could. Michaela was impressed with his knowledge and his enthusiasm that he talked about the rich history.

They entered the castle through the rectangular entryway of steep stairs. Nikolas explained to Michaela that the ancient gate was blocked and the only way to get in was to climb a ladder. It was rebuilt in 1625 from its original round shape to this rectangular gate tower that they were walking through. They entered the inner yard that contained a fountain that was hiding labyrinth of secret underground passages; Nikolas went on explaining to Michaela pointing to what looked like an old well.

They came out on the other end through a tunnel onto the park grounds that surrounded them with bushes of red roses that gave this place even more enigmatic feel. Nikolas explained that they tried to maintain the rose bushes and dahlias as these were the favorite flowers that Queen Marie during her realm in 1920s often came to admire in her gardens. They went back into the castle getting lost in the maze of this palace through different rooms, hallways and towers. They saw the hunting trophies hall, Queen Marie's music room, her bedroom, the dining room, Queen Marie's old library and many other interesting rooms with its ancient furniture that was preserved. The palace was magnificent and enormous with thick stone walls. They walked through the passage of the first floor finding their way through the maze outside again in the Renaissance courtyard with its blended Gothic style that was also rebuilt several times maintaining its striking view. They walked around the little pond and continued south on the path towards the centre of the village that let them to the Ancient Customs House Museum where they saw a display of amazing archaeological treasures and various photographs of this mysterious castle. Across from the Museum they saw the remains of the old defensive wall that divided Transylvania from Wallachia. They were lost in the maze of this magnetic place, its medieval feel and the time has stopped for them for now. When they realized what time it was; they knew they had to be on their way back finding the front entrance where they were supposed to meet the rest of the family.

"This was amazing, Nik. I'm so glad I came with you."

"Me too, Mika. I had a great time with you."

They found Nikolas' family waiting for them impatiently close to the entrance of the castle.

"Well, that's about time, you two." Mr. Senko complained. "We've been waiting here for you for ages. Let's go. It will be dark soon in the woods."

"We were really worried about you two." Mrs. Senko added. "We have not realized how huge this place is and we thought you would not know where to find us."

"Everything is fine now, so let's go see if the other families are there since we promised them that we meet with them this evening and find a spot where we could camp out. We are already running late." They all walked to the van that was parked on a side road of the small village and then drove to the agreed upon spot to see whether the Czechoslovakian and Hungarian families kept their word and would come meet with them so they could camp in a larger group. They were the last to arrive finding out that four out of five families kept their promise. They looked at the maps and decided that they would drive about another half an hour to nearby wooden area where they could drive by with cars. There they found a perfect spot to set up the tent.

The other four cars pulled up in front of them and started to settle for the night, some families decided to sleep in their cars and two families, including the Senko family decided to put the tents up for everyone to get a good night sleep. It was impossible for five people to get any sleep in the minivan and they still had a long trip ahead of them the following day. Mr. Senko grumbled something under his nose taking out the large tent out of the trunk of the van along with the sleeping bags. It was quite an operation to set up this humongous tent and Mr. Senko who was most skillful along with Nikolas in putting it together, wished he did not have to do that just for one night, but they did not have much choice at this point. At least it didn't rain, but the night was falling over them quickly surrounding them with darkness as they were surrounded by large trees from both sides of the passageway. It was getting darker fast in this part of the Alps even though it was not that late. The air was so nice and clean, but it had an uneasy feel to it perhaps because it was spookily dark and cooler than during the day, barely seeing things that were illuminated only by the full moonlight.

There was not much to do because of the darkness and cold, so the parents went to sleep shortly after their simple sandwich supper, while the three young people sat around in the tent with a flashlight, not wanting to turn in for the night.

16

Nikolas entertained the two young girls with spooky stories from Transylvania.

"Vlad Tepes, also called Vlad Dracula, the Dark Prince of Wallachia, who lived in the 15th century, here in Romania in Tirgoviste tortured and killed hundreds of innocent people. He tortured them in most inhumane ways. He cut off his victims' noses, boiled them in hot water or disemboweled them." The girls squealed with disgust but Nikolas continued in his horrific stories by putting the flashlight close to his face making a spooky grimace making the stories more dramatic.

"His favourite torture method was to impale his victims onto a stake like a shish kebob and burn them alive. Romanians say that at night, they can still hear the cries of those victims; they hear their tortured souls. People say he was a real vampire because he also drank his victim's blood to be stronger and invincible. Some say he became immortal and still roams the Transylvanian Alps; right around the area where we are right now." Nikolas looked around listening as if for the Dracula's ghost.

When Nikolas saw the girls' wide eyes and disgust in their faces, he continued.

"One day Vlad Dracula decided that the poor, beggars, crippled and disabled are not contributing to the common welfare and he had no use for them. So he lured most of them into his castle in Tirgoviste for a great feast. The unsuspecting guests ate and drank late into the night. When Dracula appeared, he asked them what else they desired and whether they wanted to be without any worry and without care, not needing anything in the world, the guests thought it would be great no more to be poor, not having to beg or suffer without anyone caring. Dracula made their wishes come true by ordering to boarder up the halls and set them on fire. No one escaped and all the guests burned alive. The screams and cries of the victims were heard far away and everyone feared the cruel dark prince. His reasoning was that they no longer presented any burden to hard working people and that nobody would be poor in his land." Nikole thought that her brother is disgusting himself for telling such horrific stories, while Michaela was quite intrigued and interested to hear more stories, admiring Nikolas' story telling ability and his knowledge of this legendary Dark Prince and this mysterious place.

Nikolas with pride continued with his story telling to further impress the girl he liked. He kept telling Michaela story after a story even after when Nikole retreated into her side of the tent and went to sleep. Nikolas enjoyed Michaela's company alone in the night but with his last story he went too far.

"Not too many people knew that Dracula had a mistress in one of the houses in Tirgoviste. This woman loved Dracula immensely and would do anything for him."

"I can't imagine a woman that would love such a cruel man. She should have run far away from him as she could", Michaela said.

"Well, don't ask me why, but she did fall in love with him" said Nikolas, "and when Dracula fell into a deep depression she wanted to cheer him up, so lied to him about awaiting his baby. Dracula had it verified by the bath matrons to find out about her lie, so he took a knife and ripped her from her groin to her breasts leaving her suffer in agony and then he drank her blood….." At that point, even Michaela had enough and did not want to hear anything anymore concluding just as her friend did, that Nikolas is disgusting and is making things up. Nikolas swore he was telling her the truth just as is the truth that Dracula's spirit is still around and who comes across it; is doomed.

"But don't worry Michaela, I'll watch over you so nothing ever happens to you." He winked at her. When Michaela went to sleep, Nikolas told himself quietly with disappointment in himself.

"Great, Nik. What a way to impress a girl. Instead of charming her, you managed to repulse her with your disgusting and disturbing stories."

That night, Michaela dreamed of Vlad Dracula how he is coming after her with his big vampire teeth to suck her blood out and heard strange noises. She suddenly woke up in the middle of the night and peaked out of the side window of the tent. She saw wagon with horses approaching on the narrow dirt road. The wagon was passing by each of the cars that were parked on the side and some dark figure was glaring into the darkness of each car where some people were sleeping. She suspected it was just few young Gypsies passing by; looking curiously at the tourists. She noticed that the wagon was heading towards their tent which was illuminated only by the moonlight. In the darkness she glimpsed something shiny;

a knife. Terrified, she wanted to warn the family to do something before they were attacked not realizing that Nikolas was already outside and as the group of three Gypsies started to jump down from the wagon sneakily approaching their tent. Nikolas stood up tall from the side of the tent and started to yell at them from top of his lungs in Slovak not caring that the Gypsies most likely did not understand a word he was howling at them, but his presence and fearlessness gave the group of Gypsies away to other families. Nikolas didn't know how the Gypsies would react and he was not aware that they had knives, but his screams woke other people from the cars and the neighbouring smaller tent and other men were coming out of their night shelters and joined Nikolas in their barks towards the suspicious strangers approaching the tent. The Gypsies were caught by surprise and cowardly jumped back on the horse wagon and went quickly on their way. The screams continued while the group retreated and a sense of pride shined through Nikolas' face especially when he saw Michaela standing beside him with shock and fear.

"Don't worry, Michaela, I told you I wouldn't let anything happen to you." Shyly, Michaela commented that he was very brave to stand up to Gypsies like that but also scolded him that he could have gotten hurt because they had knives.

"You were scared for me?"

"No, I was scared for all of us. Good night, Nik. And....thanks." Michaela's admiration and appreciation of Nik's company grew. She realized he is not the nerdy boy that she always considered him to be as she and Nikole often made fun of him, but it is a bright young man who is not easily intimidated and she felt safe around him.

The following morning after they packed up the tent and had a quick breakfast that they brought with them, the family was again on their way to the Black Sea. Mr. Senko was saying that they are not too far from the Bulgarian boarder, but when another night set, they seemed to be lost and the other families scattered their separate ways.

Suddenly they found themselves in a small town or village in the darkness. Driving up a steep hill, in the Ilfov County, Mr. Senko noticed a tractor in the middle of the road and just barely avoided crashing into it as it was completely dark and only the lights of their van disrupted the night. Luckily, the car was going at a very slow speed as the passengers were aware that they are lost in the "middle of nowhere" where only darkness surrounded them. There were no street lights or any houses to be seen. Little did they know the name of the village was Gruiu meaning "small hill."

When they finally arrived what appeared to be the heart of this small village wanting to ask for directions, they noticed many young people walking in a large group hitting sides of their van with their hands and kicking the car with their feet. They were loud and it appeared they were yelling on these intruding tourists passing accidently through their small village. The family did not speak Romanian so they could not understand the swear words that they received. The large group of people surrounded their car so they could barely drive at a low speed not understanding what was going on. Suddenly, a young man jumped up on the hood of their van with a dead cat in his arms, yelling at them. People were fiercely banging on all sides of the windows. Mrs. Senko thought they would soon break the windows and she was staring at the wild eyes of a young madman in front of them that would not stop at anything. The driver was forced to stop the car and they found themselves completely surrounded by the group of angry teenagers.

Nikolas said from the back seat, "I think they're angry because they think we killed their cat. I wouldn't be surprised if the cat was already dead and they threw it under our van just to have a reason for a fight".

At first, Mr. Senko thought he could reason with them, but when in the hot night, some young people held metal sticks in their hands and started banging on the roof of the van and its sides, the passengers quickly closed their windows, despite the heat of the un-air-conditioned minivan. This would of course not prevent them from getting hit in the head if that's what some young people intended to do. Mr. Senko kept his composure and he moved the car so that people in front had to jump aside. When he hit the brakes very suddenly the young man tumbled down from the top of the hood and jumped aside as well. Maria Senko screamed from top of her lungs when she thought her husband would kill some of those people who were in the way. Those up front of the van moved quickly to the sides probably thinking that the man is crazy enough to run them over. This created a small opportunity and a passage to get through quickly away from the angry villagers who seemed to be out of control. Whole this time, Michaela was thinking, if they hit anyone of us in the temple with those metal sticks, we would be dead.

They drove all night. Nikolas finally persuaded his father to let him drive and took the lead from him to give his father a break from driving so he could snooze with the rest of them. After their experiences in Romania they did not want to spend another night under the tent or in the van sleeping, unless it was at their destination. Early in the morning they arrived at the Bulgarian border. It was easier for them to understand Bulgarian as it is a Slavic language and somewhat similar to Slovak. Bulgarians were pleasant and helpful people that gave the family good suggestions and directions of how to get to Varna as quickly as possible. The drive seemed still quite long to Varna where the family was going camping right at the sandy beach. They stopped couple of times to eat and stretch their tired bodies.

The family arrived in Varna at the campsite just before the beautiful sunset. They picked a spot about fifty meters from the ocean. There were already many other tents surrounding them right on the sand. Michaela took her shoes off loving the warm feel of the sand on her feet. She has never been at a sandy beach before. Her mother would never be able to afford a vacation at a sea. She loved every minute of it. They started to set the tent up again while Maria Senko started the supper. The family came equipped with many canned goods, dried soups, dry biscuits and crackers. For tonight, Mrs. Senko pulled out sausages from the large cooler that were frozen when she put them there but now they were ready to cook. There was a designated camp fire area where people could cook their food. Michaela tried helping with the tent when Nikole who had no interest of helping out noticed something interesting.

"Don't look now, two o'clock one of those guys is looking right at you". Instinctively, Michaela turned her head, while Nikole scolded her quietly, hissing through her teeth.

"Which part of 'don't look' you don't understand?"

Two tents away from them was a group of three young men. One of them, a tall, skinny man was crunched down by their tent looking for something, only his bottom sticking out from the tent, half naked wearing only tongs bathing suit that showed his whole behind which Michaela found too revealing and funny to wear for a boy especially in a public place. But she was not interested in that; her gaze drew her to the man that was staring at her with an interest while a third, younger boy was talking to this man with piercing dark brown eyes. He did not interrupt the eye contact with Michaela despite his friend's words. He smiled and greeted her with a hand gesture, lifting two fingers towards his forehead to salute her. Michaela acknowledged that gesture by her shy smile and quickly turned away.

"Is he still looking, she asked Nikole?"

"Yap, he is. I think he really likes you. I think he is cute although he looks older. I see this is going to be a very interesting vacation." Nikole said with a conspiratory smirk.

When the tent was set up, Mr. Senko suggested for the girls to go for a short walk at the beach to see the picturesque sunset before it got dark, but warned them not to go too far as the supper would be ready soon. Michaela enjoyed breathing deeply the salty fresh air and feeling the water wash over her feet as she walked with Nikole along the shore barefoot. A lot of people had similar idea to go for a gorgeous evening walk when the sun was setting down.

The girls saw nearby simple wooden lifeguard booths that had a little roof to protect from the strong sun and it was one story high; high enough for the lifeguards to see as far into the ocean as they could. They noticed couple of cute life guards that greeted them while the girls giggled and ran along the shore. Coming towards them from the other side were two men that the girls recognized as their tent neighbours. When they were close enough, the men stopped and one of them said in clear German language that Michaela always admired.

"Hello, ladies. Do you speak German?" Michaela immediately remembered that piercing look of this handsome brown eyed man that was watching her earlier and his companion, butt-naked friend who changed into his shorts by now.

Mission Thrift Store

68 Allen Street
Charlottetown,PE C1A 2V8
902-894-4236

Tax # 801 026 808 RT0001

10/21/2024 3:23:40 PM   Aticia

Books Fiction
2 @ $2.50ea. $5.00 1X2
Books Fiction $2.50 1X2
Books Fiction $2.50 1X2
Item Discount 25%   ($0.63)1X2
Books Fiction $2.50 1X2
Item Discount 25%   ($0.63)1X2

SUB TOTAL $11.24
HST $0.56

TOTAL   **$11.80**
Debit Card $11.80
Item count: 5
Trans:200939   Terminal:050104016-021003

ALL SALES FINAL

(Except for defective appliances and
electronics are returnable within 3 days
Clothing is Exchange Only within 7 days.)

All returns must have the price tags
attached and accompanied by itemized
original receipt.

NO EXCEPTIONS

10/21/2024 3:23:40 PM   Alicia

MISSION THRIFT STORE CHA
68 ALLEN STREET
CHARLOTTETOWN, PE. C1A 2
902-894-4236

Purchase
MID: 80407361111
TID: 0089250008040736111303   Ref #: 87
Batch #: 578
10/21/24   Seq. #:
AUTH #: 154235   15:23:59
Debit/DEFAULT
************9501 P   **/**
Trace # 87
Total $11.80

Signature Not Required
APPROVAL 00
THANK YOU / MERCI
Interac
AID: A0000002771010
TVR: 80 00 00 80 00

CUSTOMER COPY
THANK YOU / MERCI

ALL SALES FINAL
(Except for defective appliances and
electronics are returnable within 3 days
Clothing is Exchange Only within 7 days.)

All returns must have the price tags
attached and accompanied by itemized
original receipt.

NO EXCEPTIONS

NO EXCEPTIONS

original receipt.

returned by purchaser and accompanied
All returns must have the price tags

Clothing & Furniture purchased at point of
electronics are returned within 3 days
(Except for defected appropriateness and
ALL SALES FINAL

CUSTOMER COPY
THANK YOU / MERCI
TVR: 00 00 00 80 00
AID: A000000251010
Interac

APPROVAL 00
Signature not Required
[619] $11.00
Isle # 956?1
************2201 4   **/**
Dept1/DEFAULT
AUTH #: 157532
10/21/01   15:53:58
Batch #: 518   Seq. #:
TID: 00285200080...   Ref #: 8?
AID: 8040/35111

Purchase
902-894-4254
CHARLOTTETOWN, PE C1A 5
88 ALLEN STREET
MISSION THRIFT STORE CHA

10/21/2024 3:53:40 PM   #/1019

Michaela spoke a little German because she has been learning that on her own for few years. Having lived in a Communist Country it was not a preferred language that was readily taught in schools; rather it was Russian that was mandated in Czechoslovakian schools; however, Michaela found German to be a useful language as Germany was not that far from her country and she always wanted to visit it one day. So Michaela searched in her long term memory the German words that she had learnt in the past wanting to respond but all she managed was to say "a little".

"Eduard Verner, but everyone calls me Eddy and this is my friend, Otto Tigwig, but sometimes we just call him the 'Twig' because he is so tall and thin." Eddy joked and nudged his friend in the shoulder.

"Otto", the tall thin man re-introduced himself to the girls, ignoring Eddy's introduction. He was focusing particularly on the blond girl with gray eyes he was to 'entertain' as his friend made it very clear before they approached the girls to keep away from the brunette.

"Same from both sides." Otto added jokingly about his name.

"What are your names?" Eddy asked looking again at Michaela. Nikole who was not as shy as Michaela jumped in and introduced both of them before Michaela had a chance to open her mouth. Eddy not taking his gaze off Michaela told her that he loved her name as he rolled it on his tongue repeating it back with German accent and pronunciation. Her own name sounded so much better from his lips and for the first time she liked the sound of her name.

The view was breathtaking as the sun was setting down behind the horizon giving it an orange background glow in the sky. The setting sunlight struck Michaela's natural highlights in her hazelnut hair while her friend was tossing her long dark-blond hair from side to side while she flirted with Otto. The men joined the girls on the walk.

The communication between them was difficult. It is one thing to learn a foreign language from a textbook and another to speak German with someone who is fluent and has no idea how much you can understand. The girls learned that the men come from Dresden in Eastern Germany. Nikole was surprised to learn that the Eastern Germans also had to learn Russian just as children in Czechoslovakia had to learn it in school for years. When they did not know how to say something in German they substituted the missing words with some Russian words to fill in the gaps, interchanging the two languages as needed. It was quite easy for the girls to speak and understand Russian because it is very similar to Slovak which was their first language.

Eddy was quite perceptive and when he saw that Michaela wanted to say something, he tried to guess what she wanted to say and helped her out. There was a lot of pointing, body language and laughter at how difficult it was to understand each other. They have learnt that the third guy back at the tent that they saw earlier was Eddy's younger brother, Richie who came along with them on vacation. The girls were so wrapped up in the conversation that they did not notice Nikolas approaching them. He wanted to join them on the walk but when he saw two male strangers with the girls, he hesitated and told them once he caught up with them that the sausages were ready to eat. The girls indicated that they had to go but that they will probably see them soon. After supper, Nikole and Michaela wanted to take a shower after the long trip and not having a chance to shower since Debrecen in the Hungarian motel.

They were in for a cultural shock when they learned that the bathrooms did not have regular toilets that they were accustomed to, only a flushable toilet hole over which they had to awkwardly squat down. It was very uncomfortable because this was something new and unusual for them. The shower stalls had open concept where women of all ages were lined up waiting for a free shower stall without doors. Michaela who was generally a very shy girl, felt extremely uncomfortable to shower in front of other women, who were lined-up waiting for a free shower stall.

That night they were all so exhausted from the several days of travelling that they decided to go to sleep early. For a while the girls talked about the boys they have met at the beach and that they found them quite attractive, not realizing that Nikolas who was on the other side of the spacious tent could hear most of their conversation. Little did Michaela know that Nikolas wanted to come to this trip mainly because of her and was hoping that he would have enough courage to tell her how he felt about her for some time now. Nikolas did not anticipate that Michaela might find someone else so quickly and right in front of his eyes.

Chapter 3

THE NEXT MORNING, AFTER LIGHT breakfast, Michaela and Nikole were ready for the fun at the beach. The weather was beautiful; it was hot but not humid and all what the girls wanted to do is suntan and to enjoy the ocean. Although, Michaela did not know how to swim, she still loved the warm sea water as it washed over her feet and over her body. She was always careful not to go too deep. They found a good spot near the water and set their blankets on the sandy ground, putting their shoes in every corner of the blanket so it would not blow away in the light breeze. It did not matter that there was sand everywhere. Shortly after Eddy and his friends found them and set their blankets beside them. Michaela enjoyed Eddy's company and admired the fluency of the German language with which he spoke with such splendor and ease. As they struggled through the language barrier, Eddy was teaching Michaela new words she did not understand and she picked up on it very quickly, adding to her German repertoire. It caused many misunderstandings and laughter when new words came up and they tried to figure out what the other wanted to say. There was this unspoken electricity between Eddy and Michaela that drew them towards each other. She loved his touch when he offered to put the tropical coconut suntan lotion that he applied with gentle caress to her delicate shoulders and back. He seemed to devour every minute of it.

At the same time Nikole tried to communicate with Otto who did not seem to put as much effort like Eddy into having her understand what he was saying, but non-verbally expressed his interest in her. Nikole, who was growing founder of the thin giant with blue eyes, whispered to

Michaela that it didn't matter she didn't always understand him as body language could speak louder than all the words in the world.

The four of them spent most of the days on the beach together every day. Eddy's brother at times joined them as well but often complained of the hot sun and heat and retreated into a shade or went to see the town. Every night Eddy would ask Michaela to walk with him on the beach. One evening as they were walking on the beach, Eddy held Michaela back away from the other couple and unexpectedly pulled her towards him and kissed her passionately in a way that she has never been kissed before. Nikole looked back on the couple that was behind them and smiled to herself wishing that Otto showed as much interest in her. Although a little too tall for Nikole, Otto was quite cute, with dark blond hair and a boyish smile that gave him a certain charisma. Eddy on the other hand, had dark brown curly hair and brown deep eyes that melted Michaela's heart as she was getting lost in his gaze. He already had a nice golden tan. He did not look like a typical German boy as they were usually blond with blue eyes, like Otto, but perhaps that was just a stereotype, Michaela responded to Nikole when she commented on that.

Since that first kiss from Eddy it felt to Michaela as if they were dating. They did not need to define their relationship with words; they knew that there was chemistry and undeniable attraction that drew them to each other. Now they openly held their hands when they were walking on the beach and Eddy randomly kissed her making her weak in the knees. They slowly started to separate from the other couple and would spend all days and evenings together and to Nikole, it seemed that her friend was forgetting about her.

Nikolas realized early on that Michaela did not welcome his presence at this point and spent some time surfing, reading or sketching something and watching Michaela from a distance vary of her new boyfriend, wishing that it was him spending all the time with her, which was his original intention. He could kick himself for not acting faster and not telling Michaela how he felt when he had the chance. It was hard for him because they were friends for such a long time and that is exactly where they stayed – in the 'friends zone', he thought to himself. At the same time, he wanted her to be happy and she appeared to be. On the other hand, watching her with someone else was very difficult for Nikolas, but he would not ruin her new relationship because he wanted the best for her even if it was not with him. This is why he stepped back and was hurting in silence without anyone knowing about it. Not even his own sister realized at the time the extent of his affection towards her best friend.

On July 17th, it was Michaela's eighteenth birthday. Nikolas was the first to congratulate her that morning giving her a little sketch book.

"Happy Birthday, Mika. I have a little something for you that I have been working on for a while and I hope you like it." When Michaela opened the sketch book, looking through the pages she saw beautiful pencil drawn pictures of herself and of the beach. Michaela was touched by this gesture and she never realized how talented Nikolas was in his drawing.

"Wow, Nikolas, these are really good. You have a real natural talent to draw." She was turning the sketch book pages admiring each picture with amazement.

"When did you do all this?"

"I guess I had a lot of time on my hands lately."

"Well, thank you so much, Nik. This is quite unique." She hugged him and gave him a small kiss on his cheek, pressing the sketch book towards her chest as she pulled away from him; her face still beaming with delight.

"You're welcome. You're so much prettier in real life than on these pictures." He commented and smiled back at her. Looking through the sketch book again, Michaela picked one.

"This one….definitely, this one is my ultimate favourite and I'll have it framed." She turned the sketch book his way showing him a picture of her profile with a dreamy look and a slight smile on her face looking towards the sea.

"You look very happy in that picture. I like seeing you happy, Mika." Her heart melted and she was glad to have such a considerate friend. She hugged him again and he held her just a moment longer than he intended.

"This is great, Nik. I love it. You have to draw more. You're amazing. You should draw something like that, but bigger and in colour, seeing the splendid yellow and orange glow of the sunset disappearing between the sky and the ocean." She said dreamily giving Nikolas new inspiration.

Nikole along with her family prepared a small celebration for Michaela's birthday.

"I want you to have a good time with us if you can't spend your big day with your family, hopefully you can enjoy it for now with us".

The Senko family took Michaela out to Varna downtown that was not too far from the beach. They invited her for a nice dinner in a local friendly restaurant where they ate on the patio. Michaela not having spent one day or evening away from Eddy so far invited him to join them when he found out she was going to town. Eddy gladly joined in and whispered to Michaela that he wished it was her family that he would have met and not Nikole's but he was charming and entertaining and gained the Senko family's sympathy, except perhaps for Nikolas who had a good reason to dislike him as he took the girl of his dreams away from the tip of his fingers.

Nikolas was mad at himself the most but Eddy was a good target of his abhorrence. Eddy got a small piece of white-purplish wild orchid for Michaela and he placed the flower carefully into her long hair that was now put in a fancy bun due to her birthday and due to the heat. He kissed the side of her neck right in front of the Senko family as he carefully tucked the flower into her golden brown hair.

"I love orchids", he said "because they come in different colours and shapes but especially because they symbolize love that lasts forever." He whispered in her ear.

"Eddy, I love it too. Thank you."

"Don't thank me yet, that's not your birthday present."

Soon after dinner, Eddy apologizing stole Michaela away from the family and went with her to browse the local stores telling her to pick anything she liked in the stores for her birthday which would be his birthday present to her. Michaela told Eddy he did not need to buy her anything; that being with him was already the best birthday present, but Eddy insisted. When he saw Michaela looking at an inexpensive leg bracelet with lucky charms on it, he spontaneously bought it for her without even asking. Eddy carefully put that on her ankle as she placed her foot on top of a bench in front of the store and when he was done he gently stroked her leg and placed a kiss on her knee sending shivers down her spine. There was something erotic in his touch and she wanted him to touch her all over her body like she has never been touched before. But Eddy did not pressure her into having sex and was patient and considerate.

Nikole could not say the same about his charming friend, Otto, who seduced her into having sex on the third day he met her. She resisted for a short while but eventually gave into his passionate kisses and touches. Michaela was shocked when her friend confided in her about it.

"When did that happen?" Michaela quarried when she found out that it was only after few days since they came to Varna. She was once again surprised scolding Nikole.

"Why didn't you tell me anything?"

"Well, I would have but you're always so busy with Eddy. Even the other day, I had my family to go to a nice restaurant for your birthday and then you just brushed us all off and left with Eddy. That wasn't very nice of you". Nikole chastised Michaela about her forgetting about their friendship and spending all her time just with Eddy.

"I'm happy that you found a nice guy. I really am, but you could also spend some time with me. We came here as friends to keep each other company and I feel like you're just ignoring me", complained Nikole.

"I'm sorry Niki; that was not my intention. How about from now on we spend some more time together and we do something special." Nikole already had an idea and dragged unsuspecting Michaela the following day to a group of young girls and life guards.

"What's going on here? Where are you taking me?"

"We're going to enter the "Miss Black Sea" competition. It's like a beauty contest. Please sign up with me. I really want to do it but I want you to enter as well", pleaded Nikole.

"You're nuts", said Michaela laughing. "That's totally out of my league and comfort zone."

"No, it's not. You don't even know how beautiful you are, Michaela. And besides, it's not a real thing; it's just for fun. Something they do here couple of times in summer for the tourists. It'll be fun. You see. Please,

please let's do it." Michaela who already felt that she has been neglecting their time together, finally agreed.

"Oh, alright, Niki. Stop making the puppy eyes on me; you know I can't say no to that."

Nikole happily clapped her hands like a small child that received a new toy.

"Well, that's why I'm doing it", laughed Nikole happily and went on chatting about what talent they should choose, practicing walking in high heels and what bathing suits they should wear.

"You should wear the yellow one. You look really good in that and it stands out because you're already so tan." Nikole chatted on about what she was going to wear and which dance she would do as her talent.

Michaela seeing her friend's excitement wanted to please her so she joined in the fun. They signed up for the "competition" that was going to take place in two days.

"Two days only?!" exclaimed Nikole. "That's not a lot of time, but it's doable if we spend majority of our time focusing on the competition; we can do it".

Michaela had hard time walking in high heels as she was not accustomed to that and the high heels belonged to a girl from a neighbouring tent that was coaching Niki and Michaela how to walk properly considering that she enters the competition every year when she is in Bulgaria and almost always wins. The high heels were a little tight and quite uncomfortable and Michaela felt awkward in them, but beauty and glamour had a price, so she endured her sore feet and kept on practicing her cat walk.

Eddy found Michaela on the sidewalk along with her friend and asked her what she was doing when she was promenading herself back and forth in high heels on the pavement in her yellow top bathing suit and black miniskirt. Michaela explained to him that she and Niki were preparing for the "Miss Black Sea competition" that she signed up for and thought he would be as exited for her as she was. She was quickly disappointed when he did not approve of this decision and expressed his dislike about girls that paraded themselves in front of sleazy men in their tiny bikinis.

"I don't want you to do that", he said finally.

"It's just for fun, Eddy. It's nothing to it." When he continued to frown and express his dislike about this idea, she finally tried to explain to him with difficulties, that it was not her idea but wanted to spend some quality time with her friend, Niki whom she has been ignoring. His sudden exasperated movement of his hand startled Michaela and a seagull that was scavenging nearby on the hard pavement, but then he simply ran his hand through his dark hair and retorted.

"Only sluts walk like that in high heels. But do what you want! You obviously already made your choice."

"What does that mean?" Michaela questioned puzzled at Eddy's reaction after he turned on his heal and without another word left her there wondering with her friend.

"What was that all about? I didn't even understand what he was saying. Did he just break up with me?" Michaela questioned aloud in front of Nikole.

"Don't worry, he'll get over it." Nikole tried to reassure her.

"Should I go after him?" Michaela wondered what to do.

"No, absolutely, not!" Nikole warned her. "Let him cool off. That's how men are."

Michaela hated how Eddy made her feel at that moment and did not understand where their relationship stood at this point or even if she could call it a relationship.

Nikole was skillful at distracting Michaela from her disturbing thoughts and the girls have worked hard on their individual talents. Niki was practicing a sexy dance routine while Michaela who had a lovely voice decided to sing a popular German song "99 Air Balloons". She found it quite fitting for her own situation when it came to Eddy as he did not even speak to her for the past two days. Nikole tried to cheer her up saying, "at least you had all this time to practice your song for the competition".

Nikolas helped Michaela with the music and told her that she will be the most beautiful girl in the competition and that he will be cheering for her right in the first row. In his eyes, she was his number one as he told her not so long ago and for him, she was the most beautiful girl he has ever known. Finally, he had some quality time to spend with her although sharing her attention with his sister. Seeing her excitement for the competition that she seemed to embrace, he wanted to help her. From the Varna downtown he found the song she wanted to sing in its original German version and played it for her on his small player he brought with him for the vacation. Michaela did not know where he found the song, but he did along with written lyrics that he was practicing with her although his German was quite rusty.

Where was Eddy when she needed him? She wondered quietly. He should have been the one helping her with the lyrics, which would have been so much easier for him in German than for Nikolas, but she did not see him in a while leaving her with uneasy feeling. She was grateful she had such a great friend in Nikolas who was always there for her when she needed him.

There were three parts to the competition; one was to answer a question asked by a judge in a chosen language, limited to the languages that were spoken at least by one of the judges, then walk in a bathing suit and high heels and the final one was to show their special talent. Eight girls were signed up for this competition from different countries. There were two Bulgarian girls, two girls from Germany, one from Turkey and Nikole, Michaela and another girl, who portrayed herself as the 'pro' and was helping them to prepare for the competition was also from Czechoslovakia.

Three male lifeguards were the judges as they were the ones that organized the whole event. The most challenging part of the competition was answering questions as these were presented in Bulgarian, German or Russian as these were the languages that were spoken by the judges. The girls could pick which language they understood the best. For the girls that did not speak any of these languages; it was simply a bad luck and focus was not on fairness; rather it was a great advantage for the girls that spoke any of those three languages. Michaela picked German as she was more proficient in it than Nikole and she also hoped that perhaps Eddy would show up after all. Nikole's German knowledge was quite limited, so she chose Russian which is at least a Slavic language, similar to Slovak and she has learned it in school for years although she was not proficient in it. Michaela relied on the years of self-study of German and her more recent practice lessons with Eddy which dramatically improved her communication skills within a short period of time. After all, this was a casual beach competition organized mainly for fun, so how hard could that be? Only few took it seriously. Even though Michaela knew that, she did not want to get embarrassed in front of others.

On the day of the competition, Nikolas and his parents were cheering Nikole and Michaela on when it was their turn. Michaela was very nervous and regretted signing up but there was no way out now; other than putting away her shy personality and just go through with the 'performance'. She wished Eddy was there supporting her, but obviously he was opposed to the whole idea so he would certainly not show up. Perhaps that was for the best, she thought, in case she did embarrass herself after all, like tripping and falling on her nose in her clumsy high heel walk, which she thought was a good possibility. Not seeing Eddy in the crowd she could relax and not worry about making fun of herself. It's not like there was a huge price at the end anyway.

She had no idea that Eddy was watching her intently with a frown on his face as the girls were in their bathing suits during their 'cat walk'. Nikole embraced that role and quite enjoyed showing off her slim figure, shaking her long blond hair from side to side as she walked. Michaela on the other hand, felt quite awkward and uncoordinated and she just wanted to have this part behind her. Her long golden brown hair covered her bathing suit on her back as she walked with a lot less confidence than her opponents. Little did she realize that her curves and nice tan body in her yellow bikini stood out and caught the attention of some boys, including one of the judges. She unexpectedly noticed Eddy in the crowd frowning at her as she turned the other way walking back and nearly tripped over her own foot. Damn heels, she would never get used them, she thought. Who made up high heels anyway? She suddenly felt embarrassed and did not know why. A small intermission took place after the first part of the competition to give the girls the opportunity to change from their bathing suits.

In the next part it was time to answer the questions being asked by one of the life-guard judges. Nikole struggled during this part due to some language barriers, not quite understanding the question, but did not seem to mind that she made other people in the audience laugh as a result when used an exaggerated sexy pose, flickering her long eyelashes, sending air kisses to each of the judges answering irrelevantly in Russian.

"Don't hate me because I'm beautiful." Most people laughed and she joined them laughing at herself which earned her more sympathy points even though she didn't answer the question.

When it was Michaela's turn, a young handsome lifeguard-judge smiled at her and gave her a little wink for encouragement. She did not notice Eddy's hateful look he was giving the lifeguard as she was concentrating on the question that was being asked of her in German.

"Would you marry someone who fell in love with you even though you just met him?" Michaela was not prepared for that kind of question and for a moment blanked out until she saw Eddy in the crowd watching her intently, waiting for an answer. For a moment she thought that he asked one of the lifeguards to purposely ask her this question, but she quickly dismissed the idea as ridiculous. She regained her composure and answered that it would depend whether she loved him too and if she felt that he was the one for her. Her heart was beating fast and her cheeks were burning red as her gaze fell on Eddy whose muscles in his face relaxed and she even detected a slight smile. She suddenly knew that he was no longer mad at her and knew she would talk to him that night.

During the final round the girls were to show their special talent. Most girls chose dancing or singing. There was only one girl that chose magic tricks that did not quite work out for her but the crowd took it as a good comedy. Nikole was doing her jazz routine that she had learned in her dancing classes couple years ago and was quite good at it which helped her make up for the previous round. Nevertheless, one of the Bulgarian girls, who had a reputation of a promiscuous girl who would sleep with every lifeguard on the beach and was quite a show off shacking everything that 'her mamma gave her' and doing splits, stood out to the judges the most, not to mention she was at an advantage when answering a question during previous round as it was in her first language.

When it was Michaela's turn to perform, she sang the German song by the group called Nena, "99 Air Balloons" that was an international hit from last year and it was popular all over Europe. She often heard that song on a radio and with Nik's help; she learned the lyrics of the song quite well. It wasn't a love song but that was the only German song that she knew the words to and thanks to Nikolas who bought the song for her and then shortened it for her to make it easier for her as she did not know all the verses; only about half of them, which helped her perform well. When the music started she could see that many people were familiar with that song and moved to the rhythm, which provided Michaela with encouragement. It was simply like a sing along. If she forgot the words, the little player would fill in the gaps, but she was quite good at remembering the words and carried herself with the rhythm. Michaela's lovely voice carried the upbeat tune and words splendidly because she sang from her heart. There was a long part where there was only music playing and Michaela showed few of her dance moves before she repeated the verse.

> *"Do you have some time for me?*
> *Then I'll sing a song for you*
> *About 99 balloons…"*

Michaela genuinely sang from her soul and did not see anyone else but Eddy who was admiringly looking at her. She ended the song with the last verse.

> *"………found a balloon*
> *Think of you and let it fly."*

When she finished singing, even though the melody still continued, her shyness returned and she ran into Eddy's arms. He made his way through the crowd all the way to the front. She never noticed Nikolas' disappointment as he was standing nearby cheering for her. Eddy's arms embraced her.

"I'm sorry, my love, I'm glad you didn't listen to me because you were wonderful." He whispered in her ear and kissed the top of her head.

"I had no idea you could sing so beautifully and in German! And it's quite difficult but very popular song. That was quite impressive. What made you want to sing in German?"

"You." Michaela had tears of joy in her eyes but was speechless at that moment. She had to return back to the group of girls for the judges to make their decision. The local Bulgarian 'show off' girl won the price of a cheap red wine for her advantage of understanding perfectly Bulgarian as that was her language and showing off in small bikini top that was two sizes smaller for her large breasts and being extremely provocative in her dancing earned her most of judges' points.

Nikole was looking around in vein trying to see Otto's face; hoping he saw her sexy dance routine, but she did not see him in the crowd. She was disappointed that she did not win and that Otto never bothered to come see her.

At the end of the competition Michaela ran to Eddy again and they hugged spending the rest of the evening together on the beach kissing and watching the sunset. She knew she was falling in love with him and she never felt that way about any man before. It was a wonderful feeling. She realized that she did not want to be without him another minute and realized how miserable she felt when she thought he broke up with her. Her love for him strengthened when he reassured her that he would never leave her and that she will always be his. She tried to push it out of her head that after this vacation, she will likely never hear from him again because he lives in another country and long distance relationships never work. Why would he want an ordinary poor girl from a small town in Czechoslovakia? She wondered. But for now, she tried to enjoy every minute of her time with him and did not want to think about what her life would look like after the vacation was over.

The same night, Eddy arranged for his two buddies to clear the tent for several hours and he invited Michaela to join him in his tent. Mr. and Mrs. Senko had no idea where Michaela was as Nikole was covering for her and they assumed that the girls went together to the local Disco.

Chapter 4

IN EDDY'S TENT, HE WAS whispering sweet nothings into Michaela's ear that made her feel cherished and good about herself.

"You have the most amazing eyes I have ever seen. Your eyes are like the colour of the sea, unusually blue with a hint of green. And when you're upset or thoughtful, they turn into darker blue."

Michaela knew that she was falling for him and there was no way to stop that, neither did she want to stop it. She wanted to be his. Suddenly she was so sure that he was the one for her and nothing else mattered. Michaela succumbed to his gentle kisses and touches. He did not pressure her but she wanted him; she wanted to be only his. When he reached under her miniskirt stroking her thigh, Michaela shivered with desire and whispered.

"Eddy before we go on I need to tell you something." His concerning frown and piercing dark eyes were staring into her bluish-green eyes with expectations about what she was going to tell him. Michaela continued.

"You're my first. I never…" His face immediately relaxed and he breathlessly kissed her on her full lips and her face, her eyes, whispering loving words to her, telling her that they did not have to go on if she was not ready for that. But Michaela did not want him to stop kissing and touching her and she was certain at that moment that this is the man for her and she wanted him. She wanted him to be the first. After all, she was an adult now. She already kept her promise to keep her virginity until she turned eighteen years old. She always kept her promises, even promises given to herself. She felt that she found the right person to be her first.

Eddy pulled her straps of her summer shirt down her shoulder kissing it gently, then moving to her long neck while his hand moved to her breast which hardened under his fingers. Before she realized, Michaela was completely naked under Eddy who was working his magic. She has never felt so aroused and she did not want to hold back although she was a little shy and nervous. No other man has seen her completely naked before, but with Eddy she felt comfortable and her shyness was slowly fading away. She felt a slight pain as he entered her for the first time, but the desire was stronger and she gently encouraged him with the movement of her hips to continue. Afterwards she stayed curled up in his arms, her head leaning on his manly, hairy chest where she placed small kisses.

"You're my now", Eddy whispered to her, "only mine". It made Michaela smile and she felt happy and content.

"I'm only yours", she reassured him. She drifted off to sleep still in his arms waking up with a startle realizing that she was still in Eddy's tent completely naked. She checked her watch; it was past eleven at night. She quickly sat up putting on her clothes. She woke Eddy up in the process whispering to him that she has to go as his friends might return soon.

Eddy told her that there is an agreed upon sign for the guys in front of the tent not to enter no matter what time it is until he takes it down. Eddy explained to her that they have with the boys such agreement of leaving a white shirt hanging in front of the tent to indicate that they cannot enter because there is a girl in there. Michaela suddenly felt embarrassed as she realized that his companions might be aware of their intimacy. She wondered whether he talked to his friends about things like that just like she would tell Nikole about her new experience.

On Michaela's insistence, Eddy peaked out to assure her that there were no praying eyes and it was safe for her to go out unnoticed. They agreed for a little while to go to the beach and watch the moonlight before she returned back to her tent. She went on ahead and Eddy followed shortly after her. Nikole's parents must have been inside the tent or by the campfire where they usually sat at night. Michaela was relieved that they did not see her coming out of Eddy's tent. She fixed her long hair back into the ponytail to try to put some order to them and then headed towards the beach. She sat down on the blanket watching the dark ocean, hearing its sound and thinking what just happened. She felt like a new person; she felt like a woman.

When Eddy joined her, she curled up against his chest again, happily breathing the nightly breeze. They continued their kissing and by now, Michaela was not afraid to show her affection towards Eddy in front of others. Around midnight, they both returned back to their tents so Nikole's parents would not worry and Michaela was wondering how she would tell Nikole what she experienced tonight. She was glad that they still had their special times with Nikole at night when they talked quietly in the tent about their growing loves for the foreigners who seemed to be very different from one another.

"How do you feel?" Nikole asked after she found out about Michaela's time with Eddy.

"Happy. Oh, Niki, I'm falling for him and I'm scared that after we go back home, I'll never see him again."

Nikole tried to reassure her friend saying that if he loves her as much as she loves him, they will somehow make it work. The girls chatted about how wonderful it would be to start a new life in Germany were they would have so many more opportunities and could live comfortable and maybe even rich lives. It did not matter to Michaela whether Eddy was rich or not, but the life she envisioned with Eddy in Germany, even though she did not know what to expect, was very appealing to her. She knew then that she would follow Eddy to the end of the world just to be with him if he wanted her to.

After the intimate night that Michaela had with Eddy they could not keep their hands off each other and they were spending together every minute of every day. One night they walked together, hand in hand, a little further than usual; barefoot on the sandy beach. Michaela kept her bathing suit on as did Eddy; she only put on a mini skirt to cover parts of her body she was self-conscious about especially when she was walking along the shore, although she had a nice slim figure that Eddy often commented on with interest. He led her to a more secluded part of the beach towards the rocky area where they hid behind a large rock from preying eyes, although they did not see anyone around at this late hour. Eddy put his large towel down on the sandy ground lying down with

Michaela on it making love to her in the moonlight night. Afterwards they were lying there covered partly only with a light towel that Michaela brought with her, enjoying the stars in the clear night, feeling the gentle breeze on their naked bodies.

"Let's go skinny-dipping." Eddy suddenly suggested to her.

Michaela did not understand that word, so he pulled the towel off her naked body, running his index finger between her breasts trailing it down all the way to her happy place. She moaned with pleasure and excitement. Where was this shy girl that was self-conscious to even walk on the beach in her bathing suit not along to be completely naked in a public place with a man touching her?

"Swimming.....no bathing suit." He pointed with his chin towards the quiet ocean night. Michaela giggled conspiratorially her cheeks blushing which Eddy did not notice in the moonlight. He peaked from behind the rock to assure that nobody was around; he grabbed her hand pulling her up from the ground and they ran quickly into the cool ocean that washed over their hot bodies. They left their clothes and towels where they were. Michaela squealed with joy feeling the impact of the cool ocean water washing over her belly and over her naked breasts, hardening all over again. Eddy hushed her with a passionate kiss lifting her buttocks, pulling her closer to him. Michaela wrapped her arms and her legs around him under the water and he made love to her all over again, the gentle waves washing over them. When they ran back to the shore, they dried themselves off with Michaela's clean towel and dressed quickly. Michaela first pulled on her miniskirt to quickly cover herself, then her bathing suit top that Eddy helped her tie at the back. Last she pulled on her bathing suit bottom where Eddy's hand wondered again under her skirt, reminding her of what she just experienced. When they were completely dressed, Michaela pulled towards him and whispered to him.

"I love you, Eddy." He stopped for a moment, looking at her beautiful face in the moonlight, brushing her wet hair away from her face, he whispered back.

"I love you too. You're only mine; forever." He pulled her close to him, holding her face and kissing her overpoweringly, leaving her breathless.

Her heart melted. How lucky she was having met him, she thought. When he stopped kissing her, he continued.

"You will never cheat on me?!" It was more of a statement than a question, but Michaela answered him regardless.

"I would never cheat on you, Eddy. I don't want anybody else, but you."

"Good. I could not stand anyone else touching you like that."

"You don't have to worry about that, Eddy. I'm only yours." Reassured, he took her by the hand and they walked back to their tents. It was quite late at night, but Michaela wanted to shower. She grabbed a clean towel from the tent along with a plastic bag with clean clothes, soap and shampoo and headed to the bathrooms. Nikole's parents were asleep and Nikolas probably too. She did not see Nikole anywhere, but maybe she was with Otto.

It was great how quiet it was and for the first time since they arrived to Bulgaria, she had a privacy in the open showers as nobody was around at this late hour giving her an opportunity to take time and examine her own maturing body that has changed under Eddy's touch. As she was washing her tender body after the repeated love making, touching certain parts of her body reminded her again of Eddy's intense kisses and touches that sent joyful shivers down her body. She closed her eyes under the running water and relived the special moments. Her breasts and her nibbles were tender and swollen after Eddy's rough, playful touches, but she did not mind. She loved him and she would let him do anything with her body as he would please. She wanted to please him and make him happy. She wanted him desiring only her. He made her experience pleasure that she never experienced before.

As Michaela was returning from her late night venture, Nikole was running towards her frantically from the shore scolding her like a little child.

"Where the hell have you been?" She whispered as not to bring anyone's attention in this late hour but Michaela could tell her friend was quite upset with her.

"Come on, I'll tell you inside." Michaela urged her to go to the tent as it was past two o'clock.

"I was looking for you everywhere for the past two hours, Michaela. You really make it impossible to cover for you when I don't even know where you are or what time you'll be back! You have some explaining to do!"

"Gosh, Niki, you sound like my mother. I'm sorry, I forgot my watch and I lost track of time when I was with Eddy and then I didn't see you inside the tent, so I went to take a shower." She whispered back to Nikole; the wind carrying their hushed voices in the quiet night.

"Now? At night time?"

"Yes, now. I needed a shower, alright?" It was nice. Nobody is around at this hour. Finally, I had some privacy." Nikole ignored her friend's excuse and continued with her reprimand.

"I had to lie to my parents that you're already asleep because you're not feeling well. You're lucky they didn't check on you. I've been running around, back and forth everywhere looking for you. Otto and Richie didn't know where Eddy was either so I figured you're with him, but still, Michaela, you could have told me. I thought we had agreement so we could cover for each other, but you have to be honest with me." Nikole was getting louder trying to make a point.

"Shh, ok, ok, I got it. Keep it down. You gonna wake up everyone. Let's go inside." She whispered and urged Nikole quietly into the left side of the tent where they slept, carefully not to wake anyone; they zipped up their side and continued their conversation in hushed voices. Michaela shared with Nikole what she just experienced with Eddy. Nikole already knew that her friend was intimate with Eddy, but she would never have thought that she would do it publicly and then go skinny-dipping making love in the ocean.

"I don't even recognize you anymore, Michaela. You used to be so shy and now you're running around naked. It's always the quiet ones that are the wildest." Nikole shook her head in disbelief.

"Geez Niki, keep it down. It's not like anyone was watching us. But it was great, I must add." She smirked mischievously. "You have to try it with Otto." They both giggled and her friend was back, not upset with her anymore.

"I'm the one that is not shy, but I don't think I could pull a stunt like that. Seriously, who are you and what have you done with Michaela?" Nikole joked.

"I told him I love him."

"No, no, Michaela, you don't ever say that first to a guy."

"He said it back and said he wants to be with me forever."

"Of course a guy is gonna say anything you want to hear when he wants to put his dick between your legs."

"Oh, Niki, you're so filthy."

"It's true. Trust me, I know how guys are."

"Do you think Otto is like that?"

"Probably. We'll see."

"Eddy is not like that." Michaela had the need to defend her love.

"I hope you right; because if you're not and he breaks your heart, I will have to break his legs. Ok, go to sleep now. It's late. Good night."

"Good night, Niki…..and thanks for being such a great friend." Nikole made grumbling sound as she was dozing off to sleep. Michaela could not sleep and she was staring into the darkness of the tent thinking of Eddy and how much she loved him hoping that Nikole was wrong and he did really love her back. She did not want to put any doubt into her thoughts as she was floating on a cloud of love and nothing else existed but her and Eddy. She drifted into sleep.

It was really as if nothing and nobody existed around them; just their love; their passion. They did everything together. They went exploring the town together; they would lie on the beach under umbrellas for hours and going to cool off in the ocean, kissing every opportunity that they had not hiding their affection for one another.

They decided to go see the Botanical Gardens that were about thirty kilometers from Varna. They made it a whole day trip; taking the bus, just the two of them. Nikole warned her half-jokingly at the bus station that she walked to with her and Eddy.

"You better be back before midnight, Cinderella, or I'll send a police squad to chase you down!" Then she added more quietly out of Eddy's ear shot while he was lighting his cigarette further away from them despite the fact that he would not have understood their language.

"He smokes?" Michaela shrugged. She was surprised by that too as this was the first time she saw Eddy smoking.

"Anyway," Nikole continued, "I can't believe you don't even spend any time with me anymore."

"You could come with us." Michaela offered, but in truth hoped that her friend would decline.

"Yeah, right. I don't need to be the fifth wheel. You just go, have fun. Leave me here all alone, bored to death. But don't worry I'll survive. I go and feel lonely along with my brother, but don't worry about us."

"You're not making me feel very good about myself right now, Niki. I already feel quite guilty."

"Good, you should," but then added lightheartedly, "you know I'm just joking."

"I know, but I'm sorry Otto didn't want to come too. It would have been fun the four of us. And I don't think Nikolas would have felt comfortable coming with us either.

"No, I don't think he wants to see the two love birds." Nikole thought of her brother who was lately quite withdrawn and sad looking; she has never seen him like that.

"I'll make it up to you, Niki, when go back home. I have to spend these few days I have left with Eddy. Please understand it."

"I just don't understand why he has to always isolate you from others?"

"What are you talking about?"

"At the beginning we were a pretty good group and then you two started to separate from……everyone else. You are always just with him."

"And is that so wrong that we want to be together?"

"No, I'm sorry, I said something. I don't even know anymore what I'm saying. Forget it. Your bus is coming." She looked at the approaching bus.

"Go. Enjoy yourself while you're young. Have fun and be safe."

"Yes, granny!" Michaela tried to lighten Niki's grumpy mood. She felt bad leaving her friend behind but she really wanted to be with Eddy. What if she never saw him after this vacation? They had one week left. She couldn't think of that now.

"Say thank you to your parents for trusting me to go on a whole day trip with Eddy."

"It's Eddy I don't trust, not you, but I'll give them the message."

"Your parents don't have the same opinion about him as you do. They're quite fond of him." Michaela reminded her of the birthday dinner they had together.

"That's because I'm the only one that sees through him." Michaela sometimes did not know when her friend was serious and when she was joking. Nikole often expressed her opinions as she saw things covering it up with sarcastic humour.

The girls hugged as the bus arrived at the bus stop.

"Love you."

"Me too. See you later.

Eddy put out his cigarette; fixed his cowboy hat, throwing a small backpack over his right shoulder he approached the girls.

"You take good care of her, Eddy!" Nikole warned him seriously.

Eddy gave her a contemptuous look not dignifying it with a response. They certainly did not see eye to eye with Nikole. Something about blonds ticked him off and Nikole was no exception although he did not know why. Nikole in turn did not trust Eddy although she could not put a finger on it why, either. It was one of those things she often referred to as 'woman's intuition' that she lived by. When Nikole was out of ear-shot as they got on the bus, Eddy couldn't help commenting.

"A little too bossy for my taste, that little blond friend of yours."

"Nikole? Ah, don't worry. Niki is just looking out for me. We've been friends forever. That's how she is. I swear sometimes she sounds like my mother and she is older only by five months." She smiled to herself but Eddy did not seem to be interested hearing about Nikole and to shut Michaela up he started kissing her thrusting his tongue into her mouth while they were still standing in the bus isle blocking the way of the other passengers entering the bus. She always welcomed his kisses and returned his passionate kiss when they heard someone behind them complaining to move forward rather than kissing in the middle of the isle. Although they did not understand what the man was saying, they figured out that his complains have something to do with them blocking the way, so Michaela moved ahead of Eddy all the way to the back of the bus. Eddy threw a threatening glare towards the fellow passenger to shut him up.

When Eddy caught up with her, he set down beside Michaela at the very end of the bus; her one hand in his, leaning against his chest with content looking out the window at the surroundings. He put his other arm around her shoulder cuddling her. They did not have much to say to each other, and they sat in silence during the bus ride. They did not need the words as both knew what they felt for each other.

On the bus the tour guide, who introduced himself as Ognyan, presented to the tourists the information in Bulgarian, Romanian and then German which prolonged the whole process. Ognyan informed them that they will be traveling for about forty-five minutes before they arrive at the Palace and Botanical Gardens in Balchik. He explained that there were over two thousand five hundred different species of plants and thirty three different palm trees some of them over fifty years old. One of the attractions was a collection of enormous cacti. He went on talking about the various flowers they will be able to see from colourful tulips, fifty different types of roses of various colours, but also gorgeous orchids, bromelias and the magnolias. Ognyan gave them a brief history of the Balchik Palace also called the Quiet Nest Palace which was build between 1926 and 1937 during the Romanian control of the region as the summer resort for Queen Marie of Romania. Michaela always enjoyed learning about new places, its history and culture and was listening with intent. When Ognyan mentioned Queen Marie of Romania, her thoughts wondered to Nikolas who was telling her the history of the queen at the Bran Castle in Romania during her realm with such an eloquent knowledge and excitement in his voice. Although she enjoyed Eddy's company and was quite excited to share this experience with him, somehow she missed Nikolas' presence remembering the good times and laughs they had on their ventures.

It was perhaps when she saw Eddy's bored face, exasperated sighs and constant checking of his watch certainly showing disinterest in the wealth of information that Ognyan was providing in his monotonous voice that did not seem to interest Eddy in the first place.

"We're almost there." She told Eddy reassuringly although now she was not so sure whether this trip was a good idea after all. He gave her a fake smile and checked his watch again.

When they finally arrived at the Botanical Gardens Eddy refused to follow Ognyan, the boring tour guide and preferred to walk around the Gardens with Michaela alone without other people at his back. They started on the opposite side of the Garden away from others. They first saw a stone built place surrounding them with flowers of all colours and cone-shaped trees that must have been maintained on regular basis to preserve the beauty. As they walked along they came across huge rosebushes of every colour possible. The smell of the roses was wonderful and Michaela took few deep breaths enjoying the spectacular sight. Next, they arrived at the white stoned fountain surrounded by white stone benches around them built in a circular manner where they sat down admiring the beds of flowers around them. It was a romantic place where couples could sit and relax. Eddy kissed her again passionately glad they were by themselves for a change. As they moved through the Gardens they saw the promising giant cacti as the tour guide talked about and various palm trees all over the Gardens. The most spectacular were the water lilies which were placed in a small pond surrounded with olden stone thrones. As they moved on, admiring the variety of orchids of different shapes and colours, magnolias and many other flowers, Eddy inconspicuously picked one of the white orchids with purple speckles and handed it to Michaela who instead of gratitude, scolded Eddy, which caught him off guard.

"You can't pick the flowers here, Eddy. These are exotic flowers; they're preserved here. Tourists can't just pick them! What if everyone picked a flower or two what would be left in the Gardens?!"

"So you don't like it?"

"It's not that I don't like it. It's gorgeous but it's probably illegal to do that. We can get a fine if they find out." She was trying to hide the flower in the backpack as it was too late to return it into its proper place.

"Since when do you follow all the rules?" He asked nonchalantly.

"What are you talking about?"

"Last night, for example? You and me on the beach.....naked..... making love.....skinny-dipping and making love again in the ocean?! Do you think that was not against the rules? If someone has caught us we might have been thrown out of the camp not to mention the embarrassment you would have experienced."

"Good to know. It will not happen again." She retorted disappointed that he was throwing it in her face. She just now realized that it was a big risk and she would have suffered enormous embarrassment if someone caught them.

"But I liked it and I might want to do it with you again." He said quickly.

"Then maybe we should look for a nude beach." She was not serious when she said it but wanted to quickly change the subject rather than arguing with him but he seemed to have taken it seriously; he frowned shaking his head.

"Absolutely NOT! I'm not gonna have some men drooling over my beautiful girl. This is something just for my eyes." He pulled her towards him possessively. Michaela was actually relieved that he was against the nude beach as she would not feel comfortable being naked in front of others. She did not even know why she would mention it in the first place; perhaps she wanted to make him happy thinking that this is something he would like.

They dropped the subject and walked on a stony pavement curvy-pathway that let them to the Balchik Palace. After they saw it inside and out, Eddy did not seem to be impressed saying that it looked like an ordinary old building.

"But I saw from the Palace that there is a nice beach below. Shall we go? I hope you brought your swim suit."

"I did."

"Let's go then; we have an hour and half for us before the bus leaves. Now wait a minute." He suddenly remembered. What do we do about the damn orchid that you don't want?"

"Hey, I never said I didn't want it."

She took the orchid from the backpack where it was now hiding; a little wilted but still pretty, she hid it in her cleavage.

"That's a place I would have never thought looking for orchids." He laughed; his mood changed pulling her behind him to the beach.

"That's all I wanted for you to accept the flower from me. I promise I will not pick another from here on the way out. Maybe." And he winked at her conspiratorially.

They had fun at the beach but felt a bit rushed as they did not want to miss their bus. When they returned, Eddy went to take a shower so Nikole stole some alone time with her for a change and questioned her about everything that she has seen. Nikolas, who has not spent any time with her lately since the 'Black Sea competition', joined in the conversation as Michaela described the beauty of the Botanical Gardens and the Balchik Palace of what she understood from the tour guide during their bus ride. Nikolas listened to her with interest. She finally concluded.

"Eddy was a bit bored but Nik; you would have appreciated the history and the beauty of the place." She said with wistfulness in her voice.

The following day Eddy attempted to teach Michaela how to swim again just like he already tried on several occasions unsuccessfully as her fear of water prevented her to relax in the water making it difficult. He never had enough patience with anything and quickly gave up on the idea of teaching her how to swim. Michaela was often holding her hands around Eddy's neck while he carried her in the ocean enjoying having her so close to him. He had hard time keeping his hands away from her even in the water, remembering their skinny-dipping adventure, but she did not mind. One day when they were together in the ocean as usual, the waves appeared to be stronger that day, washing over the couple which made Michaela very nervous. As Eddy was swimming with Michaela, her arms wrapped around his broad neck, kissing as usual, Michaela looked back to the shore realizing that they seemed to be somewhat further than usual and asked Eddy to go back because she was afraid of deep water. Eddy tried to stand up but he did not feel the ground under his feet. The water was already too deep.

Michaela did not know that Eddy's foot got caught on some seaweed in the process and he needed to dive under for a moment to free his leg. As Eddy went under and waves became stronger, Michaela panicked and started to yell for help, holding tightly onto Eddy who was now completely under the water trying to free himself but with Michaela's tight hold over his neck, he felt like she was drowning him and it took him some time.

Michaela could not stand the salty water in her eyes and could not see where she was or what was happening around her, but she knew she was in trouble. She realized that her only survival was Eddy and she could not let go of him or she would be gone further into the ocean as the waves carried them deeper and deeper into the endless depth of the sea.

Slovaks say that drowning people will hold onto hay in the water just to survive and that is exactly what Michaela was doing. Eddy was her only chance of survival in this overpowering mass of water as he was the closest to her and she could not let go.

Michaela's short life flashed in front of her while she was drowning. It seemed to take an eternity while in fact it took only few seconds. She saw her mother telling her before the trip not to go into a deep end because she does not know how to swim and she could drown. How much she wanted to go back in time and avoid such situation completely. She saw her grandmother who was always so loving and caring to her and she wished she was still alive. She saw her aunt Sylvie with all her strange psychic abilities as she claimed predicting Michaela's long but difficult life. How could she have been so wrong about her future that might soon evaporate completely? She saw her father in a far distance who was never close to her and she always pictured him as a black figure and that is how he flashed in her mind now; just as a black silhouette. She saw her friends laughing with her. She saw herself playing in sand as a little girl thinking how happy she was. She saw Nikolas drawing her pictures….his magnetic smile revealing his dimples. 'Breathtaking' he told her. Did he mean her? Now she could not even breathe. She saw Eddy and how much they were in love. Eddy….oh, my god, where was Eddy? She realized that she was no longer holding him and the waves were carrying her further and further into the unknown death. She tried to yell for help again, but her mouth was full of salty water that was consuming her. NO….she screamed inside; I just found my love, I only turned eighteen, this can't be the end. I haven't even started to live, I wanted to have children one day…….and the dream or reality was getting further and further away from her. It's not fair for me to die so young.

All those thoughts and images were flashing up for Michaela while she struggled to save herself and she did not even know whether she was still alive or whether she already crossed to the other side. With all her strength she had left she fought for her next breath, trying to remember Eddy's unsuccessful swimming lesson earlier today, but the waves were too strong and she was losing her strength. The waves were covering her and pulling her under the water.

Suddenly Michaela felt something reaching under her and it felt like she was flying through the air for a second, but then she was consumed by the ocean once again. This brief escape above the water gave her a chance to take her next breath before she was lost under the waves. Once again, something or someone threw her up into the air and she quickly realized that was her only hope to catch another breath to survive. She did not even know which way she was being thrown and feared that she is moving further and deeper into the ocean where nobody else will be able to reach her.

Eddy would not give up on her but because she was drowning him in a haste and panic he did not know how better to approach her to pull her back to the shore. He quickly realized that Michaela was drowning and if he had panicked it would have been the end of her. So he continued to swim under her and threw her towards the shore and then swimming towards her to do that all over again, hoping that she was conscious to take a breath while in the air. Michaela was losing her strength and saw darkness surrounding her with a white light at the end. She was drawn to this white light where she would not feel this suffering while she struggled to take the next breath. Suddenly serenity and peacefulness had overpowered her and she no longer felt the panic and suffering.

Chapter 5

WHEN NIKOLAS SAW THAT MICHAELA began to drown he did not hesitate and jumped into the ocean to help her. He swam to them and helped Eddy pull her out of the water to the shore. Michaela was unconscious by that point. Nikolas did not vacillate and provided Michaela with first aid mouth to mouth breathing and pumping her chest. His First Aid course he recently took when he completed his driver's license came very handy now. Eddy was in distress and felt completely helpless. He let Nikolas provide the CPR to Michaela hoping that she would pull through.

While Nikolas was hard at work at saving her life, Eddy powerlessly stood over her repeating, "Michaela, my love, please come back to me; don't leave me….". Suddenly Michaela spit out quite a bit of salty water and opened her heavy eyelids to see Nikolas, Eddy and a group of strangers surrounding her. She realized she has survived the drowning and that she was safe although she felt ill and very weak. It did not matter that the top of her favourite bathing suit was ripped in her struggle to survive. Eddy covered her up with his body, picking her up in his large arms and carried her to their blanket. He wrapped her up in a towel and stroked her cheek gently pulling away a strand of hair from her forehead, apologizing to her.

"No, Eddy, it's not your fault. I think you and Nik just saved my life." She hugged him. "I thought I died. I saw all my life flash in front of me…… and suddenly I was no longer afraid. It was so….peaceful." He held her for a long time as she was still shaking and realized that he could have lost her today because of his carelessness.

Michaela did not feel well that night because of all the salty water that she drank during her drowning and wanted to rest. Nikole's parents found out about this drowning incident a little later and felt horrible that they could not have prevented it. After all they carried a huge responsibility for Michaela who came with them on vacation and they promised her mother that they would look after her. They have realized just because she is an eighteen year old young woman, they still need to be more aware of her whereabouts and her safety.

After Michaela retreated into her tent, not wanting to eat anything for supper, only rest, Eddy sought out Nikolas.

"I know you don't really like me." He cleared his throat nervously and then continued. "I see how you look at Michaela, but just know; she is with me."

Nikolas looked up at Eddy shading his eyes from the sun and seeing Eddy hovering over him in all his length while Nikolas sat on a camping chair drinking pop. His German was not as good as Michaela's who seemed to have picked it up so quickly, but for what he had to discuss with Eddy it was sufficient enough.

"What do you want?" He asked. Eddy swore under his breath angry with himself as this was not what he wanted to tell him.

"I just wanted to thank you for saving Michaela's life. I don't know what I would have done if she didn't make it." Eddy tried to correct his attitude.

Nikolas retorted back.

"I didn't do it for you. She could've died out there today. If you love her, you take better care of her!"

"Well, thanks anyway," Eddy said and Nikolas nodded in acknowledgement as Eddy went on his way.

Water, water everywhere…..not being able to breathe….No please, stop…….she can't breathe……..she is dying……..Eddy saw Michaela's face under the water drowning, trying to catch her breath, fighting for her life….. no wait a minute, it's not Michaela, it's his mother's face under the water,

struggling with her own life and him standing there helplessly,.........not knowing what to do......

Eddy shook off the flashback from his past away with a chill that ran down his spine and looked around himself realizing where he was; sitting in front of his tent in Bulgaria by the Black Sea, he tried to ground himself. He put his face into his large hands and then ran them through his dark curly hair. His eyes wondered towards Michaela's tent and he hoped she was alright. His own emotions were overwhelming him. To cope with it he went into the tent and reached out for the bottle of scotch that the boys had brought with them. He has not drunk since he met Michaela but tonight he needed it.

He drank the first large shot quickly directly from the bottle to feel the immediate impact warming his heart and stomach instantly; then he poured himself another large one into a plastic cup right after that and went back outside to sit and sip his scotch, trying to gather his thoughts. He molded over and over in his head how that drowning incident could have happened. He felt like Michaela was drowning him, pulling him under the water and the only way he could save her and himself was to throw her up in the air. 'Nik was right', he thought, 'for blaming me. I should have watched over her better.' If the roles were reversed between him and Nikolas, he was sure he would have punched him up for this. Eddy could not stand the thought of losing Michaela and he realized that she is the woman for him and it is not just a summer fling. He really cared about her, he thought.

Today was a horrendous day and he nearly lost the love of his life, he thought as the scotch was getting into his head. He headed towards the bathroom to relieve himself where he bumped into his younger brother.

"Hey, Ritchie....what's up?" He exclaimed.

Ritchie frowned at his brother with a concern telling him he should not be drinking.

"You know how you get when you drink, Eddy."

"Hey, what's it to you, little brother? You gonna lecture me? Do you have any idea what I've been through today? Do you get it that I nearly lost my wife today?!"

"Eddy, you're drunk. I don't know what you're talking about, but Michaela is not your wife and she never will be."

"We'll just have to see about that, won't we? I always wanted to marry young, beautiful Slavic chick that would adore me, take care of me, listen to me and not be mouthy and bitchy like the German girls and she would have my babies. It's not like the cold, ugly German girls that are soooo opinionated that my head hurts. Besides, you know that these Slovak chicks are so eager to get married and move away from their country to have a better life that they would do anything for their men. I know Michaela would follow me; all I have to do is ask her to marry me and then she'll live with me. It's really simple."

"Where would she live with you? At mom's apartment....you can forget about that. You can't even take care of yourself; still living at home at twenty-five." He laughed, and then continued to further provoke his older brother. "How are you going to take care of someone else?

"Shut up." Eddy warned him, but Ritchie ignored it.

"You're kidding yourself if you think mom would ever accept her into our family. She is not German. She'd never fit in." His brother's dark blond head was shaking in disbelief.

Eddy hit the side of the toilet stole where Ritchie was standing. That did not seem to scare him and he continued to aggravate his brother.

"Let's face it, you're fucked up. No woman would ever want you. Did you tell Michaela? Did you tell her about what you've done; where you've been? Does she know?" Eddy got pale in his face and started shaking with rage, while Ritchie overlooked his brother's reaction and continued to be his pesky old self.

"I think she should know if she is the one, don't you? Or you think she'll never find out?"

Eddy grabbed his brother under his neck and hissed at him two inches from his face.

"Shut up, you shut your peep hole, you little bastard.....understand?!"

"Let go of me, you asshole", his brother hissed losing his breath. Someone came into the bathroom at that moment and Eddy let go of his brother glaring at him with disdain.

"I think it's time for you to pack up and go home little brother." Eddy said and let him there gasping for air. Ritchie splashed some water over his face, checking out the redness on his neck. His brother could be a real jerk when he was drunk and thought what he should do next. He did not want to return back to the tent tonight as Eddy was probably getting drunker by the minute. He would sneak out his backpack with his sleeping bag if Eddy was not around and would sleep on the beach tonight. Tomorrow he would decide whether he would go back home or whether he would stay a little longer. This was his summer vacation and he would not let Eddy ruin it for him. The tent belonged to Eddy and if he decided to kick him out, he would not have another choice but to go home anyway. He thought he should not have gone with his brother on such a long trip on the whim. Either way he did not want to provoke him further tonight; he knew that his brother could push it too far.

When Ritchie left the public bathroom, Nikolas opened the bathroom stole that he was using minutes before Eddy and Richie had their altercation. He waited until they left, not wanting to get in the middle of it, but he wished he did not witness their argument. But he did witness it and was not sure what to do with this information. He thought of Michaela who was in love with Eddy, who did not even deserve such a great girl. Today, she could have died because of him, he thought. Tomorrow he can grab her by the neck, just like he did his brother. Nikolas decided to talk to Michaela tonight. He had to warn her; he had to protect her from this crazy guy. He promised her that he would always be there for her and he meant to keep his word. This was his way of protecting her.

When he came into their large tent, he hesitated, looking at the zipped up part of the section where Nikole and Michaela slept every night. It was only 7:30 in the evening but Michaela has been through a lot today and she might be sound asleep. He called out her name, not too loud as not to wake her in case she was asleep. She unzipped her side of the tent looking at Nikolas with tired blue-green eyes that nearly last their spark today.

"How are you feeling?" He asked.

"I've been better. My stomach hurts from the salty water and I still feel shaken and weak, but I'll be fine after some rest. I'm glad to see you though", she added. "I never had the chance to thank you for saving my life today, Nik."

"I saw you in the distance. I knew right away, you were in trouble, so I ran quickly to the water to help you. I could not even imagine if something happened to you."

Michaela touched his arm in affection and thanked him again. Nikolas nodded and hesitated to go on, but Michaela's intuition told her that he wanted something more than just to check on her.

"What is it Niko?" He loved when she called him that. She pointed to a spot on the blow up mattress where they normally slept. He took his flip-flaps off and sat down, crossed legged across from her, holding her by both hands. She could see concern in his face.

"Come on Niko, how long have we known each other? Most of our lives....", she answered herself. "You can tell me whatever it is. You know that, right?"

"Alright", he regained his audacity to tell her what he believed she needed to know. "I know this is probably not the best day to tell you this, considering what you've just been through.....but I don't think there is going to be an easier time to tell you this any day."

"What, Nik? You're starting to scare me."

"I'm sorry, Mika, that's not my intention to scare you but........."

"Oh, come on Nik, I'm scrapping that out of you like a sticky candy from a fuzzy blanket. Just spill the beans. How bad can that be?" Normally he would have laughed but the situation was too serious.

Nikolas continued in quieter voice keeping in mind that Eddy's tent was not that far away although they spoke in Slovak and he knew Eddy did not speak that language.

"Mika, you know that I care about you a lot and I always have. I never told you that but I loved you for as long as I can remember."

Michaela smiled at him with affection, "I love you too, Niko, but..... as a good friend."

"I know." He paused and took a deep breath as if to intake some courage from a thin air that was nowhere to be found.

"I wish it was more than that, but that's not what I wanted to talk to you about." He quickly changed the subject, feeling embarrassed.

"I was a witness of some unfortunate altercation between Eddy and his brother tonight that I thought you should know about." He started.

"What happened?" Michaela frowned concerned.

"Well, I was in the men's bathroom when Eddy became quite aggressive towards his brother. Listen, Michaela, he was drinking tonight and said some things that concerned me. He said that he always wanted to marry a Slavic beautiful girl that would take care of him and have his children because German girls are……well, not the same."

Michaela raised her eyebrows questioningly at Nikolas.

"And… what's wrong with that?" At this point Michaela pulled her hands away from his.

"Nothing, I guess, but the way he said it….I don't know. There is more to it than that. His brother was saying something about some secret or something like that, questioning Eddy whether he told you about it. It seemed to be something bad, something important although I don't know what, but Eddy got really angry at his brother for bringing it up. He tried to hush him and he wasn't very nice about it".

"Oh, come on, Nik. I'm sure it's nothing. Stuff like that happens between brothers."

"Mika, Eddy grabbed him by his neck to shut Ritchie up. There seems to be something important that he doesn't want you to know."

"Like what?"

"I don't know what it could be, but I don't think Eddy is a nice guy as he presents to be."

At this point, Michaela felt she needed to defend Eddy whom she loved so much and told Nikolas off.

"First of all, it's not nice to eavesdrop; second of all, this is none of your business and third of all, I'm sure it's nothing."

"Mika, I'm just worried about you. I think Eddy doesn't have a very good past or track record."

"You know what, Nik……just stop. I'm starting to think that you're just jealous of Eddy, so you try to portray him in a bad light and that's not very nice of you. You know how I feel about him." Unfortunately, Nikolas knew how she felt about Eddy. He wasn't blind; Michaela never hid that from him.

"I would never lie to you, Mika." He continued with concern in his voice.

"I didn't say that, but you are assuming Eddy is a bad guy, without having any basis for it. It doesn't even have a head or a tail what you're telling me. You don't know what they were really talking about, do you?"

Nikolas was getting frustrated with himself that he probably took a wrong approach to explain it to Michaela what he witnessed and repeating it in different ways would create more distance between him and Michaela who seemed to be so defensive of her new boyfriend. He finally added.

"Mika, I care about you and told you I'll always be there for you. I just don't want you to get hurt. Please be careful." Michaela softened towards Nikolas and finally said.

"Don't worry, Niko; I can take care of myself. You don't have to be concerned. If I need your help, you'll be the first that I call, ok?" She said it only half-jokingly to lighten the atmosphere.

They parted at that as Michaela wanted to be by herself to gather her thoughts. She needed fresh air and decided to go for a short walk on the beach to look at the ocean that nearly took her life today. Despite what she experienced today, the sound of waves watching it from the shore calmed her down. She glanced towards Eddy's tent, hoping to see him there, but he was nowhere to be seen, so she went for a walk. She thought about what Nikolas just told her and she didn't know what to make out of it. She had mixed feelings about it. Nikolas professed his love to her. She thought that he might have a crush on her the way he often looked at her, but he never acted on it and she assumed for the longest time that they were just good friends.

She thought about Eddy and tried to think what 'secret' he could have, if any. She was not feeling herself and concluded for now that Nikolas is probably just jealous or is overreacting to something that does not mean anything. With those thoughts, she returned back to the tent. She did not see Eddy at the beach either and she wished she could talk to him tonight, although she did not know what she would say. She was not sure whether she would say anything or ask him anything what Nikolas was talking about, as it did not make much sense to her. And she wouldn't bring up Nikolas in conversations with Eddy as she sensed the two had a natural dislike for one another and she would not break Nikolas' confidential observations. She concluded that if there was something important, Eddy would tell her about it himself. She did not see Eddy or his buddies anywhere so she retreated to her tent and turned in early. Nikole was still somewhere out, probably with Otto.

The following day, Michaela decided not to ruin the last week of their vacation that was remaining before they had to go back home. She did not want to confront Eddy and she just tried to enjoy his company and his affection. Quickly, she put out of her mind the conversation she had with Nikolas and her own affection towards Eddy was growing.

It occurred to Michaela that she barely knew Eddy or anything about him. She did not even know what Eddy did for a living and tried to have a conversation with him about it. He attempted to explain to her what he did, the jobs he has held in the past, but she had difficulties understanding it as it seemed that he did a little bit of everything.

Michaela having graduated from nursing school was taking the summer off and then she was planning to find a job most likely in a hospital or a doctor's office. Her mom worked as a nurse in the hospital and Michaela thought she would continue in her mother's footsteps when it came to her career. She tried to explain to Eddy that in her country young people from grade nine were going to 'collages' or in other words middle schools either for four year diplomas with a specialization or some people went for three years schooling to learn some specific job skills for a specific profession such as a mechanic, cook/baker or a hairdresser. She told Eddy that she just recently graduated from four years college getting her diploma in nursing. Eddy did not seemed to be impressed or even interested in her career choices and pointed out that she would be busy one day as a wife and a mother and deserved better than work eight to four every day.

It did not matter to her when she learned that Eddy finished only Grade ten High School education and did not have intentions to go further. He appeared to be quite bright and more street smart than book smart. He told her that at age twenty-five he would explore other opportunities after he returned from vacation although he was not sure what he wanted to do with his life.

Eddy's friend and his brother wanted to go back to Germany days ago, but Eddy wanted to stay with Michaela. Otto had to go back to work as his vacation was ending and his brother did not want to stay with Eddy alone under one tent considering his rapid changes in moods and violent temper and despite having more than a month of summer holidays before he went back to school, he decided to spend it in Germany instead. They all came by train, so it was not like they were missing out on a ride when Eddy decided to stay another week, just to be with Michaela longer.

Now that the boys were gone, they had his tent all to themselves and spent a lot of time there together making out. Michaela could not believe that she could fall in love so much with someone whom she just met less than a month ago.

When it was time for them to part and go their separate ways, Michaela had tears in her eyes thinking she might never see Eddy again and her love would simply end, although Eddy tried to reassure her that he would write to her often and eventually they will end up together. She didn't argue that but she was not sure how realistic it was. She wanted to believe it so much but had her doubts. Perhaps it had a lot to do with her insecurity.

He was kissing her tear covered face and then hugging her tightly, holding her for a long time, not wanting to let her go. They exchanged addresses and phone numbers and he said he might even show up at her door steps one day surprising her.

Otto made similar promises to Nikole week earlier but something told her, she might not see him again when they were saying their goodbyes.

Michaela pressed her slender body in Eddy's embrace for a long time and then gave him a last passionate kiss good bye. It was excruciating for Nikolas to watch it so he busied himself by helping his dad load their things into the van.

"Don't cry my love", Eddy whispered to her, "you hear from me soon".

She watched Eddy from the back seat of the van. He was just standing there his hand raised in the last greeting to her as the van was on its way. Eddy's figure was getting smaller and smaller until he completely disappeared out of her sight and she wondered this time out loud whether she would ever see him again. Nikole wondered the same thing about

Otto last week but was not as emotional when they were saying their farewell. Nikole took this brief relationship with Otto with a reservation that this might have been just a summer fling and that it is likely that neither of them will see the German boys again, but she kept her thoughts to herself as she did not want to upset Michaela, who was already quite emotional. Nikole just hugged her in silence for a while, letting her cry in the back seat.

Nikolas wished he knew what to do in such situation or whether to do anything. It was so awkward for him. He wanted to comfort her somehow, but he knew it would be futile. He was hurting inside as he felt the distance between him and Michaela growing even though she was just couple meters away from him sitting at the very back seat.

He sat in the van sulking quietly, withdrawn from the world. He tried to read his book, but his thoughts wondered and he had hard time focusing on anything else but on Michaela. At times he took over the drive from his father so they would get home faster and this time they decided that they would not stop anywhere overnight. So Nikolas napped during the day and drove during the night when Michaela was asleep on the back seat. That way he avoided talking to her for the most part. The trip back home was uneventful and somehow it seemed faster almost by two days as they drove non-stop with just few breaks in between.

Nikolas realized that he had missed his chance with Michaela and was mad at himself that he should have acted on his feelings sooner. Now it was too late and he could only wish to go back in time. He knew that he has lost the love of his life and he will never get her back because her heart belonged to someone else. Michaela was quiet too as she was not feeling physically well but she attributed it to her broken heart and loneliness.

Chapter 6

Back at home, Michaela if she were to expect a surprise it would have been for her belated birthday party, but instead her mother prepared her a different and quite unexpected surprise by introducing her to a new boyfriend whom she met while Michaela was away on vacation. Her mother was so thrilled that she considered moving him in soon. Klaudia Martenz said that they went to college together years ago when David wanted to become a medic, but dropped out of school early not finishing it as he found out he didn't have the stomach for seeing blood on regular basis. They have lost touch with one another for years. He was divorced as well and had a daughter from his first marriage, just like Klaudia had her daughter. Klaudia admitted to Michaela that she had a crush on him back in collage and could not believe that he came back to her life so unexpectedly bumping into him in a store. They immediately 'clicked' and had many things in common.

Michaela knew that after her father left them when she was only six years old that her mother was very lonely and although she had an occasional boyfriend, she did not present him as Michaela's step-father, nor she move him in. David Kovalik was a man in mid-fifties with a beard resembling Chuck Norris. He wasn't very tall. His bushy eyebrows and bushy chest that was showing through his half way unbuttoned shirt were giving him a little bit of a caveman look, Michaela thought to herself. She was polite and accepting of her mother's decision because she wanted her mother to be happy but perhaps because he was suddenly moving into their home; it gave Michaela an uneasy feeling.

"Michaela, this is David Kovalik. David, this is my beautiful daughter, Michaela, but we often call her Mika for short". Her mother introduced them.

"You do have a very lovely daughter. It's very nice to meet you, Miska."

"It's Mika or Michaela." She said sternly and frowned at David. She hated when someone called Misa or Miska as it meant a little mouse in Slovak language and when she was younger, kids made fun of her and that's why her family and close friends called her Mika.

"Oh, perhaps I didn't say that much." He scratched his reddish beard.

"No of course, you couldn't have known." Klaudia came quickly to his defense when she saw her daughter's frowning face.

David stayed that evening for supper and cake celebrating Michaela's late birthday. He was asking Michaela all kinds of questions that she did not feel like answering and she often just gave him a forced polite smile or answered with one or two words.

"Michaela is a very shy girl especially with new people, but once you get to know her she is a chatter box." Klaudia said when she noticed her daughter being quite withdrawn.

When they were alone, Klaudia asked her daughter.

"So what do you think?" When Michaela just shrugged, Klaudia continued to build her case in her favour.

"I've been trying for so long to find you a good father to take care of you after your father left us and never turned back. Unfortunately, it just didn't happen that way. I think this guy could be it even though he is coming a little late into your life." After a long pause she continued.

"Please say something, Mika. I need to know how you feel about it."

"I don't need a father, mom. We were doing so well, just the two of us. And why he has to move in after such a short time?"

"Oh, sweetheart, you're growing up so fast. You just turned 18 years old. Before I know it you'll find someone and move away and I'm not getting any younger. I don't want to be alone in my old age. Please try to understand that. Besides it will greatly help us financially. You don't think I'm going to let him mooch off of us. And he is not like that; he is actually a very generous man. He has a car and he will help out financially once he lives here. So that's a big part of it too. You know well how hard it has been for both of us. Life can be better from now on." She took a deep breath and when Michaela was quiet looking down at the floor, Klaudia continued.

"I'm tired of working two jobs and always living in poverty. If you one day have a chance of a better life, I'll tell you 'go and start a better life, don't even think twice about it'. I feel like this is my chance. Look, it's not like I'm marrying him tomorrow", she joked, but only partly. When Michaela was still silent, Klaudia went on.

"Look, darling, both me and him had our share of bad relationships that did not work out for either of us and neither of us is that young that we can waste years dating. So, yes, we are jumping into it quickly, but you'll see that when you find the one, it will not matter how long you have known him. Michaela I haven't felt so alive for such a long time. He makes me laugh, he is really nice to me, he buys me nice things, he is a good father to his daughter and I know he will love you too. Not to mention that my heart skips a beat when I'm around him." At that, Michaela looked up and smiled at her mother thinking of Eddy. She now knew how it felt to be in love and how hard it is to let go. She has to tell her mother about Eddy, she thought.

"Mom, I understand how you feel and why you're doing what you're doing. If you accept him into our small family; then so will I." She hesitated for a moment gathering her thoughts how she would tell her mom about Eddy and finally she simply said.

"Mom, I met someone too. And I fell in love with him while I was away." It was Klaudia's turn to smile.

"That's wonderful, Mika. Who is it? Tell me all about him." So Michaela did tell her mother about Eddy, how she met him, that he was from Dresden from Eastern Germany vacationing with his friend and with his younger brother in Bulgaria and happened to be in Varna at the same time she was there with Nikole's family. She avoided telling her mother about the drowning incident as not to worry her. But she told her that she believes that Eddy too fell in love with her, but that she worries that she will never see him again, considering the distance and language and cultural barriers. Her mother reassured her.

"If he loves you, you'll hear from him soon and if you don't than he wasn't the one".

Within a week David moved in and around the same time, Michaela got her first unexpected letter from Eddy. All her worries vanished and the letter she got melted her heart. Eddy's handwriting was difficult to read because it looked like chicken scratches, but Michaela didn't mind and once she got used to his handwriting recognizing his curly 'y's and 'g's, it became easier and familiar to her.

August 6, 1984

My Dear Michaela,

I'm back in Germany in my mother's home in Dresden. For now, you can write to me here but I'm looking for a new place for me and hopefully for you too one day. I feel like I'm not too far from you, yet too far to touch you. I can't stop thinking about you. I miss you so much. I miss your smile, your kisses and your touch. I miss looking into your blue-green eyes just like I miss the sea where I've met you. I miss our nightly adventures on the beach. I know you worried that you would never hear from me again, but like I promised you, I am writing to you to tell you that I don't want to be without you. I know you're the one for me, so I really hope you haven't forgotten about me.

I miss you so much and I wish I could just hold you in my arms. I will call you soon when I get the chance.

Forever Yours, Eddy

Michaela must have read his letter at least fifty times. Not necessarily because of the German language difficulties. Well that too, but mainly because she could not believe that he wrote to her such a beautiful love letter. She did not expect it. It was so romantic and thoughtful of him. Just as he mentioned it in his letter, she did not expect to hear from him. She often thought that it was not realistic to have a relationship because of the distance and because of her own insecurities thinking that he could have any girl he wanted. He is so handsome with his dark brown eyes, thick curly hair and full kissable mouth. Any girl might be all over him; so why would he pick her? Why would he want an ordinary girl from a small town in Slovakia? All her self-doubt was wiped out with this love letter. She never had a serious boyfriend before although there were some that were interested but Michaela never gave them a chance because nobody made her feel so special; made her feel important. She sat down immediately wanting to write back to him. She wanted him to know that she is thinking about him and misses him a lot. With the help of German/Slovak dictionary to assure she didn't make many mistakes, she wrote back to him.

August 11, 1984

My Dear Eddy,

> *My heart skipped a beat when I got your lovely letter. I am so happy to have heard from you so quickly. Of course, I'm thinking about you. I think about you all the time. I miss you very much and I feel lonely without you here. I love you so much, Eddy. I really hope that we'll see each other again.*

> *A lot has changed for me here at home. My mom has a new boyfriend and he is unfortunately moving in but it's great that my mom is happy again too. I am still trying to enjoy the rest of the summer and soon I will start looking for a job.*

> *I wish you were here with me. I think about our time together in Bulgaria. I would go back in a heartbeat if I could be with you again. You can be proud of me as I have been studying German, learning new words every day, so we can talk more easily together. Write back soon. I'm looking forward to hearing from you again.*

> *Forever yours, Michaela*

She wrote down Eddy's address in Dresden and without sealing it she placed the letter carefully along with his letter into her gray purse and headed over to Nikole.

Enthusiastically, Michaela rang the doorbell of Nikole's house, Eddy's letter in her hand to share with her the wonderful news of hearing from him. Nikole was happy for Michaela, she really was and wished that it worked out for her, but at the same time it reminded her that Otto never wrote back to her even though she already sent him a post card the first day she came home. She gave him her address, but he didn't write yet.

Michaela read Eddy's letter to Nikole, word by word, translating it to Slovak language and asked Nikole what she thought about it. Then she read her letter that she wrote as a response back to him before she sent it out.

"This is so romantic. You're very lucky, Mika. I wish Otto remembered to write to me as well. I thought I wouldn't care if I never saw him again, but I do care. I sent him a postcard, but I haven't heard back yet." She no longer could hold it in her. Michaela suddenly realized that she has not even thought of Nikole falling in love with Eddy's friend and felt quite selfish.

"I'm sorry, Niki. I feel like a horrible friend right now. I should have considered your feelings about Otto and here I'm bragging about my relationship with Eddy. But you never know, he still might write to you. Maybe it just takes him some time to write back."

"Yeah, right." Nikole said doubtfully.

"I'm sure he has thought about you but maybe he is not much of a writer. Not too many guys like to write. And besides, you still might hear from him. It's been only a week since we've been back." Michaela tried to cheer her friend up.

"Don't worry about me. I kind of thought that I might never hear from Otto again, but it sure would have been nice. In a way I feel used by him. You know....him sleeping with me and now probably just forgetting about me." Michaela wanted to comfort her friend but did not know how. This easily could have been her situation as well.

Telling Nikole what she wanted to hear might make her feel good in the moment but it might be a lie. So, she decided to change the subject and asked about Nikolas, which she soon regretted as that was another sore subject, this time for Michaela.

"You know, Nik, will be Nik. Annoying brother as usual, but I think you broke his heart, Michaela Martenz." Nikole only called her by her full name when she was serious about something.

"He doesn't talk about it and tries to hide it, but I know him well enough that it bothers him a lot. He always had a crush on you and I think he went to the vacation only to make a move on you." Michaela felt bad for Nikolas because she never wanted to hurt him. She did not even realize at the time she met Eddy that Nikolas was interested in her. But now it made all sense to her why he was so attentive to her, why he wanted to go hiking with her and entertaining her on the way to Bulgaria and how protective he was of her. He saved her life and she will never forget that. At the same time, her self-esteem has grown this summer considering that she had two guys that were interested in her. Her mother always told her, "We can only chose from those that want us, so as women we are at a great disadvantage. You have to wait for the man to make his first move." That is why she did not write to Eddy first. And now she had two men that were interested in her but since Nikolas did not make his move fast enough, she made her choice way back in Bulgaria. Her heart already belonged to Eddy and her mind was already in Germany picturing her new, wonderful life with him.

Michaela was invigorated by the letter from Eddy and she was highly motivated to continue to study German language to assure that she became more fluent in her conversations and wanted to surprise Eddy how much improvement she has made. After visit at Nikole's she rushed to the nearest post office to mail her precious letter to Eddy.

While Michaela busied herself with studying German during her summer holidays, David made a comfortable home for himself in their two bedroom apartment.

Michaela's mom was still working the afternoon shift at the hospital as a nurse and was glad that Michaela would not have to spend the evenings alone. Michaela did not know why but felt quite uncomfortable around David, whom she barely knew. He told her she could call him 'dad', but she was far from being ready for that and she probably never would be. Perhaps it would have been different if she had grown up with him, but at this age she could not image calling him that since she just met him. All her life when someone asked her about her dad, she would say that she didn't have a dad because she did not have any contact with her biological father. He never made the effort to see her although she knew he lived in the same town as her and could have come any time he wanted to, but didn't.

David was very generous to her and to Klaudia and he brought a lot of nice things into their home from his old apartment and he showered them with gifts and attention. Michaela noticed that there was more delicious food in the fridge. Not that she had ever gone hungry, but the food was expensive and her mother would buy only bare necessities. Often that meant living on potatoes and flour based meals or pasta. Fruit and meat were a special treat. Only the seasonal fruit was available in stores and when oranges or bananas were imported, there was always a long line up on the streets and it was overpriced. They never had that in abundance. They ate meat usually only once a month, but since David moved in, they had enough fruit, meat and meat products and other goodies that they could not normally afford. Life with David, Michaela noticed, just like her mother told her, became easier at least when it came to finances. Her mother could afford to quit her weekend job and instead they drove in David's car as a happy family to High Tatras or visited surrounding castles. Michaela enjoyed it a lot and even though she was eighteen years old, she did not feel the embarrassment to tag along with her family like other teenagers often did. She was past that stage being embarrassed by her family. Perhaps because she seldom had a chance to get out of their town and she quite enjoyed it. So in that sense, life was easier.

David's daughter, Marcela at times came with them on these trips or spent the weekends with them. Michaela enjoyed her company and for the first time she felt that she has a complete family. She always wanted to have a big sister and now she did. Marcela was twenty-one years old and lived with her own mother, but it still felt to Michaela that she gained not only a big sister but a good friend.

In turn, Michaela learnt that she would have to compromise with David's highly critical demands of her. She felt it was never good enough how she cleaned or how she prepared the meals when her mother worked, but to her it was part of life and necessity. Perhaps because of David's criticism and judgment she was not as fond of him but tolerated him as her mother's partner.

One Friday evening, while her mother was still at work, Michaela wanted to watch some TV in the living room, but as she walked in, David was already sitting on the sofa only in his robe watching some pornography. As soon as Michaela realized what David was watching, she started to back out of the living room when suddenly David called out to her.

"Hey, Miska, you're old enough, you can watch this. Don't worry, I won't tell your mom. I bet she would never let you watch something like that. Am I right?"

Michaela did not want to watch it with David and felt quite embarrassed walking in on him while he was watching it. But David didn't feel embarrassed at all. When he saw her hesitate, he ordered her to sit down.

"You might learn something new. You have a boyfriend, don't you, such a pretty young girl? Don't you want to make him happy; learn what makes a man excited and crazy for you?"

Michaela was no longer a virgin but felt quite inexperienced, especially with Eddy who was a great lover and had so much more experience than her. She did not have much to offer to Eddy but herself. Although she did not think it was appropriate what David was doing by inviting her to watch it with him, she noticed that David had been drinking and there was some intimidation in his voice. She did not know whether it was fear or curiosity that won over her, but she sat down in the armchair, pressing her knees together uncomfortably and watched with David for a while. She would have never thought that looking at such revealing scenes would actually turn her on. She felt even more embarrassed that she couldn't control her body's reactions to it. She wished Eddy was here with her making love to her instead.

She saw a girl in her early twenties slide into bed completely naked under the covers beside an older man pretending she fell asleep, while he fondled her and then climbed on top of her. David told her that the guy making love to the 'sleeping girl' is her step-father. They stayed alone because her mother died as David explained the events in the 'movie'.

"Look, how much she is enjoying it even though she knows it's wrong, but he knows she wants it."

She had to leave, she thought, it was wrong on so many levels, but when she tried standing up David stopped her by touching her knee and gently pushing her back into the armchair with his other hand. He sat back down crossed legged on the sofa across from her, his robe half way open revealing his bushy chest as his shirts often did. Her face was burning red when she noticed that he was completely naked under the robe revealing himself to her without any ignominy. He noticed her quick glance at his penis and her burning red cheeks. She quickly looked away, pretending she hasn't noticed; she felt embarrassed. He smirked at her and opened his robe further.

"Do you like what you see? I bet you haven't seen such a big one before. You can touch it if you want." He completely revealed his erection to her now touching himself with pleasure and stupid grin on his face.

At that point, she had enough. She was going to be sick. She stood up quickly and went to her room. She felt guilty that she stuck around to watch the porn even if for only a brief moment and for seeing David naked, touching himself. What was she thinking when she stayed in the living room, Michaela questioned her common sense. She knew that it was wrong but quickly dismissed it that he was just drunk and he wouldn't do something so inappropriate if he was sober. That night, she turned and could not sleep, hoping that her mother would come home soon from work. David's presence in the apartment felt more uncomfortable than ever and Michaela did not know what to do about it.

The following morning, David grabbed her by her arm whispering to her to be quiet about last night as nothing happened anyway. He surprisingly apologized to her saying that he shouldn't have drunk so much and act so stupid and that he only missed her mother. Michaela decided that for her mother's sake she would give David another chance and wouldn't tell her anything or to anyone else for that matter. She felt that she should have known better. After all she was now a young adult, yet she somehow became part of something so disturbing and although he did not touch her, it gave her an eerie feeling.

In the afternoon, David bought Michaela a box of chocolates, winking at her and putting his index finger towards his lips indicating for her to be quiet about it when her mother was not watching. When Klaudia saw the chocolates, she asked what it was for. David quickly offered an explanation.

"Well, I never got Michaela a birthday present as she was away. So it is a small belated birthday present."

"That's so sweet, David." Klaudia said and kissed him on the cheek.

"Her own father did not even remember her birthday." Her mother commented. That certainly did not make Michaela feel any better not only about her mother not seeing through David's double faced personality but also her own father's lack of interest in her that her mother didn't have to remind her of.

Michaela was uneasy about the whole situation and hoped that last night was the first and last incident. She was glad it was the weekend and her mother had couple of days off.

Lately, Michaela was feeling down about her life and about the whole David situation. Not knowing what to expect is daunting. The only console she felt she had was Eddy's love letter that she read every day before she went to sleep thinking about him and wondering what he was doing at the moment. Other than that, she started to dislike her own home and David had a lot to do with it. Besides, she did not have anything to look forward to other than hoping to hear from Eddy again. There was no school or job for her to go to, but at least she still had Eddy somewhere in a distance. Who knew when or if she would hear from him again? Eddy was her hope, her love and her way out of depressing life; far away from David and the disturbing memories that he planted in her head. Eddy, although far away, became the center of her universe and the only other focus she had was on improving her German that Eddy inspired in her to progress in quickly and thinking what life with him would look like. She could not focus on anything else and she felt unhappy without him. It did not help that she felt physically ill almost every day. Usually she felt nausea in the morning that eventually went away and she wondered whether she was coming down with a flu or was simply disgusted with David's looks checking her over and licking his lips every time she passed by and when her mother wasn't looking. Perhaps it was just her paranoid imagination working over time because she disliked that guy.

"What's wrong with you?" Nikole asked her one day when she saw Michaela's pale face after returning from the bathroom.

"I don't know. I haven't been feeling well since we came back from the vacation. Maybe I caught some bug on the way; flu or something. I just keep throwing up at least once or twice a day."

"When did you have your period?" Nikole queried with worry.

Michaela paused thinking about it for a while. Why she has not thought about it?

"I didn't have it since….the first week in Bulgaria…..so that's what? Hmm,…….about six or seven weeks."

"Have you been late before?"

Michaela's head started to spin and she thought she would get sick again.

"No, I haven't. You don't think I'm….." She could not make herself say those words.

"Pregnant?" Nikole finished her sentence.

"That can't be. He is hmm……..experienced. He knew what he was doing. I know Eddy was being careful." Michaela said with hesitancy and a scorn in her face.

"Careful? Careful using protection or careful making sure nobody interrupted you?" She questioned sarcastically.

"Oh my god, Nikole, we didn't use any protection." As if it just occurred to her.

"He promised he would be careful and I thought he was. How could he do that to me?"

"I'm sure he didn't do it on purpose, but you should have used something."

"Well, excuse me; I didn't plan on having sex on the beach so I didn't pack any condoms. What am I going to do, Nikole?"

Nikole tried to think rationally as she saw her friend panicking.

"Ok, ok, let's think it through. You don't know for sure that you're pregnant so the first thing you have to do is get the pregnancy test and find out."

"Let's go." Michaela stood up and commanded with urgency in her voice. "Pharmacy…now, you're coming with me. Come on, I never done this before."

Once they brought the test back to Nikole's house, Michaela was relieved when neither the parents nor Nikolas were home. She couldn't deal with him too. After she took the test, waiting five minutes felt like an eternity that would change her life forever.

"It's a plus sign." Michaela cried out and almost passed out. She sat down on edge of the bathtub, putting her head into her hands, she started weeping. Nikole tried to support her stroking her head and saying reassuring words although she was not sure what to say in such a situation. She was not sure what she would want to hear if she was in her shoes. They were so young. When she had no more tears left, she flooded Nikole with questions that neither of them had any answers for.

"What am I going to do now, Niki? I messed up my whole life. What if Eddy never writes again? Never comes? What if I don't ever see him again? How could I be so stupid? Trusting a guy to be 'careful'? Really? How stupid a girl could get?" Michaela was beating herself up with self-pity and guilt. Nikole had few consoling words to offer that Michaela did not even hear and continued on her tangent.

"I don't want to be a single mother. I had so much that I wanted to do in life. I'm not ready for that. And what will Eddy say to that? Maybe that will bring him to me faster. Yeah, right…what am I thinking, he probably runs the other way." Michaela continued in her monologue.

"Oh, shit….shit, what do I do? Do I tell him? Or should I just ask him to come and tell him in person? If he of course calls at all! Or should I go to Dresden to see him; to tell him in person? Oh, my god, my mother will kill me! How do I tell her?!" When Nikole had a chance to say something, she offered her unsolicited advice.

"You know you have some other options."

"WHAT?! Are you kidding……..you mean….like what….abortion?!" She exclaimed, nearly hysterical.

"I could never live with myself if I did that......it's a human being.......
growing inside me......oh, god; neither could I give it away, not care about
the baby.........just like my own father doesn't care about me. There is just
no way out." And the tears poured down her cheeks again.

It's as if this news was not tough enough for Michaela to deal with,
David was making her life at home miserable. On one hand he was
showering her with gifts that she didn't want from him, smirking and
winking at her, making her really uncomfortable and giving her the
creeps. And on the other hand he would criticize everything that she did
or did not do portraying himself as a parent in power that he was not.
But he was smart about it because in front of Kladia he acted as a caring
and supportive step-father. It turned Michaela's stomach upside down
thinking how uncanny and hypocritical he was, but she could not deal
with him right now. She had a bigger problem to focus on that she did not
know how to handle. If only Eddy called her. She didn't want to write it
into a letter.

Her heart skipped a beat when she received a small package from
him. She held her breath while she struggled to open the package, her
hands shaking with anticipation. There was a regular cassette tape from
a portable tape recorder that she saw in Eddy's tent back in Bulgaria and
another letter. She did not know what to attend to first. She decided to
read the letter first he wrote her and then she would listen to the tape. As
always, she pulled out her German/Slovak dictionary, just in case she
did not understand something. Lately, she has been using it a lot. She lied
down on her stomach, opened Eddy's letter and read:

August 16, 1984

My Love,

> *I received your lovely letter. It made me very happy that you
> still think about me and want to be with me. I'm writing you this
> letter to let you know how much you mean to me and how much I
> want to be with you. You're always on my mind. I made you a little
> tape with some German lessons for you to practice new words and*

to improve your German. Sorry for the poor quality but that's the best that I can do. I've put a lot of work into it, so I hope you'll like it. I want to see you again. I'm crazy about you. I'll call you this coming weekend, so I hope you'll be home.

I can't wait to hear your angelic voice.

Love Eddy

Michaela was ecstatic that she received another letter from Eddy. The letter was not as romantic as the first one; but it was a very loving letter and it gave Michaela hope that she will see him soon. She wished she could tell him about being pregnant but she needed to do it in person if she ever got the chance. She had no idea how she would deliver to him this unexpected news or how he would take it. But one thing she knew, that she had to tell him at some point. Surely, he would know what to do. Or would he? She just might have ruined her chances of a better life with this unexpected conception. But at least, there was a good chance he would come.

She inserted the tape into her small play deck and put all her attention on listening to the tape. The static was bad. She heard some melody in the background; she readily recognized the "99 Air balloons" song that she sang in Bulgaria. 'Oh, he remembered', she thought, when suddenly strong Eddy's voice sounded too close to the microphone on the tape overpowering the song.

Hey my love. I thought you might like to hear my voice for a change. I wish I could hear your beautiful voice and see your lovely face. I miss you so much. I prepared some German conversational lessons for you to listen to and wanted you to understand everything and to practice what you would answer in return. That way we don't have to plug in the Russian words for things that you don't understand in German.

Eddy went on to use conversations in his German 'lessons' he created about what they have experienced in Bulgaria and conversations they have had there. He used some more complex words to help expand Michaela's vocabulary that he thought she might not know. How well he knew her after such a short time remembering her repertoire of her limited German vocabulary. He even translated it into Slovak in small parts which was most impressive. Slovak is a very difficult language and the fact that he took time to look it up trying to pronounce it was quite impressive to Michaela. He must have bought himself a German/Slovak dictionary and even though his Slovak pronunciation was really bad and incorrect, she still understood what he was trying to say and it was the sweetest and most considerate thing that anyone had done for her. It didn't matter he sounded funny when he tried to say some Slovak words in a strong German accent. She loved him for that even more. Often it made her laugh remembering their times in Bulgaria how they struggled with conversations which was actually a lot of fun. This is exactly what she needed at this time considering how she was feeling lately.

On the tape he asked questions that he wanted to know about her and her family to get to know her better so she had time to prepare answers in German. She was quite amazed how much she has learnt in such a short period of time since she met Eddy; more than she has learnt in three years on her own. Love is certainly a great motivator she speculated.

He asked her questions such as whether she had any siblings and how close she was with her family. What she liked doing for fun, what was her favourite food and what music she listened to. He wanted to know her values and even how many children she wanted to have. Wow, he was thinking about children, Michaela was surprised and pleased because she always wanted to have a family of her own one day, but not quite yet. Although, now the situation she was in, she might not have much choice about it.

He wanted her to prepare answers so they could have flowing conversations together. The very last question on the tape took her by surprise completely and it gave her a lot to think about and it gave her glimmer of hope for the future.

I'd like to know if you would ever come to live in Germany with me? Could you imagine your life with me? She listened through it few times assuring that she really understood what he was asking her. She understood exactly what he was saying, but she had difficult time believing it. What would she tell him? Isn't it what she actually wanted? Isn't it what she hoped for? Is this even possible that her dream would come true? Her head was spinning with happiness. Although sometimes a self-doubt crept in telling her "that's impossible, I've never been so lucky." But if he was really serious and if the baby didn't scare him away, she made up her mind that she would follow him to the other end of the world without any hesitation. She loved him so much and that's all that mattered along the fact that she carried his baby under her heart. She hoped that would not turn him away from her and change his mind.

She did not know what she would do about David. Should she tell her mother? It will be her word against his as she was sure he would deny everything; all his inappropriate misdemeanors. And he actually has not done anything to her, other than giving her some lascivious looks that she did not know how to interpret and an occasional light slap on her buttock that he ventured in passing. When she gave him a disapproving look, he dismissed it as a joke.

"Oh, my, you're so sensitive, Miska. Can't you take a joke?" He gave her another slap on her bottom as to urging her to go do what she was supposed to do.

"Get me a beer!" He ordered her. Things like that became quite common on daily basis and soon Michaela started to normalize it, although she despised him. Perhaps that's how fathers treated their daughters when they did not know how else to connect or interact with them, she wondered. Michaela would not know because she never had a father-daughter relationship. Perhaps it was not a big deal. He did not reveal himself to her again and despite the occasional slap on her buttocks and some suggestive comments about her body, Michaela thought that the incident with the porn was a onetime thing because he was drunk but would not dare do anything else. After all, he was her mother's partner and her supposed step-father. Although she developed a dislike for him for apparent reasons, she thought he was quite harmless especially when she spent time with Marcela who visited them most weekends. Michaela was fond of her and they became quite close.

To Michaela who was an only child and always wanted to have a sister; it was the coolest feeling to suddenly have a 'big sister' or at least it seemed to Michaela that she finally had a sister that she always wanted, especially when she got along well with her. She would often talk to

Marcela about Eddy and asked her what she thought about him. When Marcela gave her positive feedback from her reaction to her experiences with Eddy, Michaela was content.

A thought occurred to her that she could ask Marcela if her dad ever done anything sexually inappropriate to her when she was younger, but she quickly dismissed the idea that she might lose a 'sister' and a good friend. She started to feel like a complete family although Marcela didn't live with them. It was her and her mom for such a long time and she always felt that her family was incomplete despite Aunt Sylvie being big part of her life.

Michaela thought surely, David could not be such a bad guy if he has such a lovely daughter that adores him and has such a close relationship with him. She tried to accept David the way he was especially as her mother adored him and spoke about him quite highly.

She quickly put David out of her mind with all his impropriety when she received the long awaited phone call from Eddy. Michaela nearly screamed into Eddy's ear from joy when she heard his deep voice.

"Hi, my love! Do you still remember me?" Eddy's deep voice sounded so sexy over the phone. Michaela was ecstatic to hear from him.

"Hi. I would always remember you! Thank you for the letters and for the creative tape. I love it. I listen to it all the time. I just sent you another letter in response. You should be getting it soon."

"That's good. And you're welcome. I miss you, sweetie. I can't talk long, but I just wanted to let you know that I found a new place for us; it could be our new home. I want to come see you very soon. I'll stop in Prague first before coming to Kosice. I heard Prague is gorgeous city." Eddy said enthusiastically. He is such an adventurer, she could not help smiling.

"That's wonderful. Yes, Prague is really beautiful....." Michaela agreed with him.

"Yes, but not as beautiful as you, darling. Anyway, after Prague I'll come directly to your home town and perhaps you can show me around.

"With pleasure."

"I was wondering whether I could stay overnight in your home when I come or should I go to a hotel?"

Without hesitation and without asking her mother, she answered quickly.

"Of course you can stay here. Why would you waste money on a hotel?"

"That's great. I can't wait to see you my love. I wish you were here with me."

"Me too, Eddy, it's so good to hear from you. I miss you so much. I have to tell you....."

"I'll talk to you soon" Eddy interrupted her suddenly. "I don't have more change....Love you......." and the line went dead. Michaela was still holding the phone in her hand, staring into the space, listening to the peeping sound of the disconnected phone line. He must have been calling from a pay phone. She did not have a chance to tell him she was pregnant and perhaps that was better that way, she thought. Telling him face to face might be better just to see his reaction and then she would know what to do. He still might leave her, but at least she'll know what she is dealing with. She has to wait for a little while longer. Hopefully he will come see her soon as he promised.

Michaela was as if in a seventh heaven after hearing Eddy's voice over the phone. It reassured her that he still thinks about her and hopefully is really serious about their relationship. She continued to listen to his tape and read his love letters several times each day. Just like a drug addict needs his daily fix, she needed to feel ongoing connection with Eddy and right now that was the only way. It gave her assurance about their love and kept her going. She could not wait to see him again. Every night was so lonely without him. She wished he could wrap his hands around her and plant his gentle kisses all over her face and body.

Not seeing Eddy for a period of time and longing for him, she often idealized him, not even realizing that she was ascribing characteristics to him that he might not possess, not aware how little she actually knew him. But all that mattered to her was their love. She was often day dreaming about him and at night she would twist and turn thinking about him, yearning for his touch.

Another night full of dreams of Eddy touching her, making love to her, feeling his hands all over her.....she woke up with a startle or was she still dreaming?

Gabriela Elias

"Shhh, hush. I'm not gonna hurt you. We're just gonna have some fun together. I can see it in you that you want it too. I like how your body is responding to my touch....you're already so wet and hot........I know you want it," she heard him panting close to her ear, while his hand wondered under her blanket. She realized her legs were spread apart and she no longer had her underwear on.

Chapter 7

*E*DDY? SHE THOUGHT IN DARKNESS, half asleep. *That can't be.* *It's just a dream……..no it's a nightmare…..*She realized it was David when she felt his weight on top of her. NO, she screamed but no sound came out of her lungs; only a muffled noise. This must be just a nightmare and she will wake up any second now, but she didn't. It was dark; she tried to adjust her sleepy eyes in the darkness completely awaking into a cruel reality. She was living the nightmare that she had never even imagined. Her mouth was covered by his hairy large hand and the other hand was touching her under her nightgown that he suddenly pulled up to her neck, revealing her naked body. She was fully awake now, twisting and turning her head from side to side trying to fight him off.

"Don't fight it, you know you want it, you pretty little whore. You think you gonna provoke me with your tight ass and I wouldn't get a piece of it?" He hissed in her face.

She smelled alcohol on his breath. He was unbuttoning his pants…… she was hitting him with her free hands and scratching him with her fingernails and pushing him off of her in futility. He had to restrain her hands. Freeing her mouth, made her scream loud while his one hand grabbed both of hers holding them above her head.

"You can scream as much as you want, nobody can hear you. Your mother won't be home for another two hours. I just spoke to her. Don't worry; we have plenty of time to play." She wanted to push his heavy body off of her but she was completely restrained. She felt absolutely powerless. He was still holding her both hands with force in his left hand and his strength surprised her. She wanted to kick him off but her legs were spread apart being held by his legs and by his body weight that was hovering over her. Her screams were futile as nobody was at home and she knew nobody would help her. Soon she gave up her screams and tears rolled down her face changing into pleas as he entered her, thrusting into her with force. She couldn't believe this was happening to her. Although it seemed to her to have lasted a life time, he didn't prolong her agony as he was done quite quickly. He finally let go of her hands, zipped up his fly and stood up, freeing her body that felt light as a feather, like if it was not even her body anymore. She quickly curled up into a ball, covered herself with a blanket, shacking with shock and crying quietly. He bent over her and whispered into her ear.

"This is just between us, do you understand? Or next time I won't be so gentle with you." Michaela looked up at him with hatred in her eyes.

"My mother will never forgive you for what you just did."

"Your mother or anyone else won't ever find out about it or it would be the last thing they hear." He lowered his voice in a malicious way.

"You wouldn't want me to have to hurt your mother, now would you? I kind of like her, she is a nice lady. So I hope you'll be smart. Sweet dreams." He exited her room, closing it behind him, leaving her with fear, shock and fury. She was curled up in a fetal position, shacking in shock what seemed to be an eternity. When she regained some serenity she had the sudden urge to get rid of his smell. She needed to get rid of the disturbing traces of his touch. She needed to use the bathroom and she had the compulsory need to wash it all away along with the disquieting memories of what just happened.

She glanced at her watch. It was 11:23 p.m. Her mother would be home soon. She had to get to the shower before she was home otherwise she might wonder why she is using the shower so late, when normally she is already asleep at this time. She peaked out quietly out of her room. It was dark and quiet. David must have gone to sleep. Very slowly and silently she made her way to the bathroom that was adjacent to the bedroom where she heard the monster soundly snoring. Relieved that she does not have to face him again, she locked the bathroom door behind her and in the shower her tears continued to mix with warm water that could not possibly wash away what she just experienced. No matter how hard she scrubbed her aching body, she couldn't get rid of the disgust.

She could not understand how someone would do such a horrible thing to a young girl, especially, someone who was supposed to be in a fatherly role. This was twisted; this was wrong and that was an understatement. Was that her fault? Did she really provoke him? She didn't think so, but he certainly perceived it that way. Or was that just an excuse to him? She never saw him so callous, so violent.

She heard about things like that happening even in the best of families; she never thought it would happen to her. As she was drying herself with a thick towel, she examined her body. Although there was some redness around her inner thighs and on her wrists, there did not seem to be other signs of struggle. Her head was spinning, her whole body was aching and she suddenly had the urge to throw up. She ran to the toilet and after the immediate relief that her stomach could no longer take; she was reminded of her pregnancy hoping that the trauma to her body and soul did not harm the baby. She thought for a second and did not notice any semen on her body before she showered or on the sheets. Did he wear a condom? She hoped he did. She changed her bed sheets because she could not stand any trace of him lingering or his smell. Although her window was wide open, it did not get rid of the eerie atmosphere her room has provided her with. This was always her sanctuary and now it was tainted with something unspeakable.

Once in bed in her flannel pajamas, buttoned up to her neck, chair leaned against the doorknob of her room as it did not have a lock on it, she covered herself up to her neck. She still could not fall asleep. Her thoughts wondered to innumerable situations. She thought that if she did not make love for the first time only recently to Eddy, David would have stolen her innocence, her virginity. What if he had made her pregnant? She could not even imagine that. She was relieved that it was Eddy's baby. Oh, god, the baby! She hoped this incident did not harm the baby. She needs to see a gynecologist on Monday. All kinds of disturbing thoughts were emerging in her mind preventing her from sleeping. She finally heard her mother coming home from work. Should she tell her? What if David hurts her or both of them? Was it a rape if it was done by someone she knows?

Should she go to the police? Would she endanger her mother or herself by doing that? She couldn't think anymore. She was exhausted and knowing that her mother was back in the home, she dosed off into a restless sleep.

In the morning Michaela still did not know what she would do about David. She needed more time to think about what she would do. How can he sleep in the same bed as her mother after what he has done? She wondered. Should she talk to her mother? Would David follow through with his threats? She would not have thought that he was capable of raping her despite her unnerving feeling she had from the beginning when she met him, but he did. Who knows what else he was capable of if she told anyone? Undecided, she stayed lying in her bed most of the morning, depressed, not wanting to come out of her room and face her mother and see David.

Before noon when Michaela was still in bed, she heard a knock on her bedroom door of her small room and stiffened with fear. When she heard her mother's voice she realized that her mother was off work for few days before she started her day shift. She quickly wiped her eyes and blew her nose.

"Are you awake?" She heard her mother on the other side of the door.

"I'm sorry, mom, I'm just really tired."

"I just thought....well it's almost noon and you haven't even eaten yet."

"I'm not hungry." Michaela quickly put the chair back in case her mother tried to open her door and she didn't want her to question why she barricaded it. During the day with her mother at home for few days, she wasn't as scared.

"Are you ok, Mika?" Her mom sounded concerned.

"I'm not feeling well."

"Can I come in?"

"Just leave me alone, mom." Despite Michaela's protest, Klaudia entered her room and sat down on the bed next to her seeing her pale face and puffy eyes.

"What's wrong baby?" This would have been the perfect moment to tell her mother if only David wasn't hovering in the doorway and his threatening presence made her sit up and cover herself with a blanket over her chest.

"Is everything ok?" He quarried. *What a hypocrite!* Trying to avoid David's gaze she answered her mother.

"Nothing mom, I….didn't get a good night sleep", which was the truth, "and I don't feel that good. Maybe I'm coming down with something." Klaudia placed a hand on her daughter's forehead.

"You don't seem to have a fever. I hope you feel better soon because we were planning to go for three days to Hungary, to Miskolc. They have such wonderful thermal waters and spas there; it might actually make you feel better. David is taking us this afternoon and Marcela is coming too."

"I don't feel up to it. Besides I've been there recently with Nikole's family."

"I thought you would want to go if Marcela was going. You always came with us on the trips."

"It's not Marcela……..I'm just not going", Michaela said sternly raising voice at her mother, which took her by surprise. She quickly added with more calm in her voice.

"I really don't feel that well. Perhaps some other time, ok, mom? Besides, Eddy might call me this weekend, so I want to be home."

"Alright but I don't want to leave you here alone if you're sick."

"I'll be just fine, mom. Don't worry. I'm eighteen years old. You don't have to treat me like a little kid anymore." Her voice was rising in frenzy again. "Just go for the weekend to Hungary and don't worry. I'll be fine." She repeated, trying to reassure her mother.

"Ok. We're leaving around two thirty today if you change your mind."

"I wouldn't change my mind. Have fun. I really mean it, mom. I just need a weekend for myself. When I feel better, I probably spend some time with Niki.

"Alright, then. If anything, you can always ask for help from Niki's mom or call aunt, Sylvia. You know my sister has always been there for us and treats you as her own daughter." It was true that Aunt Sylvie was like her second mother, often spending time with her when she was younger while her mother worked two jobs. Aunt Sylvia did not have her own children and devoted herself helping her sister raise Michaela when she was younger.

"I'm sure everything will be just fine, mom, but thanks, I'll keep it in mind." With that Klaudia kissed her daughter on the top of her head and left her room.

Michaela was relieved when they finally left on Friday afternoon, leaving her to her misery. She finally got out of bed, washed her tear stricken face, looking up at a ghostly reflection in the mirror. This was not even her face anymore. Her eyes were swollen from crying, dark circles under her eyes and her face was still pale. She felt like she has aged a decade in less than twenty four hours. She wasn't planning to go anywhere so she pulled on a pair of sweats and a baggy t-shirt. She needed to gather her thoughts and to take it easy. She did not want to think about what happened last night and needed a distraction. She shuffled through her mother's books finally picking up a historical novel hoping to get her mind off things. She read for a while but found herself re-reading the pages over again as her thoughts wondered and she did not even know where she was.

She nearly jumped out of her seat when the phone rang in the silence of the apartment startling her from her troubling thoughts.

"Hello, my love. How is my best girl?" Eddy's enthusiastic voice felt like a breeze of fresh air.

"Oh, Eddy....I" Her voice broke down and tears threatened to roll down her cheeks again.

"What's wrong, Michaela?" Eddy heard in her voice that something was not quite right.

"I have to talk to you....soon. So much has happened...." Where should I begin, she thought and decided that this was not something she could discuss over the phone.

"But I don't want to do it over the phone...." She continued.

"Are you breaking up with me?"

"NO, no Eddy, on the contrary. I love you so much. I just wish you were here with me right now. I need you so much...."

"Ok, Listen, I'll get on the first train today and come to Kosice to see you. I shouldn't be there later than tomorrow around noon or so."

"Ok, it will be just the two of us here when you come. I'm here by myself for the weekend anyway....hurry Eddy, please....I really need you...." Michaela had a sense of urgency in her voice and tears threatened to fall again.

"Just you and me, baby", Eddy sounded in the distance "Nothing else matters. I'll see you soon. I love you."

"I love you too, Eddy."

Michaela felt so much better after the conversation with Eddy and she was ecstatic that he would come see her soon. The following day she woke up early in the morning, but felt rested and better about herself. Perhaps because she didn't sleep in her own bed, but on the sofa, so at least it was a night without nightmares. She had to put herself back together and be somewhat presentable before Eddy arrived, she thought. She was hoping that he would come today or at least before her mom returned with David. She showered and washed her hair. She applied light make-up; just little bit of mascara and a blush to cover her pale cheeks. She put some light make-up under her eyes to cover up the darkness and puffiness under her eyes. She thought she has lost her spark and her eyes looked dark blue with concern. She applied a touch of beige and brown eye shadows which made her eyes stand out and a pink lipstick to balance it out. She styled her long hair for a while and when she was satisfied with the end result, she sat down and ate hungrily, realizing that yesterday she did not have any food in her mouth. This can't be good for the baby. It's not just her that she has to worry about. No wonder she felt sick and light headed all day yesterday. After a hardy meal she felt energized and refreshed with a new outlook on life. Eddy is coming....she has to tell Nikole. When she dialed her number, Nikolas picked up the phone, which she did not anticipate. Darn, she thought. She was not prepared for a conversation with him, right now.

"Hi, it's Michaela. Is Nikole home?"

"Hi, Mika." She heard Nikolas' pleasant voice on the other end. "She went to town with her mom. She will be home in a few hours." Before Michaela had a chance to end the brief talk, Nikolas quickly added.

"I haven't seen you for a while. I....I missed you. How are doing? She paused for a moment.

Not so good, Niko, I'm pregnant with Eddy's baby and I'm scared. I don't know how he will react to it or how I will tell him about it. I'm scared he will leave me and I'll be a single mom. On top of everything else mom's boyfriend just raped me and I don't know what to do about it. And I'm terrified.

"I'm fine." Michaela lied. She wished she could talk to him about it. What happened to them? They used to be pretty good friends and she was always able to talk to Nikolas before.

"How are you doing?"

"Well, as you might know, I have to go to the army for two years. It sucks that it's mandated. I'm not looking forward to that, but hopefully it will keep my mind off things. I hoped to have had a nice girl like you to write me some love letters when I'm away, feeling all alone……but that will not happen." He said with regret.

"Nikolas. I never wanted to hurt you. I hope things go well for you, Niko."

"Thanks. Have you heard from Eddy?" He quickly changed the subject as they were on a thin ice going into discussion about them further. There wasn't 'them'. They were just friends and nothing else and he knew it.

"Hmm, yes. He's actually coming soon. That's actually what I wanted to talk to Niki about. Have her call me, ok?"

"Sure. I'll let her know you called." After some hesitation, he added, "Mika, I hope you're happy…..anything you need….anything, I'll always be here for you." Damn, why was she so oversensitive lately, as her eyes started to fill up with tears again, realizing in a way she has hurt him. She did not even deserve for him to be so nice to her.

Maybe you could have helped me, but I can't tell you. I can't ever tell you, Niko because I care about you and I don't want to hurt you even more.

"Thanks, Niko……for everything. You're a wonderful guy and I do care about you. I hope you find happiness too. Take care of yourself, Nik."

"You too. Goodbye Michaela." *Good bye, love.*

Michaela looked up to the ceiling and took few deep breaths after the conversation with Nikolas. She can't cry again, she cannot cry.

Stop doing that to yourself; you'll ruin your make up. She told herself. She needs to focus on Eddy and how she will tell him about the baby. She decided she would not tell him about David but would see a gynecologist soon.

Less than twenty four hours later after their conversation, Eddy rang the doorbell of the small apartment on the fifth floor where Michaela lived. Her heart jumped with joy when she saw through an opening in the front door that it is him. She opened the door nearly knocking him over as she jumped into his arms, hugging him around his neck. She could not believe that he was here. He really came and only because of her. She pulled him quickly inside and without a word they kissed for a long time.

Chapter 8

WHEN THEY SEPARATED FROM EACH other, Eddy stepped back still holding her around her waist looking at her with curiosity. "What?"

"Let me look at you, how much prettier you got since I last saw you. Really, you're even more beautiful than in my memory." Eddy was shaking his head in disbelief.

Make up works wonders, Michaela thought, considering that few hours ago she looked like a ghost without any colour in her face and her eyes deeply sunk in. Now her eyes were sparkling with joy and excitement. It seemed to her as if she has not seen him in ages, but in fact, it's been only five weeks since she last laid eyes on him from the moving van that was leaving him behind.

"I can't believe you're here."

"I told you I would come."

"I missed you so much." When she wanted to kiss him again, he held her back.

"I am really dirty from the trip and need a shower. Do you think that would be a problem?

"No, no problem at all." She showed him to the bathroom and gave him a clean towel.

"Meantime, you can make me something good to eat, I'm starving."

"Sure." Of course, Michaela was suddenly embarrassed that all she wanted to do was make up with him while he had some basic needs that have not been met. She ran to the kitchen with enthusiasm and decided on scrambled eggs with a toast. She cut up some tomatoes and green peppers that were in season to go with it. She was almost done when Eddy came out only in a towel around his waist, his hair messy and wet. She enjoyed the view. He was nicely built, his chest covered with a trail of dark hair mainly in the middle of his chest; a little down to his stomach all the way to his happy trail that disappeared in the yellow towel.

"Do you want to get dressed first?" She asked hoping he would say 'no'.

"No, I'm quite comfortable. Hmm, what do we have here?" He smelled the scrambled eggs as he sat down on one of the kitchen chairs.

"I hope you like scrambled eggs."

"That's perfect. I'm so hungry I could eat a horse." He sat down and ate it all up in few bites. "A little too runny for my taste, but don't worry, you'll learn." He said with a wink.

"You didn't complain when you were licking up the plate." Michaela joked as he pulled her closer to him.

"Come here, you." He took her into his arms and pulled her onto his lap, looking at her closely.

"What's that mud on your eyelashes?"

"It's called mascara. You know....make-up?" She further mocked him but he became serious.

"You don't need to wear make-up at all. You're beautiful the way you are." He frowned at her. Michaela remembered that in Bulgaria she usually did not wear any make-up because she did not want to smear it up in the water.

"Yeah, I already licked up the goop out of your lips when I came. Your lips taste better without it." He took the napkin that she prepared for him and he tried to wipe off the rest of her lipstick with it.

She put her arms around his shoulders while still sitting in his lap nuzzling her head against his neck. He lifted her face with his shoulder finding her mouth and started kissing her again. She knew he was eager to make love to her but she needed to know whether he was serious about her. She needed to know how he would react once she told him that she is pregnant.

"Wait, Eddy."

"What is it?" He scowled at her. "I thought you missed me, that you wanted me."

"I missed you so much and I do want you, but…."

"What's the matter? Your family will be home soon?"

"No, they're in Hungary this weekend and will not come until tomorrow night. No, just….listen….it's not easy for me to say it."

"You're making me very anxious, Michaela. What is it?"

"Ok, there is really, no easy way to say it……I'm pregnant."

"WHAT?" He screamed in disbelief nearly knocking her down from his lap. "How? I thought you said you were on a pill."

"NO, you misunderstood, I told you I was NOT on a pill because there was nobody else before you, so….there was no need for a pill……I thought you knew…….I thought you were being careful." Eddy ran his hand through his thick curly brown hair in exasperation.

"Oh my god, Michaela. Are you sure?"

"Yes. I took a pregnancy test because I was late and it was positive."

"And are you sure it's mine?!" He looked at her quizzically. This was the kind of reaction she was most afraid of and she was upset that he even questioned that.

"Of course it's yours! There's nobody else I love, but you. And I don't sleep around!" She had tears in her eyes, not sure whether it was because of what David did to her or because Eddy doubted her. She thought that the incident with David should not be considered as sleeping around, because that was not her choice. He forced her, but she would not be able to explain all that to Eddy, especially after the way he just reacted. She also knew the baby was Eddy's for sure because it happened before David raped her. Either way, she decided not to tell him what David did to her; trying to deal with one major issue at a time.

"Ok, ok. I'm sorry." He finally said, disrupting her from her disturbing thoughts. "You just took me by surprise. I did not expect this." After a short pause, he continued. "I don't understand…..what are the odds…… we only slept together……..what?………five, six times?"

"It was a lot more than that, but it doesn't matter. It only takes once. Look, Eddy, I didn't expect it either." Michaela made her way back into his lap hugging his broad shoulders tears threatening to fall. "I'm scared. I didn't know whether I was scared of being pregnant or….," her voice broke down and tears started to pour down her face.

"Or what?"

"Or that you would leave me."

"Oh, Michaela, sweetie, I would never leave you." He embraced her, holding her for a while. Then he leaned back on the chair and ran both of his hands through his hair, thinking about the unexpected news and what to do about it. He finally decided and with relief he announced.

"We have to get married."

"Eddy.....we barely know each other."

"I don't think we have much choice now, do we? Unless you don't want me?"

"It's not that. I do want you."

"Then what is it?"

"It's just so complicated. My mom doesn't even know. Your family doesn't know. I don't even know them, except for Richie, but that's beside the point."

"So what is the point?" Eddy was getting impatient.

"The point is that we never even talked about 'us'. What it would look like? Where would we live? How would we raise this baby? There are just so many unanswered questions that I don't have answers for and it scares me." Michaela went on.

"We'll figure it out as we go along. I already have a place of my own. I always thought that you would come with me if I asked you to. We can get married here if you want. Translate the marriage certificate to German and the rest of the immigration documents we take care of once we are in Germany. I'll help you with that."

"It's not just that, Eddy."

"What else bothers you?"

"I don't know. It's not the way I pictured our start into our relationship."

"Well, neither did I but I won't let you abort my baby. You hear me?!" He said seriously and took her chin in between his thumb and index finger squeezing it tight. He released her as she pulled her head away from his pressing fingers.

"I would never do that!"

"I'm glad we agree on that." The atmosphere suddenly felt very heavy. He tried to relax a little and asked her.

"So how would you picture it now?"

"I just didn't think that your proposal would be so casual, if I can even call it that."

"Well and how did princess, Cinderella picture it? Me, going down on one knee in the towel to propose?" He said sardonically reminding her that he was still naked underneath.

"Never mind. You're right. Considering the unexpected development, I should be happy that you don't run the other way." He was amused by that statement.

"Is this really what you thought about me?"

"I don't know any more what I thought. I'm just so glad that you're here, Eddy. Just hold me." And he did. He held her in his arms for a long time while she snuggled in his chest, his long arms embracing her protectively. After a while they started kissing each other again. His hand slid under her shirt touching her gently. Desire was strong for both of them and she felt it rise under her legs as she was still sitting in his lap.

"Which way is your bedroom?" Michaela pointed adjacent to the kitchen, but then quickly remembered the horrible memories from two days ago and did not want to make love with Eddy there. There was no way. It was tainted with violence and shame. She could not go back there. Not with Eddy. She did not want it to abolish their love by telling him, so all she managed was to say, "not here" and pointed instead to the living room.

"Why not in your room? Wouldn't we have more privacy there in case they came home early?" Eddy questioned with a surprise in his face.

"I don't want to talk about it." When he quizzically looked at her she added to distract him. "It's dirty and I don't feel comfortable there." In a way it was dirty; she did not lie about that but not in the way he interpreted it. He seemed to accept this answer for now as desire was stronger than curiosity at this point. He carried her in his arms. She always seemed so small and light in his arms. He seated her down gently on the sofa, kneeling beside her, still wearing the yellow towel; he took her hand into his and unexpectedly asked her.

"Will you marry me, Michaela Martenz?"

"Oh, Eddy.....", tears of joy in her eyes, "yes, I will marry you." He leaned and started to kiss her passionately falling back onto the sofa.

He skillfully unbuttoned her shirt and wanted to kiss every inch of her body savoring everything about her. When his hand moved to her inner thigh lifting her long skirt and pushing her legs further apart, Michaela squirmed in pain.

"What's wrong?" Eddy asked surprised from a daze of foreplay that was suddenly disrupted. When he looked down where he just touched her on her thigh, he noticed a large bruise. He looked at her other leg and there was another similar bruise.

"What……..what are those?" He pointed to the bruises. Michaela quickly sat up and pulled her knees towards herself hugging her legs with her arms while covering her breasts with the blue blouse that was still unbuttoned.

"Michaela, what's going on?"

"Eddy, I don't want to talk about it." This was so much more difficult to explain than the pregnancy that both of them had something to do with. This was just her problem and she did not know how she was going to explain the bruises to him. She wished he never noticed them. Things developed so well between them. He just asked her to marry him. It was better than she could have even imaged. Telling him about David's rape might ruin everything. Seeing Eddy's stern look told her that was not a good idea, but Eddy would not let go of that.

"How did you get those bruises? Tell me!"

"It's nothing." She lied.

"It's not - NOTHING!" He raised his voice. "Don't disparage me!"

"What's that? I don't understand that word."

"Now, you suddenly don't understand!? Yeah, blame it on the language barrier. It means, don't fucking mess with me. Don't make an idiot out of me! Do you understand that?!" He was screaming at her and without waiting for a response he continued. "Did you cheat on me?"

"Eddy, I would never cheat on you."

"Liar, you wouldn't have bruises on your inner thighs if you…." He could not finish the sentence getting red in the face with rage barely catching his breath. Michaela could not take it anymore herself. She covered her face with her hands and started weeping. He suddenly noticed the bruises on her wrists and took them into his hands to examine them, pulling them away from Michaela's face.

"And what the fuck are these? Did he restrain you? You like it…… kinky? Playing a naive virgin?" Michaela had enough but the self-pity and guilt turned into a rage and she burst out with the horrific incidence she endured and did not want to ever say out loud. Especially, she did not want to convey that to Eddy. But he would not let go of it and he turned it against her, blaming her for something that was not her fault. The least she could do was explain what really happened and then it would be up to him what he did with that information. The situation escalated to a point where she could not turn back and she had to tell him the truth.

"Yes, he restrained me and then he raped me; in my own home, in my bedroom. That's why I didn't want to go in there with you. It's tainted and I don't know how to get over that. I screamed and screamed but nobody could hear me. Nobody could help me and he knew it. You want to know more? You want to hear the gruesome details? He snuck in my room at night while I was sleeping when my mother wasn't home. He first placed his filthy hand on my mouth, while sitting on me with all his weight pressing on my inner thighs………touching me……. That's how I got the bruises."

Eddy did not want to hear any more details having tears of rage in his eyes but Michaela continued to throw it in Eddy's face for not trusting her, for accusing her of cheating, for not believing in her and in their love.

"When I tried to push him off, fighting with all my strengths, hitting and scratching him with my hands, he restrained them while he raped me. I didn't want this to happen. I have nightmares about it and I'm still terrified of him. Is that enough information for you? Is this what you wanted to hear?

"Geez, Michaela, you think this is what I wanted to hear? That's the last thing that I expected……" He was lost for words. Finally, when he recovered from the sudden shock he asked almost too quietly.

"Who is the fucker?" When she did not answer right away, he howled. "Who is that fucking asshole that did this to you? And how come he was in your home; in your room?" She did not want to protect David and what he did to her. She hated him for that.

"It was mom's new boyfriend that recently moved in."

"What a piece of shit! And your mother doesn't do NOTHING about it?" He was outraged.

"She doesn't know yet." Abruptly something horrific occurred to Eddy and another wave of rage erupted.

"How do I know it's not his baby? God, it could be his….this is so fucked up, Michaela.

"Because I got pregnant in Bulgaria, with you, before all this happened. I knew about the baby before he raped me, so I know it's yours. And because he did it less than 48 hours ago when I already knew I was pregnant with your child!" Michaela cried trying to have him understand but Eddy was furious and irrational.

"I don't know why I should believe anything you say."

"Eddy, please, I'm telling you the truth. This was not my fault. And I know hundred percent that you're the father of my baby."

"This is so fucked up, Michaela." He repeated because he was running out of what to say before he went on an angry tangent. "I came quite a distance to see you because I thought we had something special. I thought we would have some good times together, get to know each other better. I thought we would see where this relationship could go, but I didn't expect such a fucking drama. First, you tell me you're pregnant with my baby and then you tell me that another guy fucked you. Oh, yeah, but, I forgot, you didn't like it. Who knows, you probably provoked him." Michaela thought through the haze of her tears and Eddy's screaming that this was exactly what David told her; that she provoked him. Perhaps, he was right. Maybe it was her fault, she thought but she could not say anything as Eddy continued his outrageous accusations.

"The dog wouldn't fuck if the bitch didn't give it to him." He was raging; he hit the side of the wall in the living room with his fist knocking down a small picture of a forest path that was hanging above. Now it was on the ground, glass scattered all over the hardwood floor. "I have enough of this bullshit." With those words, he grabbed his backpack, closed the bathroom door where he quickly changed into his clothes storming out of the bathroom and without another look at Michaela uttered.

"I'm out of here". He slammed the outside door behind him, despite of her pleas, leaving the distraught girl crying.

Chapter 9

EVERYTHING WAS GOING SO WELL and she certainly did not expect such a sudden twist of events. When she calmed down and had no more tears to cry, she tried to process what actually happened and could not help thinking that this was it. Eddy has left her for good. This is something he would never be able to get over; he would never forgive her. He blamed her. And perhaps she was to be blamed for what happened with David, she thought, although deep down in her soul she knew that there was no reason and no excuse for what David did to her. Nevertheless, he ruined her life; he destroyed her and her love she shared with Eddy. Her life would never be the same again......It was over and she could only wish that she could turn the time backwards and be again in Bulgaria with Eddy and the rape had never happened. She cried as she was sweeping the broken glass from the picture frame being startled out of her sorrow when the phone rang.

"Hey, how are you? Nik told me you called?" Nikole cheerfully twitted into the receiver.

"Hmm, yeah." Michaela took a deep breath and cleared her throat to try to cover up her devastation in her voice, but Nikole knew her friend well enough to know something was not right.

"What's wrong, Mika?"

"Nothing!" *Should I tell her?* She wondered. She needed someone to talk to her about everything that happened within such a short period of time.

"Eddy was just here."

"You don't sound very happy about it. What happened?"

"I don't even know where to start, Niki."

"How about from the beginning? Did you tell him you're going to have his baby?"

"Yes, I did."

"Oh, I see, and he didn't take it so well, I gather."

"Well, not at first, but then he came into terms with it and he even asked me to marry him……but then everything was suddenly ruined when he found out……." Her voice broke off and she was incoherently crying into the receiver.

"Mika, don't cry, it's going to be ok. I'm coming right over." Within ten minutes, Nikole knocked on her door. She hugged Michaela on the hallway of their two bedroom apartment when she was still sniffling. When they sat down in the kitchen after Nikole made strong Turkish coffee for both of them, acting as if she was at home. After all she was at Michaela's place often enough since they were little girls and the apartment was as familiar to her as her own home.

"Now, tell me again, what really happened. You said that Eddy asked you to marry him. I thought that's what you wanted?"

"No, yes, that part was amazing, but it was all ruined." She stared blankly into the black coffee looking at the swirl that her spoon was creating.

"Mika, I never saw you that way. Did he hurt you?"

"Yes, but not the way you think, although he was quite furious with me."

"Why?"

She finally looked up at her friend and knew she could tell her anything because her friend would understand and she would stand by her.

"You know David? My mom's new boyfriend that recently moved in?"

"Yeah, well I saw him briefly in passing the last time I was here. Why?"

"Well, the bastard raped me. Niki, he really hurt me."

Niki was dumbfounded and for the first time in her life she did not know what to say to that. When she regained from the initial shock of this horrific news that Michaela just shared with her, she finally said.

"You have to report it to the police. You have to tell your mom." When Michaela did not respond, continuing to mindlessly steer her coffee appearing to be somewhere else, Nikole touched her arm gently and persistently asked.

"Did you? Did you tell anyone?" More silence. "You told Eddy, didn't you? That's why he is not here now, right? He didn't take it so well, I gather."

Michaela turned her wrists showing Niki the bruises.

"I had to tell him. He saw these. And there are bigger ones on my thighs he saw and questioned me about them."

Niki sat beside Michaela on the kitchen bench where she was sitting and hugged her friend as Michaela continued.

"Eddy blamed me for it that I cheated on him. That I sleep around. He doesn't even believe that the baby is his. But I never wanted David to touch me. He raped me. He forced me to have sex with him by restraining my hands and my legs."

"I'm so sorry, Mika this happened to you, but you have to tell your mom and you have to report it. This is so wrong what he did to you."

"I'm so scared, Niki. You can't tell anyone." Niki stared at her in astonishment.

"What?"

"He threatened me and he threatened to hurt my mom if I told anyone. Oh, god, I shouldn't have said anything."

"He can't do that, Michaela Martenz! This is a crime and you have to report it."

"I don't know what my mom would do if she knew. She likes him so much and here I'm ruining her new relationship she had after such a long time."

"Listen to me, Michaela; this is NOT YOUR FAULT. Do you hear me!?" Nikole nearly yelled in exasperation to put some common sense into Michaela's brain.

"He raped you and that's a crime. It's wrong what he did and it is not your fault. He needs to be punished for what he did to you. Who knows how many girls he already did this to? You have to stop that. You have to stop him. He deserves to go to jail. What a piece of shit!" Now Nikole was on the row while Michaela was weeping quietly. Lately this was all she could do.

"And listen Mika, if Eddy blames you for this then he is not the guy for you anyway. You should then kick him to the curb and forget about him. He has no right to blame you for any of this. Gosh, you're the victim in this."

She took a huge gulp of her coffee nearly burning her whole mouth and feeling the hot liquid hurting her all the way to her stomach. She then continued with her unsolicited advice.

"You have to go to the doctor, Mika. You know.....to get checked out. To make sure you're ok. Make sure the baby is ok. Oh, man, I can't believe this happened to you. This only happens in bad movies. When? When did this happen?"

"Day before yesterday."

"Forget about Eddy for a moment, you have to deal with this first. It's Saturday today, we'll go together to the doctor on Monday, alright?!" Nikole could be quite bossy, but she knew her friend was right and had the best interest in her mind. After more persuasion, Michaela finally agreed to go to the doctor on Monday and talk to her mother on Sunday night as soon as she came back home regardless whether David was here or not. Her mother would know what to do next. Nikole called home to tell her mother she would stay over at Michaela's as her friend was alone and needed some company. Maria Senko did not find it unusual as Nikole slept over at her friends' home plenty of times before.

In Kosice downtown, Eddy was browsing through the streets thinking he should find a hotel. In his experience, there was always someone somewhere that understood at least a little German and was able to give him directions, which he hated to ask for. He noticed a pub so he walked in and ordered a scotch. As he had the habit, he drank the first shot quickly ordering another one and another shortly after that. The place smelled of spilled beer and the wooden table was sticky, but Eddy did not care. He needed this now. Why did he even bother to come such a long way? He could not think clearly; his head hurt and he did not care right now. All he wanted to do was to forget about what he just heard from Michaela; forget about her and drink himself to oblivion. That was what he liked to do; that was what he was good at. At the barstool a lovely girl with fake peroxide hairdo sat with her nice long legs crossed.

Her hairdo looked larger than her whole head, typical 80s look, but she had an attractive little face. Eddy sat beside her already a little inebriated.

"Hey, pretty girl, are you a screamer or are you a moaner?" He used his funny pick up line that often stupid young girls giggled about, but this girl did not understand him, but she was attracted to Eddy's well built body and handsome face with dark eyes.

"Another scotch and for the lady too." He yelled at the bartender slurring his words. Even in his drunken state he knew when girls were checking him out and he was certainly not oblivious to that. He did not have to understand her language. Her eyes, her lips and her large breasts told him everything he needed to know. Even how she sat on the high barstool, her right leg crossed over. He did not need words. As he was checking her out from head to toes, returning to stare at her large breaths instead of her face; he shamelessly placed his large hand on her naked thigh, just below her 'way too short mini-skirt' and kissed her on her mouth, greedily, aggressively. She let him; she responded positively when he thrust his long tongue deep into her mouth and soon after led him to the nearby hotel.

Michaela set up a pull out sofa in the living room for her and Nikole. It would be just like the old times when Nikole was younger and used to come for sleepovers. Except, they would not laugh at silly things tonight; there was nothing to laugh at this time. The situation was too serious. But they would still talk through most of the night. There were just so many things they had to discuss. Michaela was grateful that Nikole was such a good and supportive friend.

"I can't believe Otto didn't even send you a post-card back. I'm sorry." Michaela shook her head in disbelief.

"I didn't expect nothing more. Really. What can you expect from a foreigner that can disappear and you never hear from him again?"

"I was so happy when Eddy showed up and when he asked me to marry him. It was so romantic. I don't even know where it went wrong so quickly, one minute he was so nice and gentle and shortly after he was so mean, so........scary."

Nikole laid back on the pull out sofa, put her hands under her head and looked up, noticing something different in the room.

"Where is the picture of that forest path? It was my favourite."

"It fell because Eddy hit the wall just before he stormed out of here." She pulled the broken picture frame with the picture still intact from under the small coffee table showing it to Nikole. "That's what I mean. He was quite scary in that moment, but I know he had a good reason. What was I thinking telling him about it? But he somehow knew something was wrong. It was the damn bruises that gave it all away. I never wanted him to know. I wish it never happened like that. We could have been still together."

"Hey, don't cry again. You deserve better. It's probably for the best that it turned out the way it did."

Michaela thought for a moment that her friend is jealous of her because Otto never showed as much interest in her as Eddy did towards her, but she quickly dismissed that thought because Nikole was a really good friend to her and was here to support her throughout a difficult time.

"I just miss him so much, you know…..and with the baby on the way……..I don't know what I'll do without him."

"I know. It's not easy." Although Nikole did not have a clue, she tried to console her best friend. She held her hand comfortingly like an older sister would do to a younger one that was afraid of monsters. Michaela fell asleep into a dreamless sleep forgetting about everything, at least until she had to face the reality the next day.

The following day Eddy woke up on the other side of the town with a startle from his restless sleep looking around himself, trying to figure out where he was, feeling disoriented. He tried to remember what happened last night, but there were gaps in his memory replaced with a black hole that consumed part of his night. Looking down at a sleeping blond girl lying on her stomach legs splattered in opposite directions, he vaguely remembered picking her up at the bar. He did not even remember talking to her. Maybe they haven't talked. He pulled the covers off himself, revealing his naked masculine body. He used the bathroom, splashed some water on his face trying to remember where he was and how he got here, but in vain. The image in the mirror stared back at him with a frown and without any answers. He looked around wondering where he was. Was it the girl's place or a hotel, he wondered. He looked around and noticed '*Slovan*' logo on the towels, on the little bottle of shampoo and soap with the same logo gave it away. Ok, so he was in a hotel. The hotel was right in the Kosice downtown. He remembered passing it before he went to the nearby pub. He wondered how much that night would cost him.

When he came back from the bathroom the stranger girl started to stir peaking up with one eye checking out his naked body that was now standing close to the bed. She enjoyed the view. He did not bother to put on any clothes, feeling quite comfortable with his own body, looking down at her with contempt; he sternly said.

"Get out!" One would have thought that his demanding tone of voice and his frowning face which created a little 'V' shape in-between his eyes, would have said it all, but she did not seem to be intimidated and instead, turned onto her back, putting one arm under her head and started to touch herself with the other hand, looking at him lasciviously. Completely naked, bending her knees and spreading her legs wide she gave him a full view. She moaned and muttered something sweetly in her language that Eddy did not understand but he did not care. He did not need words to know what she was saying. Her body said it all. Just now he realized that she was a really pretty girl. Although unnaturally blond with roots showing, she had a great body that was waiting for him in anticipation. She looked him up and down as he was hovering over her, stopping at his large erection. She licked her lips, calling him towards her with her index finger. He could not stand it anymore. He could not resist a beautiful woman that wanted to fuck. So he did; he fucked her hard, getting all his rage out in the process. He was harsh with her, but she didn't seem to mind. It felt good. He could feel like himself again. It was different than with Michaela. He didn't have emotions other than rage, no care for this stranger, no tenderness. He didn't even know her name and he didn't care. It didn't matter. She asked for it, so she got it. It wasn't even his fault. She practically seduced him. And it's not like he got lucky last night with Michaela after their fight. All that mattered was how he felt in the moment. He could be rough with this girl and he liked it. He had to be gentle with Michaela who was a virgin when he made love to her the first time and she was always so full of emotions and tenderness. Last night didn't count with this peroxide girl since he didn't even remember it. Today, it didn't count either. This was strictly physical pleasure, 'a MAN thing' that Michaela would never understand. He didn't like that Michaela was getting mixed up in his thoughts at this moment, so he turned the girl on her fours and fucked her from behind squeezing her hanging breasts that didn't even fit into the palm of his large hands. Michaela's were so much smaller, he thought. He didn't want to look at the girl's face; he didn't want to feel any guilt. All he needed was a good release. He didn't know whether he satisfied the girl and it didn't matter to him. She was a tease; a hooker; an object; a means to an end. Sex relaxed him and made him feel good. He had his needs that had to be met or he would explode. What Michaela doesn't know, doesn't hurt her he justified it for himself. He put Michaela out of his mind for a moment before he came, pulling out of her in time, splashing his release over one half of her buttocks. He slapped her hard on the other half of her bottom, leaving a slight redness of his palm on her white skin.

"Now you can go!" He pointed to the direction of the door with his chin. He lay back on the bed, still naked he threw part of the blanket over the lower part of his body to cover himself. He leaned back against the solid border of the bed supporting his head with a hard pillow; he lighted a cigarette.

Finally the girl got the message and started to dress, but before she left, she put her left leg provocatively up onto the bed beside Eddy sticking her little hand under his nose in a 'pay up buddy' gesture. The body language across the cultures has to be the same because Eddy understood immediately what she wanted and why she was still sticking around.

"Fucking whore," he muttered under his breath and reached out for his wallet in the side of his backpack. He pulled out three green twenty German Marks with the philosopher, Johann Wolfgang von Goethe on them, tossing it onto the bed beside her leg. She grabbed it greedily and tucked it in her bra. The German Marks, although from East Germany had to have more value for her than he thought, but he was glad she did not demand more.

"Now get out!"

When she left, he showered and shaved and put on clean clothes. He ordered breakfast and felt like a new man. Now he can face life's challenges. Michaela was constantly playing in his mind and he knew that with her, it was different. There were emotions involved. He cared about her, he told himself. Especially now, that she carried his child under her heart. He liked her innocence, her caring nature and her loving touch. He knew she loved him and he knew that she would be a good mother. Not like those whores that were always throwing themselves at him. He liked the casual sex; he liked it a lot, but with Michaela it was serious. It was so much more than just sex. He always wanted a nice girl to be his wife and to have his children and decided that Michaela fit perfectly. He had to go back. He had to fix it with her.

Chapter 10

NIKOLE WAS ON HER WAY out the door when the doorbell rang startling them both standing on the hallway of the apartment so close to the outside door. When Michaela opened the door Eddy was standing there with a bouquet of dark purple orchids in his hand, with a puppy look on his face. Nikole did not buy into it but when she saw Michaela's face lighting up and a smile on her face after sullen and tear stricken night, she stepped back. She greeted Eddy briefly but he barely acknowledged her as usual and she made her way out the door leaving them alone with a scornful remark.

"I'm sure you two got a lot to talk about. Give me a call when you need me, Michaela." With that she disappeared behind the corner of the elevator. There was something that irritated Eddy about blonds and he certainly felt annoyed by Nikole, but he did not give her a second thought.

Michaela stood in the doorway looking at Eddy confused and torn in her emotions. She wanted to jump into his neck like the last time and start kissing him, but she could not make herself to make the first move. She was still angry at him for not trusting her and for blaming her for the rape and for not believing that the baby is his. She wasn't surprised that he got angry. It was a lot to take in, but she did not expect anything to that extent. He hurt her and she did not deserve it. She decided it was his turn to make the first move, and he did. He stepped closer to her; close enough to kiss her.

"I'm sorry, my love. I overreacted yesterday. I reacted like a fool because I didn't expect anything like that. It was just too much at once for me. I love you and I don't want to lose you." With that Michaela pulled Eddy inside the apartment closing the outside door avoiding curious ears or praying eyes of the neighbours that might be glued to the doors whenever there is some commotion on the hallway.

"I love you too, Eddy. You really scared me. I never saw you that angry. I didn't deserve to be treated by you like that."

"I know. I'm sorry. I was angry, but I misplaced my anger at you and that was wrong. I'm still angry at that fucker that did this to you. I want you all to myself. How dare he put his filthy hands on such a beautiful girl like you?"

She kissed him hushing him for a moment. When he caught his breath again, he said.

"I want to take you away from here. I want you to come with me. I want to marry you. I meant it when I asked you the first time." He placed his hand onto her belly that was not visible yet, indicating that he is thinking about the baby she was carrying under her heart.

"Oh, Eddy, you don't even know how much I dreamed about this moment. But you have to promise me that you will never hurt me like that again; that you never yell at me like yesterday and that you never leave me. I thought you left me for good, Eddy." Tears in her eyes again threatened to fall.

"Wow, so many demands from such a small girl," he teased.

"But alright, if that makes you happy, I promise, baby. I would never leave you. That was circumstantial……hmm, unexpected turn of events, but I do trust you and I know you didn't cheat on me. I know it wasn't your fault. Forgive me?"

"I already have." They kissed passionately ending up in the unmade sofa bed in the living room that Michaela did not have time to clear. He made love to her gently touching and kissing her just the way she liked it. He loved her. She was the one, he decided. She was the one he was going to spend his life with; the one that was going to have his children; one already on its way.

After they have made love, which seemed as such a long time since they last made love in Bulgaria, Eddy tugged his hand into his hair behind his ear, lying sideways beside her, looking at her intently.

"I can't believe how much your German has improved. We could actually have a good fight without you searching for words to translate to German. I'm impressed." He smirked.

"I had a good teacher."

"So we have our first big fight behind us and we are still here…. together. I think that says something, what do you think?"

"Technically, it's our second fight." Michaela pointed out half-jokingly.

"Oh, now you want to fight about how many fights we had?" Eddy queried lightheartedly and kissed her to shut her up without waiting for an answer. After a while he became serious again and said.

"Let's elope."

"Elope?" That was a new word for her and she did not understand what he was saying without much context to figure it out.

"And here I'm praising you for your improved German." He laughed. "You know, to get married, quickly, just the two of us with couple of witnesses and then we'll go to Germany or marry in Germany. I really don't care. I just want you to be mine. We'll be married fast and avoid huge expenses. I hate how girls in Germany plan these huge weddings that cost a fortune. I don't think we need that. What do you say?"

"Oh, I can't do that Eddy, as much as I want to. I do want to marry you but I do want my mom to be there. I'm her only daughter and I know she always dreamed about the day I once marry. I can't do that to her. Besides, I think my mom has been already saving some money for my wedding since I was a little girl."

When she saw his solemn face, she added.

"But I don't think we need a lot of time to plan the wedding. In fact, I don't want a big wedding either. So we just invite my immediate family and perhaps couple of friends and your family. I have a very small family, so it will not cost so much."

"I hope that doesn't include the fucker that raped you."

"Eddy, please don't swear. I don't like that."

"Well, there is no other title that is more deserving."

"Well, that's true." Michaela agreed.

"I could kill that guy if I get my hands on him. When are they back?"

"Eddy, you're side tracking from the topic. Don't worry; I already figured out how to deal with that. You don't have to worry about anything. He is good as gone out of my life." Eddy sighed and let it go, for now.

"Ok, fine, have it your way, but just so you know, I don't have much money left for a wedding." He tugged a lock of her hair behind her ear and added, "I'd rather build a life with you than spend it on the wedding."

"I like that."

Throughout the day, they stayed inside talking about their future plans. Eddy told Michaela that he had a little house in Dresden fully furnished and he could go back to his job at any point when he returns. She still did not understood what it was that he exactly did but it didn't matter to her. It did not really matter to her if he was the janitor. She loved him and was happy that things were falling into place.

"We have to plan the wedding soon."

"Why?"

"Well, several reasons, Michaela. First, I don't want people to know that you're pregnant and think that this is why we're getting married, because there is so much more to that than this. And you know that. Second, I have to get back to Germany soon and start working to be able to support you and the baby and I'm running out of my savings."

"I don't care whether you are rich or poor. I love you regardless."

"It's not about that, Michaela but we need to think about how we'll survive."

"I can go to work too, you know."

"You're pregnant! And besides, it will probably take some time with the immigration papers until you will be able to work even after we get married. It's not that simple."

"Oh, I didn't think about that. I don't even know how that works."

"First of all we need to get married for you to get a Status to become a permanent resident and get a working permit and so on. So, how about if we get married by next Saturday? You said you don't mind a small wedding. So why long standing preparations that will cost a lot of money?"

"Wow, Eddy, this is crazy. It's moving too fast. I haven't even introduced you to my mom yet."

"You said she is coming back tonight, so I'll meet her soon and we announce our decision then. You don't have to tell her right away that you're pregnant, unless it becomes necessary, if she was against us getting married after such a short period of time."

"Well, what about your family? Don't you want to invite them to our wedding?"

"Well, we can have a small dinner when we are back in Germany. It's just my brother and my mother and we are not that close."

Michaela was getting more and more anxious by the minute as her mother's and David's arrival back home was quickly approaching. She needed to deal first with the 'David situation', which she still didn't know how she would tell her mother about it. Klaudia knew about Eddy, but has never met him and had no idea that he came to see her this weekend while she was away.

"Don't worry, Michaela, she'll see me here and you'll introduce us. It's not such a big deal." Eddy tried to simplify it for her forgetting that she first needed to talk to her mother alone about what David did.

They spent all day inside and Eddy made himself feel quite at home, putting his feet on the small coffee table, relaxing, drinking David's beer from the fridge that Michaela brought him and flipping through the few channels that they had. When he did not find anything interesting, he turned it off and put attention back to Michaela who was standing in the doorway of the living room.

"So this is how it is going to be? Your feet up, watching TV, drinking a cold beer and me....slaving over the stove in the kitchen?" She asked jokingly after she prepared a dinner for them and for her mother before she came home from her trip.

"Yes, that's right. That's exactly how I picture it. And that's how it should be. Don't you think?" They laughed, but little did Michaela know that Eddy was quite serious about it as this was what he saw at home when he was growing up. This was what he saw his mother doing. She would always take care of her husband, cooking meals, doing his laundry, cleaning and taking care of two little active boys that often misbehaved as far as Eddy could remember. This is how he envisioned his home life and not once he considered that marriage was a partnership between two people that loved each other. He wanted Michaela to stay at home raising his family and taking care of him and thought that loving her and supporting her financially would balance everything out. They never talked about these things and they were rushing into marriage quickly without even talking about their values or their needs. They had a great physical attraction and strong feelings for one another and never considered that there might be more to the marriage, merging two lives together and creating a new one.

"Darn, I didn't even get you a ring yet. I'll buy you one once we are in Germany, ok?"

"Oh, Eddy, you're so sweet. Don't worry about it. I don't need anything fancy. You know that's not why I'm marrying you." Eddy was sure of that. He was also sure that any other German girl would not give him the time of day when it came to serious relationship because he did not even have a car, a house, as he told Michaela he had and he was out of work for a while. Good looking or not, as soon as girls found out he was broke, they turned the other way. He spent most of his savings that his mother had for his college education that he never attended. No German girl would want him without a diamond ring on her finger, at least not a nice, intelligent and beautiful woman wouldn't. Michaela was all of that. She was gorgeous, young and she had an innate intelligence that sometimes worried him but it also attracted him to her. She was nothing like the simple-minded girls that usually threw themselves at Eddy because they wanted a one night stand because they were attracted to him. Yeah, that was fun for Eddy; it was playful, but they never considered even going out on a date with him as soon as they found out he did not have anything. Michaela was modest and although bright, she was quite naive in many ways. She wanted a fairy tale life; she wanted someone saving her out of an abusive situation and she picked him to be her 'hero'. She wanted him and wanted to have his children regardless who he was, what he did or what his past entailed. Well, she didn't know anything about his past, but she was sure that it would not have made a difference to her because she loved him unconditionally. She should be glad he was marrying her being pregnant and all, he thought to himself. Maybe one day he will tell her about his troubled childhood and outrageous youth, but not now;

not before they were married. He would not dare to risk it all again. He needed someone like Michaela who loved him wholeheartedly with all his flaws and worshiped him no matter what he did. He needed someone loving and caring to take care of him. Michaela disrupted his thoughts.

"You should go, Eddy."

"What? You're throwing me out? You said on the phone that I could stay overnight."

"No, I'm not throwing you out, but you know that I need to talk to my mom about a lot of things, especially about what David did and I think it would be better if I did it by myself." She said it slowly, making a puppy face watching his reaction carefully.

"Is David gonna be here too?"

"Well.....yeah, he lives here now."

"There is no way I'm leaving you with this asshole here alone."

"I will not be alone, Eddy. My mom will be here and he will not do anything to me in her presence."

"No! I'm not going anywhere. I don't even want you near him!"

Michaela signed partly with relief that Eddy was reluctant to leave. She felt protected by him and perhaps it was better that he stayed. She was not sure whether she would have had the courage to tell her mother when David was nearby. She remembered before they left for the weekend how he was hovering by her bedroom door behind her mother threatening her with his ominous look on his face for her to be quiet. There was a definite threat from him. She was so focused on how she will tell her mother about this horrible incident that she did not even consider that Eddy might have a strong reaction to David. She simply assumed that he would be on his best behavior considering that he was going to meet her mother for the very first time. She was wrong.

Chapter 11

WHEN HER MOTHER CAME IN calling her name cheerfully right from front of the entrance, completely unsuspecting what she was going to experience, Michaela quickly stood up from the sofa in the living room where Eddy was kissing her just seconds ago. David was sauntering unsuspectingly behind Klaudia with couple of bags on his shoulders. Michaela came to greet her mother; Eddy was standing tall by her side whispering to her.

"That's him?" Michaela nodded her agreement. She knew exactly what Eddy was asking her. Before David had a chance to assess the situation and before any introductions could be made, Eddy launched at him with a leopard speed and with all his strength he punched David between his eyes breaking his nose knocking David down to the floor. David tumbled and hit a wall with his shoulder falling to the ground. Klaudia who up until this point had a friendly smile on her face was staring in shock and disbelief along with Michaela who did not expect that. And neither did David. He did not have a chance to recover from the first blow; receiving another one and another.

"Eddy, stop…..that's enough…..enough, you're going to kill him……" Michaela was shrieking in German trying to pull Eddy away, tagging on his large shoulders. "He has enough. Let him go. He's not worth it." She continued.

Klaudia, who was just standing in her own home in a shock, not understanding what her daughter was saying or why all this just happened or who the stranger was punching her partner out, wanted some answers. Klaudia quickly recovered from her astonishment looked questioningly at Eddy and then to Michaela waiting for an explanation.

"What's going on here? Who is this, Michaela?" Michaela did not know where to start and before she had a chance, David scrambled to his feet, holding his blood stricken face with a handkerchief that he pulled out of his pocket.

He spoke in Slovak so Eddy did not understand; quickly putting two and two together assuming that Michaela told her friend about what he did to her.

"Nice boyfriend your daughter brought home. Really, you raised your daughter well, Klaudia!" He said sardonically, wiping his bloody nose.

Klaudia looked confused, still waiting for an explanation from her daughter. Michaela only briefly looked at David seeing his ominous look, but this time she ignored it and blurred out in front of all of them feeling safe with Eddy by her side.

"Mom, David raped me." Tears were in her eyes as she relived the horrific scene.

"WHAT?!" Her mother was now in more shock than before, speechless to say anything at the moment. She looked at David with disbelief, her eyes wide open. He quickly responded trying to distract her from what just came out of Michaela's mouth before Klaudia had a chance to believe what she just heard.

"You're going to believe this crap? This is ridiculous!" He ventured.

When Klaudia recovered from this unexpected horrific news that followed David's beat up face, she looked from Michaela back at David saying with a flat affect.

"Yes, I believe my daughter."

"Klaudia, you know me. You know I would never do something like that. She is lying because she doesn't want me around."

"GET OUT! GET OUT NOW, before I call the police!" She shouted at him in frenzy.

With all the commotion in the small apartment with paper thin walls, the neighbours must have had some show lately, but that was least of Michaela's worries.

"You can pick up your stuff tomorrow." Klaudia added and she stepped towards Michaela who was shaking and crying. She hugged her for a long time, rocking her from side to side to calm her down and to calm herself down. How could she not see it sooner? How could she has

Gabriela Elias

allowed such a monster to enter their lives and hurt her only daughter in an unthinkable manner?

David scattered out of the door quickly slamming the door behind him seeing Eddy's threatening expression on his face, scared that he would receive another blow. He took only his one bag that fell on the floor when Eddy launched at him unexpectedly knocking him to the ground soon after he came inside.

"I'm sorry mom," Michaela finally managed to speak.

"You have nothing to be sorry about. I am sorry baby. I'm so sorry that I allowed this monster into our lives. I'm sorry, I didn't know about what was happening to you. I should have seen some signs. This is not your fault." Both of them became oblivious to Eddy still standing there leaning now in the doorway between the living room and the hallway of their apartment feeling quite uncomfortable, but he did not dare move or say anything. He waited there patiently even though patience was not one of his virtues. After some time, when both women recovered from the emotional impact that this had on them, Klaudia looked at Eddy with her composure intact telling her daughter.

"You're lucky to have such a great friend that protects you and defends your honour. Otherwise, I would have had to punch David out myself. Why don't you introduce us?"

Michaela wiped her face from tears, giving Eddy a half crocked smile.

"Eddy, this is my mom."

"Mom, I want you to meet Eddy, my fiancé. You know the man I have met in Bulgaria that I told you about?"

"Fiancé? Wow, when did that happen?"

"We just got engaged....I know it's sudden."

Eddy not quite understanding the interchange between mother and daughter as they spoke Slovak, he stepped closer to Klaudia taking her hand and kissing it gently like a perfect gentleman.

"It's nice to finally meet you. I'm sorry; it was under such an unconventional of circumstances." Michaela tried to translate his response to her from German.

He indicated to Michaela to keep translating as he explained his behaviour.

118

"I'm sorry, for the commotion, but I only had the best interest in mind when it comes to Michaela." Michaela smiled at him as she was explaining to her mother what he was saying.

Klaudia, recovering yet from another shock of learning that Eddy is her daughter's fiancé accepted his introduction with grace and approval asking her daughter to translate her response.

"Please call me Klaudia. I think Michaela is a very lucky girl to have found such a fine man. There is so much we need to talk about." She led the two young people into the living room where she pulled out small crystal glasses and poured all of them a shot of Becherovka, a common Czechoslovakian drink. It was not very strong; it was a sweet, herbal drink. Klaudia was not a drinker but had couple of bottles of alcohol ready for the guests. Today, it was a special situation and she would have a drink or two with the guest and her daughter to recover from the initial shock of what she just experienced. She took immediate liking to Eddy as he was quite charming and polite; not to mention tall, dark and handsome, unlike most German boys. He had a certain male magnetism and charm that drew women of all ages towards him. He helped his daughter; he protected her. Klaudia thought that they really made a beautiful couple and even said that aloud.

"Cheers to the two of you. You have my blessing although I don't think you need to rush into things right away." And she turned the crystal glass upside down and emptied the content making a horrible face.

"Come on guys. Drink it up."

Nobody needed to prompt Eddy twice; he followed Klaudia in the same gesture and emptied his glass bottom up. Michaela looked at Eddy and told him in German that she could not drink this. He understood immediately what she meant. When Klaudia went to the kitchen to bring some juice, he quickly drank her glass as well so her mother would not suspect anything or ask questions why she did not want to have at least one symbolic drink to celebrate their engagement. Michaela put her hand over her glass saying to her mother she did not want more.

"Thanks but I had enough."

The three of them talked for a long time with Michaela's translating skills for majority of the evening about the engagement, what their plans were for the future, why they were rushing into marriage so quickly. They did not tell Klaudia that Michaela was pregnant. It was too much, too fast. When she asked why they wanted to marry so soon, Eddy stepped in and provided a good reason.

"I love Michaela and I'd like for her to come to Germany with me as my wife, so we can start our life together. I believe distance relationships are very difficult to maintain especially when it is in different countries. The immigration takes a while to sort out and I want Michaela to have all the rights like a German citizen or landed immigrant, but in order to get that process started, we need to be married first."

After Klaudia understood what Eddy was telling her, she still did not feel convinced; he continued.

"I fell in love with Michaela back in Bulgaria and I could not stop thinking about her ever since and that's why I'm here. I knew she was the one for me. Klaudia, I know you and Michaela didn't have the easiest life here. I can provide a better life for her in Germany than she has here. I'll take a good care of her."

"So you want to marry because both of you love each other?" Klaudia tried to make sense out of it after her third drink.

"Of course!" Eddy said with a surprise on his face.

"Well, I still think this is a little rushed, but you have my blessings. I think Michaela does not need to be scared with you, considering how you handled……" She broke off, not being able to say David's name. Either way, for now she accepted Eddy's reasoning.

They've talked for several hours, Klaudia asking Eddy about his family and about what and where he worked. Eddy shared that he had a younger brother by five years and his mother lived in Dresden. He said that he has a home in Halle where they would live and her mother can come and visit them. After all, he said, it was not that far. When asked about his father, it was obvious that it was a sensitive topic and he simply said that he died when Eddy was a teenager, but did not elaborate on any details and Klaudia or Michaela did not ask out of consideration for his feelings. Michaela was learning about Eddy as much as her mother was as there were many things that she never discussed with Eddy. When Klaudia asked what he did for living, he said that he is now in-between jobs, mostly sales, but again was quite vague. Klaudia attributed it to her daughter's limited German vocabulary.

Klaudia invited Eddy to stay for supper that Michaela prepared earlier. She made cooked chicken in a homemade sauce with pasta which was quite tasty. Eddy ate well as much as he drank along with Klaudia.

Klaudia who as a single mother for many years struggled to provide for her small family the basic necessities, always wanted so much better for her only daughter. Michaela had the opportunity of a life time to have a better future in a country that was economically more prosperous with more opportunities where she would not have to live in poverty. Although she knew she would miss her daughter, she put her own needs aside as her daughter would be living so far away from her, but she kept in mind that she would have hopefully a better life once she immigrated to Germany. More importantly, she seemed to be engaged to a fine man.

"Alright, you'll get married, but I'd like for Michaela to marry here, in her home town, having her immediate family and some close friends at the wedding. Perhaps your mom and brother could come? I have some money saved…."

"That sounds like a wonderful plan, Klaudia." Eddy interrupted her excitedly with a smile on his face. She smiled back at him.

"Call me 'mom'."

"With pleasure, 'mom'." Eddy said with his most charming smile on his face.

As it was getting late, Michaela asked her mother if Eddy could stay at their place rather than paying for a hotel.

"Of course you can sleep here. You're practically a family. I know you're engaged, but the two of you, be good, ok?"

Michaela prepared the pull up sofa in the living room where Michaela slept the past two nights and hoped to sleep here again, this time besides Eddy.

Meantime, her mother continued to drink with her future son-in-law and they seemed to have bonded quite well. Klaudia who was not accustomed to drinking at all and after fourth drink; she was quite drunk, telling both Eddy and Michaela how much she loved them and what a beautiful couple they were. She even went to the balcony and smoked a cigarette that Eddy offered her smoking along with him even though she normally did not smoke. Michaela was glad that her mother accepted Eddy so quickly and liked him a lot. That certainly was a good sign. But she never saw her mother drunk and thought that this must be so terrible for children whose parents drink every day. She knew from her mother's stories about her father who was an alcoholic, although he never admitted to it or received any help for it. Perhaps that is why her mother normally never drank. But today, it was an exception and a good reason to have a drink or few. It was a lot for her mom to take. Michaela would have had few drinks as well if it was not for her pregnancy but she would not dare to do anything to harm this precious baby that was growing inside her.

First time in her life, Michaela had to put her mother to sleep as she was too drunk to get to bed by herself. Eddy helped carrying her. The alcohol did not seem to affect him in the same way as it did her mother, but then he was almost two meters tall and was quite masculine.

When her mother was in bed, she and Eddy closed the living room door snuggling together in bed and made love again. She stayed with him all night. She did not want to return to her room.

"Mom.........oh, my god, MOM....... Leave her alone! Let her go! STOP......STOP.........you're going to kill her!" *Her eyes are closed, her face is pale; she is unconscious or dead? NO....NO.........NO....this cannot happen! He has to do something. He has to save her.......he has to......Oh, god, so much blood. He is lying in the pool of his own blood......*

"Eddy......EDDY! Hey, Eddy, answer me. What's wrong? Where did you go?" Michaela was tagging on her fiancé's arm calling his name, over and over again concern on her face. Eddy nearly jumped out of his seat nearly knocking Michaela out of the chair when he finally focused at her in confusion looking around realizing that he was in her apartment. There was no danger. Nobody was being hurt. Nobody was getting killed. He starred at her in bewilderment, frown on his face, he quickly hugged Michaela.

"I'm sorry baby, you startled me. Everything is ok, everything is ok." He repeated breathless more for his benefit than for hers. When he pulled away, she asked him again.

"What just happened, Eddy? Are you ok?"

"Yes, yes, I'm fine. It's nothing. I….just got caught deep in thought…… and…..but I'm fine. Everything is ok." He was reassuring himself and Michaela at the same time.

"It's like you were somewhere else, Eddy. You didn't even answer when I called your name several times." Michaela explained with concern.

"I was just thinking of my….parents. That's all. And for a moment I forgot where I was. It happens to me sometimes, but I got it……I got it under control. Nothing to worry about, baby."

He quickly changed the subject.

"I'm going to get some fresh air and go for a little walk around the lake that I saw when I first came here. I just need to be alone for a little while." Michaela lived close to a small lake that she could see from the 9th floor of their apartment building. It was a nice walk to go around it, which did not take more than an hour. Michaela herself often went for a walk or a jog with Nikole to keep in shape.

"Are you sure that you're ok to go out now?"

"Yes. Stop worrying. I'm fine. I just need some fresh air!" He snapped in frustration running his hand through his dark hair. Then he added more calmly, "I'll be back in about an hour for lunch. Anyway, I'm sure you and your mom have a lot to talk about. I'll see you soon, baby." He kissed her on her lips; he put on his running shoes and went out.

Michaela dropped it for now but it was bothering her when she saw Eddy's terrified face, dilated eyes, not recognizing her for a moment, reliving something horrible that she was not aware of.

Eddy was right, she needed some alone time with her mother to talk to her about the recent turn of events. She went to the kitchen to find her mother who was preparing lunch. She automatically started helping in the kitchen without her mother asking her. She grabbed the potatoes and started peeling them.

"Where is Eddy?"

"He just went for a walk around the lake."

"I'm glad I finally have a chance to talk to you alone. It's been difficult to get a moment with you alone as the two of you are inseparable."

She sat down beside Michaela, thinking how to begin.

"I really like Eddy. He seems like a nice guy. You can tell he really loves you."

"I know, mom. And I love him too. I'm so lucky to have him…."

"I just don't understand why you have to get married so young."

"Mom, please. We talked about it. I thought you were ok with that, just the other day."

"Well, now that I had some time to think about it with a clear head….I just don't get why you want to marry so young. At least if you waited a year or so. If he loves you he would wait for you until you're a little older."

"Mom, we love each other and we want to start our life together in Germany. The immigration papers will take a long time before I can do anything. I really don't want a long distance relationship. I'm scared to lose him."

"If he really loves you, he wouldn't pressure you into marriage."

"He is not pressuring me into anything. Remember when you told me that if I found someone special that you would not try to stop me from moving on?"

"I know I said something like that before, but I've also been wrong so many times in my life, Michaela. I just don't want you to repeat the same mistakes I've made."

"Don't worry, mom. I'm not you and Eddy is not like my father."

"It's just seems to me he is…….hmm……more experienced. How old is he anyway?"

"Twenty-five."

"Hmm, that's a bit of an age difference."

"It's only seven years difference. Why does it matter how old he is? You told me my father was nine years older than you."

"Well, look how that ended up."

"That's not why and you know that. He was drinking…..right?"

"Yeah, that's true. Anyway, Eddy seems to really care about you." After a pause, she added. "I'm glad he was here when, I came back with David…." Her voice broke down, not being able to finish the sentence. She eventually continued.

"I'm so sorry, Mika, this happened to you. You know the thing……with David. It's my fault."

"No, mom, it's not your fault. You couldn't have known."

"Yes, it is. I should have seen some signs but I didn't. He was always so nice and generous and he helped out financially." She thought back on the times she was with David. She shook her head in disbelief about her own horrible decisions and added sardonically.

"I know how to pick them, don't I?" When Michaela was silent, Klaudia continued. "Why didn't you tell me right away? I always told you that you can tell me anything."

"I don't know. I should have told you but I was so scared. He threatened me….and he threatened to hurt you. I didn't know what to do."

"When did he do that?"

Michaela told her mother how he started with inappropriate comments, showing her pornography and revealing himself one night when she was working. She also told her mother about his gifts he bought her but also that he did it with a threatening demeanor. She told her mother how she wanted to tell her about the rape the following morning when she came to her room, but he was staring at her threateningly and she was afraid what he would do in that moment.

"That's terrible……what happened to you, I mean. You're coming with me to the hospital on Monday morning. Dr. Novak will take you without an appointment. She's a good friend of mine and a great gynecologist." Klaudia said decidedly without even asking her daughter what she thought about that.

"Oh, mom, I don't want to go to your work to see someone you know."

"Why not? At least, you don't have to wait for an appointment. You need to get checked out as soon as possible!" She stood up and went to the stove to stir the stew.

"It's just….embarrassing."

"This is serious, Michaela. We have to make sure you're ok. Stop acting like a little kid. You're going and that's final." Klaudia concluded it with a scowl on her face creating wrinkles on her forehead.

"Alright, fine." Michaela pouted, but continued to peel the potatoes with concentration, while her mother was adding some spices to the stew.

She knew she would not win this argument with her mother. She didn't mind going to the gynecologist. She was planning on doing it anyway, but she did not want her mother to know that person as she would likely find out that Michaela is pregnant. She wanted to delay the inevitable until after the wedding or little bit later. Little did she know that she would not have to wait until Monday for her mother to find out as the doorbell rang.

"That must be Eddy." Michaela quickly rinsed her hands and ran enthusiastically to the door.

"Check who that is first." Her mother warned her as always, more out of habit. How ironic, Michaela thought, that her mother was always wary of the strangers when it was at times those that were closest to us that we needed to fear.

"Mom, I'm not a little kid. Stop lecturing me."

"Ok, ok, I just thought....David......and all......I just want you to be careful. That's all."

Michaela surprised opened the door to see her smiling Aunt Sylvie's face.

"Hi, darling." She kissed Michaela on her cheek with a really loud kissing sound that hurt Michaela's ear. She hated when Aunt Sylvie did that but she never said anything because she adored her aunt, who was like her second mother to her.

"Please, come in. I have big news to tell you, Aunt Sylvie."

"I know, Michaela. Your mother invited me for lunch. We need to talk."

Michaela led her aunt to the kitchen wondering what her mother has revealed to her sister. All Michaela wanted her to know was about Eddy, his proposal and the wedding plans and her plan moving to Germany. That was plenty of news at once that a relative could take during one lunch. She tried with caution to find out what Aunt Sylvie already knew.

"What did my mom tell you?"

"Don't worry, sweetie, she didn't have to tell me anything. You know me and my darn premonitions. I already know you're pregnant."

Klaudia was just coming out of the kitchen pale as if she saw a ghost.

"What did you say, Sylvia? My daughter? Pregnant?" She turned to Michaela questioningly.

"Is that true, Michaela Martenz?" She said sternly. Michaela wide eyed now was looking from her mother to her aunt, confused how her aunt knew that; but of course, it was Aunt Sylvie and her dammed psychic abilities that quite often proved to be true. Sylvia tried to come to Michaela's rescue as she saw her sister's dumbfounded face.

"I thought you knew, Klaudia. Look at her. Just look at her. She is glowing. There is a different aura around her……new energy…….new heat….new life inside this precious girl. I felt it as soon as she opened the door. I don't know how you don't sense these things, Klaudia. You're my only sister crying out loud and you're nothing like me. It's like we didn't even have the same parents. You're always so clueless."

Aunt Sylvie was not helping the situation at all, as Klaudia did not recover from this new information. But she had a good point and was right on target with her sister often being clueless. With that Sylvia made her way into the kitchen, sat her purse on the kitchen bench and put on a pot of coffee just as if she was at home. Klaudia was still standing with her daughter in front of the kitchen motionless. She finally repeated the question.

"Is Aunt Sylvia right? Are you pregnant?"

Michaela nodded quietly, confirming her mother's worst fear.

"And when did you plan to tell me this wonderful news?" She said sardonically.

"Mom, please don't be angry with me."

"Why would I be angry, Michaela? For you not telling me that you're pregnant although I think today you had a perfectly good chance to tell me when we were talking about the gynecologist just minutes ago. Do you think I wouldn't find out from the doctor tomorrow? Or should I be angry for the cheer fact that my only daughter has not used protection and got pregnant at eighteen?" Klaudia had tears in her eyes but they were not tears of joy.

"Why is Michaela going to see a gynecologist?" Sylvia asked with suspicion in her voice, but she met with Klaudia's scathing glare who was ignoring her question turning back to her daughter.

"No, Michaela, I'm not angry with you. I'm disappointed. That's not how I envisioned your life. I thought you would go to university, but now you tied yourself down with a baby. I'm not angry, Michaela. It's your life. You're the one that will have to raise this baby."

"I know mom. Eddy and I are prepared to raise this baby. That's why we wanted to get married so quickly. But that's not the only reason. We do love each other….and we would have probably gotten married at some point anyway."

"Oh, please Michaela, stop. You don't know anything. You think Eddy's going to help you with the baby? You don't know what you don't know. You're so young and so naïve." Her mother's voice was rising in frustration. Sylvia was annoyed with herself that she put Michaela in such a tense situation with her mother, but at least it was out in the open. But she should have known Klaudia had no idea about the pregnancy. She and my big mouth, Sylvia thought to herself; how come I didn't see that coming. It would be better if she could only control what or how much she sees. She and Michaela should have prepared Klaudia for such shocking news. Sylvia tried to calm the situation down that she in a way contributed to.

"Hey, hey, hey it's not the end of the world. She is not the first or last teenage mom. At least she didn't have it at 17 like her mother. Right, Klaudia?" Sylvia distracted Klaudia's attack on her daughter by bringing the attention to her own teenage oversight.

Michaela never knew her mother's age. It never even occurred to her to ask and she never knew that her mother gave birth to her when she was only seventeen years old. She only knew that her father was older by nine years as her mother once mentioned it but it never occurred to her to ask how old her mother was when Michaela was born. Now it started to make sense to her why Aunt Sylvie, who was quite older from her mom has lived with them for several years when Michaela was little and why her mom needed so much help raising her. She simply accepted it as normal when she was growing up, never having to question it. Now she had a good reason to query about it.

"So, you were a teenage mom?" Without waiting for an answer she continued. "And you're trying to lecture me about it? At least I'm a little older than you were when you had me."

"I'm not lecturing you, Michaela about anything. I'm just worried about you and the little one exactly because I know how hard it will be for you. It's so hard when you're so young and you haven't even figured out what you want to do with your life."

"I always knew I wanted to be a mom one day, so I just started a little sooner than planned, but don't worry, everything will work out."

"So, I gather that Eddy has been informed about it?"

"Yes, mom, he knows."

"That's nice. So he knows, and your own mother has to find out from her peculiar psychic sister because you always keep things from me." She said it with sarcasm and hurt in her voice.

"I'm sorry mom. I just didn't want to put so much on you at once, considering all the recent events." She hugged her mother, who returned her embrace, softening towards her daughter. Michaela did not want to go further into details in front of Aunt Sylvie although you never knew what visions she was getting and how much she already knew. Aunt Sylvie usually had to meet someone in person and then she would get some sort of vibe about that person and sometimes she would see or sense things. Nobody was really taking her seriously and considered her unique skills a little dubious, but she never cared about that as she knew what she knew and nobody could tell her otherwise. There were many times when Aunt Sylvie told people things that came true and rarely was she wrong.

"So when am I going to meet your prince Bajaja? Is he around or do I need to drag him here by his ears?" Sylvia asked bluntly breaking the heavy atmosphere and they all laughed.

"You'll meet him very soon. He is from East Germany, so he only speaks German, but I'll translate for you. He is actually here."

"And you're hiding him in the closet or what?" Sylvia turned her head mockingly pretending to look for him.

"No, no." Michaela laughed lightheartedly. "He will be here soon. He just went for a little walk. He'll be back for lunch."

Aunt Sylvie queried more about Michaela's fiancé cheerfully. Klaudia listened with intent learning about her potential future son-in-law all over again even though she already heard the story how they met and fell in love with one another. When Eddy walked in, meeting Aunt Sylvie her smile quickly disappeared replacing a deep concern in her eyes as she met Eddy's dark intense eyes. Michaela knew that look of concern and concentration of having one of her visions.

Chapter 12

S HE LOOKED AT MICHAELA WITH a shocking expression on her face as if she was seeing her for the first time.

"Hello, I'm Eduard Verner." Eddy introduced himself when nobody was saying anything and an overwhelming silence was suddenly soaring over them. When Aunt Sylvie did not respond to him rather told Michaela, completely ignoring him as if in trance.

"I need to speak with you alone, NOW." She said with urgency in her voice. Michaela tried to cover up her aunt's unconventional behavior towards Eddy and quickly introduced her despite her insistence to be with her alone.

"Eddy, this is my Aunt Sylvie. She is my mom's sister that I'm very close to." Sylvia was tagging at her shirt like a small impatient child that has no regard for the guest.

"Please excuse me, Eddy. I'll be right back." Aunt Sylvie headed already to the living room without another word or acknowledgment of the guest; Michaela following her on her demand.

"Aunt Sylvie, that was quite rude of you. You could have at least greeted him."

When she saw her aunt's stern look, she added. "Don't tell me you got another of your visions."

"Sit." She ordered simply reminding Michaela of David's harsh order at the exact spot when she walked in on him watching pornography. She tried to shake that memory, but nothing escaped intuitive Aunt Sylvie. She looked around the room as if she was looking for something.

"Something bad happened here; in this room; in this apartment. I can feel it! We'll have to talk about that at some other time. Right now, I have to warn you about another dangerous man."

"Another dangerous man? Aunt Sylvie, you're scaring me. What are you talking about?" Sylvia was an odd lady; an old spinster without her own children and many people often found her a little strange because of the intense glare she would give people when she saw something. To Michaela, Aunt Sylvie was familiar, loving and caring and despite her odd premonitions she sometimes had and the intensity that she always presented it with; she loved and respected her.

"I'm talking about the man that you chose to marry. I'm talking about 'him'!" And she looked in the direction of the kitchen where Eddy was helping himself to some coffee. Michaela did not know how Aunt Sylvie knew that she was planning on marrying. Perhaps her mother told her over the phone when she talked to her or perhaps Aunt Sylvie simply knew.

"Mika, darling, you can't marry this man. He is not good for you!"

"Aunt Sylvie, what are you talking about? This is the father of my unborn child. This is the man that I love and he loves me."

"That may be, but he is…….troubled……….his soul has been wounded too much……….he is dangerous. Michaela, darling, I saw some very bad things that he is capable of."

"Aunt Sylvie, I know you're just trying to look out for me, but come on, Eddy is not dangerous. He would never hurt anyone."

"Darling, he already has and he will again and again. Listen to me. If you marry this man, you will be very unhappy and even your life may be in danger." This is why people usually did not believe Aunt Sylvie, Michaela thought, because sometimes she talked nonsense and dramatized things. Michaela signed exasperatingly, shaking her head.

"Ok, that's enough. You know I love and respect your opinions a lot Aunt Sylvie, but I'm not going to listen to this gobbledygook. We will now go back into the kitchen and you will be nice to Eddy and try to get to know him. He deserves for you to, at least, give him a chance. I'm sure you will change your opinion and first impression of him. You can't judge a person from just looking at them for few seconds. It doesn't work that way." Aunt Sylvie gave Michaela, 'I know what I know' look and said obstinately.

"You're making a mistake, my child. Don't say I didn't warn you. You're at the crossroads and you can choose your Life Path now. I think you'll make the biggest mistake of your life if you marry this man and go to Germany with him. He is not the one for you."

And be a single mother? Michaela thought to herself. There was no way she would give up her love and the father of her unborn child for some stupid predictions or bad first impression of her aunt, who is for sure blowing things out of proportions. Michaela interpreted Aunt Sylvie's concern to the fact that she is planning to leave and start a new life in a foreign country, far away from her family and she was sure that this was not an appealing idea to Aunt Sylvie or to her mother. But her family has to realize that she is an adult now with a child on the way and she has a right to create her own future that includes Eddy in it.

"I know you're worried about me, but everything will be just fine, Aunt Sylvie, you'll see. Eddy is really a nice guy."

Sylvia shook her head either not agreeing with Michaela or simply trying to shake away what she just saw minutes ago when she looked into Eddy's striking but troubled eyes. Without much choice, she followed Michaela back into the kitchen to see the man that frightened her and her niece's future. Sylvia's eyes conveyed a look of suspicion and disapproval when she looked at Eddy who was sitting across from her during the lunch. The atmosphere was tense, but nobody mentioned it.

Eddy did not need to understand Slovak language to know that Aunt Sylvie despised him, but he was marrying Michaela, not her aunt, so it did not matter what she thought of him. He thought she was a little crazy as she was giving him vary looks. He mentioned it to Michaela that evening after Aunt Sylvie left.

"Your aunt hates me."

"She doesn't hate you. She is just……protective of me."

"Well, that's my job now. So she can back off." Michaela thought that Aunt Sylvie was trying to protect her from him, but she did not say that.

"What were you two talking about in the living anyway?" He queried suspiciously.

"She was telling me what a handsome man I found for myself and if you have an older brother." She joked tickling him.

"Yeah, right." He said sardonically and pulled her towards him looking at her intently.

"You know, she is very different from everyone I know, but she is very loving and caring person. She helped my mom raise me. Did you know that?" Instead of answering her he said.

"I will not let anyone or anything ruin our future together. Make sure your family is clear on that." Without waiting for a response he kissed her possessively.

From the weekend overnight visits, Eddy's stay stretched out to a whole month due to the wedding preparations. They agreed why have Eddy run back and forth to Germany when he can just stay at Klaudia's apartment and spend more quality time with Michaela. They did not plan a big wedding, but invited Michaela's and Eddy's immediate family and very close friends only. Eddy said that his mother would not be able to come but his brother Ritchie and his best friend Otto whom Michaela met in Bulgaria would come to the wedding. Michaela invited naturally her mother, aunt Sylvie and Nikole's family with whom she was always close. As she was handing her the wedding invitation she told Nikole enthusiastically.

"Otto will be here for the wedding too." She expected an exciting response from Nikole, instead she saw her shrug it off indifferently.

"So?" Surprised at her reaction, Michaela commented on her friend's phlegmatic attitude.

"I thought you would be happier about it."

"Why should I be? He never bothered to write or call me. He is not coming here because of me, but because of his best friend's wedding. If anything having him at the wedding while I'm there will be quite awkward."

"I thought you liked him." Michaela said with a disappointment in her voice. What was she expecting that both of them get married to the German boys at the same time, move to Germany and live next to each other for rest of their lives? Fairy tales did not exist and Michaela was still wondering how lucky she was to have found Eddy.

"I did like him. A lot. But I guess he doesn't feel the same way about me." She shrugged again, pulling a chocolate ice-cream out of the freezer.

"Want some?" Michaela shook her head with a concern on her face.

"But….you are coming to my wedding, right? I wanted to ask you to be my maid of honour." She looked at her friend expectantly.

"I wouldn't miss it for anything in the world!" They hugged, Nikole wiping her tear off her cheek that Michaela did not notice; then she pulled away opening the invitation.

"Let me see the gorgeous invitation. When is the big day?" Michaela pointed to the card that her friend was examining.

"Saturday, October 5 at 3pm in the Old Town Hall in Kosice Downtown."

"Town Hall? But you always dreamed getting married in the in the gorgeous Cathedral of St. Elizabeth in downtown! You always drag me to go inside whenever we go to town." It was Nikole's turn to be quite surprised. This time Michaela shrugged sadness in her eyes.

"You're right. I did want to get married there, but I just found out that Eddy is not Catholic. He is not even baptized so we can't marry there."

"He could get baptized for you, especially when you dreamed about a beautiful traditional church wedding ceremony since you were a little girl."

"I don't want to push him into something he doesn't feel comfortable with." Nikole tried to change the subject and lighten the mood.

"Hmm, remember when we were little girls and we played 'weddings'?" She laughed.

"I wrapped you in a toilet paper and made Nikolas to be the groom wearing his dad's big white shirt. He looked like a ghost; you couldn't even see his hand that's how long the shirt was. And you looked more like a mummy than a bride." They both laughed remembering.

"Oh, yeah, I remember. And you were pretending to be a priest marrying us." They fell silent for a moment.

"I always thought that one day you two would get married and you would become my real sister." Nikole had tears in her eyes again. "Darn you! You're going to move far away from me and I'm gonna lose my best friend."

"You're not going to lose me, Niki. I always will be your friend." The friends hugged again. After a while Michaela suddenly asked Nikole.

"How does Nikolas feel about my wedding?"

"I don't know. Why don't you ask him yourself? He is home." Michaela was not prepared for a conversation with Nikolas. She just thought she would talk to Nikole, give her the invitation for the whole Senko family, but she knew deep down she needed to have a conversation with Nikolas. She came close to his bedroom and hesitated at the doors taking a deep breath before she knocked on his door. Nikole was watching her from across her room. She heard a male voice yell out in annoyance through the closed doors.

"What?" She slowly opened the door ajar, peaking in, her stomach in knots.

"Niko? Hi. Can I come in?" Nikolas has obviously not expected any company, virtually jumped out of his bed, his book falling out of his clumsy hands onto the ground.

"Oh, hi Mika." He said breathlessly. I'm sorry, I didn't expect...... Sorry, it's a mess here. He quickly started tidying his scattered things from the chair. She grabbed his hand, stopping him from his momentary distraction. He looked at her standing close to her, looking into her big blue-green eyes.

"Don't worry about that Niko, I won't stay long." He put the clothes back and pointed for her to sit down. She sat on his hastily made bed that had one of the covers dangling on the floor, pillows scattered carelessly on top.

"I wanted to talk to you in person." Expectedly, Nikolas sat down beside her.

"I brought my wedding invitation for your whole family and it would mean a lot to me if you were there too." It was like a slap in the face for Nikolas who did not expect such a sudden turn of events. When she saw his stunned face, she clarified as if he could not have figured out the details.

"I'm marrying Eddy in three weeks."

"Wow. That's.....fast. I did not expect that." He was lost for words.

"I need to know how you feel about it."

"Why? Does it matter how I feel?"

"It matters to me. You know I care about you."

"Just……not enough to be with me." He concluded despondently.

"Nikolas." She said with a pleading intonation in her voice. "You know you mean a lot to me. You're one of my best friends. We can't control who we fall in love with." She shrugged her shoulders as if to indicate that she is powerless to control her own destiny.

"No…..I guess we can't." He said with sadness in his voice.

"Can't you just be happy for me?"

"And are you? Happy?" He asked her honestly wanting to know.

"Yes." She said quietly nodding her head, tears in her eyes; because she knew that she hurt Nikolas all over again. She never wanted to hurt him, but he had to know the truth. He moved closer to her embracing her in his arms.

"Don't cry, Mika. Don't cry. I am happy for you if you're happy." He held her for a little while longer; she didn't pull away from him and found comfort in his embrace.

"He better be good to you, otherwise he will have to deal with me." He said it half-jokingly, but he really meant what he said. He worried about Michaela, the argument in Bulgaria between Eddy and his brother replaying in his head.

"You call me if he doesn't treat you right." Michaela was grateful to have such a great friend who cared about her so much. She thought for a moment what it would feel like if she had started relationship with Nikolas before she met Eddy. If she had not met Eddy, she probably would have. But just like she said, 'you can't help who you fall in love with'.

"Thank you for always being there for me, Niko." She kissed him gently on his scruffy cheek which he did not shave for days and was leaving his room. She then turned in the doorway.

"Nikole has the invitation with all the information. It would mean a lot to me if you came to the wedding." She repeated.

When Michaela left, Nikole turned to her brother who was watching them from the hallway, leaning against the wall staring at the door that closed behind Michaela.

"I was always hoping that it would be you; marrying my best friend. She was always like my sister to me anyway. Trust me. I'm not thrilled about her marring Eddy either." When he did not say anything just looked down at the floor, she continued.

"I'm sorry Nik, you lost her." He looked at his sister and retorted with sorrow in his eyes.

"You can't lose something you never had." With that, he turned and went to his room, closing the door behind him; wanting to be alone.

Michaela busied herself with the wedding preparation. She decided to wear her mother's old wedding dress that she never got rid of. They just needed to have few alterations made, but it was certainly a lot cheaper which made her decide on that dress despite of Nikole's warning about being it a bad luck as her mother's marriage did not survive. Michaela did not believe on superstitious tales and she refused to believe her Aunt Sylvie who until the last minute was trying to talk her out of this marriage. Klaudia finally told her sister off.

"Just leave her alone. They love each other and they are going to get married. Just stay out of it, Sylvia!" Klaudia was fond of Eddy from the moment she first saw him punching out her ex-boyfriend who hurt Michaela in an unspeakable way. Because of that she held Eddy in high regard and also thought he was quite a 'catch' being so handsome and from Germany. The situation with David fell far into the past unfortunate of experiences about which Sylvia never found out despite her sixth sense and some intuition. They decided not to press charges as not to ruin Michaela's wedding and her chances of immigrating. Those kinds of things usually dragged on forever and there was little proof according to Dr. Novak, who did not note anything suspicious other than the fading bruises on Michaela's thighs. The gynecologist said if she came right away and if there was semen found it would be enough of a proof, but it was all washed away which seemed to be so long ago, although at times it reappeared in Michaela's nightmares quite vividly. Otherwise, Michaela was healthy and so was the baby. They estimated the due date on April 24th of next year.

Michaela one evening while cuddling with Eddy on the pull out sofa watching some German channel suddenly remembered that there was nobody to give her away. She did not have an older brother, or a male cousin and she always pictured her own father as a black silhouette as he had no part in her life.

"Maybe you should go see him." Eddy suggested it nonchalantly one evening when she brought it up.

"I don't know what I would tell him."

"I don't know, Michaela. You just tell him that you're getting married. You can invite him to the wedding. I can go with you if you want."

The following day Michaela made the decision to call her father after twelve years of not seeing him or talking to him; barely remembering him. She looked up his name in the yellow pages and with shaking hands dialed the number. Eddy was standing beside her with encouraging look to go on.

"Hello?" A little girl's voice answered. Michaela was taken by surprise. She suspected that her father probably found someone else over the years, but was this her half-sister that just answered the phone that she never heard about?

"Hi. Is your daddy there?" She ventured on her hunch.

"Mommy." She heard the little girl yell close to the receiver." Michaela wanted to hang up the phone, not knowing what she wanted to say. Eddy not understanding what was happening was raising his eyebrows, looking at her questioningly. Suddenly a female voice on the other side of the line answered.

"Hello? Who is this?" Was this her father's wife; the other woman for whom her father has left her mom? She could not hang up. She had to answer.

"I'm sorry to bother you. I'm not sure whether I have the right number, but I'm looking for Michael Martenz.

"This is the correct number, but he is……not here. Who is this?" The young woman repeated the question on the other end of the line.

"It's Michaela Martenz, his daughter."

Chapter 13

THERE WAS A LONG SILENCE on the other side of the receiver before the woman answered. For a moment she thought that the woman hung up but then she surprised her.

"Michaela, you do have the right number. Why don't you come for a visit tomorrow evening; let's say around six?" When Michaela did not know what to say to that, the woman on the other end continued.

"My name is Svetlana. I was married to your father and the little girl you have heard is your half-sister, Julia. We certainly have a lot to talk about. Please come." Something in Svetlana's pleading voice broke and Michaela could not say 'no' to the invitation. All that she managed to say was, "Alright. I will come with my fiancé if that's ok."

"Of course. That would be lovely. I'm looking forward to meeting you Michaela." The woman had a pleasant and welcoming voice. When she told her mother about going to see her father the following day, as well as his wife and her half-sister that she knew nothing about until few minutes ago, her mother did not seem to understand why she would want to go.

"I don't understand Michaela. Why would you want to see someone who didn't care about you whole your life? All these years, he could have come to see you, but he didn't."

"Mom, please, I want to ask him to give me away at the wedding. He is my father after all."

"Why are you doing this to me, Michaela? Why are you trying to hurt me? You know how I feel about your father. I am glad I didn't have to deal with him for several years. Of course, he hasn't paid child support for you for years, but now it doesn't matter because you're eighteen years old. He didn't do anything for us but cause pain." Klaudia said with vehement disdain in her voice.

"Mom, I am not trying to hurt you." Michaela said softly. "But this is not about you. This is for me. It's my wedding and I get to chose whom I invite. I would appreciate if you could put the past behind you for one day and showed some respect. Besides, he might not even come. I haven't even talked to him yet."

"Fine. I'll never understand why you have to go see him after all these years, when he never cared about you, but do what you want. He is practically a stranger to you." She turned and walked into the kitchen again leaving Michaela wondering whether she was doing the right thing. She wished her mother was more supportive of her decision to re-connect with her father, but her own pain prevented her from understanding why Michaela had to do that.

It was true that her father never called her, never visited her and never even sent her a birthday or Christmas card. Michaela did not know why she wanted to see him, but somehow she had the need to fill the black hole in her life. She had the need to fill in the black figure that was always playing in her mind. She needed to find something good in him because she was part of him. She did not choose him for her father, but she was the one that suffered consequences of her parents' decisions. She needed answers and she needed closure. If he slammed the door in her face; that would be an answer too and at least she would see for herself. But somehow she doubted that he would be so mean to her. His wife seemed to be quite open about it; inviting her into their home. Michaela wondered whether her father ever talked about her.

The next day Michaela picked up a navy blue dress matching Eddy's only dress shirt which he had with him. It brought up the colour of her eyes.

"Are you sure you want to come with me?" She asked Eddy for the third time as her nerves were getting the better of her. Perhaps if he changed his mind, she would cancel the whole idea. But Eddy wanted to meet her father and ask him for her hand. Michaela explained to Eddy that she never had a relationship with her father, so it would not matter if he asked him or not because her father did not have any say in it anyway.

Eddy had old fashioned ideas ingrained in him and insisted on meeting her father and asking for her hand. Michaela looked at Eddy nervously as they climbed the stairs of second floor of a tall building that stood up on a hill, her hand hesitating by the door bell.

"We can still leave." She said timorously although she knew that it was too late when they heard a dog's barking behind the closed doors. Without answering her, he impatiently pushed the doorbell making the barking more intense as it must have ran from another room closer to the front door. They heard a child's voice trying to quite the little snow white shiatsu that was now jumping up and down, continuing to bark at the unknown visitors when a short woman with reddish-brown hair opened the door. Although she was not very pretty, she was considerably younger than her father. She welcomed them with a friendly smile on her face.

"You must be Michaela. Hi." She extended her arm offering her brief embrace right at the door. "Please come in. I'm Svetlana; we spoke on the phone. And this must be your fiancé."

"Eduard Verner. Eddy." He extended his hand to the young woman poking Michaela with his elbow in her back to say something. Michaela regained her composure and introduced herself.

"Dunco" be quiet, Svetlana sternly scolded the little dog that was still jumping and barking all over the place excited about seeing new people.

"Please don't mind him. He is just a puppy that gets easily excited and hasn't been fully trained yet." Michaela bent down and stroked the little white shiatsu on its head looking at a little girl that was tending to the dog. Was that her half-sister, with the hazel green eyes looking up at her shyly?

"Hi. I'm Michaela. What's your name?"

"This.....is your half-sister, Julia." Her mother stepped in to introduce the child when she wasn't saying anything. She is very shy in front of strangers, but she is a little chatterbox that will not stop talking once she feels more comfortable.

"Please come in." Svetlana urged them to sit down in the living room where she has prepared open sandwiches with ham, Russian eggs and pickles on top along with cookies beside it on another plate. When they walked into the living room an older man was sitting in a comfortable armchair putting his glasses back on his nose squinting at the people around him showing his fake teeth that he tried to readjust nearly dropping them out of his mouth.

"Michaela, this is your father's father, your grandfather. I don't know if you remember him at all. I thought you might want to see him again." The old gentleman supporting himself on his cane hugged six years old Julia who tried to escape his embrace.

"Michaela, sweetheart. You haven't changed a bit since I last saw you." He exclaimed looking at the little girl who was able to move away from his awkward embrace.

"No, no grandpa. This is Julia. Remember, you see Julia every time we visit you in the nursing home? This is Michaela, grandpa." She said loudly, pointing to Michaela indicating that this was the other granddaughter that he wanted to greet.

"Michaela!" He exclaimed again surprised how much his little granddaughter has grown since he last saw her.

"I remember you when you were this little." He touched Julia's top of the head who was crunched down beside the shiatsu.

"Look at you how grown up you're now. It means I'm getting old." He chuckled as he got a glimpse of clarity for a moment, but then got distracted as his legs were giving in from under him and he needed to sit down again. As grandpa was sitting back down in the armchair, barely listening to the conversation, Svetlana noted.

"Unfortunately, his memory is not very good. He has beginning stage of Alzheimer's. Sometimes he forgets who we are and gets confused, but at times he remembers so many things from the past. I'm glad he remembered you. Please sit down. We have so much to talk about, even though we actually never met." Svetlana noted, pointing to the burgundy sofa across from the armchair where grandfather seemed to be quite comfortable. They all sat down; Julia sat in her mother's lap with the puppy in her arms who occasionally barked but stopped jumping around, sitting now contently in Julia's arms.

"Is my father here?" Michaela finally asked.

"That's what I wanted to talk to you about." Eddy, who did not understand a word what they were talking about, looked at Michaela questioningly. Svetlana took a deep breath, kissed her daughter's back of the head and she told her daughter.

"Julia, darling. Why don't you go play with Dunco in your room for a little while?" Julia jumped off her mother's lap and carried the puppy with her to the other room. Michaela was looking behind her new found sister; then again at Svetlana, with curious look on her face.

"I didn't want to say anything over the phone. This is not something you discuss over the phone especially when we have never met."

"What thing?"

"I'm sorry, Michaela, your father is not here because he passed away four years ago." Ignoring the shocked look on Michaela's face, Svetlana continued.

"He got into a single vehicle accident. He was drinking that day and hit a tree, getting killed on the spot. He didn't suffer at least and luckily nobody else was around to get hurt." Svetlana said with sadness in her voice. She continued to explain.

"Julia doesn't even remember him. She was only two at that time. I haven't talked to her about it and she never asks about her father. As far as she knows, it was always just me and her. Michaela was shaking her head the realization did not hit her yet and she did not show an emotion about her father, perhaps because the relationship was non-existent for so many years during the majority of her life. She unexpectedly blurred out.

"Julia should know who her father was. You should talk to her about him. It's terrible for little girls not to know about their fathers." Michaela thought of herself as a little girl, how difficult it was for her growing up without a father and now her baby sister would endure a similar destiny. She felt bad more for her sister and for the little girl within her who has missed so much when it came to their father. She was angry at her father for getting drunk and getting himself killed as a result. She was suddenly angry with him for abandoning her when she was six years old, just her sister's age and never calling her; never taking her for visits; never spending any time with her. And now she will never get that chance because he is gone and she will not even get a chance to see him ever again. All the questions that Michaela had for her father, had vanished unanswered. She will never have any relationship with her father; she will not even have any closure. He yet, abandoned his other daughter, this time because of his carelessness and irresponsibility just as her mother often accused him of when she talked about him.

"You might not remember much about your father, but he was not always a nice man. He drank a lot and sometimes………unfortunately, he was quite physical with me. I know that's not what you probably came to hear, but it is the truth. The truth is, he never spend much time with Julia even though they lived in the same home, so don't be surprised that he didn't spend any time with you. Your mother was the smart one to have ended that relationship. I feel like I got the rotten deal. I know we should talk about the dead only in good ways and I shouldn't be saying this, but to be completely honest, I was relieved when he died." Svetlana wiped her single tear off with the back of her hand.

"You don't know how terrible it is for a little girl not to remember; not know anything about her father; good or bad. When she is older; she will wonder who her father was and why she doesn't know anything about him. When I got older I always wanted to know. I always wanted to find out something good in him and I always heard just the bad things from my mother. This is why I came. I'm part of him too and I'm thinking that there must have been something good in him, but now I will never know what it was."

Michaela took a deep breath and continued with a chuckle on her face remembering her childhood.

"I always envied my friends who spent time with their dads. I never got that. At least I don't remember it because he left when I was so young. Julia was even younger when she lost him. Svetlana, you have to talk to your daughter about him because she will never know him. She needs to know that there was something good in him because she is part of him too." Up until this point, despite the one tear she shed since she started talking about her deceased husband, her face was quite stern; emotionless. After Michaela's words that came from somewhere deep within her, Svetlana became quite emotional and excused herself mumbling that she will make some coffee and quickly left the room. Grandfather was snoozing in the comfortable armchair, oblivious to his surroundings. Michaela looked at Eddy who was getting bored because he was clueless about what just transpired. Michaela briefly filled him in, surprising him about her father's death and summarized the conversation she had with Svetlana translating it to her best abilities to German.

"Maybe we should go." He suggested after they were alone with sleeping grandpa for about ten minutes. Michaela felt uncomfortable as well. She got an answer, but nothing prepared her for that and she would have expected either a friendly greeting or a blunt rejection, for either she was prepared. Nothing has prepared her for his death. He was dead for four years and nobody even let her know. Her grandfather who barely remembered her and at times forgot his own name was not much help either; although she was glad that she got to see him again. She saw him last time when she was about six years old visiting in their old house. She was running in his garden, climbing on the cherry tree, eating right from it spitting seeds on the ground. That tree was her sanctuary; her safe place when her parents were fighting. Nobody disturbed her there and she could sit in that tree for hours. She suddenly remembered glimpses from her early childhood. Why did she stop visiting her grandfather? She did not remember her grandmother from her father's side; that has died when she was a baby. But she remembered visiting the old house where she often spent part of her summer with her grandfather, going to town for ice-cream.

As Eddy prodded Michaela to stand up and leave, interrupting her thoughts, Svetlana came back into the living room apologizing for leaving her guests alone for a while. Instead of coffee in one hand she was holding Julia's hand and in the other, she held a large envelope. Her entrance woke up sleeping grandpa who was looking around confused trying to remember who was who. Svetlana made some room on the glass coffee table pushing the plate with sandwiches to the side that only Eddy had indulged in. She finally took out the content of the white envelope.

"I think it is time for the two sisters to learn about their dad and maybe also about each other." She took a picture out after another talking about their father; his sense of humour; his love of fishing and his love for soccer. Svetlana showed them pictures of their father when he was in the army as a young man. He looked so young and handsome on that picture, Michaela thought. She showed them pictures of their wedding.

Then Michaela saw random pictures of him and Julia; him holding Julia in his arms in the hospital shortly after she was born; a proud look appeared on his face. She showed them other pictures when Julia was a toddler her father holding her hands, helping her walk and "playing soccer" with her when she was slightly older in her cute flowery dress pointing for her to kick the ball. Svetlana then pulled another smaller envelope that Michaela did not notice at first. She scattered black and white pictures of different sizes all over the table.

"That's all the pictures your father had of you." Michaela kneeled down to the low coffee table examining each picture closely seeing herself as a little girl. He had pictures of her, she thought. He didn't just forget about her. Michaela picked up a black and white picture of her father holding out a little brown teddy bear to her seeing his smile and her excited face of a little girl with two ponytails. She turned the picture automatically to see whether there was something written on another side just as her mother often wrote on pictures. It said *'July 17, 1970, Michaela's present from her dad'*. It was her fourth birthday.

"I still have this teddy bear at home. I never knew it was from my dad. Can I have these pictures?" She asked Svetlana. Michaela did not have any pictures of her father, especially not pictures of her and her dad together in one photograph. All the pictures that Michaela remembers were of her mom and wherever her father was in the pictures, she only saw the body of a tall man, the head cut off in each picture. She could not even remember him until now. Now she could put a face to the dark shadow that she envisioned as her father. Looking at the happy pictures, seeing her father smiling at her, seeing her and him happy together, even if there were only few moments, they looked like a happy family at one time. Although her father has gotten lost and eventually died because of his love for alcohol, seeing these pictures, she thought that he must have loved her at one time. She came here to find her dad and was shocked to find that he was gone and she would never have a relationship with him; she would never get a chance to know him better; she would never see him again. But in a way, even though he was gone, she has realized that at one point in her life, he was there and she must have had some loving moments together with him. She has learned some things about him;

some bad, but some positive things that she will take with her. She might not have seen him again in person because he was gone forever, but now she has a memory of him; a face that she can say was her father. When they gathered the black and white pictures back into the small envelope, Svetlana handed it to Michaela.

"Your father was holding on to these pictures and every so often, he would look at them. I'm sure he would want you to have them now." She handed her the old yellowish envelope with its contents.

"This means so much to me. Thank you." Michaela said with tears in her eyes and the two young women hugged each other, while Julia was chatting and explaining to her grandfather that this is her as a baby.

Michaela told them that she and Eddy set their wedding date for October 5th but questioned whether she should change it because of her father's death. Eddy, who was quite supportive to Michaela about her loss, was now getting upset with her when she suggested postponing the wedding; scolding her in German refusing to change the wedding date. The brief interchange created a brief friction between them and a tense atmosphere. Michaela felt embarrassed in front of Svetlana and her half-sister and even her grandfather who seemed to pay attention for a change. Svetlana must have sensed it or perhaps she understood some German, because she quickly interjected the argument.

"Don't be ridiculous changing your wedding plans. I know you just learned about your father's death, but he has been long gone, Michaela. He wouldn't want you to make changes because of him." When she translated it back to Eddy who was sitting tense like on pin nails, getting upset by the minute, she saw him relax almost immediately, giving Svetlana some sympathy points for averting a possible disaster.

"Alright, then." Michaela agreed. "But you have to come to the wedding." She turned to her younger sister and asked her.

"Will you be my bridesmaid, Julia? I have a very long dress and I need someone to help me carry it so I won't trip. Would you do me the honour?" Julia excitedly clapped her little hands.

"Can we go, mom, pleaseeee!" Julia whined.

"Are you sure about inviting us, Michaela?" Svetlana queried with a concern in her face.

"Of course, I'm sure. I want my sister there and I want you to be there too, as her mother and my friend", she added. Michaela was excited to have found a little sister that she always wanted to have. That was not a step-sister; this was her blood; even though just partly.

"What would your mom say about it?"

"It's our wedding and she will have to accept it. How can you hold a grudge against a man that is long gone?" Michaela was able to forgive her father for abandoning her when she was six years old. She did not want to hold a grudge or hatred towards him anymore. She has done that all her life and it hurt her in the end. She needed to forgive him; not for him, but for herself. She might have come looking for her father; instead found some answers she needed and although she might have lost him forever, she has gained something new. She was re-united with her long last grandfather, who when he remembered her, showed his affection towards her and she found a sister and a new friend.

Chapter 14

ALTHOUGH MICHAELA'S MOTHER WAS NOT thrilled about her ex-husband's wife and her daughter attending the wedding, Michaela was adamant about it and Klaudia eventually accepted it with reluctance. Now she was sitting in the first row in anticipation of her only daughter who would walk down the narrow Old Town Hall isle at any moment. Even though Klaudia always envisioned her daughter getting married in the magnificent Gothic style Cathedral of St. Elizabeth in Kosice having a traditional Catholic ceremonial wedding; she came to terms with the fact that her only daughter was getting married in Kosice's Old Town Hall; a white nice looking building with its unique historical touch surrounded with fountains at the front.

Klaudia wore a long evening, off the shoulders olive green dress with a small orchid pin in the cleavage of her dress; a present from her soon to be son-in-law. She put all her negative emotions about her ex's wife who was proudly standing with Nikole as the other bridesmaid. Klaudia accepted her daughter's choices when it came to the wedding plans, stepping back becoming an observer; rather than a person of interference. Nothing else mattered to her but her daughter's happiness which she saw in Michaela's face at the back room just before the ceremony. Sylvia sat beside her sister wearing a large navy blue hat that abstracted the vision of the small crowd directly behind her. The below the knee dress matched the colour of her hat with long see-through silk sleeves which were the best feature of the otherwise plain style. Aunt Sylvie did not look happy about Michaela's wedding on this sunny fall day but felt that she gave her niece enough warning to change her destiny, yet she still chose to marry Eduard Verner.

All she could do at this point was to look at Eddy with chagrin in her eyes gnawing at her inner cheek hoping that her predictions were wrong.

Eddy was standing tall feeling restless and edgy, especially when he noticed Nikolas standing at the end of the hall leaning against the back wall; his arms crossed; a bouquet of roses tucked into the curve of his arm sticking out; waiting for the ceremony to begin just like everyone else. He was not sitting with his parents as he had just arrived minutes before the ceremony began. He debated with himself to the last minute whether to attend or not, but thought of Michaela's words of how much it would mean to her for him to be there; so he put his feelings aside and came to see his best friend's wedding no matter how difficult it has been for him. Seeing Michaela gorgeous in her wedding dress, happiness in her face; he was glad he postponed his army duty by a month due to this wedding.

Mr. and Mrs. Senko sat on the bench beside Klaudia, from the left side, showering her with pleasant smiles. Nikole and Svetlana as the bridesmaids were standing on the left hand side wearing amethyst purple long dresses with thin straps and small bouquets of purplish orchids in their hands.

Otto and Ritchie stood across from the bridesmaids in their black suits, with Eddy slightly ahead of them, who seemed to be quite anxious waiting for his bride to be. Ritchie was rubbing his forehead trying to ease his headache after a night of drinking that he was not used to.

Otto winked at Nikole smiling at her broadly while they waited for the bride's entrance. Yesterday afternoon when he arrived in town with Ritchie heading to Michaela's apartment where he knew Eddy was staying; Otto anxiously rang the bell of Nikole's house seeing her angry face, hands placed firmly on her hips when she saw him at her doorstep. Neither of them said a word. They stood there staring at each other for a moment when Otto's tall figure took a step closer opening his long arms waiting for an embrace from her. She did not expect to have still such strong emotions for him, but she did. For a moment she pretended to be still mad at him for not writing to her or calling her, but that has quickly vanished when he added puppy face eyes still holding his arms wide open for her to jump into. Nikole pursed her lips to the right corner of her mouth, thinking for a moment how to react, but soon she gave in to his boyish charm and jumped into his arms, embracing him tightly, all her anger dissipating. He lifted her in the air for a couple of seconds giving her a loud kiss on her lips. When he put her down, she remembered why she was so angry with him in the first place and hit him with her small fist into his shoulder for letting him know that he cannot treat her like that. But he was quickly forgiven when they made love that afternoon before her parents came home from work. Now, waiting for the ceremony to begin, he had a big smile on his face whenever his gaze wondered towards Nikole, who was returning his smiles back, her eyes sparkling with happiness.

The wedding melody sounded throughout the small Town Hall room where the ceremony would take place. The bride appeared in the entrance in a long, old fashioned dress with long sleeves and a long trail, making her way slowly towards the front where her fiancé was anxiously waiting. Julia behind her, proudly carried Michaela's long trail of her dress that otherwise would have dragged behind her on the ground. Michaela held a beautiful bouquet of vibrant mixture of colours from white and purple-speckled orchids, lavender and amethyst shades and dark purple orchids in both hands conveying the message of eternity that the flowers were promising. The flowers went with the purple theme of the bridesmaids' dresses. Even Julia wore a purple long dress, made out of the same material as her mother's dress that was standing up front smiling at her little girl. Julia looked like a little princess.

Michaela had one of the Dendroc-dy orchids from her bouquet placed in her carefully styled hair that was put up in a bun showing her long neckline. Few curly strands of her hazel-brown hair were hanging purposely from her fancy bun. Eddy also wore a small purple orchid in the packet of his black jacket, from the bouquet of his bride that was arranged by Nikole the last minute before the ceremony.

Nikolas stood up straight when Michaela made her entrance, passing by him with a big smile on her face that was not directed at him. She did not notice him in the back corner; her eyes were fixated on her future husband to be who now returned her smile mouthing the word "Wow" on his lips. There was nobody to give Michaela away but that made her entrance more dramatic with a cute little girl behind her that remained standing there patiently throughout the whole ceremony holding her long trail patiently. Quiet whispers carried in the room competing about the bride's beauty and the cuteness of the little girl questioning who she was.

The guest list was very small just with Michaela's immediate family and few of her friends as they agreed during the wedding plans; however, some other acquaintances consisting of Klaudia's and Michaela's other friends and neighbours that either the bride or her mother mentioned to them about the wedding in passing attended the formal part of the wedding. From Eddy's side there was only his best friend, Otto and his brother, Ritchie with whom Eddy seemed to have made some piece since Ritchie arrived for his brother's wedding. Along with Otto who returned later in the evening the other night from Nikole's house took Eddy out for his bachelor's party in town; on the whim as they usually have done things. The boys got drunk below recognition; especially Eddy whose excuse was that this is the last time he gets to do it. They invited couple of hookers into the nearby hotel room where they all stayed last night. The last thing that Eddy remembered was the stripping of the girls; one of them giving him a lap dance and everything else went black again. The boys pledged in the morning that whatever happened last night will stay between them bonding the brothers again in the process. The boys got ready in the hotel without letting Michaela see her fiancé saying that it was a bad luck for the groom to see his bride in the wedding dress before the wedding. Otto came to gather Eddy's suite and other essentials in the morning to get ready for the wedding; while Nikole as the maid of honour helped Michaela with the hairstyle and make-up.

Eddy was disappointed not having his own mother attend his wedding, but he shook the uneasy feeling of his mother's lack of acceptance of his bride that she has never met and looked at the city official who started his speech. Michaela hired a professional German/Slovak translator to assure that Eddy understood everything and to make the wedding valid. Eddy barely listened to the translator; he just wanted to get it over with; wanting to get to the fun part of his wedding; the drinking from last night did not seem to faze him like it did his brother who was suffering from a hangover.

Michaela was nervous but ecstatic at the same time. Luckily her morning sickness was gone by this point; otherwise she did not know how she would have gotten through with the ceremony; although it was shorter than the typical church weddings.

The brief speech of the city official marrying them was not as special as Michaela had envisioned if she were to be married by a priest in a church, but when she gazed lovingly into Eddy's eyes exchanging the wedding bands that her mother purchased few days ago for them, she could have not felt happier. The couple did not prepare any wedding wows, so the city official simply said at the end.

"Now I pronounce you husband and wife. You may kiss the bride." At that, Eddy took Michaela into his arms, bent her backwards and gave her a passionate kiss that made some people feel awkward as it took longer than it should have.

Nikolas must have had an innate instinct to stand close to the exit as he had to go out during the last part to get some fresh air, thinking that coming here might not have been such a good idea after all. But he made it this far, so he would stick through this wedding for her. He came back to the room after few minutes seeing a line-up of congratulants kissing the bride and the groom on the cheeks wishing the couple happy lives together. Michaela's mother and aunt had tear-stricken faces, for different reasons, as they were hugging Michaela one after another, barely able to utter their congratulations to the bride. Nikolas joined the small group of congratulants, being the last one to congratulate the happy couple.

"Nikolas. I'm so glad you came." Michaela exclaimed with joy of seeing him as she did not notice him standing at the very back with all the busyness of the wedding ceremony.

"I wouldn't have missed it for the world, seeing you so happy." Then he leaned closer to her embracing her and whispering to her ear out of Eddy's ear shot despite the language difference.

"I hope you always stay this happy." He kissed her on both cheeks noticing Eddy's visible displeasure about him being there in the first place. Michaela smiled at her friend, taking the lovely pink and red roses from him that he was handing to her.

"Thank you, Nikolas." The way she smiled at him could have easily made jealous man like Eddy murderous. But Eddy held his composure enduring the formalities.

"I wish you all the best, Mika." Out of courtesy he moved towards the groom who was not thrilled to see his unspoken rival, but the men shook their hands with respect, Nikolas expressing his congratulations to Eddy in German.

"You're a very lucky man, Eduard. You just married a very special woman. Take good care of her." Eddy looked at him with umbrage in his eyes that would have knocked him down if looks could kill.

After the main ceremony at the Old Town Hall, the group with the bride and groom in the lead moved out into the small park-like area with beautiful fountains nearby where they decided to take some wedding pictures. Shortly after few pictures, majority of the attendees scattered away and went their separate ways leaving only a small group of people that were awaited in the nearby restaurant were the wedding festivities would begin. Eddy noticed Nikolas talking to his friend Otto and Richie who were listening with curious intent. He seemed to be quite fluent in German and the boys were chuckling and nodding in agreement. Eddy would have given everything he had, although it was not much, to know what Nikolas was telling the boys, but they were standing out of his ear shut and with the noise of the fountains with added classical music that started to play through the speakers that surrounded the fountains, he had no chance of hearing anything. When Richie went to the bathroom in the restaurant, Eddy took the opportunity and excused himself, heading to the men's room after his brother. He caught up with him behind the doors of the bathroom, holding him back by the arm askance.

"What was that asshole telling you and Otto earlier today?"

"What are you talking about?"

"Don't play dumb with me, Ritchie. I saw you and Otto talking about something with Nikolas. What bullshit was he telling you?"

"Nothing, Eddy, he was just telling us about some Slovak wedding traditions; that's all. I swear." He added to persuade his brother lifting two fingers in a promise.

"I hope you're telling the truth. I can easily find out, you know." Eddy warned him; still feeling suspicious that something else was going on, but he let his brother go and returned back to his new bride and the wedding guests transforming his face back into a smile that felt phony even to him.

He remembered Michaela telling him about their wedding traditions couple days before the wedding and begged him to participate in them. One of them he experienced right at the entrance of the restaurant where the owner purposefully broke a plate, scattering the pieces all over the front hall of the restaurant. He handed the groom the broom while the small crowd was cheering for Eddy to clean it up, while Michaela was holding a sweeping pen waiting for Eddy's cooperation; smiling at him with encouragement. She warned him about this tradition explaining to him the belief or the reasoning of this tradition was that the potsherds bring the young couple good luck and they get a good start into their marriage indicating equality in their relationship with shared household responsibilities from both of them.

Eddy had quite a different opinion about equality of the sexes when it came to house chores as he believed that it was the woman's job to attend to the housework, cooking and taking care of the children as well as her man, but he kept his opinions to himself, reluctantly participating in the tradition that seemed to be important to Michaela.

Michaela also told him about couple of other eastern Slovak traditions that she could think of from attending Slovak weddings in the past. She told him that she would change into a red, shorter dress after midnight as the tradition prescribed before the bride and groom went away on their honeymoon, but before they left, everyone present, men and women alike would get the last chance to dance with the bride during the "Bridal Dance" and each person would have to pay something for the dance. Eddy could hold a box, a plate or a hat collecting the money while Michaela danced their national polka dances. Eddy liked the part where he would collect money from guests, but did not like the idea that everyone would dance with his wife. Eddy found it a little strange, especially the part that even women would be dancing with Michaela; however, for her dancing with every men in the room sounded to him even less appealing.

"Eddy, come on, it's an eastern Slovak wedding tradition that has been in existence for a long time and we can actually make decent money on it. Don't worry; the dances are fast and short-lived."

"Well, I thought that the wedding would continue all the way till morning." Eddy further expressed his dislike.

"Yes, of course it will. We don't have to leave right after midnight but the dance is usually done at that time, but we can stay as long as we want." At Michaela's persistence, he eventually agreed to it although somewhat grudgingly.

Eddy was at loss when Michaela asked him about some German traditions as he could not think of any other than that the bride's father should pay for the entire wedding. This reminded Michaela that she never had a father present in her life and now he was gone forever; her mother paid for the entire wedding instead. She would not have her father-daughter first dance at her wedding which she always dreamed about. There was no other male old enough to be Michaela's father that was invited to the wedding; other than Mr. Senko. She did not even consider inviting David or even his daughter, Marcela to the wedding. They cut all contact with them; not wanting to have anything to do with that family even though what David did to Michaela was not by all means Marcela's fault; she did not even know about it.

Instead, Michaela decided to ask Mr. Senko, whom she adored and who always called her "my little bride" to have the first dance with her in place of her father although he was the father of her two friends and not hers.

"It would be my honour. You were always like my own daughter. I told you that before." He responded to her when she asked him before the wedding and he kept his word. Michaela and Mr. Senko danced to the song *"My Girl"* by *"The Temptations"* that made its popularity from North America all the way to Eastern Europe as one of the popular American songs. While Michaela danced with Simon Senko, Eddy danced with his new mother-in-law since his mother failed to attend the wedding.

The restaurant was nicely decorated with white and purple orchids in vases at each table with purple ribbons above the bride and groom where they were seated. Although it was a modest wedding, everyone received several courses with beautiful platters starting with homemade chicken noodle soup with the traditional German touch of various garnishes to make it more appetizing served with a traditional farmer's bread. Michaela and Eddy were encouraged to feed each other first few spoonfuls from each other's plates and each other's spoons. The second course consisted of schnitzel with potato-salad with pickles on the side. For the third course, they have served the traditional Slovak sheep cheese gnocchi with pieces of bacon in the middle even though the guests were already quite full from the previous meals.

Klaudia Martenz could not afford a live music, but Nikolas arranged a friend who worked as a DJ and was playing some traditional polka music as well some modern dance music that people often danced to in a circle. Few times, Michaela danced with Otto, Ritchie and even Nikolas was able to steal one slow dance when Eddy went out for a smoke, coming back glaring at him with disdain. The married couple danced mostly with one another in a slow motion as dancing was not really Eddy's forte but with each drink he loosened up and did not seem to care whether he could dance or not. Nikole enjoyed Otto's company at the wedding and they often snuggled together during a slow song.

At midnight, just as Michaela explained the tradition to Eddy, she went to the back room to change from her long and awkwardly uncomfortable wedding dress that she could barely move in. She came out in a red mini-dress with white polka-dots and comfortable red shoes with open toes and a strap around her ankle which extended her endless legs, giving it a sexy look. It was time for the Bridal Dance that the DJ announced playing upbeat polka music encouraging the wedding guests to participate in. First it was the mother of the bride that twirled her daughter around few times, then embraced her and threw five-hundred Crowns into Sylvia's hat which was used now to collect the money for the Bridal Dance. It was a lot of money for Klaudia especially after paying for the entire wedding, but she had been saving for a long time for her daughter's wedding, wanting her to have fond memories. Next was Michaela's Aunt Sylvie who hooked her forearm into Michaela's and turned around several times in a fast Polka dance. When she was handing the two-hundred Crowns into her own hat that Eddy was now holding; she hesitated for a moment giving him an inhospitable look, muttering something under her breath that Eddy neither heard or understood, but then she tossed the money into her blue hat and turned on her heal to the other side of the room; far away from Eddy. He did not need to hear or understand to know that Aunt Sylvie still did not warm up to him although he did not understand what he did to her to deserve such adversity from her. The few guests lined up one after another dancing briefly with the bride as the DJ was advertising loudly through the microphone.

"The bride is for sale. The bride is for sale. Last chance to dance with the beautiful bride…."

Although Otto and Ritchie were not familiar with this tradition, Nikole quickly explained it to them and they pulled out some German Marks and went to dance with the bride. Nikolas just like during the congratulations was again the last one in line to dance with the gorgeous bride that he wished was his. He paid thousand Crowns for a dance with Michaela ahead of time; tossing it in the hat provocatively and then enjoyed every minute of the dance despite Eddy's hateful look. The only reason why he did not step in was because Nikolas paid the highest amount of all the guests. Unexpectedly, Nikolas scooped Michaela into his arms like a feather and carried her to the back door of the restaurant where the owner and Ritchie were covering for them. Eddy not understanding what was happening, he grabbed first the money from the hat showing it into his pocket and ran behind them while the owner and his brother tried to stop him explaining that it was a bridal kidnapping. Eddy pushed them away in time to see his best friend, Otto behind his Volkswagen driving away with Michaela and Nikolas.

"What the fuck….?" He swore, while other guests joined him to see what was happening.

Although the 'kidnapping of the bride' was a common eastern Slovak tradition and even in some small villages across Germany there were similar ideas of 'bridal kidnapping' and hiding her usually in a nearby pub while having the groom look for his bride, Eddy was not familiar with this tradition. Once the groom found his bride in a nearby pub where the rest of the guests would be invited and the groom would have to pay for the drinks and for getting his bride back. These kinds of pranks; however, did not end well, especially with a jealous man like Eddy who did not know at first that it was just a prank of a wedding tradition; overreacted by swearing and grabbing his brother and then pushing him against the wall with his forearm with an unbelievable strength of a madman.

"Where are they? I know, you know. Talk!" Still holding his brother with his forearm, he pressed harder on his chest.

Nikole who caught up with Eddy at the back of the restaurant, tried to calm the situation down explaining him in her broken German that it was just a typical Slovak wedding tradition and that they would be just in one of the pubs or restaurants waiting for them and that he would have to pay back for his bride. Eddy did not have any intention of paying in monetary value to Nikolas for kidnapping his wife; but he certainly planned to 'pay him back'. He pressed on his brother's chin in a threatening manner repeated the question.

"Where are they?" His lips pursed into a thin line and his 'V' shape appeared in the middle of his eyebrows.

"Golem." His brother said breathlessly. He let his brother go. Nikole still trying to calm Eddy down offered her help.

"It's a local brewery pub. Come Eddy, I'll take you there. It's only about twenty minutes from here on foot." She tried to keep pace with Eddy but she ended up running beside him as the fury was pushing him faster and faster.

"Eddy, please don't be angry at my brother. It really is a wedding tradition around here." He stopped for a second turning to face her that unexpectedly scared Nikole.

"So I supposed to be just fine with it that your brother is having the time of his life with my new wife?!"

"Eddy, it's just a stupid prank. They are probably sitting there, having a beer and waiting for you." He did not listen to her anymore and hurriedly walked ahead not waiting for her directions. Walking in the brisk fall night he felt the alcohol evaporate out of his head leaving only rage. Nikole could barely keep up in her long narrow dress that was now getting in her way, running behind him with small steps as her dress permitted; she nearly twisted her ankle in her killer high heels. Seeing Eddy's angry face, she was worried that he would hurt her brother rather than laugh at the prank. While Eddy was rushing through the walking zone of the Kosice downtown peaking into nearby pubs that were open, Nikolas, Michaela and Otto sat comfortably in a micro-brewery restaurant called "Golem" famous for the best beer in town. Nikolas ordered Golden Pheasant in a large pitcher claiming that this was the best and famous beer in whole Czechoslovakia.

They drank the beer with its foam rising high from the tall glasses; still chuckling at Nikolas' kidnapping idea. Otto who knew his friend quite well was concerned but not to the point of not participating in it. He was a jokester and if someone organized a prank, he was first in line. He thought it was quite ingenious idea; tradition or not and he could not wait to see Eddy's face when he found them. He clicked the bottom glass with Nikolas'.

"Cheers, buddy. You're fine guy. Too bad I knew you for only such a short time because Eddy's gonna kill you. He must be frantic now, looking for you everywhere."

"That's for marrying the girl that I always loved." He winked at Michaela conspiratorially. Nikolas, who had enough to drink all night, was frank about his feelings and enjoyed the few last moments with Michaela without Eddy hovering in the background before she forever disappeared from his life. Of course, his joy was short lived when Eddy stormed into the pub finding Michaela at the wooden table with Otto and Nikolas. He looked at her sternly yet with surprisingly collective voice said to her.

"Wait outside the pub."

Chapter 15

NIKOLAS PUT HIS FEET ON the table, pursing his lips and shaking his index finger at Eddy.

"No, no, no. Not so fast. You have to first pay the ransom. How much are you willing to pay to have your lovely bride back?"

"You want me to pay for my own wife?" Eddy asked menacingly, still in a low voice that held more threat than if he was yelling. But Nikolas did not feel intimidated by this nearly a head taller man with venom in his eyes.

"That's right. It's part of the tradition. You pay to the kidnappers the amount that you think your bride is worth; otherwise you don't deserve her." Eddy had enough of Nikolas' attitude.

"I'll pay you alright." He yelled at him this time and launched at him with his right fist, knocking him off his chair, hitting Nikolas in the lower part of his face. Blood spattered all over his shirt. Michaela who had no intention waiting outside was standing to the side watching what would transpire, gasping in astonishment when Nikolas fell down backwards from the blow to his face. Her caring nature told her to run to Nikolas who carefully wiped his bloody side of his lips, but she did not dare move when she saw Eddy's furious expression.

"STOP! If you want to fight, you can do it outside, but not here, young men." The bartender was yelling at them in Slovak trying to push all of them out of the pub, not wanting any trouble; although nobody was paying attention to the small old man that was getting frustrated with his guests. When he saw that the fight did not escalate, as Nikolas did not retaliate, he threw his hands up in the air in frustration slapping a white dirty towel on his leg; returning behind the counter.

"That's enough, Eddy. Come on, give the guy a break. It was just a prank and quite a good one, I must add." Otto who was taller than Eddy, stepped in-between them stretching his long arms in both directions separating Eddy away from Nikolas who had no intention on fighting with Eddy.

"You better stay out of my way. You were in on it too. I can give you a bloody matching set to go with your new friend here." He pointed abruptly at Nikolas who sat back down, wiping his bloody nose on a napkin. Eddy reprimanded his best friend but did not put his hands on him.

"Eddy, come on. It was just a joke; calm down and just pay." Otto told Eddy calmly putting his hands on Eddy's shoulders in a friendly way. Eddy grabbed Otto's wrists and pushed them away from his body. Nikole along with Ritchie who was following them with a safe distance, so Eddy would not beat him up during his fury, caught up with the group of young people inside the pub; they came in time to witness the interchange. Nikole stood close to Michaela hugging her now, checking whether she was alright. Nikolas although with a swollen lip and bloody nose, sat back down and put his feet back on the table as before and repeated the question to Eddy with a coolness in his voice.

"How much is she worth to you?" Eddy, who was held by Otto by one shoulder, reached in his pocket and pulled out a five Crown coin tossing it towards Nikolas. The coin hit the edge of the table and rolled down somewhere under the chairs. Nikolas put his legs down looking at Eddy intently.

"That's how much you value your wife?" He did not let his eyes of Eddy, not bothering to pick up the coin.

"Stop it already, Nikolas." Nikole interjected. For once he listened to his sister and dropped the issue.

"You want a beer, asshole? It's on me." Nikolas said with a chuckle, running his tongue over bottom of his sore lip. Without waiting for an answer, Nikolas yelled out to the bartender.

"Hey, Josef, bring us a jug of Golden Pheasant and a jag of Budweiser and glasses for everyone and come join us as well. We have a wedding to celebrate." Josef, the bartender was glad that the fight did not continue and that it ended up the way it did. He quickly went into his working mode, serving the young group of people with skillfulness. Everyone seemed to have calmed down and they all sat down behind a rectangular table. When they were drinking beer, saying their cheers and now laughing at the prank, Nikolas told Eddy.

"Next time, you learn our traditions. You married one of the feisty Slovak girls."

"Yeah, I wish I had heads up. I still don't like what you guys pulled on me." Nikolas touched his lip making an exaggerated face in pain.

"Tell me about it."

"Sorry, man about the fat lip."

"I guess I had it long coming." Nikolas said it with chuckle and clicked the large beer glass with Eddy's. "No hard feelings?"

"I don't think we'll be friends, but no hard feelings, asshole." Eddy returned the insult and they were even.

The men had another round of beer before they returned back to the other wedding guests who were anxiously waiting for them; not knowing what has happened. When Maria Senko saw her son's bloody shirt and swollen mouth, she reprimanded him.

"Did you get into a fight, Nikolas?"

"No mom, I ran into a metal pole." He said jokingly kissing her on the cheek, he thought. *Metal pole called Eddy's fist.* But he did not say that aloud; instead he reassured his mother.

"Don't worry, everything is alright."

The wedding festivities continued till early morning as was customary. Eddy and Michaela were spending their wedding night at her mother's home, while Otto and Ritchie walked to the hotel where they spent the previous night. Klaudia went to her sister's place for the night giving the young couple an empty place for their wedding night.

Michaela's wedding night was anything but romantic; certainly nothing like she has envisioned in her dreams. Eddy jumped on top of her performing routine movements, satisfying himself quickly in the process without any consideration for what she was experiencing at the moment. Afterwards he fell down on his stomach, face down on the pull-out sofa sliding off of her soundly falling asleep. Michaela never realized how much Eddy snored at night but she loved him, so she should not be bothered by that, she thought. They had a long day and a long night behind them and she knew Eddy was drinking a lot at his wedding. She was surprised that he could actually still walk, not let alone to make love to her. She did not let her disappointment of the wedding night bother her too long. She was tired and needed to rest. She tried to fall asleep but despite her tiredness her thoughts kept her up. She starred in the dim light at her hand where Eddy placed her wedding band less than fifteen hours ago. She never received the promised engagement ring and the wedding bands were bought by her mother with Eddy's promise that he would repay her. It was embarrassing that he did not purchase it himself, but that was not what the marriage was all about. She did not need a fancy, expensive ring to know that Eddy loved her.

She was now a married woman. Even in her mind it sounded strange. She was so young, but at the same time it was the coolest thing that she could have imagined. Her former classmates that came to the ceremony congratulated her with envy whispering to her.

"You didn't say he was so handsome." She heard another girl whispering in her ear shortly after the ceremony.

"You're so lucky, Michaela. You get to move away from this God forgotten shitty place." Yet another commented when they were gathering outside to take pictures.

"German? Way to go girl. He must be rich."

Michaela did not know anything about Eddy's financial means or assets, but it did not matter to her. She was always embarrassed to ask him such questions and he never volunteered it on his own. She would soon find out where they would live. She did not care if he was poor as a church mouse. She married him because she loved him and because now they will be a complete family. That was what she always dreamed about; a beautiful, complete family with a mom and dad and a little one running around them. They will help support each other and as long as there is love between them they could overcome any adversity; whether it was not having jobs or money, language barriers, or even his mother's acceptance or the lack of it. She still wanted to meet her as soon as they came to Germany and would tell her how much she loves her son and will be always by his side. There is no person that dislikes her, she thought. She is a nice young woman that has a unique ability to have people like her no matter what. She was sure she would gain Mrs. Verner's acceptance even if she was not German.

As Eddy turned on his back, his snoring increased. Michaela kissed the left side of his cheek, snuggling close to his hot body. She was thinking of all the things that she still had to do before she went to live in Germany until she finally drifted off to sleep.

Ritchie and Otto went back to Germany the following day in Otto's 1978 Volkswagon Scirocco. To help out the young couple, Otto took some of Michaela's trousseau that her mother has been collecting for her throughout her life such as new bedding, dishes, pots and pans and other small household essentials that her mother insisted for Michaela to take rather than buying everything from scratch. Going through the wedding presents, they discovered a coffee machine, an iron, a toaster and other small things that a couple could use in their new household. These were nice gifts, Michaela thought and despite Eddy's rolling eyes he agreed to bring the items as he did not have majority of these things or they were not in a good shape. Until recently, Eddy lived with his mother, so he did not need anything at that time.

One of the wedding presents was a large thin package that Michaela unwrapped excitedly. She knew right away it was from Nikolas. It was gorgeous oil painted picture of a beach and ocean in the background, with an orangey-yellow sun set with a young woman with long hazel brown hair walking away on a shore; just as if she was walking away from the artist with only a slight turn of her body, appearing to look back.

"He did draw it in colour for me." Michaela said to herself under her breath, thinking back to Bulgaria when Nikolas gave her the sketchbook with pencil drawings of the beach and of her portraits. She loved the picture and it reminded her of beautiful times in her life. Eddy did not catch what she was saying as she said it in her language.

"What is it?"

"Look, Eddy. Isn't that beautiful?" Michaela asked him excitedly turning the picture towards him as he was sitting on the sofa across from her looking at a small set of salt and pepper shakers in the shape of ducks' heads making a duck face. He looked up and questioned her.

"Who is it from?"

"Nikolas painted it himself. He is really talented. I want to take it with me to our new home. Otto can take it in his car."

"Forget it." Eddy retorted coldly.

"Come on Eddy. I really like it. And it's a gift."

"You like the picture or that jerk?"

"You don't need to be jealous Eddy. I married you, not him." She stood up, leaning the picture gently against the wall putting her hands around his shoulders she placed gentle kisses on his slightly scruffy cheek that he did not shave since the wedding.

"I'm not jealous!" He said sternly. "I just don't like the guy."

"Ok, you don't have to like him, but can we take the picture with us? Please? It reminds me of the beach where I fell in love with you. Please, Eddy." She made a puppy face flailing her long eyelashes at him. Eddy made a grumpy sound; then he shrugged. Michaela interpreted it as a yes and kissed him on the lips. He pulled her passionately into his lap kissing her back. Suddenly, he thought of something.

"How was our wedding night?"

"You don't remember?"

"Ohm, I was really tired and it is kind of a blur." He admitted reluctantly.

"We made love, although I experienced a better performance from you before." She said with a reproach in her voice. Eddy's ego was touched and he pushed her away, pretending to unwrap another present.

The best present Eddy thought was the cash that was given to them either in the cards or from the Bridal Dance. Nikolas' contribution alone increased the amount. He kept it with him, not showing Michaela how much profit they had made at the wedding and he did not have an intention paying anything back to Michaela's mother who never asked for any money from him; not for the wedding or the wedding bands or for living at her home for over a month.

Few days after the wedding, Michaela checked all her documents, including the marriage certificate, her civil identity document and the two large black suitcases she had carefully packed with all the essentials for her new life in Germany that she would begin with Eddy. Eddy complained about who would carry the suitcases considering that they were going by a train and they would first stop in Dresden where his mother lived.

"I can't believe you're moving so far away from me." Her mother protested at the train station when they were boarding the train.

"It's not that far mom. I'll call you when we get there and I promise I'll write all the time. Besides, it's not at the end of the world. You can come visit us at any time."

She watched through the window, waving back to her mother who was standing by herself at the platform as the train set into motion. Aunt Sylvie did not care to see Eddy again. Attending the wedding where she had to tolerate the groom was already a huge sacrifice for her. Michaela visited her aunt the day before her departure to reassure her that she is very happy and she has nothing to worry about.

"You come back home if he ever lays a hand on you." Aunt Sylvie warned her. "You know that this will always be your home and me and your mother would always help you, no matter what." Michaela smiled at her aunt who was almost a head shorter than Michaela; she told her she will write to her soon.

The same day, Michaela went to say good bye to the whole Senko family. She caught up with Nikolas who opened the door looking handsome, dressed in his army uniform, ready to start his military duty for the next two years as it was mandated in the Communist country. His chestnut brown eyes lit up when he saw Michaela in the doorway, whom he thought would not see again. His light brown hair was cut short, hiding under his military hat giving him more serious look.

"I came to say goodbye. I'm going away to Germany."

"I'm glad I got to see you before you left. I'm leaving tonight to Bratislava where I will be stationed in one of the military barracks."

"I hope it goes fast for you there. I know how much you despise going."

"Don't worry about me. Maybe it will be good for me……to forget some things."

"Nikolas, I wanted to thank you for your beautiful picture you painted. It's the best gift I got."

"I'm glad you like it." He barely finished the sentence when his sister appeared interrupting their conversation.

"You mean the wedding album I got you was not as special?" She asked scornfully, giving Michaela hug and pulling her inside her room. The girls chatted for a while remembering the fun things they have done this summer.

"I would have never thought that you would be the first to marry and leave me here behind. Still waters run deep." Nikole pouted.

"Well, now that you and Otto seem to get together again, maybe there will be another wedding."

"I don't know. I don't understand that guy. I take him with reservation."

"Either way, Otto or not, I hope you come visit me. I'll send you the address as soon as I find out where Eddy actually lives."

"You don't even know the address where you're gonna live?"

"Well, we're going first to Dresden because his mother lives there. I believe he has a new place in the town called Halle, but it's a surprise, I guess. So I don't have any details."

"Take care of yourself and call if you need anything, ok?"

"I will." The friends hugged as Michaela was making her way out the door saying goodbye to the parents as well.

Saying farewell to her new found little sister was probably the hardest as the little girl was hugging her big sister with tears in her eyes. Michaela made promises that one day she would come visit her in Germany which stopped the tears.

Now sitting with Eddy in the Express that went directly to Dresden, she looked wistfully at the passing scenery of her beautiful country. They would travel all night and Michaela was glad that they got the sleeping wagon. Another young couple joined them in the same wagon in Bratislava; they were heading to Hamburg. She was German and the young man was Czech so Michaela could easily communicate with him. The couple had dated for about three years but they were in no hurry to get married anytime soon or have children. Michaela proudly shared that they just got married and are on their way to honeymoon. She did not know what Eddy had in store for her. He had made promises that he will take her for honeymoon, but did not say where or when. Perhaps it would happen after their visit with his mother that she started to dread.

The train ride was quite long but Michaela was sleeping comfortably through the night with the rhythmical rocking and monotonous noises of the train; it made the trip quite enjoyable despite Michaela's anxiety of the unknown.

"I have a surprise for you." Eddy said in the morning while they ate small breakfast they bought on the train.

"What kind of surprise?" Michaela's eyes lit up with excitement.

"Don't be so curious, you'll get old too fast." He mocked her brushing his index finger on her nose.

When they arrived in Dresden in the morning, the weather was chillier. Michaela was glad she brought her jacket with her. She dragged one large suitcase and a smaller handbag in the other hand. Eddy pulled her other large suitcase behind him. His backpack with few of his belongings easily fit into one of the suitcases with Michaela's things to avoid additional luggage. Eddy waved to the nearby taxi and gave him the address.

"Are we going to your mother's place?"

"Not yet. I'm sure you will like it."

Michaela looked around the town as the taxi was passing on the busy streets even in the early Friday morning. Some people were waiting for streetcars in both directions. Michaela was familiar with streetcars as they are commonly used in Kosice, but she noticed that there were no lights, no gates when coming to the streetcar crossing; just a row of poles. They passed a stunning horse carriage that considerably slowed down the traffic; the horses setting their own pace regardless of the rush hour. They passed through a long bridge with two large triangular peaks typical of the Blaues Wunder Bridge in Dresden giving it a wondrous appeal. Michaela looked intently around the beautiful city as well as a river that was flowing below them. When they arrived at their destination, Eddy announced.

"We're here." He took out their language from the back of the cab, paid the taxi driver and carried one of the suitcases towards a two story brick house with spacious front lawn that was beautifully maintained.

"Is this your mother's house?" Michaela quarried as she pulled her other suitcase awkwardly behind her, tripping over her high heels which were a bad idea to wear on this long trip. But she wanted to look good for Eddy and make nice first impression.

"No, it's not. I already told you we are not going now to my mother's house. Come on." He reached out under a large stone-like matt with the carvings "Willkommens" in a burgundy colour with carved glass opening in the door that gave the front entrance a magical allure.

"Welcome to a palace." He announced. The house looked newly built and very clean.

"This is your place?" Michaela asked surprised as well as impressed with the beauty of the house.

"Do you like it?"

"It's beautiful, Eddy. I love it." She exclaimed with excitement and jumped into Eddy's arms kissing him.

"Come I show you the rest of the house." She noticed in the hall an expensive piano, which surprised her. Does he know she plays piano, she thought. She might have mentioned it to him in Bulgaria, but would he just buy it for her? She touched the oak banister with the hardwood flooring and followed Eddy up the stairs. There were two large bedrooms on the top floor and a wonderful huge bathroom with a bathtub, separate shower stall and amazing round Jacuzzi filling the middle of the spacious bathroom. Michaela never saw such a large bathroom; it was incomparable with the little bathroom in her mother's apartment. There was a double sink with large mirror and the toilet was within the same room, which she found a little strange but it was hidden behind a two meter tall stone wall with its separate window. There were flowers in the windows across the whole bathroom that overlooked the backyard. Michaela peaked out the window to see a spacious backyard with lawn chairs and rectangle glass table with an umbrella in the middle of the table. She stretched her neck to see the right corner of the yard noticing children's swings and some toys on the grass.

"Eddy? Why...." She turned around and noticed Eddy left the bathroom. She went down the stairs finding Eddy in the wooden covered kitchen that led to the backyard. From here she had a better view of the yard. She opened the glass door finding herself on a large deck. She stepped down from the three wooden steps and sat down on the larger swing, stretching her tired legs.

"What do you think Michaela?" She stood up and walked towards the little ducky on wheels with a string attached. She bent down and picked it up remembering she had a similar toy when she was a child. She looked at Eddy and with disappointment in her voice, she stated.

"This is not your house. Right?"

"Why? Are you disappointed?" He was watching her curiously. She shrugged.

"It would have been nice to have such a beautiful house." Michaela said with wistfulness in her voice.

"So, I'm not good enough for you if I don't have a big house and money?" Eddy was getting irritated.

"I didn't say that Eddy. I love you no matter what, but you didn't have to make me believe that this was your house."

"I never said this was my house. I told you I have an apartment in Halle." That was true, Michaela thought; but neither did he dispute it when she asked him where they were going as soon as they arrived and he skillfully avoided her questions.

"I guess you would rather be with that punk from the train. You seemed to hit it off with him."

"Who are you talking about? The couple from the train we met?"

"Oh, so you do remember him. I saw how you were looking at each other. How you were flirting with him."

"Don't be ridiculous, just because we speak similar language. I wasn't flirting with him at all." Michaela did not realize until this moment how jealous Eddy was. When she saw he was getting upset, she quickly added.

"Eddy, you have nothing to be worried about. I love you and I'm not interested in anyone else." He grabbed her roughly and held her hands behind her back kissing her harshly uttering between his kisses.

"You're ....my.... now. Only..... mine." He stopped kissing her for a moment looking in her eyes with his intense gaze. "You understand? I don't want you looking or talking to other guys. It drives me crazy. I'm crazy about you. I love you so much. You are my forever." To prove his point, he stripped her from her clothes rather quickly revealing her naked body. She never understood how quickly he could undress her. He made love to her right on the kitchen floor to prove his point. Michaela was taken by surprise but succumbed to his passion. She did not know whether she should be flattered or frightened. She tried to lose herself in Eddy's arms that were holding her tight at times. They lay on the cold kitchen floor in an embrace for a while; only the heat of their bodies and their recent love making was keeping them warm.

"So, who lives here?" She ventured again, turning to face Eddy who was still embracing her.

"My uncle lives here with his wife and two kids. They went away on vacation for two weeks and let us use their house meantime. So I thought that might be a nice place to spend our honeymoon here. It's free; all we need is to buy some food and I can show you around the city where I grew up."

"As long it's alright with your uncle and his family that we're here, then I love this idea too. And just for the record, I don't care if you're rich or poor. I love you no matter what." He kissed her again, but this time more gently. Now this was the Eddy that she knew. Gentle but passionate; it was her Eddy and she had a life time to figure him out. She loved being with him even when his demeanor sometimes scared her.

"Are you hungry?" He changed the topic.

"Famished."

"Come. I know some nice restaurant not too far from here. We'll eat there and later we can go buy some food." He grabbed her hand, pulling her up from the cold floor.

"Come on, you have five minutes to get ready." He ordered putting on his jeans and buttoning his flannel shirt. He opened the side door that led towards the garage.

Michaela followed shortly after she fixed her hair and used the bathroom. She entered the garage finding Eddy there sitting on a Jawa Babetta moped. He picked up a blue biker's helmet and put it on. He opened the electronic garage door, indicating for Michaela to sit down.

"You're not serious. Michaela looked at the tiny little seat of the small motorcycle behind Eddy, no additional helmet and gave him a questioning look.

"What? Our transportation methods are not up to your standards, madam?

"It's not that, but are you allowed to use it?"

"Sure, Uncle, Albert wouldn't mind. I rode it before many times. Put your jacket on; it can get a bit cold with the wind. Come on already."

"What about a helmet for me?"

"You can have mine. Here!" He took of the helmet running his hand through his thick curly hair and stuck the helmet roughly onto her head. "It's more like a bicycle than a real motorcycle. It will be fun." When she hesitated, he continued with sarcasm in his voice.

"Or you can bus-it." Michaela reluctantly sat down straddling the moped behind her husband. She was glad to wear her comfortable jeans. She thought of changing her heels to running shoes, but saw Eddy's impatient look so gave up on that idea quickly, feeling quite uncomfortable. She wrapped her arms around his waist holding him tightly as the moped slowly set into motion.

"Now that's what I call travelling in style." He yelled out to her through the noise moving his back against her breasts. "I like having you wrapped around me." Michaela smiled to herself thinking that this is the Eddy that she loves so much.

It did not take long before they arrived at the Altmarketkeller restaurant for lunch. They chose to sit outside despite the early October breeze but the sun was high now, warming the cooler air that she felt earlier in the morning when they arrived. The place was relatively cheap, serving traditional German sausages, roast pork and other meat based meals along with variety of beer.

"German sausages with sauerkraut twice, one Pilsner and orange juice." Eddy ordered without much consideration for what his wife wanted to eat. He ordered quickly for her assuming she did not know what the best meal at this restaurant was. Michaela who did not like sausages that much was pouting, trying to complain.

"I can pick for myself, Eddy."

"Don't be ridiculous. You can barely read German and besides I know this place has the best sausages in town. You'll like it." Without waiting for her response, he continued.

"After we eat, we can walk to the Old Market and buy some food for the week." They waited quite a long time, but the food was decent despite the fact that this was not what Michaela would have chosen. But she was hungry, so she ate everything on her plate, confirming Eddy's assumption that she will enjoy it.

"Are you sure you can have another one? You have to drive us back." She commented when Eddy was ordering a third beer.

"We'll take a streetcar back. There is no way we can carry the groceries on the bike and I'll come get the moped later tonight." He lit up his cigarette blowing the smoke in the other direction away from Michaela. She wished he did not smoke but never told him that. After their shopping at the old Market Square, just as Eduard told her; they had taken a streetcar back to the house; both of them carrying few bags of groceries.

"I'm gonna get the moped from the parking lot." He told her later that evening.

"Don't wait up. I'll be back late." Michaela did not like being alone in someone else's house by herself. What if his uncle returned back early with his family, finding a complete stranger in their house? Eddy reassured her that she has nothing to be worried about as his uncle knows about them, but would not be back for next two weeks.

When Eddy came back, she was concerned how he drove the moped back as he was more intoxicated than before he left. She needed to say to him what was on her mind otherwise; she would regret it if something ever happened to her beloved husband.

"How dare you drink and drive, Eddy?"

"Shut up, you don't tell me what to do." He told her off.

"Eddy!" She was both shocked and appalled at his reaction, but she would not stop there.

"You know well that my father died in a drunken accident and because of that, I never got to see him again. I don't want the same thing happening to you."

He dismissed her with a careless wave of his hand.

"Nothing is going to happen to me. See? I'm just fine." He threw his hands in the air and the heaviness of his arms made them fall back rapidly to his sides, nearly making him fall.

"I'm hungry. Get me something to eat, woman."

"Eddy, I didn't think…..to cook anything. You said you would be late."

"So now it bothers you I'm home early? You supposed to take care of me! That's why I married you." Not that she had much experience with drunks, but her instincts told her not to argue with him. She ran off to the kitchen, yelling back to him.

"I'll be right there with some food, Eddy." She prepared a large sandwich for him with ham and cheese, but when she came back to the living room, Eddy was already sleeping on the sofa, snoring loudly.

The following morning when Eddy woke up he tried to remember what happened. He squinted in the early morning sun that was penetrating the left side of the living room. He looked around to see Michaela sleeping across from him on a loveseat sofa. She never went upstairs to the king size bed without him. The sandwich that she prepared for him last night was still sitting on the wooden coffee table on a plate covered in a plastic bag so it would not dry out. He vaguely remembered returning back for the moped at the restaurant where he saw an old friend from high school. The two friends did not see each other for at least a year and Eddy wanted to fill him in about recently getting married to a Slovak girl and recently returning from Czechoslovakia. They sat in the small restaurant drinking one beer after another. He did not remember how he got back to the house. He did not even remember driving the Jawa. He got up and peeked through the side doors into the garage. The moped was not there.

Chapter 16

"**S**HIT." EDDY SWORE ALOUD WAKING Michaela in turn.

"Oh, Eddy. You're up. What's wrong?"

"Nothing." He harrumphed and pondered back to the sofa where he spent the night in an uncomfortable position. He put his face in his hands and then ran them through his hair as he often did, trying to remember. He hated those blackouts.

"I'm sorry, sweetie about last night. I just saw an old friend that I haven't seen for a long time and we got carried away. It won't happen again." She gave him a wry smile.

"I'll make you fresh breakfast and coffee."

"Just coffee for me. I'll gobble the sandwich from last night. Let's not waste food."

After Eddy showered, he came to the kitchen, poured himself a cup of coffee, taking it out to the porch where he had his routine morning cigarette. Michaela did not like that he smoked as she never picked up on that habit despite the peer pressure at school and she certainly would not start now. She was bothered by the smoke, but most of the time, Eddy tried to smoke outside, perhaps because of the consideration of the unborn child. Despite the smoke that quickly evaporated in the fresh air, she joined him outside sitting beside him sipping her own coffee.

"This is nice, the two of us just enjoying the coffee on a deck."

"Let me make up to you the last night. I have an idea of what we could do today. I'm sure you'll love it. I always loved to go there when I was a kid. Do you like dinosaurs?" She looked at him quizzically, lifting her eyebrows curiously.

"Dinosaurs?"

"Yes, life size dinosaurs. Come on, get ready, we'll leave in half an hour."

Within an hour they were sitting on the city bus going to the Saurier Park near Bautzen. It was only about twelve kilometers east of Dresden through lovely countryside, surrounded by farms. The park consisted of life-size plastic dinosaurs that were a great attraction for the children as well as for adults, although it was quite commercialized but Michaela did not care about that. She enjoyed every moment she spent with her husband whom she loved dearly despite of his rough demise when he drank.

They went to the hedge maze that was across from Saurier Park and they chased each other like little children. When Eddy caught her, he pushed her into dead end corner where she could not escape and started kissing her. She reciprocated his passion. She loved when he was playful with her. He could be so loving and passionate.

The honeymoon they spent at his uncle's house was great. Eddy took her sightseeing in the town, to the museum and they often went for walks in the park or nearby forest. Eddy did not drink throughout that time, since the moped incident which he retrieved from his friend the following day. He promised Michaela he would not drink and drive and kept his promise thus far. To please her husband, Michaela cooked lunch for them every day and resumed the responsibility of shopping for food without asking for his help to carry the groceries as she quickly figured out was not one of Eddy's favourite things to do. They did not have much money as Eddy was only on social assistance and he did not work for more than six months. Michaela's small savings she brought with her to Germany were quickly spent on food and outings.

Towards the end of their honeymoon they just stayed in the house and only went out occasionally for a walk. In the evenings Michaela often entertained them with classical music on the piano which Eddy often admired. One night when Michaela was playing Beethoven's famous *"For Elisa"* piece, Eddy simply announced.

"Tomorrow we'll go see my mother. She wants to meet you." Michaela stopped playing and looked up at him.

"Oh, alright." She agreed although she would have liked a little more heads up to at least buy her mother-in-law, whom she has never met, some present. She managed to get flowers the following morning before they caught a bus travelling to the other side of the town.

Her mother-in-law was pleasant and quite welcoming or so it had appeared. Eddy told his mother how they met and about their wedding day. He did not share with his mother that Michaela is pregnant. Despite fifteen weeks into her pregnancy, she was still able to hide her tiny belly under loose t-shirts. Despite her well-covering attire, she did not fool her mother-in-law. After lunch his mother asked Eddy to go to the store to buy dessert, saying that she has forgotten to buy that.

"You go, Eddy, I need some alone time with my new daughter-in-law." Eddy kissed his mother on the cheek and whispered to her something in a German dialect that Michaela did not catch, and then more intelligibly he said.

"I won't be long." With that he put on his light jacket and left leaving Michaela in the hands of his mother waiting with anticipation what her mother-in-law wanted to tell her.

Eleonore Verner cleared her throat, waited for the outside door to close after her son before she spoke.

"You're very beautiful young woman, Michaela and I can see why my son would fall in love with you. But I must tell you I was quite against this marriage." She paused before she continued.

"I see you trapped my son." Michaela looked at her with puzzlement in her expression.

"Don't look at me so innocently with those big eyes of yours. You think I'm dumb and haven't figured out that you got pregnant probably on purpose? Besides you're starting to show. Am I right, are you pregnant?"

"Yes, you're right. I'm pregnant although we didn't plan for it."

"Hmm, obviously! That doesn't change the fact that you ruined my son's life." Michaela had to say something to protect her relationship with Eddy and her dignity or what was left of it. She rehearsed the speech for many days now and she needed to get it off her chest changing what she was originally going to say considering the circumstantial verbal attack of Eddy's mother. She needed to clear the air with her mother-in-law once and for all.

"Mrs. Verner, Eddy and I love each other very much and although the pregnancy came unexpectedly and perhaps earlier than we would have wanted, we are very happy and I don't think I ruined his life. If he didn't want to marry me, he wouldn't have." She paused to catch her breath, but Eleonore saw a window of opportunity to interject.

"You know him for five minutes and you jump into something not even knowing what you got yourself into. How much do you even know about Eduard's life?" She caught Michaela of guard and left her feeling dumbfounded that she could not respond quickly enough perhaps because it was the truth that she did not know anything about Eddy's past, his childhood or teenage years. Meantime Eleonore continued increasing Michaela's concerns.

"I love my son very much, but did he have the audacity to tell you that he murdered his father?" That news came to her like a bombshell and she opened her mouth in astonishment hoping she misunderstood.

"What did you say?"

"You heard me right. He killed his father. Well actually, it was really his step-father, Anton Verner but nobody knew it at that time. Although Anton who was a typical German man with light blond hair and blue eyes always suspected that Eduard was not his son. Ritchie, looks like Anton with his darker blond hair and bluish-gray eyes. Eddy on the other hand with his dark brown eyes and dark brown curly hair did not look of course anything like Anton although he always called him 'dad' and thought that it was his biological father." Michaela listened with shock and intrigue learning about Eddy and his family looking wide-eyed at Eleonore Verner who continued her story, reliving her experiences. She was no longer looking at Michaela; she was back in the past telling her about horrific experiences.

"You see, I was in love with a man a very….very long time ago. He was from Spain travelling through Germany when I met him. His name was Eduardo. Eduardo Carlevaris." Eleonore said his name with wistfulness in her voice. "Oh, it was love at first sight, brief but passionate. Of course, once he left Germany he left his memories behind as well as leaving me pregnant with my first son. He never even found out that I had his baby; I never heard from him again." She took a deep breath and then continued.

"Back then, even today, it was a great shame for a young unmarried girl to be pregnant. And there was Anton, a boy who always had a crush on me. All I needed to do is to reciprocate his affection. We didn't date very long before we got married. He was there for me when I needed it most. He thought the baby was his when he found out I was pregnant. He was a proud father; happy when I gave him a son. But even when Eddy was very little, Anton always suspected that he wasn't his and treated him differently than Richie who was born five years later. Eddy was always the one that got the beating, even when it was Ritchie who did some mischief. He would beat Eddy with his fists, belts, wooden spoons wherever he could get him and sometimes for little things that I can't even remember why. It could be because he didn't clean his room or had gotten into a fight or brought bad marks from school. Whenever I stepped in trying to stop Anton, I got the same treatment." A single tear rolled down her cheek, nodding to herself as if to confirm the story; she then continued.

"He beat me often senseless for minor things; if the dinner was late or the beer was not cold enough; if I put too much make up or when the boys misbehaved. It was always my fault. And I believed it for a long time."

Michaela's empathy for her new mother-in-law had grown tremendously and she ventured to ask.

"Why didn't you leave him?"

"Why? Hmm, that's a good question. I don't know. Many reasons; I guess I was scared; I hoped he would change because he loved me. I believed that children, especially boys needed a firm hand; they needed a father. I wanted to keep the family together. But you're right; I should have left. I would have prevented a disaster that followed when Eddy was sixteen years old. He did not deserve to go to the Juvenile detention for nearly a year for involuntary man slather." She took another breath as if to gather her thoughts that were getting scattered.

"See when the boys were little; I tried to protect them, although I know I failed miserably. Anyway, as Eddy grew older, stronger and a lot bigger than Anton, he became my protector. Eddy was my savior in many ways and he paid the biggest price." Eleonore took a sip of her white wine as if to gain more courage; then she went on.

"That fatal night, Eddy came home just in time when he heard my screams upstairs from the bathroom. I don't remember where Ritchie was at that time. I think he was at his friend's house at a sleepover. It was lucky for him, but not so lucky for the rest of us. Anton and I had a huge fight; as usual he was accusing me of Eddy not being his son as he did not look anything like him. Eddy doesn't even look German, he told me. He told me I was a whore and a piece of shit; pardon my German, but that how he often talked to me. He was drinking that night and I don't know what I was thinking but I was fed up with the abuse and challenged him by telling him the truth of what he suspected all those years. I told him, Eddy was a product of a love affair I had with a Spanish tourist who disappeared shortly after but before I started dating him. Obviously, that was a huge mistake. His eyes changed; I can't even describe it but I saw something…. something evil in his eyes and I knew that I shouldn't have said that.

There were many similar violent outbursts from Anton, but that night I realized he was going to kill me. I screamed out of top of my lungs when he cornered me in the bathroom grabbing me by my throat. Eddy must have heard my screams and rushed to the upstairs bathroom. I tried to fight him off, pushing him and scratching until he pushed me into the tub. I fell on my back hitting my head on the tub and probably lost consciousness for a moment. I came out of it when my head was covered under the water his hands squeezing my neck tightly. I couldn't breathe." She spoke in a monotonous voice as if it was someone else's story that did not concern her. Michaela was terrified and did not realize that she had tears rolling down her cheeks as she listened intently.

"Then he released his grip of my throat, but not because he wanted to, but because Eddy was hitting him from behind trying to pull him off me. I got a chance to catch a breath and fight my return to life. I was too weak to do anything else. I couldn't even climb out of the bathtub. They end up fighting with one another. Anton hated Eddy because he wasn't his son and Eddy hated Anton in turn for all the abuse he had inflicted upon our family." Eleonore got silent for a moment when Michaela prodded her to finish the story.

"What happened after that?" Her voice was hoarse; she barely recognized it.

181

"Well, obviously, I survived and Anton didn't. As they fought, Eddy pushed him off of him and Anton accidently hit his temple on the edge of the bathroom counter being killed instantaneously. There was a lot of blood from his head injury as the impact opened his skull as he fell to the floor." Eleonore skipped the details of the police being called and concluded the horrendous story.

"After long court proceedings, Eddy got two years but served only eleven months with some community service, considering he was a minor and it was in defense of me."

Michaela wiped her tears; her eyes conveyed compassion for Eleonore, Eddy's childhood and his innocence that was stolen from him because of years of abuse from his step-father and for the murder that occurred.

"I'm so sorry, this happened to you and to Eddy."

"Yah, well if that will not have you run in the direction far away from Eddy and our screwed up family, then I don't know what will."

"I would never leave Eddy because of his past. I love him no matter what. This was not his fault. He was a child and he saved your life."

"Yes, you're right. He did save my life and took another one in return." Michaela felt perplexed by her mother-in-law's reaction. Was she upset that the man that abused her during all of their marriage was killed? Eleonore must have noticed Michaela's puzzled look in her face as she went on answering Michaela's unspoken question.

"For years I have wished throughout our marriage that something bad would happen to Anton; that he would just die or was killed somehow. And when that occurred, I was all alone; I was lost; I didn't know anything.... how to take care of the boys; how to support us or anything else. I didn't even know how to pay the bills. Anton always took care of everything. I was miserable and devastated about my family's life and how things turned out. I'm even more heartbroken today for Eddy who was probably impacted the most." Then Eleonore switched her demeanor and there was some malice in her voice when she said.

"Like I told you; you don't know what you got yourself into. Did you get to see Eddy's monstrous side yet?"

"What do you mean? Eddy is not a monster! How can you talk about your son like that?" Michaela was dismayed about the change in

Eleonore's behavior, seeing again the distant and cold Mrs. Verner that she has met only few hours earlier when Eddy first introduced them.

"I love my son dearly", she repeated again, "so don't tell me what I can or can't say. If you haven't seen the dark side of him; his temper especially when he drinks, then you don't really know him."

"If you try to scare me away from this marriage, it will not work." Michaela said stubbornly standing behind her husband. "I married your son for better and for worse. I only feel love and compassion for him and I can understand if he has a little temper considering what he has been through."

"You're a sweet girl and I quite came to like you, but don't fool yourself, dear, if you think he will change."

"I don't need him to change. I want him the way he is with all his flaws."

"I think you're very naïve, but you made your bed; you might as well lie down in it. My parents tried to warn me about Anton too and I would not listen. Don't forget I was pregnant too so I had the pressure from the society to be a married woman. You will learn on your mistakes too, but don't come crying to me." When she saw Michaela's miserable expression, she softened again towards her daughter-in-law.

"I told you about it first of all because you have the right to know as Eddy's wife, if my son didn't have the audacity to tell you himself. But maybe you're right that I told you partly because I wanted you to run the other way and not look back. I guess I should be happy for my son who found himself a beautify wife that loves him so much."

"Thank you, Mrs. Verner." Michaela's expression relaxed as well and she even attempted a sad smile.

"Please call me 'mom'. I never had a daughter." And Eleonore returned Michaela's cheerless smile. Then suddenly if she remembered that Eddy was coming back with a dessert as she heard the key in the door; she whispered to her quickly.

"Please don't tell Eddy that Anton was not his biological father. That's something he never knew." Michaela considered for few moments Eleonore's plea as Eddy was getting inside.

"Maybe it would help him to know the truth about his father." Eddy only got a part of Michaela's sentence as he entered the kitchen with a large white box in his hand.

"What truth about my father? What are you two talking about?" He queried suspiciously looking from his mother back to Michaela. His mother interjected.

"Eddy, I had to tell her what happened in our family." He looked at her for a moment as if her gray eyes spoke the unthinkable words. He knew exactly what his mother meant. After he regained some composure he admonished his mother for exposing their family's shameful secret.

"We talked about this! This was not to be talked about with anyone. EVER! Nobody else needed to know about this. It's a long forgotten story and I served my dues to society for that, though unfairly. This is just a family matter."

"Eduard, she is now a family. She is your wife. Maybe it wasn't my place to tell your wife, but you surely wouldn't have told her. She had the right to know." But that did not console Eddy. On the contrary, he was fuming. He threw the box with cake on the table and looked at Michaela with arrogance in his face.

"So, I guess, this is it! Thanks mother for ruining my life." He said with fury in his voice. Without waiting for a response he looked at Michaela and quickly added. "You can now go back to your mamma." With those words, he turned and left her there with his mother. Michaela looked at Eleonore confused, but her mother-in-law did not seem to be the least surprised. She certainly knew her son well. She gave her the 'I told you' look and opened the box with cake to see the damage.

"Should I go after him?"

"This is what I meant about his temper. He is hot-headed and needs to cool off, but I would still go back to his uncle's place and just be patient with him. He is pushing you away; yet he needs you now the most." This was the nicest thing that her mother-in-law told her since she arrived.

"Here, dear, have a slice of cake. It's little bruised up, but still tasty." She licked the coffee cake off her thumb as she was handing Michaela a plate with the cake on it.

"I'll pack half of it for you and Eddy for later. This is way too much for me." She spoke casually as if the horrific story never happened. Michaela ate the cake but did not enjoy the taste as she was trying to process all information she has learned this afternoon and Eddy's reaction to it.

When Eddy did not return back within two hours, Michaela decided to go to his uncle's house. She wanted to call but his mother discouraged her from doing that as she was sure he would either not pick up the phone or he would slam it in her ear as soon either of them called. Eleonore gave her careful directions to her brother's house and which bus she needs to take and reassured her that with a little time, Eddy will come around. All she needs to do is to reassure him of her love.

"I think he acted that way because he does not think he deserves someone like you. You can show him that he is wrong about that." She smiled at her daughter-in-law and although from the beginning she was determined to dislike this young woman; she could not help it but came to like Michaela rather quickly.

When Michaela arrived at the house where they were staying, finding her way with little difficulty, she rang a doorbell with a shaky hand. When nobody answered, she tried again and again; coming to a conclusion that Eddy was not inside. There was nowhere for her to go and she didn't want to go back to her mother-in-law all across the town again. She went for a little walk around the community admiring the beautiful houses and a family in the front of one of the houses with their two children playing soccer. Will she have a happy family like this family appeared to be? She wondered. When she came back from the unsettling walk, Eddy was still somewhere out. So she reached from behind the backyard hook and opened the wooden gate. Closing it behind her, she walked through the spacious back yard. There she sat down under the gazebo on one of the lawn chairs, waiting for her husband to return. As the darkness was setting in she started to feel cold as the chilly air consumed her body. She was tired, hungry and needed to use the bathroom. She ate some cake with her fingers that her mother-in-law carefully packed for them as nausea was returning to her whenever she was hungry. She licked her sticky thumb and index finger. This is not right, she thought. There were no lights inside so she knew that Eddy still had not returned from his quest wherever that was. The smell of the sweet cake did not satisfy her hunger.

While Michaela curled her legs towards her body in the nippy October night protected only from the wind in the gazebo, Eddy sat alone at a barstool drinking his favourite scotch that appeared to warm up his insides although he felt chill inside his heart. He persuaded himself that a beautiful young woman like Michaela could do so much better than him and that after finding out that he murdered his father, she surely would not want to stay with such an atrocious person. He was disgusted with himself. How could she love someone like him? He tried to drink his sorrow away thinking of his brother's words *"Let's face it, you're fucked up. No woman would ever want you. You can't even take care of yourself. How are you going to take care of someone else? You're fucked up. No woman would ever want you......"* It was ringing in his head like a mantra. He drank another shot of scotch feeling the impact of the warmth in his throat and stomach. He decided that it was time to get his wife back and he would fight to have her stay with him, if that was the last thing that he did. He paid the bartender with a hefty tip and plunked his feet on the ground leaving the pub.

Chapter 17

IT WAS GETTING DARK AND really cold outside and Michaela wondered when Eddy would be back. What if he was out all night? She could no longer stand the cold. She was starving and her bladder was going to explode. She would have gotten a motel if she had enough money but she did not and she did not even know where the nearest one was. She thought about what she should do. She remembered a small coffee shop that she has passed when she walked from the bus stop. She quickly got to her feet and headed towards the coffee shop. She only had less than ten Marks with her; certainly not enough for a taxi and a motel, but at least she could buy something to eat. The small coffee shop at the corner was not too far from the house. The surrounding houses were lighting up as she walked along the sidewalk looking around. She made a plan to first eat and drink something; then she would go back to see if Eddy returned. She decided if he was not back by then, she would take a bus and go back to her mother-in-law for the night even though she did not want to do that. That was the only other person she knew in this town. She knew that Ritchie lived in Dresden as well but she did not have their contacts.

In the cozy coffee shop with low lights, she sat down on a chair looking out the window that was facing the street corner in the hope that Eddy might walk by from either direction. She bought herself a bagel with cream cheese and a hot herbal tea to warm her cold body. She bit into the bagel with appetite and placed her cold hands on the steaming cup of tea to warm them up. It felt nice, at least her basic physical needs were met but on the inside she really worried about Eddy. She wished she knew where he was. What if something happened to him? Intrusive thoughts were entertaining her not helping her situation.

When she was finished, she used the bathroom one more time. She washed her face and hands looking at her reflection thinking how unfair life was. Poor Eddy, it was horrible what he has gone through. How he could think that she would leave him, she thought.

She hurried back to the house hoping Eddy was back. Her heart skipped a beat from happiness when she saw a flicker of light from the living room which was facing the front entrance. She ran to the door ringing the bell excitedly. Very quickly she regretted her decision to come back; her expression changing instantaneously when Eddy opened the door. He reeked of alcohol; welcoming her with a chagrin on his face. He abruptly clasped her hand firmly pulling her inside.

"Where were you?" He queried with suspicion in his voice. She could not believe her ears. He was questioning her where she was when he was the one drinking out somewhere for hours leaving her out in the cold. Strong minded as Michaela was, she could not keep it inside her and threw her query right back at him.

"How dare you question me when you first left me at your mother's and then you went out drinking?" Unexpectedly, his hand flew up in the air, landing across Michaela's face. She instantaneously, put her hand on her cheek not so much because of the pain but because of the shock that her bellowed husband just hit her for the first time. She did not have time to mold over what Eddy just did as his hand was up in the air again threatening her again if she did not answer his questions quickly enough with the right answers.

"I called my mother and she said you left about five hours ago. So think what you answer me when I ask you WHERE THE FUCK WHERE YOU?????" He yelled at her out of top of his lungs, making her curl up in a ball on the sofa in a fetal position protecting her baby she carried under her heart.

"Eddy, please don't." She put up a hand to protect herself from another impact that landed on her shoulder as she turned in time to avoid another slap on her face or head. She was scared but she had to tell him. She had to make him understand. Before Eddy had a chance to inflict another blow, she quickly said.

"Eddy, I was waiting for you on the backyard for hours. I got cold and hungry so I went to the coffee shop to eat and use the bathroom and came right back." His raised hand that almost inflicted more pain had dropped to his side shamefully. He dropped to his knees beside Michaela who was still wary of her husband's reaction. Just as unexpectedly he slapped her across her face for the first time; now he embraced her around her waist placing his head on her belly as she was crunched down on the sofa watching his every move. He started weeping like a small child needing reassurance.

"I'm so sorry, my love. I don't know what came over me. I'm so sorry. Please forgive me; for everything." She surprisingly felt bad for him and automatically hugged him around his neck while he continued to hold her around her waist still kneeling on the floor beside her; both of them were crying together for a while. When Eddy looked up at her with his striking dark eyes splattered with tears, she could not help but feel love and compassion for him despite the fact that he hit her. She was not this woman that would tolerate being beaten by her husband and he needed to know that at the beginning.

"Eddy, you can't ever hit me again. I will not take that. It's wrong."

"I know, I know. I'm so sorry. I swear I will never lay a hand on you again. I don't know what came over me. Maybe it's the alcohol or maybe because I thought I have lost you forever. I couldn't stand loosing you, Michaela. I love you so much. Please don't ever leave me."

"I wasn't planning on leaving you, Eddy. I love you. Why did you tell me at your mother's to go back home if you don't want to lose me?"

"I don't know what I was thinking. I was angry at my mother for telling you and I thought I don't deserve you. I thought that once you knew who I was; what I was capable of, you would not love me anymore. That's why I was so angry when my mother told you about our family secret." Remembering Eleonore's story, she felt deep empathy for him.

"Eddy, you were a teenager who protected his mom and you saved her life. I'm sorry you had such an abusive childhood." He hugged her tighter.

"So you're not going to leave me even though I killed my own father?"

"It was in defense. If you were not there that night, your mother believes that Anton would have killed her. And besides it wasn't your….."

She quickly stopped herself remembering her mother-in-law's plea not to tell Eddy that Anton was not his biological father. She had a lot of time to mold things through when she was waiting for him and believed that it would help him to know that his father was someone else but it was not her place to tell him.

"It wasn't my.....what?" Eddy queried with curiosity over her unfinished sentence.

"Eddy, it's not my place to tell you that, but I think you should ask your mom about your father." He gazed at her suspiciously with the 'what are you not telling me' look.

"You can't bite into a sentence and then not finish it. Tell me!"

"Eddy, please, your mother asked me not to say anything. Just ask her." He pulled away from her sitting beside her on the sofa running his hand through his hair in exasperation.

"NO, Michaela; I'm asking you. My mother never considered my pleas when I asked her not to talk about our horrendous family secret to anyone and it was not her place to tell you. So I think it will be even when you tell me what she told you about my father?"

She was tired and sore and besides she thought that Eddy had a good point. It was not worth another fight with him, so she gave in.

"Anton Verner was not your biological father." Eddy sat with that information for a while trying to replay his childhood with the man that abused him for years. Learning that he was not his biological father was shocking although it was a relief for him even though it did not change anything. But at least he knew now that he did not share the same DNA with that brutal man.

"Did she say who my father is?"

"She said it was a Spanish tourist who was passing through Germany at that time. His name was Eduardo...ah, something; I forgot his last name. But your mother never heard from him again. He never even knew your mother was pregnant with you at that time when he left. She married Anton instead letting him believe that you were his son and let him raise you as his own.

"He always treated me differently than Ritchie. I didn't understand why. I thought it was because I was older or because I had dark hair and dark eyes and did not look anything like him. Now it makes so much sense." He turned to his wife.

"Thank you for telling me. I'll talk to my mother about it someday. Maybe she has more information about my real father." He got up and walked to the kitchen returning with an ice-pack when he noticed Michaela repeatedly touching her sore cheek.

"Let me see." He looked at her red cheek. "Here; put that on your face. It will prevent it from swelling." He gently placed it on her face that made her wince in pain but once she got used to it; it felt good. He kissed her hand that was holding the ice-pack; whispering his regret.

"Please don't leave me, my love. I can't live without you. For you I will try to be a better man." He started kissing her face that had now tears pouring down her cheeks ending up in a passionate kissing and love making. Michaela never understood why 'make up sex' felt always so much better. She hated the fights, but the passion that followed afterwards made it all worth it. Perhaps it was the intensity of the emotions; both bad and good that they felt for each other at the same time.

The following morning when Michaela looked at her reflection in the mirror, she barely recognized herself. She saw a little bruise forming on her left cheekbone. It felt tender and swollen, despite the ice-pack last night. She gently washed her face and tried to apply some foundation and blush to cover the bruising. She still could not believe that Eddy had hit her. But he was drinking and thought she would leave him. He was furious when his mother told her about the murder in the family; obviously, Eddy did not want her to know about this horrendous incident because he believed she would not love him. How could he think that she would leave him because of his unfortunate past; because of his abusive childhood? How ridiculous of him to think that. Does he not see that he was just a kid who tried to protect his own mother; that he is the one who saved his mother's life? Doesn't that mean something to him? With these concerning thoughts, Michaela made her way to the kitchen where a wonderful aroma was coming from.

She could not believe her eyes when she saw Eddy with an apron around his waist humming a song she did not recognize. He was turning around in the kitchen preparing wonderful breakfast when he noticed her standing in the doorway; still holding a small pan with scrambled eggs that he was going to divide on the plates. The table was already set up with plates and cutlery; coffee brewing in the coffee machine. A gorgeous purple orchid was placed in the middle of the table in a flowerpot.

"Good morning." She barely recognized her croaky voice that was a result of the crying last night. Eddy smiled at her surprised to see her.

"Hi, Sweetie. I thought you were still sleeping. I'm not quite ready; the bacon is still cooking. I was going to bring it up for you to eat in bed."

"Wow. It looks and smells wonderful. Thank you, Eddy. It's very sweet of you to do that for me." She walked over to him and kissed him on his cheek.

"I just wanted you to know how sorry I am." He quickly placed some eggs on her plate and put the pan down. "Come, sit down." He pulled out a chair for her to sit. "I hope you like bacon and eggs."

"This is perfect and what a beautiful orchid."

"Beautiful flower for a beautiful girl. Coffee?"

"Yes, please." Michaela could not believe Eddy woke up early in the morning, went to the bakery for fresh buns and to a flower shop and prepared her a wonderful feast.

"I'll do the dishes today too, so today you just sit, put your feet up and relax."

"Wow, you're really spoiling me. I could get use to it, you know."

"I do anything for you, my love." He kissed her on her lips as he was sitting down to have his breakfast as well. After they ate, they took their coffee cups outside as Eddy wanted to smoke. It became a routine for them to do this together even though Michaela did not smoke but she kept him company when he did.

"Ah, look a cake." He noticed surprised.

"Oh, I forgot it outside last night. At least you see I was here before."

"I'm sorry I didn't trust you."

"You have to trust that I'll always be by your side, Eddy. I married you for better and for worse." He tugged a wavy strand of her hazelnut hair that fell into her face behind her ear and hugged her tightly.

"I'm so lucky to have you."

The last few days that they had left at Uncle Albert's house were great. Eddy was much more helpful and caring towards her. He even helped her with groceries when Michaela went to buy some more food for them. The bruise was slowly fading away although the memory of that night when Eddy hit her was lingering in her head. She has long since then forgiven him; she has forgiven him the moment he dropped to his knees pressing his cheek on her pregnant belly asking her not to leave him. Since that day their relationship has not only improved, but their love seemed stronger. Michaela thought if they went through something like that; they could make it through anything. As her love for her husband grew, so did her belly.

When it was time for them to leave, Michaela cleaned the whole house, from top to bottom so the owners would not regret having someone over for such a long time. They left the remaining food in the fridge with a note of thank you on the kitchen table. It was easy to pack up their clothes as they practically lived out of their suitcases, so the few items were quickly gathered. Michaela washed and changed the bed sheets in the bedroom and carefully made the bed. Eddy locked up and threw the key through the mail slot as he told his uncle he would do. Michaela wistfully looked back towards the cozy little house. She was curious about the apartment in Halle and was looking forward to settling in their new place where she would finally unpack her things after two weeks of honeymoon.

"It's nothing fancy, but that's all I can afford right now." Eddy warned her with worry in his eyes on the way to Halle as they were riding on a bus.

"That's not what's important. I'm sure I'll love it because you're going to live with me there." She smiled at him.

She did not expect luxury but what she saw was barely meeting the basic needs in a civilized country, such as Germany.

Chapter 18

I T WAS AN OLD BUILDING in the old part of Halle which was mainly a student town. Eddy told her that if they wanted to save up for some nicer home, they would have to live here for a while as it was a lot cheaper. They climbed up to the fourth floor carrying the heavy suitcases with them all the way to the top floor as there was no elevator. Each floor, Michaela noticed had an old fashioned sink on the hallway which she found strange, but did not comment on it. When they finally reached the top apartment, Eddy unlocked the door to reveal his modest one bedroom apartment. The door opened straight to the large living room revealing a disarray of boxes, scattered clothes and dirty dishes all over the living room area. The place needed to be aired out as nobody was inside for a long time and it smelled of old and stale furniture that was in the living room.

"I'm sorry, for the mess, but I was here only couple of times myself when I got this place. I see Otto brought some of our things." He pointed to the boxes and gift bags that looked familiar to her. Michaela stood frozen in the doorway with a suitcase still in her hand. She did not know whether she wanted to cry or run away. The place was cold and impersonal with barely any furniture in it, other than an old sofa and a small table in front of it and a wooden closet in the corner of the room. She had difficulties concealing her disappointment but did not say anything. Eddy urged her to come in and close the door behind her. He showed her the rest of the apartment. Their supposed bedroom was empty of furniture consisting of only a double blow-up mattress and blanket thrown on top as an indication that Eddy had spent at least one night here before. She recognized his blow-up mattress he used in Bulgaria in the tent where they made love. There was no window in the bedroom.

Next to the bedroom a door led them to what Eddy called a kitchen containing an old fashioned coal oven, few cupboards and a small sink with boiler above it. A small window from the kitchen was facing the yard of the inner part of the building that Michaela peeked through. The kitchen was long, but narrow. Dirty plates of different designs and other dishes were placed all over the counter creating more disarray and clutter. Few flies were having a feast on the leftover dried up food and sticky jelly-like leftover juice in a glass.

"The previous owner left some dishes behind that we can use. At least we don't have to buy new ones, but they need to be washed." Eddy explained apologetically when Michaela was looking at the mess with horrified expression.

The other door from the kitchen led back to the living room; there were no other rooms or doors.

"Where is the bathroom?"

"Oh, you have to go? Ok, come." Eddy took her by her hand dragging her back through the front door, relocking the door and going down the stairs.

"Eddy, where are we going?"

"You said you needed to use the toilet, so...."

Michaela stopped on the stairway interrupting him.

"You mean there is no bathroom in the apartment?" Eddy stood between the floors on the steps looking up at her standing still on the top of the floor, shock in her eyes.

"There are flushable toilets downstairs. Come I show you." Michaela walked behind Eddy as if in trance, still refusing to believe that the apartment did not contain a bathroom. They walked all the way to the bottom to the back seeing the small yard that contained garbage bins and a small concrete pavement with an attempt of keeping flowers around in one corner that were dying out as nobody seemed to take care of them. On the right before they walked all the way to the yard were three toilet stalls and a small dirty sink at the end. Michaela needed a moment to gather her thoughts from the cultural shock she has just experienced, so she entered one of the toilet stalls while Eddy waited for her on the yard, looking around.

She did not come from a wealthy family by far and her mother had to fight tooth and nail for their two bedroom apartment in Czechoslovakia after their father left them, but they had everything in there what they needed for comfortable living. They had running warm water, radiators and most importantly they had toilet, bathroom with a bathtub and a wash machine. This place had nothing. Where would they bathe? Where will they do their laundry? Was this a coal furnace that she saw in that small kitchen if she even could call it that? And the bedroom had nothing, not even a window. How was she going to live there with Eddy? Can she actually live under such conditions? How was she going to raise a baby in such an environment? She did not want to stay here a moment longer. What should she tell him?

Michaela knew that there were people who lived in worse conditions than this. Somewhere in Africa, she thought, people did not even have a drinking water or only small huts over their heads, but this was not Africa. This was not a third world country. This was a prosperous and economically one of the best European countries. She had not even thought that there might be parts of some old German towns with such old buildings living under such harsh conditions like people lived in before the Second World War. She had no idea that this is what she had signed up for when she said her famous 'yes' to the man that she loved with all her heart. She felt betrayed; she felt cheated and lied to and she felt a great disappointment. She hoped for a better life in Germany with the man she fell in love with; but this was not 'better'; this was far worse than it was in her own hometown; in her small room back home in her mother's apartment.

But at least she had the love of her life with her and that was what should matter the most, she told herself. She was angry at herself because she was never a materialistic person and should accommodate to the new situation; to the new environment; to her new home and try to make the best of it working towards something better in the future. As long as she had Eddy by her side, she was willing to do what she needed to do. 'For better and for worse' they have promised themselves at the wedding ceremony. So perhaps, this was worse, but she was sure this was not the place where they would live for the rest of their lives. It will have to do for starters. With these thoughts she made her way out of the toilet stall walking towards a small sink nearby with only one faucet of cold water. She rinsed her hands. There was no soap or paper towel anywhere so she dried her wet hands on her jeans finding Eddy smoking and impatiently waiting for her on the small yard where the surrounding apartment windows were facing. He looked at her with a frown and concern in his face.

"You hate it here. Don't you?" *Yes, Eddy, I HATE it, but I love you.*

"No, Eddy, I don't hate it." She lied. "Yes, it's different than back home, but….." The words froze on her lips as she did not know what to add as she had no words left for this place.

"Michaela, I promise you that we will not stay here forever. This is just our starters place until we get on our feet. I will find a job soon. We'll save some money and we'll find something better. I promise." He hugged her, digging his hand in her long hair that was hanging on her back. She once again saw his fear in his eyes; his fear of her leaving him. She could not do that to him. He probably did the best he could afford and she told him so.

"I know Eddy you did the best you could. I just don't know where we will shower? And I'm worried about how we are going to raise a baby here?"

"It's not that bad, Michaela. The woman that lived in our apartment before us had a water and sink installed on the inside along with a boiler to heat up the water. She had a small child too and she managed just fine."

"Really?" Michaela said surprised trying to imagine how she was going to manage going up and down to the toilets with an infant at her side.

"Yeah, Michaela, we have actually one of the better apartments in the building as the other apartments don't even have running water inside. The superintendant told me that when I was renting it out. Most of the other people in the building get their water from the hallway sinks and it is only cold water." Eddy pointed out to the sinks as they walked back upstairs to their apartment.

He agreed that the place needed a good cleaning and organizing and they needed some basic supplies. Otto dropped off the boxes that her mother had carefully packed up for Michaela as a dowry for her only daughter along with bags and boxes with the wedding presents that he carried in his car dropping the key in the mailbox downstairs. Now Eddy presented the spare key to Michaela to her new home.

They went out shopping for food but did not buy a lot; only for one day as Michaela realized that the place did not have a fridge. How they will manage without a fridge, she thought. They bought some cleaning products and sponges and towels. They looked at some beds and mattresses but that was too expensive for them to buy at this point. So the camping double blow up mattress would have to do for now. They bought a small and large bassinettes so they could wash dishes in one and themselves in the bigger one. Michaela could not imagine how they would do that. She pictured the French historical movie 'Angelica' from sixtieth century how they were bathing back then. It was sad; Michaela thought that in the 20th century she still had to use the old methods being grateful that they had at least running water in the apartment which was apparently a luxury in the building.

When they were coming back from the store, walking up the stairs, on the second floor they met a neighbour who was getting water from the hallway into her bucket.

"Hi. Have you just moved in?" The woman in her mid-thirties with perm in her dark blond hair asked them as they were passing by her door.

"Yes. Eduard Verner." He freed up his right hand from the big bags and extended it to her. "And this is my wife, Michaela."

"Hi, nice to meet you." Michaela smiled at her.

"I'm Verena Meswig. This apartment building is something else, isn't it?" She gave them a conspiratory look. "Sharing the toilets downstairs and all, you don't see that often, but at least it's clean and cheap place and the area is not too bad either. You're lucky, you have the better apartment; as only two apartments in this shitty building have running water installed inside. Not me though, I can't afford to do that but it would be damn nice. Anyway, you might want to know who is who in this building. Well, let me tell you." The couple never asked but Verena seemed eager to share that information so they stood there out of politeness listening to this chatty woman. "The first floor is occupied by some young punk university students on both sides that make a racket sometimes when partying, but it's not too often. I don't really know them that well as they are usually in and out of the building. Right across from me", she pointed with her long bony finger, "lives Rayner, but I call him Ray. He is a truck driver so you will not see much of him as he comes here only about once a month to sleep for few days before he goes back on the road again. Really nice guy though. The third floor is full of old folks. Honestly I don't know why they still live there if it so damn hard for them to walk up and down the stairs. There is this old couple in their fifties in the apartment on the left and they are alright, real quiet folks and as you might already know the guy is a superintendant of the building so you have to give him the rent money. On the right, across from them lives this old grumpy guy that spills his feces all over the hallway stairs; real disgusting guy and nobody can talk any sense to him. Turns my stomach if you ask me." She made a repugnant face and continued to gossip, as Michaela exchanged glances with Eddy at her last comment, not sure what she had meant by that, but they did not ask her to elaborate. As it was, Michaela had already difficulties keeping up with the cadence of her monologue that was ringing in her ears, but without the regard of the listeners, Verena went on. "You must be way on top floor across from that weird guy on the right that doesn't talk to anyone. Trust me I tried to engage him, if you know what I mean, but it was pointless. He is really wacked in the head", she twirled her index finger beside her temple to indicate that their next door neighbor is crazy. "He 'planted' a branch in a garbage bin on the yard. Can you believe this? I mean, who does that? If he likes to plant things, fine, he might as well take care of the half dead flowers that nobody gives a damn on the yard, but NO, he plants in the garbage a dried up branch. I'll pee my pants if that ever blooms. And don't you dare touch it; he might slice your throat if you do. Anyway be real careful around him." She must have been breathing through her ears Eddy thought as this was the first time he noticed her take a breath before she went on again. "You get used to this crazy place soon. It's not so bad though, except when your butt starts to freeze to the toilet seat in the winter as there is no heat there." She giggled stupidly at her own joke or perhaps it was a reality check; not a joke at all and then continued to chitchat as Michaela wanted to run from this God forgotten old place. "Anyway, I don't want to keep you. I'm home most of the time if you need anything, eggs or cup of sugar. I mean a*nything.*" She emphasized the last word while looking at Eddy and chuckled again with her annoying piercing sound that visibly annoyed Eduard who barely listened to her and was ready to leave.

"Thanks." Eddy forced a fake smile and kept walking up the stairs, carrying heavy bags that were cutting into his fingers, eager to be away from this exasperating woman. Michaela followed, hauling her own load of new things they have just bought. Verena stretched her thin neck looking after them before they disappeared out of her view and then returned to her tedious task that nearly overflowed from her bucket when she did not pay attention.

"What an irritating and ugly woman." Eddy commented behind their closed doors once they reached their apartment.

"Eddy! That's not nice to say. I thought she was very friendly and quite informative."

"Whatever. I like you better." He placed his hand under her long hair that were hanging down her shoulders and hugged her around the back of her neck kissing her. As always, she returned his kisses.

"I would hope so." She said jokingly in-between the kisses.

"Come. I want to make love to you." He announced seriously and pulled her behind him to the bare bedroom leaving all the bags at the doors adding to the disarray of the apartment. He lay her down gently to the blowup mattress, undressing her skillfully. Michaela started to protest.

"Eddy, we should unpack and clean up first. There is so much to do."

"That can wait." He said ignoring the fact that she was feeling quite uncomfortable in this messy apartment that needed so much work, but soon succumbed to his desire. After their passionate moments Michaela needed to wash up while Eddy went out to the small yard for a cigarette. She set up the small boiler waiting for the water to heat up while she unpacked some of the things they have bought. She carried the large washbasin they have bought pouring some cold water in it; hoping there would be soon some hot water for washing. She found a bucket under the sink that helped her fill up the basin faster. While she waited for the water to heat up, she piled up all the plates and cups that needed to be washed discovering on the counter a two top mini stove with oven which she did not notice before because of the mess. This would come handy for cooking as the coal oven looked complex to get started and she would have to ask Eddy how to use it. It might come handy to heat up this place in the winter, she thought as she did not see any other heating in the apartment.

When the water was hot, she added it to the basin, mixing it with the cold one. She put her hair up in a bun so it would not get wet. She would have to figure another way to wash her long hair at a different time. She underdressed herself and submerged into the warm water, washing her body. There was not much space in the basin and she would not be able to rinse but she felt cleaner. Eddy walked in and offered to wash her back.

"I'll buy a small hose that we can attach to the faucet so you can rinse off." It was strange washing not only in washbasin but in the middle of the kitchen.

"We might have to use the same water for both of us as the boiler is really small and does not heat up a lot of water at one time. As Michaela dried herself up and was getting dressed in clean clothes, she said.

"The water is still warm. Hop in and I'll wash your back for you." She offered but Eddy instead put his leather jacket back on and shuffled through his backpack until he found what he needed.

"What are you doing?" She was observing him with curiosity.

"I'm going to the gym and I'll shower there." He mumbled grumpily.

"Oh. I didn't know you had a membership at the gym."

"I don't. I'm going to sign up today."

"That's a great idea. Can I come too? That might solve our showering problems for now."

"Come on, Michaela, don't be ridiculous, you are getting so fat with that belly of yours and you want to exercise? I noticed that you put on a good junk of fat lately. You should cut down on the sweets."

"I'm not fat, Eddy. I'm pregnant with your baby. Remember?" She said with a hurt in her voice, offended at his harsh remark.

"Don't get smart with me. I can't believe how stupid you can get thinking that's a good idea to pay for an extra gym membership for you when you won't be able to use it. You could hurt yourself or the baby and besides once the baby comes, you won't have the time. Don't you have enough work to do here now?!" He said it with admonishment in his voice and knew she would not be able to persuade him otherwise so she did not even try. It was pointless to argue with him that mild excise was good for her and for the baby and that she would at least stay in shape, but she already knew the answer. He was quite clear about it. Besides, maybe Eddy was right; she was feeling tired anyway and had a lot of work inside the apartment that she wanted to have done before the end of today. Obviously, Eddy was not keen on helping her out; he believed that house chores were women's work, so she accepted the position out of necessity. When she was quiet, he added.

"Make me some dinner when I get back. See you later."

"Bye." She called after him as the outside door slammed behind him. He did not kiss or hug her this time. He seemed quite agitated and she did not know what she did to deserve such treatment. To distract herself she set to work starting with the huge pile of dishes that needed a good soaking and washing. She boiled some water on the electric mini stove, using the medium basin for dishes they bought earlier for this purpose and set to work.

Verena must have had a lot of free time on her hands it seemed as she was often around on the hallway getting water or coming in or out of her apartment every time Eddy passed by her door whether he was just going for a smoke or to use the bathroom or whether he was returning back home from somewhere. Perhaps she was watching the peephole in her door like people watch a soap opera of what neighbour was doing what at a given time to add to her repertoire of gossip. Or perhaps she was just watching out for the one neighbour in particular that she grew fond of although Eddy would give his hand in the fire that she slept with most of the other guys in the building minus the senior citizens on the third floor.

Sometimes she would bump into him on the stairs or downstairs at the toilets, squeezing through the narrow path, brushing against him. A man would have to be a fool not to notice that she was interested. Eddy was not particularly attracted to her. He did think she was ugly. *Damn German blonds*, he thought. He never liked them but used to have a casual sex with them. But now it was different; now he was married although he often argued with himself that it was unrealistic for a man to ask to be monogamous with one woman for rest of his life, especially when the wife started to look like a fat cow. Eddy was turned off by Michaela's pregnancy as she entered the second trimester. She would eagerly ask him to touch her belly to feel the baby's kicking or wanting to make love to him but he was always reluctant to do it. He often escaped to the gym or to the corner pub. He said he found a new job at a construction site and she saw him less frequently.

Michaela felt lonely and had nobody to talk to. She kept writing to her mom, her aunt and to her friend, Nikole about what a wonderful life she had in Germany and how happy she was. She was too ashamed to tell them the truth about her husband and the living conditions she had to endure. It would be admitting to Aunt Sylvie that she was right from the beginning and she did not want to hear 'I told you so' from her. She avoided telling them about Eddy's troubled history or the fact that he has slapped her on few occasions when he was drunk and even when he was sober. It was not as bad as the slap in Dresden that caused her cheek to bruise up, but it was something she did not bargain for; something that should not be happening in a loving relationship. She did not even want to think about the collection of names that he sometimes called her that sent her off crying into the corner of the room feeling worthless. The 'fat cow' or 'chunky pig' were mild comments despite the accompanying sounds Eddy was making when he said it; it was tolerable compared to the vicious attacks on her character and personality that he was frequently showering her with. Sometimes he was so annoyed with her crying he would slap her to give her more reason to cry while at other times he showed remorse and apologized profusely promising her it would not happen again, crying with her in the process. He would bring her flowers and small gifts to make up with her the following day; making love to her with care and passion that held the promise of a better relationship. He could be so loving and compassionate when he wanted to be and she loved that part of him and did not want to let it go in a hope that it would stay that way. But it never stayed that way as the tension between them started to build up.

She hoped this was just a difficult time in their marriage due to the harsh conditions in the apartment and due to the pregnancy that caused them to have intimacy less frequently, but she thought once the baby was born, things would improve.

Eddy seemed to be excited about the baby when he agreed to buy the crib and other essentials for their unborn child. He often spoke about wanting a boy, picking up boy names. Michaela decided after seeing a gynecologist in Halle that she did not want to know whether it was a boy or a girl and refused to go for ultrasound. Eddy had his moments when he was quite considerate, generous and nice to her but it usually did not last longer than the bloom of the orchid that he often bought her when he tried to apologize; eventually the flower died along with his promises. These moments were quickly gone before she started to feel the tension in their relationship again that followed with him yelling at her for small things. If only she would not have burned the dinner and only if she had cleaned away her shoes away from the door so he would not had tripped on them swearing at her when he came in. If only she would do what he told her to without defiance, everything would have been just fine. But that was not Michaela's personality as she often spoke her mind and expressed her emotions which usually turned against her and quickly shut her down. So Michaela tried and tried harder to perfect their lives and their home to avoid unnecessary battles; changing who she was; changing who she wanted to be. Michaela started to lose her confidence and self-esteem; changing into someone she no longer recognized just so her marriage would survive, for the sake of their unborn child.

One night when Eddy was climbing up the stairs of his building, a little tipsy as he stopped in the local pub to eat some sausages flushing it down with few beers right after his workout at the gym which clearly defeated the purpose of exercise, but he was not worried about it just like he was not worried about Michaela's complains when he came home late and drunk. He had another flashback at the gym when he used the treadmill running.

A little boy was running from his step-father who easily caught up with him hitting him with a belt anywhere he reached him.

"Please, daddy, stop. I will be good." Little boy was screaming and pleading for him to stop, but he never did.

"I'll teach you respect, you little bastard." Little boy was helplessly crying crunched down in the corner feeling every hit of the belt on his back, on his shoulders, on his head.

"Tough guys don't cry. You want to cry, I'll give you reason to cry." Anton yelled at him as he was beating him ruthlessly.

Eddy needed few drinks and the cold beer felt good, helping him forget for a moment about his past. When he finally made it to their apartment building, Verena opened the door as Eddy was walking through the second floor.

"Hello handsome." She said seductively.

Chapter 19

HE TURNED TO SEE VERENA standing just outside her doorway in her skimpy miniskirt, with her dirty bare feet and no bra that Eddy immediately noticed. The white t-shirt with a silver sign "Great Catch" on it was barely covering her nibbles that were hard in the chilly November night, but she did not seem to mind the cold. He did not like her face with her big crooked nose and thin line instead of her lips that gave her a harsh appearance with painted on eyebrows with permanent colour that were much too dark in comparison to her blondish hair which did not suite her. Her small eyes were set way too close together making her look more like a monkey. But he did not fail to check her slim body from neck down. Despite her large manly feet with bright red toenails he liked the rest of her figure; her breasts and the curves of her hips that swayed from side to side when she walked over to him.

"Hey there, neighbour." Eddy said still staring at her breasts rather than her face which did not escape her attention. She knew how to seduce a man and Eddy was no exception. She ran her fingers from her bottom non-existent lip through her neck to the middle of her breasts that Eddy's eyes got stuck on as he did not enjoy looking at her face.

"Can I ask you for a favour, Eduard?" Before he could say anything she hurried to say what she had in mind. "I was in the mood to open the red wine but it has a cork that always gives me trouble. Would you help me open it?" *What a lame excuse*, he thought, but followed her inside.

"Sure, no problem." *That was easy*, Verena thought to herself as she got him where she wanted to. She closed quickly the door behind them as Eddy entered her living room where candles were lit up and a soft slow music was playing. Two wine glasses were set up as if Verena was expecting a company. When Eddy commented on that while opening the wine, Verena said.

"The man I was expecting couldn't make it tonight. His wife was giving him hard time." Whether Verena was giving him indication that she was in fact expecting a married man who did not show up or wanted him to know that she did not mind sleeping with a married man, he did not know and he did not really care.

"Why don't you have a glass of wine with me, since it's already open? I don't want to drink it alone." He looked at her suspiciously, but poured two classes all the way to the top, passing one of them to her.

"What do you want to drink to?" He asked carelessly.

"How about two neighbourly helping hands?" She took a sip of her wine looking at him provocatively then she sat it down taking his hand and placing it nonchalantly on her left breast. Eddy without pulling away his hand drank most of his glass, then set the glass down beside hers and unzipped his pants. She pulled him towards her wrapping her bare legs around him. *Gosh, she doesn't even wear any underwear.*

"This is the kind of helping hand you had in mind?" He asked while thrusting into her. She giggled with her annoying chuckle. He wished her skirt was long enough to cover her face so he wouldn't have to look at it.

"Yes, that's exactly what I had in mind." *Why was it always the blonds that threw themselves at him? And why the hell were they so annoying although good enough for a quick uncommitted sex? At least, this one did it for free.* Eduard's mind wondered to his childhood when he was only thirteen years old and caught his father cheating with a blond woman who laughed annoyingly.

'*Get the fuck out of here, you little bastard*'. His father yelled at him, throwing a pillow at him before he had a chance to close the door of his father's office on the bottom floor of their house. His father never even bothered to stop despite the interruption and the blond bitch just laughed and found it entertaining saying, '*Let him watch, maybe he will learn something.*'

He always wondered whether his mother knew that her husband was cheating on her right under her nose. If she knew, she did a good job of pretending that it was not happening. Eduard shook those memories away as he zipped up his pants back up making his way to the door when he was done. And he knew if he came back another time, she would gladly open her legs again.

"Don't be a stranger neighbour." She called after him before he opened the door and without turning back he left. *Whore.* He went down to use the toilet and wash his hands before he went back home. He was a little drunk but not to the point that he blacked out like he sometimes did in the past. He checked his watch. It was late and Michaela seemed to be asleep on the blow-up mattress. He made his way to the kitchen wanting to have something to drink; trying not to wake his wife but he had hard time locating the light switch knocking all the plates off the counter top that were drying up. The racket woke Michaela up instantaneously and she rushed into the kitchen finding Eddy standing there helplessly with most of the broken dishes all over the floor, a puppy face eyes looking at her innocently. She never knew how he would react; whether he would yell at her for not putting it away blaming her for his mistakes or feeling guilty for whatever he did trying to apologize and fix it. It was the later reaction that night that she much rather preferred. He even attempted to joke.

"At least you don't have to wash them."

"They were already clean. Step aside carefully so you don't cut yourself." She grabbed the small broom and sweeping pan bending down with her growing belly beside his feet sweeping the broken dishes away. She wanted to ask him where he was that late, but she knew that it would be futile as he was drunk. She preferred the sweet puppy dog face that looked guilty than the angry aggressive Eddy that she has experienced at times during his wrath. She did not think he would hit her again as he has promised her but the promises never lasted very long and she knew better not to provoke him.

It was not enough for Verena that she seduced Eddy who did not show any resistance in the first place, but she put on her friendly neighbourly expression and did her best to befriend his unsuspecting wife who was clueless about Eddy's sexual endeavors.

"Why don't you come over for a coffee and some banana bread?" Verena offered one afternoon when she saw Michaela coming up the stairs. When she saw her hesitate, she added.

"I don't have many friends around here since I moved from the other side of the town. It would be nice to talk to someone. But if you're in a hurry, I...."

"No, actually, I don't have any friends around here either. I don't really know anyone." Michaela smiled at Verena hoping to have formed a new friendship; she joined her for the coffee and cake as Verena promised. At least she had someone to talk to and made it a routine of connecting with her new friend every day. At times, Michaela invited her to her modest home, which was better looking than Verena's. They seemed to have common interests and Michaela was often telling her about how she met Eddy in Bulgaria and instantly fell in love with him. She told her everything that she would have shared with any other friend, except, she reserved Eddy's violent temper for her own knowledge only. Nobody else needed to know their problems. She always thought that marital problems are between the couple and not other people's business. She was well aware though that the older couple, Mr. and Mrs. Ziegler that lived below them must have heard some of their fights through the paper thin walls. Whenever she saw Michaela on the hallway whether it was by the mailboxes that Michaela anxiously checked for letters twice a day or just passing her on the stairs, Mrs. Ziegler with friendly round face always asked her.

"How are you doing, my dear? Is everything alright? How are you feeling?" And Michaela always reassured her with a smile that she was doing just fine. One time she engaged in a longer conversation with Mrs. Ziegler, telling her that she wished she could work as she was still waiting for her working permit and money was tight despite Eddy's new job. Besides, even if she had a working permit, nobody would likely hire her without any experience and five months into her pregnancy. Mrs. Ziegler offered to pay her money for few chores such as cleaning of their apartment or shopping for food. Every day, early in the morning when Michaela went to buy fresh buns for her and Eddy, she brought the Ziegler family fresh rolls and pastry as well, which was a great help to the elderly couple and Michaela earned small amount of money that she saved up to purchase new things for the home or for the baby.

Michaela had a unique ability to build great relationships with almost everyone in the building. Even grumpy old Mr. Ehrlichmann that Verena could not stand became quite fond of young Mrs. Verner. Michaela met him for the first time when he was carrying a full bucket of smelly liquid of urine and feces. She quickly learned that because of his bad knees and old age, he did not have the energy to go up and down the stairs every time he needed to use the bathroom and instead used his bucket as a toilet that he tried to empty three or four times a week. Although he covered the bucket when he tried to carry it on the stairs, he could barely support himself, spilling some of it accidently on the hallway. What Verena was telling them about the smell on the hallway had made sense. Michaela, despite her pregnancy, still had enough strength and energy and did not hesitate to offer Mr. Ehrlichmann to carry it for him; which whole building was grateful to her as nobody else wanted to help with the nauseating task. She would wash it out for him, bringing him clean bucket and would check on him everyday offering to help him empty the bucket before it was full. It was not surprising that grumpy old Mr. Ehrlichmann became quite fond of her inviting her over for some tea and cookies and to keep him company during his lonely days. Michaela felt lonely herself and liked spending time with the intelligent and experienced veteran who survived so much in his life.

In a way, Mr. Ehrlichmann reminded her of her own grandfather who too served in the war. Mr. Ehrlichmann often talked about his life during the World War II and how he survived while his friends were dying around him.

"I jumped from crack to crack where a bomb had already exploded because the likelihood of it exploding again in the same spot was very slim. This is how I survived the war." One day Mr. Ehrlichmann told Michaela one of his stories that she took to heart admiring the old grandfather whose own family has abandoned.

"Never treat anyone badly, Michaela." Mr. Ehrlichmann was providing her with a life lesson from his own experiences. "There was this young Jewish boy that was captured by our troops and would have been beaten to death right in front of my eyes. I saw a lot of death in my days but something about this young boy did not allow me to let him die. He was an enemy and that's how you supposed to look at it when you're in the war, but he was so young; he could have been no more than seventeen years old and was there by mistake. Well, six years later when I was in my late thirties and the war was almost over, the Russians captured me as well as four of my comrades. They put us against the wall and started shooting us one by one, like rabbits. It was like life had no meaning whatsoever. I saw them die right in front of me and I knew I was next in line. I have long forgotten about this Russian young boy that was beaten so badly years back when I pulled him off a death's row, but he remembered me and yelled out an order 'Not this man' and he took me aside saving my life that day. He became a general by that time when I saw him again. So you see Michaela even the lowest of the low people that appears to be the most insignificant person in the world to you at any given time or the one that seems to be your enemy can one day help you or even save your life. Life swings like a pendulum and once you're down but then you come back up."

Mr. Ehrlichmann had interesting life stories with good lessons that he learned from his own hard life and Michaela enjoyed listening and learning from him. In turn, Mr. Ehrlichmann was glad someone had visited him as everyone else seemed to hate him in the building.

Michaela had tears in her eyes when Mr. Ehrlichmann told her the story of famine when he was captured. He had to walk many kilometers barefoot, starving. He saw an apple core on the dirty ground that if he were to pick it up would have been shut on the spot for not keeping up with the pace of the prisoners. So he carried that mud-splattered apple core in between his dirty toes and bent to pick it up when nobody was looking risking his life for a filthy scrap of garbage he could put in his mouth because he was famished and dying from hunger and thirst. Stories, such as these put things into perspective for Michaela and despite the modest life that she lived with Eddy, she was grateful for what she had appreciating the good times she experienced with her husband.

She visited Mr. Ehrlichmann everyday to help him with the bucket at the end of the day and for that he would give her small change that she was reluctant to take from him as she knew he did not have much, but he insisted. The Ziegler family was also helpful as they provided Michaela with a part time work and an opportunity to earn some extra cash despite being pregnant and not having her working permit making her unemployable at this point.

Since Michaela was constrained to the building and did not know anyone else in town, she quickly became quite popular with the residents in her apartment building. Even the young students that she occasionally saw gave her a friendly smile and quick 'hello' which made Eduard jealous when he saw one of the young students at the main entrance greeting her. He frowned at Michaela questioning her when the young man was out of sight.

"How the fuck do you know him?"

"I don't really 'know him', Eddy. He just says hello when I see him; that's all."

"Are you sleeping with him?"

"NO. Of course not! Why would you think something like that?!"

"Well, I don't want you to talk to these young guys. Understand?!" He simply ordered expecting Michaela's compliance. She nodded not understanding why Eddy would over-react for no reason at all.

The only person that scared her at least at the beginning was the neighbour right across from them who never answered her when she greeted him and seemed a little odd with his nervous twitching and bad nail biting habit. He would just look at her timidly through his ashtray-thick glasses, then turn away and hurry back to his apartment. Michaela greeted him anyway and tried to give him a polite smile when she saw him. Soon she found out why he never answered her when she saw him using sign language with another man on the street.

Michaela was lucky that she had a good pregnancy during her second trimester with enough energy and strength to do the chores and additional work for the neighbours that brought a small income to purchase some essential things and help her safe some money.

Just before Christmas holidays, Eddy decided to visit his mother in Dresden and bring her some Christmas gifts. Michaela begged him to take her with her, but he refused.

"It's not good for you to travel in this state. You're six and half months pregnant. Even the doctor told you that." It was true that when she asked her new gynecologist, Dr. Hynes, about travelling to Czechoslovakia during the third trimester as she wanted to spend Christmas with her mother and aunt; he told her it is better if she stayed in town. She thought a smaller travelling distance to Dresden would be alright, but Eduard was adamant about her staying put.

"But you'll be back for Christmas, right?"

"I promise, I'll only stay at my mother's two or three days and be back before the Christmas Eve."

"I hope she likes the scarf I bought her."

"I'm sure she'll love it. I'll call you when I get there." Finally Eddy bought a phone and paid for the service. Michaela felt safer with a phone in the apartment especially when Eddy was out late most of the nights and now she would be left completely alone in a foreign country for few days.

"Tell your mom, I'm sorry I couldn't come."

The three days and nights that Eduard was away seemed long and very lonely. She was very cold in the apartment as the December snow was covering the ground and their windows. Verena was right when she said that going down to use the toilets felt like your butt was freezing to the seat. The little metal coal oven would heat up mainly the kitchen and if she left the door open, some heat escaped to their bedroom. They still did not have a bed but they bought a mattress so they would not have to sleep on the floor, but during cold winter days like tonight, Michaela would sleep in the sleeping bag despite getting a small portable electric radiator which took some time to warm up the place.

Michaela had the Christmas dinner ready when Eddy finally arrived on Christmas Eve. She made his favourite potato salad with schnitzels and a sauerkraut soup which was their traditional holiday meal and Eddy seemed to be quite fond of it. Their Christmas holidays were surprisingly peaceful and uneventful as Eddy was relaxing at home and did not go to work for rest of the year. Instead of presents their first Christmas together they agreed to buy themselves a mattress for the bedroom where they could sleep more comfortably along with blankets and pillows. That was the best present they could have bought for themselves and Michaela was really happy about it as it was getting difficult for her to stand up from the floor blow-up mattress every day as she was getting uncomfortable with her growing belly. She was glad she got to spend the Christmas with her husband whom she adored although she missed her family. On the other hand she thought that things started to normalize between them as they have not argued once during the holidays.

Shortly after the New Year, which they spent at home in front of a small black and white TV that someone threw out, but it was still in a good working condition, Eddy got upset over their expenses.

"Michaela." He yelled as he ran from the mailbox with the phone and electric bills in his hand. "What the hell is this?" He threw the bills on the small coffee table in the living room. When Michaela looked at him with her big blue-green eyes questioningly, not understanding why he was upset; he pointed angrily with his fingers.

"This....the electric and the phone bills. You can't use the radiator twenty-four seven. Do you know how expensive electric heating is?"

"It is really cold here otherwise and the small coal oven in the kitchen does not heat up the whole apartment."

"And then you called Czechoslovakia three times when I was away in December?!"

"Well, yes.....I called my family to say Marry Christmas and wish them all the best in the New Year."

"Three times? And each conversation lasted almost half an hour?"

"Yes, I called my mom, Aunt Sylvie and Nikole. Come on Eddy I haven't seen them since October."

"Nikole? She is not even your family. Did you enjoy talking to her smartass brother?" He said sardonically with a hint of threat in his voice.

"I only spoke to Nikole when I called her house. Stop giving me the third degree." Michaela retorted with annoyance.

"Don't pick that tone with me! I'm the one who supports you so you call when I let you call. Do you understand?" He grabbed her chin and squeezed it hard leaving a red thumb print for few seconds on her chin. She pulled away from his hand freeing from his rough handle.

"Stop it Eddy."

"Stop it?! I told you not to call long distance. Didn't I tell you that?! We can't fucking afford you calling all over the place and we can't afford to pay so much for heating either. You ran a hundred Marks bill just on the phone and another two hundred on the electricity? I lost my job in November and you tell me to STOP IT?!!! I'm gonna solve the problem right now." He yelled and grabbed the phone smashing it against the wall, leaving a small dent in the wall missing Michaela's face by couple of inches. Then he slammed the door and left her there crying and shaking helplessly for rest of the night.

When Eddy did not come home whole night, Michaela started to worry about him, considering the angry state that he has left in. She did not have a phone and even if she did, there was nowhere to call. She did not dare call her family again and she did not want them to know about her marital problems, if that could be called what Eddy sometimes did. She distracted herself with her daily routine. She turned on the boiler to heat up the water so she could wash up in the washbasin. It was becoming more difficult for her as she was twenty-eight weeks pregnant and her belly grew considerably. After she washed herself, she dressed and went to the bakery to buy some bread and buns. She stopped at the Ziegler's apartment and at Mr. Ehrlichmann's to check if they needed anything as she did every morning. She was content when she could help others; it brightened her otherwise lonely life. She only wished that someone would help her, but there was nobody. She was completely dependent on Eddy. The little money that she has earned from her neighbours for chores she tried to safe for emergencies or other necessities. She quickly learned that Eddy would take it and spent it on his drinking. She learned not to tell him everything. She hid the money behind Nikolas' picture frame of the Black Sea where she was so happy.

She often thought of Nikolas and wondered whether she had made the wrong decision marrying Eddy and thought how different her life would have been if she had stayed in her country. At least she would have her family and friends close by. Here, she did not have anyone; other than the few neighbours that she befriended. She felt lonely and depressed when Eddy still did not show up by lunch time the following day. She ate alone again; wondering where he went. Perhaps he was looking for a job somewhere or drinking. She hoped nothing happened to him. She needed someone to talk to; not necessarily about her problems, but just to have some company. She knew Verena was always home as she did not work and although she was quite older from Michaela, she might have understand her better as a woman who also might feel lonely. She went down two floors and knocked on her door.

"Hi, Verena. Can I come in?" Verena, who was often openly inviting her every time she saw her, now hesitated, nervously looked over her shoulder, but then smirked and said.

"Sure, come on in." She pulled her in by her arm. Michaela was glad to have a friend that was available anytime she needed a friend. Although she did not have an intention to talk about her problems, she could not help but ask her casually.

"You haven't seen Eddy today, have you?"

"No, why do you ask."

"Ah, it's nothing." She sat down on the sofa when her eye caught a blue checkered material stuck in the closed closet doors. It looked like a piece of shirt that her husband wore the night before. It couldn't be, she thought, but she stood up automatically and walked to the closet opening it, not noticing Verena's horror in her face.

She opened the closet door to find her husband standing there crunched down in the small closet.

"So, this is where you spent your night? Cheating on me, with my only friend that I have here? Bastard!" She yelled at him and her hand automatically flew up slapping him across the face.

"I can explain." He attempted surprised at her volatile reaction that he never saw from her before. But Michaela did not listen to him; she turned to Verena with tears in her eyes at the betrayal by her husband and by her new found acquaintance.

"I thought you were my friend, but I should have known better." She ran out of the apartment crying. Eddy pushed Verena out of the way when she tried to stop him and caught up with his wife on the top floor just before she had a chance to open the door of their apartment that became her crying sanctuary way too many times. He grabbed Michaela by the arm forcing her to the ground nearly falling off the stairs as his threatening

216

fist came over her head. She instantaneously knew that slapping him was a big mistake that would have dire consequences.

"What the fuck are you doing embarrassing me in front of the neighbour?! You want to fight, let's fight." His screams reverberated off the walls of the building heedless of attracting unwanted attention. Michaela was covering her belly with one hand and her face with the other nowhere to escape; she was expecting the blow to come any moment when his fist was hovering over her in a threatening manner. She surrendered to his superiority without much choice.

Chapter 20

H E WOULD HAVE LANDED A punch at her if it was not for a male hand grabbing him from behind giving Michaela a chance to scramble to her feet.

"L...leave h...her a...a...alone." The short nerdy looking man with glasses was still holding Eddy's arm stuttering at every word trying to speak with great difficulty. It was the weird neighbour across from them that never spoke to anyone. Eddy forcefully pulled away from him then ushered his wife to go inside their apartment glaring at the older man. Michaela was surprised that her husband did not pick a fight with this nerdy looking man whom he could easily overpower with one hand behind his back. Clearly he was no match for Eduard and one slap over his face would have brought him to his knees; nevertheless, he did not back down. Michaela looked at her neighbour with gratitude, yet with fear in her eyes not sure whether for her or for her new savior. He stepped one step closer in a protective manner, but was put off by Eddy's more masculine and a lot larger body and menace in his dark eyes. Eddy pushed Michaela inside and forcefully slammed the door in his face leaving him on the hallway with a concern.

She thought of Mr. Ehrlichmann's words 'Never treat anyone badly; you never know who could help you'. She was glad that she has always treated everyone with respect and kindness even when she did not always receive it back. Now this last person that she would have expected it from has helped her in the moment when she felt most vulnerable, while lying down pregnant on the dirty hallway floor with an ominous fist over her head. She has made a mental note to thank her neighbour whose name she did not even know, next time when she had a chance, but for now she still had to deal with her current crisis situation at home.

She stepped back placing her hands protectively on her belly watching Eddy's every move, every facial expression to figure out what he would do next. Should she run? But where would she go? Or should she try to calm him down or rather not say anything at all? She did not know what to do so she just stood there in the corner of the room watching him carefully. His instantaneous rage seemed have vanished in the thin air, once he closed the door behind them as if they stepped into a new dimension; his anger has been replaced with sorrow and remorse. He slammed his heavy body down on the sofa putting his face in the palms of his hands ashamed to look at his wife who was still standing there watching him for a moment longer. When he did not move, she came closer to him and sat beside him at the end of the old couch touching his shoulder. As soon as he felt her beside him, he clutched her hand in his as if he never wanted to let her go and started to kiss it possessively. He then looked at her with tears in his eyes and embraced her. They were sitting there together in a tight embrace for a long time, Eddy whispering to her.

"I'm so sorry, my love. I don't know what's wrong me with. You must hate me so much. I know I hate myself."

"Don't say that Eddy. I DON'T hate you, but you did hurt me a lot. I thought you loved me."

"Oh, God, I do. I do love you, so much. I don't know why I do what I do. I didn't cheat on you, I swear. She invited me in when I was walking by and I was so upset with you, so I went in. Maybe I just needed someone to talk to. But when I heard your voice I panicked and I didn't want you to get the wrong idea, so I hid in her closet. Stupid, isn't it? So childish. I made everything thousand times worse. I don't know why I did that, but there is nothing between me and her. She doesn't mean anything to me." When she did not say anything as she was trying to process what just happened, he added. "I wish you believed me."

"I want to believe you Eddy because I love you, but....." He quickly interrupted her before she would say something that he could not deal with; something that would change his life forever.

"I love you too. I'm so sorry I yelled at you, but when you slapped me, I.....I just got so angry. I don't know what to do with my anger sometimes. I don't know how to control it."

"I shouldn't have slapped you. I'm sorry too." She gently stroked his cheek where her hand landed ten minutes earlier. "I should have given you a chance to explain. I thought you were cheating on me."

"No, no, my love. I know how it must have looked...but I only want you. I know I don't deserve you. How can you even love me?"

"I do love you, but you can't treat me like that. Sometimes you really scare me, Eddy."

"I know. I know and it will not happen again, I swear."

"Maybe you need some help, Eddy."

"No, no. All I need is YOU by my side. I need you to believe in me that I can change. Nobody ever believed in me. NOBODY! You can't leave me, Michaela. I need you so much. I promise I change. I change because of you. I can change for you; for our baby." He started kissing her belly. She stroked his thick hair while he still held her around her waist kneeling down beside her as he often did when he was asking her for forgiveness.

She did not tell him that, but she often thought about leaving him, except she could not make herself leave; she could not simply throw away the love that he could give her, especially during times like these. She did not know what she would do without him on her own with the baby and she was too ashamed to go back home after such a short time of their marriage having to admit to Aunt Sylvie she was right about Eddy all along. No, she would not give up that easily; she would not give up on their love; she would not give up on Eddy and she would not take the father away from her unborn child. She wanted to believe that he would change. When Eddy showed remorse, compassion and love she was filled with new hope and she wanted to hold on to that. She wanted to help him. Nobody ever believed in him; nobody ever loved him as she did and she did not want to take that away from him. He needed her and she had to help him. He must have sensed her vacillation about what she would do about their relationship and he had to safe their marriage; he had to make it better.

"Michaela, my love, don't leave me." He pleaded. "I know you deserve better, someone better than me. I promise I will try to be a better husband.

I'll do anything for you, just don't leave me. Give me another chance." He reached up to her face and started kissing her cheeks, her eyes that were slightly swollen from her tears that fell down her face getting mixed up with Eddy's tears. He finally found her full lips that got red as the blood rushed to them when she cried and started to kiss her passionately. She could not help but return his kisses that she loved so much. His gentle touch, from her neck to her breasts and rest of her body that he started to undress, was like a healing balm on her wounded soul. They made love slowly, gently but passionately right on the sofa in their living room and afterwards they stayed lying there together in an embrace while Michaela's head was resting on his hairy masculine chest dosing off.

After a while, Eddy gently picked her sleeping head and placed it on a pillow while he slid down from the sofa and got to his feet. He caringly placed a blanket over his wife, kissed her forehead and made his way to the small sink in the kitchen. He washed his face in cold water to clean away the dried up tears and the guilt that he felt. He hated the hypocrite that he has become; he hated the lying man that was now staring at him from the mirror. He would change; he had to change, just like he promised. Michaela was the best thing that ever happened to him, why is he ruining it for himself, for them and for their unborn child? With new determination he left their small apartment leaving Michaela sleeping after the exhausting turn of events.

Eddy looked around and listened for any sounds on the hallway of the second floor before he knocked on Verena's door. Verena did not hide her surprise when she opened the door finding Eduard on her doorstep. Without invitation he went in and closed the door behind them.

"Back so soon? A little too eager, aren't you?"

"Shut up. You already caused enough trouble. I just came to tell you that you better keep your mouth shut in front of my wife. Do you understand?"

"What? Are you afraid that I might tell her what a great lover she has at home? She might not be aware of that. If she took better care of you, you would not have come here in the first place." She tried to touch his hair, but he pushed her arm away. Verena was an incorrigible flirt but Eddy quickly brought her back to reality.

"I told you to shut your mouth! You will not talk about us to anyone. Nothing happened between us, ever." He held her chin threateningly squeezing it tighter.

"Do you understand?" Her small gray eyes that got bigger with fright were staring at him and she looked even uglier than when she tried to flirt with him.

Only after she nodded her agreement Eduard let her go and then he continued.

"When my wife asks you what happened here today, you say that I just came for coffee to talk to a neighbour as you invited me and nothing else. I only panicked and that's how I end up in your closet, but nothing happened between us. Got it?

"Sure. If you think she'll believe that bullshit…." He interrupted her.

"If you ever talk, I'll squeeze your chicken neck and nobody will give a dumb about you." He gave her an ominous look to let her know he was serious.

Verena tried to be more persuasive so she changed her demeanor and said keeping her sarcasm at check.

"You have nothing to worry about, neighbour. I don't want to ruin your marriage; I just like to have some fun. And I know you're not opposed to that." She chuckled starting to flirt with him again but Eddy stopped her with his menacing look.

"I mean it. It's over and there is nothing between us. And never was. One word, Verena and I swear……"

"Don't worry, Eduard. I'll be quiet like a grave." She twisted her fingers as if she was locking her mouth shut and throwing away an invisible key.

"Good. Otherwise you might end up in one." He threw at her another warning look and then made his way out of her apartment making sure that no nosy neighbour saw him leaving or worse, Michaela making her way downstairs.

When he came back Michaela was already up tidying up in the kitchen.

"Hey beautiful! Did you have a good nap?"

"Yes, I guess I really needed it. The pregnancy is making me tired."

"Come on; leave the cleaning up for another time. Get ready and we'll go shopping."

"Shopping?"

"Yes. You deserve some nice things. You can pick anything you want and for the baby too."

"Wow, Eddy. That's so sweet of you, but can we afford it?"

"Don't worry about it." Michaela was worried about it because Eddy was out of work for about two months and her small income that she earned for cleaning and helping with other chores for the two elderly families would barely cover the rent. Besides, she did not know how long she would be able to keep doing it as the third-trimester was becoming more difficult for her due to the weight and back pain, but Michaela never complained. Remembering how Eddy over-reacted recently because of the bills that had to be paid, she objected to his generosity this time.

"But Eddy, you're out of work right now."

"I know. You don't have to remind me about it. We pay by credit card. I'm starting a new job through a temp agency next week; some forklift job. I got my forklift license years ago so it will be a good job for me. Don't worry." He repeated. "We'll be alright. I just want to buy something nice for my beautiful wife that deserves so much more." He came to the kitchen where she was still putting away the dishes and he stood behind her, pulled her long hair to one side kissing the back of her neck.

As Michaela was getting ready for their shopping spree, Eddy set down on the sofa in the living room finding the broken phone he recently threw against the wall. He examined it trying to put it together coming to a conclusion that it was beyond repair.

"We'll buy a new phone today and you can call home."

She peeked out of the bedroom with surprise as she was pulling a large pullover over her belly.

"Thank you, Eddy. You don't know how much that means to me."

They took the streetcar to the Leipziger Street which was the main shopping street in downtown Halle and they walked from store to store. They bought a simple table rotary phone that would serve its purpose for the seldom use. Michaela enjoyed buying baby clothes, new-born diapers, wipes, bedding for the crib and baby blanket and other essentials that she might need for the baby when it comes. Michaela was the happiest when Eddy agreed to buy the baby stroller with attached car seat. Even though they did not have a car at this point, they would need a car seat to bring the baby home in the taxi from the hospital. Michaela chose neutral colours for the baby things. The clothes were mainly yellow and white and a light brown blanket with cute teddy bear on top. The stroller was the colour of white coffee with different shades of brown as a design as they did not know whether it would be a girl or a boy, but Eddy refused to buy anything pink believing he would have a son soon.

Eddy often spoke about wanting a boy and called the baby junior. He came up with a list of German boy names that he liked for their child, not even thinking that it could be a girl. Michaela went along with that; happy to see her husband's excitement about the baby after such a long time. She enjoyed every minute of having the Eddy she fell in love with back again. She was ecstatic not because of the shopping, although she was excited to be getting ready for their new arrival; but she was thrilled because it has been a long time since she went anywhere especially with her husband. She usually went only to the bakery, grocery store or Laundromat. On occasion she went for a walk in the nearby park as her form of exercise and to get out of the lonely apartment. Today was different though; today she was spending quality time with her husband that she has not experienced since their honeymoon in Dresden. She did not care if she did not get anything for herself despite Eddy's encouraging words to pick something just for her. She eventually picked some nursing bras that Eddy did not find one bit attractive, but it was a necessity as Michaela was planning on nursing the baby for a while. She also picked up a nursing pillow and a changing mat for the baby although they did not have a changing table. Michaela said that she could change the baby on the floor on the mat and the baby at least would not be at risk of falling down.

They placed majority of the things into the new stroller as they made their way back home. Eddy called a taxi from a pay phone as they had too many things to carry by a streetcar and stopped at the local café for coffee and desert while they waited for the cab to arrive. Eddy held Michaela's hand at the café.

"I wish you bought something nice for yourself too."

"I did."

"All that stuff", he looked at the packed up stroller, "is for the baby".

"Eddy, it makes me so happy that I could get that for the baby. I don't need much. It means more to me that you came with me and we had some nice time together."

"Good. I want you to be happy with me. I told you I wanted to be a better man because of you." She stroked his cheek gently and said honestly what she believed.

"I know we can be happy together, Eddy. I know we can make it work."

At home, Michaela busied herself with unpacking all the new things and finding a proper place for them. Because the apartment was small, the baby would have to sleep with them in the same room and Michaela felt more comfortable with that. Eddy sat down on the sofa, opened a Budweiser that they bought on their way and placed his feet up on the small coffee table reading the newspaper. Their brief interactions once in a while had a feel of an old couple that had been together for many years and had not much to say to each other. Despite that, Michaela was content; nesting for the arrival of their baby that was still weeks away. Although Michaela wrote to her family and friends at least every other week, she was thrilled when they got a new phone and she could call her mother.

"Hi mom."

"Michaela, darling. Oh, my, I'm so glad to hear from you. I tried calling you but there was no answer."

"Ah, our phone was not working, but we have a new one now."

"How are you doing? How are you feeling?"

"I'm doing just fine. The baby is growing and kicking. You would not even recognize me with my big belly." Michaela laughed with delight and so did her mom with tears in her eyes.

"I wish I could come see you." Michaela hesitated for a moment before she responded. She did not want her mother to see the shabby apartment. And although Michaela made it homier, some things she could not change.

"Ah, well, maybe you could come after the baby is born to see your grandchild."

"I'd love that. And have you been going regularly for your check-ups."

"Yes, mom. Don't worry. Everything is fine and Dr. Hynes is really good."

"You should go to prenatal classes, Mika." Her mother suggested with a concern about her daughter not knowing anything about what to expect about the childbirth or about the baby.

"Ok, mom, I'll look into it."

"Darling, I miss you so much. At least you write to us often. You take care of yourself and the little one. Say hello to Eddy."

"I will, mom. I miss you too. Love you."

Their life together seemed to have taken on a new meaning after the last incident and it was much more peaceful and calm. Eddy started a new job the following week and Michaela spent her time with daily chores seeing her husband in the late evenings and sometimes she would be already asleep by the time he came home. He told her that he stopped at the gym and showered although she knew that occasionally he went to the local pub instead. It was better not to confront his occasional drinking and let him sleep it off. She had carried a keg of beer from the store at least once a week to have him home more often.

Despite their modest little apartment with old furniture Michaela made sure everything was nice and tidy. She even painted the whole apartment by herself without Eddy's help. He was not around to help her anyway as he was either at work, in the gym or in the pub. She decorated a small corner of their bedroom with baby things. She had everything ready for her baby and could not wait to hold it in her arms. The pregnancy and her back problems prevented her from helping with the cleaning chores for the Ziegler family and the older woman did not want her to do it either worried about Michaela's advanced state of pregnancy.

She had to argue with Mr. Ehrlichmann who also did not want her to do his filthy chore for him, but Michaela argued that it is not so hard if she does it every day as she needs to go down to the washroom anyway.

Despite Verena's nosy nature, she seemed to withdraw into her apartment and whenever she knew Michaela was around, she walked the other way or avoided coming out of her apartment in the first place. Michaela did not talk to her since the incidence and she had no desire to do so now. With friends like Verena she did not need any enemies. Although Eddy reassured her that nothing happened between them, she did not trust this cougar like woman that would seduce any man that walked by. Verena hinted that way the very first time she met them but she did not pay attention to that at the time, but now it all added up.

One time when she was going down the stairs, she met her neighbour from the fourth floor who courageously helped her by stopping her husband in a crucial moment of what could have ended in a disaster and for that she was very grateful to him.

"Hi. I'm sorry, I didn't have a chance to say thank you." Michaela stopped him before he disappeared from her sight.

That was the first time she saw a glimmer of a smile revealing his crooked yellow teeth. He nodded that he understood.

"Y....you ok?"

"Yes, I'm fine. Thank you." This time Michaela nodded her agreement. "What's your name?" He watched her lips concentrating on what she was saying.

"W....Wal....Walter." He uttered his name without offering to shake his hand with her; hiding them in his pockets of his oversized coat. Michaela smiled at him and slowly mouthed her name to him, placing her hand to her chest. He again nodded although she was not sure whether he understood as she was sure he could not hear her. Without another word, he disappeared behind the door of his apartment.

Michaela took the streetcar to the hospital. A familiar route that she had learned very quickly as she had to rely on herself to go see Dr. Hynes every two weeks. He checked her urine sample and blood pressure that were always in a great condition as she was healthy young woman with no complications during her pregnancy. She inquired from him about prenatal classes and he had her fill out some documents and told her where to sign up. The course was starting next Wednesday for the next four weeks.

"You still have a lot of time to complete the prenatal class." Michaela signed up right after she left Dr. Hynes' office. The classes were two floors down in the hospital which was convenient. The nurse encouraged her to bring her partner and to bring a comfortable pillow and comfortable clothing for the class. She could not wait to tell Eddy about it, but was disappointed when he did not share her enthusiasm.

"Why do I have to come? You're the one that gives the birth, not me."

"For support I guess. Besides, you could learn things about the baby too. It's not just about the labour."

"We'll see. You know I have to work and then I like to go to the gym to workout. I don't know if I be able to go."

"It's in the evenings at seven and you're done work long before that. It's only once a week for four weeks. Please Eddy."

"I do my best, alright?" She knew the conversation was over at that point and persuading him further or pushing him into it would be futile and most likely ending up in an argument. She hoped that he would attend with her, but when the first class started and Eddy was supposed to meet with her at the hospital after work, she waited at the side entrance of the hospital for him in vain a small pillow clutched to her belly; she felt ridiculous. She was pacing back and forth hoping that he would come any moment now. She saw another pregnant woman entering the hospital with a pillow under her arm. When she saw Michaela standing there with a pillow, she stopped and asked.

"Are you also going to the prenatal class tonight at seven?"

"Yes, I'm."

"That's great. I always get lost in the catacombs of the hospital and never go to the right doors. Do you know where the class is?"

"It's just to the left of the building behind that small cafeteria."

"Thanks. By the way, I'm Juliane Bergsman." The young woman with dirty blond hair and chestnut colour eyes smiled at her revealing tiny dimples that gave her otherwise ordinary face a friendly appeal.

"Michaela Verner. It's nice to meet you." She offered to shake her hand.

"Are you waiting for someone?"

"Yes, my husband, but I don't think he will make it. It's already seven. I don't think he is coming." She said with a disappointment in her voice. Juliane tried to encourage her.

"I'm sure he had a good reason. At least you have someone that is there for you during the pregnancy. I'm a single mother of already one little girl." She pulled out her wallet with a picture of her five year old daughter.

"She is very cute."

"Thanks. I love her dearly, but you would have thought that I have learned the first time around, she placed her hand on her medium sized belly to indicate her expectancy of another child. But that's a long story for another time. Let's go. We're already running late."

The women walked together to the prenatal class. They came a little late and they were the only two women without a partner. They sat to the side listening to the nurse explaining what they need to pack when they come to the hospital to deliver their babies. They watched a video of a childbirth that looked quite gruesome but realistic. It was not a pretty sight, especially when the pregnant women imagined that this is the kind of pain they will have to go through but at the end there was a tiny miracle that cried its lungs out and they saw a happy although exhausted mother that was proudly holding her newborn baby boy.

"Do you know what you're having?" Juliane whispered to Michaela with genuine curiosity.

"No. I want it to be a surprise although I know my husband Eddy hopes for a boy."

"Hmm, guys!" Michaela smiled back at her new found friend.

After the class the young women decided to go for a tea and pastry at a nearby café just across from the hospital.

"You look so young, Michaela. How long have you been married?"

"Just about five months. Yeah, I know you adding it up. Yes, we had to get married even though I'm just eighteen."

"I was just a little older when I got married and had my daughter at twenty."

"You said you were a single mom. What happened, if you don't mind me asking?"

"Not at all. It's nice to talk to someone who doesn't judge you."

"Yes, I know what you mean." Michaela said and smiled at her new acquaintance.

"We were so much in love and I really thought that we will spend the rest of our lives together. But shortly after we got married and I got pregnant with our daughter, he started to call me names and putting me down; it really had a great impact on my self-esteem and I believed him every word he said that I'm not good for anything." She took a deep breath and then continued her story. "When I was four months pregnant, he kicked me in the stomach so I would lose the baby and when that did not work; he beat me senseless until I ended up in the hospital with a broken arm, bruises all over my face and body. It was a miracle that I did not miscarry that night. When my daughter was born prematurely, I did not think she would make it and I always blamed myself. I named her Hannah because it means hope and that's all I had at that time. I don't know what I would have done if she had died. But she pulled through and today she is a little five year old opinioned princess that I just love to pieces." Michaela listened to Juliane's story with a great interest and thought about her own relationship with Eddy questioning whether it was abusive at times. He had called her nasty names on more than one occasion and he had placed his hands in anger on her, slapping her and threatened to punch her. He never seriously hurt her to a point that she would have to go to a hospital like Juliane had described but once she had a small bruise under her eye when Eddy slapped her harder promising never to hit her again.

She still had nightmares about the time when Eddy stood over her threateningly with his fist over her head and if it was not for the neighbour in that moment, she knew he would have punched her and he would have punched her hard. Juliane ate few bites of her Danish before she continued interrupting Michaela's thoughts.

"That night when I had to go to the hospital; that was a breaking point for me and I made up my mind I would leave him as soon as I got out of the hospital. And that's what I did. I went to the shelter and lived there for about three months. I did not want my daughter to live in that kind of home and I was fed up with it." She took another bite of her cherry Danish and sipped her tea before she continued again.

"It's funny that I found very similar man couple years later and got pregnant again. That's the father of this baby and although he was not half as abusive as my first husband, I would not put up with any name calling or little slaps over my face when things agitated him. So this time I went to live with my mom. It was too late to abort and I wanted to have another child. So this is how I ended up being a single parent." She concluded and asked.

"What's your story, Michaela?"

"I met Eddy just in summer of last year in Bulgaria."

"Oh, is this where you're from? You have such a lovely accent. I knew right away you were not German."

"No, I'm from Czechoslovakia; from the Slovak part of the country. I was there on vacation with some friends and so was Eddy and we just fell in love." Michaela got quiet for a moment, distracting herself with her own pastry in front of her that she ate without much appetite before she spoke again.

"Your story reminds me a little of my own. Not to that extend of course. I never been in the hospital with any injuries and Eddy would never kick me in the stomach but...."

"But what, Michaela?"

"But he has called me names before and he has slapped me on few occasions although usually for a good reason."

"Michaela, there is never a good reason for a man to hit you."

"It's not always like that. Actually, it is very good between us now."

"It's just a honeymoon period."

"Honeymoon period?"

"Yes, that's what they call it when the abuser begs you for forgiveness and the woman forgives him believing that everything will change for the better because they love each other. And it is the nicest and sweetest time in the relationship. But it never stays that way. Soon you will notice more tension building up in your home and you will feel like you're walking on egg shells just to make him happy before another incident occurs. Trust me Michaela, I lived through that so many times and did not even know about it until I left and went to counseling at the shelter."

"I don't think I could ever leave Eddy. I know he loves me and I love him."

"I know this is not easy. But I don't want you to get hurt or worse, I don't want your unborn child to be hurt."

"That's not going to happen. Eddy has changed and besides, I don't know why I'm talking about it to a complete stranger. I never talk to anyone about my marital problems. That's all that this is. Every couple has some problems."

"Yes, Michaela every couple has problems but what you seem to experience when he puts his hands on you when he is angry or calls you names is abuse and that should not be ok with you."

"I have to go. I'm already late coming home. Eddy will wonder where I am so long."

"Michaela, I don't want to intrude in your life. I thought we clicked and it was great talking to you. Here is my number if you want to get together sometimes and if not, I will see you at the prenatal class next week and that might be all. But I just don't want you to get hurt. I'm here if you need a friend." Michaela hesitated before she put her coat on.

"I appreciate it and you're right, I felt very comfortable talking to you even though I just met you. I could use a good friend. Besides Eddy I don't have anyone in Halle."

Juliane handed her a napkin with her phone number.

"Call anytime. I know how it is to feel completely alone."

"Thanks. I'll see you next week in class."

When Michaela came home, Eddy was already at home anxiously waiting for her.

"Where the hell were you?" He yelled at her as soon as she opened the door. She would not have any of that and retorted back to him.

"I can ask you the same thing. You knew today was my first prenatal class and you were not there even though everyone else's partner was there." Eddy ran his hand through his curly dark hair in exasperation.

"Shit. I forgot, alright. I'm sorry. But still," he checked his watch, "it ended at 8:30 and it's almost ten. Where were you for over an hour?" He looked at her askance.

"I went with one of the women for some cake and tea. She was there by herself too and we had such craving for something sweet. You know my cravings since I have been pregnant." She tried to smile at him to lighten the mood.

"I know you eat too much junk." He scolded her like a little child. "You're not gonna be able to shed the extra kilos after the baby is born if you eat like that."

"Alright Eddy, I'm too tired to argue now. I just want to wash up and go to bed." She headed towards the kitchen, when Eddy caught her by her shoulder.

"Don't walk away when I'm talking to you. You always complain that we don't communicate and when I want to talk, you are too tired and don't want to deal with our problems." At that Michaela stopped and turned back to face her husband with a tired expression on her face.

"Ok, Eddy, I do want to talk but I don't want to fight."

"Hey, we're not fighting, we are just talking. All I wanted to say that I don't want you out at that hour. You don't know how dangerous it is here lately even though we live in a quite student area. There are these Nazi skinhead gangs that are roaming the streets looking for anyone who is not German; believing in 'white power'."

"So? I'm white."

"It's not just a different race, but different culture. You don't look anything like a German woman and your accent would give you away along with your not so perfect language even though you speak now quite well. They can smell the foreigners and last thing I want is them to get hold of you and hurt you. I was born here and speak German perfectly and they had picked a fight with me because I don't look anything like a typical German man." Michaela thought Eddy had a good point. He was just worried about her and probably for a good reason. She had seen some young groups of men in downtown with shaved heads often tattooed in black leather jackets with offensive graphics or writings and in black steel toe shoes or combat boots. They had an ominous presence and people tended to avoid any eye contact with them as not to provoke a fight, hurrying away from them.

"I appreciate your concern. I've seen the groups before and you're right, they do look quite scary, but I go the other way when I see them from far. Maybe next time you can come with me to the hospital?"

"Alright, I'll come." They hugged and kissed before Michaela went to wash up thinking that her marriage was not so bad. Eddy genuinely seemed to care about her and was upset with her because he was concerned for her safety. It did not escalate to a big fight as it easily could have; this was just a small exchange of opinions that happens in any marriage. Even arguments between couples are normal and to be expected, Michaela reasoned with herself and this was not even a fight.

She was not Juliane and she had a different life than her new found friend. She felt bad for what Juliane went through along with her little girl, but this was not her life and she has to remember that. Sure, she had problems and things were not always the best, but Eddy was never abusive to the point that Michaela would have to go to the hospital; she never had any serious injuries. She knew that Eddy had a temper that he sometimes had hard time controlling, but he was trying to change and if she did not provoke him, they could have a great life together. If he beat her everyday sustaining any injuries, she would definitely not stay with him no matter how much she loved him.

Somehow they were even surviving the cold winter days in the little apartment that did not have a toilet or a shower inside the apartment and the heating was a great challenge but she learned to accommodate to the new exigent conditions. Their problems, she thought were often based on little petty things that she could change and avoid Eddy's harsh words and his strong hand that was quickly raised to her face when he was angry with her. But even that did not happen in a while and she hoped it would not happen again. Or was it a honeymoon period just like Juliane suggested?

As she was getting ready for bed, she remembered Juliane's phone number on the napkin. She carefully wrote it down into her paper phone booklet and put it back in her purse tossing the napkin to the garbage bin in the kitchen. She said good night to Eddy and quickly fell asleep only being awakened couple hours later with Eduard's yelling. He put the bright light in the bedroom having her sit up and adjust her eyes to the light.

"What's going on? She tried to adjust her eyes to the bright light. Eddy's tick in the right corner of his mouth and heavy breathing was a good indication of his rage.

"What's going on? You tell me!" He was waiving the white napkin from the café with Juliane's phone number on it, but it did not have her name on it; only her number.

"What is it?" Still not fully awake she tried to comprehend his reaction.

"I can't fucking believe it! You asking me what it is?!" He crumbled it hitting her with it in the face; she opened the old napkin to see what it was, remembering that it was from Juliane.

"It's the phone number from my friend, Juliane from the prenatal class. You know the one I mentioned I went for a dessert with?" Michaela tried to explain over Eddy's cadence of accusations that he was throwing in her face.

"So you go on dates with who knows who and I worry about you at home?"

"No, Eddy, you're not listening to me." She was right about it, he was not listening to her; all he heard was a trace of fear in her voice.

"Are you sleeping with him?"

"Eddy, calm down, there is no 'him'." But it was too late he lashed out at her slapping her across the face with such a force that she fell back on the bed hitting her head on the edge of the board. She did not know what hurt more her face or back of her head. And just as quickly, the honeymoon period was over. So much for his promises, Michaela thought with great disappointment. And as usual he left her there in shock, pain and in distress. She did not even cry this time; she was still in shock as she tried to apply some ice to her cheek and to the back of her head.

She did not know again where Eduard went. He might have gone to his old 'friend' Verena for a console or he went drinking or he might have left for good. She did not know and she did not care at this point. She was angry with him but she was furious with herself that she believed he would change. She placed her head on the soft pillow from the other side where he hit her, thinking that tomorrow she would go back home to Czechoslovakia regardless that it was not recommended for her to travel at this stage of her pregnancy. She needed to leave and the sooner the better.

She did not expect Eddy to come back the same night or not anytime soon and especially sober, but to her surprise, her husband returned within twenty minutes a lot calmer and remorseful. He reeked of cigarette smell. She was still awake because she was afraid to fall asleep in case it was a concussion.

"Oh God, what have I done. I don't even remember hitting you. I'm so sorry, Michaela. The rage was stronger than me when I thought you cheated on me, but now I remember you telling me that it was the girl's number."

When Michaela was quiet giving him an unforgiving look, he suddenly knew that he went too far this time. When he continued to explain himself about his blackouts and that he did not mean it, Michaela did not want to hear it anymore.

"Eddy, just stop. I can't do this anymore." Sudden fear grew in his eyes that made them even larger.

"What do you mean?"

"I mean, I had enough of your abuse and of your apologies and I'm done! I'm going back home tomorrow."

"THIS is your home. You can't just leave. You are going to have the baby in seven weeks. You can't just leave me."

"You can't treat me like this. I haven't done anything bad to you. I just loved you and you treat me like crap." She tried to stand up for herself although she could no longer control her tears that were rolling down her cheeks when the self-pity set in.

"I said I was sorry and that I did not mean to hit you. If you just told me about the phone number upfront I didn't have to over-react like that. But what was I supposed to think? I could not stand if you ever cheated on me."

"You will not have to worry about it anymore because I will not be here to blame, to accuse of things I haven't done, to yell at me and hit me." She was yelling at this point back at him and she did not care if he hit her again for being mouthy with him. She needed to tell him that. She was not going to just forgive him this time. She knew if she did, the abuse would simply continue. Juliane with whom she shared few things about her relationship assessed the situation better than Michaela has from the beginning and she was right; Eddy was being abusive and what she experienced for couple of weeks of peace was just a honeymoon period.

"You're not leaving!" He said decisively.

"What are you going to do? Hit me again?" She knew she provoked him but she could not help it. He hurt her so many times; this was only trickle of what she was doing to him.

Eddy had tears in his eyes but this time it did not faze her; she was determined. She could not go on like that.

"Michaela, please. You can't do that to me. You can't leave me. I can't live without you. I get help. I will. I can see now I can't do it on my own. I need professional help. I'm sick; I'm messed up in my head. I don't know what's happening with me. Please, you said you will always stand by me; that you will never leave me."

"Eddy, please just stop the charade. I can't do this anymore. You always beg me to forgive you and when I do it's good for a little while but nothing really changes. I can't do that anymore." She repeated. "You've hurt me too many times. I think we need some space away from one another."

"No. NO, YOU'RE NOT LEAVING!" He yelled at her with fury in his eyes; then he quickly disappeared in the kitchen for a moment returning with a large kitchen knife in his hand.

Chapter 21

"**Y**ou're not going to leave me!" He repeated, but this time in a lower hoarse voice that presented more threat than ever. He took a step closer to her.

"Eddy, please, don't....." Michaela was terrified not just for herself but for her unborn child. Would he really hurt her? She was pressed against the wall in the corner of the mattress nowhere to escape; she was looking at him in disbelief with her big bluish eyes.

"You know why you're not going to leave me?" Without waiting for a response, he continued in a husky voice that she barely recognized. "You're not going to leave me because.......I will leave before you do." He said with dilated tearful eyes of a crazy man, holding the knife to his neck. A trickle of blood in one spot where he was pressing the point of the knife with a shacking hand appeared on his neck. This got Michaela to her feet and this time she did not fear for her own life but for his. She never realized how troubled her husband was.

"Eddy, please, put the knife down."

"I don't care if I die. I will be death anyway if you leave me, so what's the point of going on? I told you I can't live without you and I meant it."

"Eddy, please just put the knife down. Please. I don't want you to kill yourself."

"Then don't leave me! Stay with me! Or I swear...." And he pressed the knife a little harder at his neck showing more blood.

"Alright, alright, Eddy, I will not leave you. Just give me the knife, ok?" She reached out her hand to him waiting for him to hand her the knife. He was about to pass the knife to her when suddenly their doorbell rang accompanied with some banding on the door. Eddy startled touched Michaela's hand accidently with the tip of the sharp knife cutting her hand that started to bleed.

"Open up, it's the police!"

"Shit."

Eddy dived towards the door, not realizing his knife still in his hand when he opened the door. Two policemen noticed the knife in his hand as soon as the door opened and quickly disarmed him, bending his right arm behind him and putting handcuffs on his wrists. Michaela emerged from the bedroom in her long nightgown. One of the young officers asked her.

"Are you alright, madam?"

When the police saw her standing there in her white long nightgown looking pale as a ghost with the exception of her left cheek that was red and swollen and her right hand bleeding, he repeated the question. But she did not respond. She placed her bloody hand on her stomach staining her white nightgown; her body folding down to the ground and darkness surrendered her.

When Michaela woke up she did not recognize her surroundings. A nurse was checking her IV.

"Where am I?"

"You're in the Bergmannstrost Hospital in Halle." An older nurse with thin lips answered her. Michaela automatically placed her hands on her belly in a protective manner.

"What happened? Is my baby alright?"

"The doctor will be with you shortly." The nurse told her with an unreadable face, placing her lips in a thin line then made her way out of the hospital room. Michaela looked around. An older woman was lying on a bed by the window sleeping. The IV did not allow her to get up, so she stayed lying down waiting for the doctor to arrive. Within ten minutes, Dr. Adler appeared in his white coat. He had a friendly smile with sparkly white teeth. What teeth whitener he uses, Michaela wondered as he spoke to her.

"Welcome back. Can you tell me your name?"

"Michaela Mart....I mean Verner. Michaela Verner."

"Mrs. Verner. You were out for four days."

"Four days?"

"Yes. You suffered a severe contusion to your head but there was no cerebral swelling and it luckily did not affect your brain activity." Michaela still feeling a little disoriented tried to sit up higher on the bed. Your right hand had a superficial cut that should heal relatively quickly but it might leave a scar." Michaela looked at her bandaged hand.

"Is my baby alright?"

"Yes, the baby will be just fine. We put you on the IV to keep you hydrated. I'll tell the nurse to bring you a Popsicle you can start with or ice-chips today and in the evening you can have some soup."

"What happened with my husband? Mr. Verner?"

"I'm sorry; we were not able to contact any of your family. Mrs. Ziegler had come to see you the second day you were in the hospital. She was the one that called the police. Constable Meinrad wanted to talk to you but I told him that was impossible under the circumstances."

"Constable?"

"Mrs. Verner I would not worry about it now if I were you. You need a lot of rest now. Do you have any other family that we can contact for you to let them know that you're here?"

"No. My family lives in Czechoslovakia and I don't want to worry them."

"Who is your family doctor, Mrs. Verner?"

"I have only been seeing Dr. Hynes, a gynecologist because of the pregnancy."

"We will notify him that you're here and about the injuries that you suffered."

"When will I be able to go home?"

"We'd like to keep you here for observation for at least another day. You can press this button to call the nurse if you need anything." He pointed to a button beside her bed. Get some rest, Mrs. Verner. You were very lucky." He added with a concern in his gray eyes.

In the afternoon, Constable Meinrad called the hospital about Michaela's state as he wanted to question her the last few days. When he learned that she was awake, he made his way over to the hospital poking his head into her room.

"Mrs. Verner?"

"Yes?"

"Constable, Meinrad. Can I come in? I have few questions regarding your husband." Michaela was anxious to know what happened that night before she was taken to the hospital and she wanted to know what happened with her husband.

"Yes, of course."

He pulled up a chair that was close by for the visitors. He pulled out his block of papers and pen and then looked up at her.

"Mrs. Verner….Michaela, can I call you that?"

"Certainly. What happened with my husband?" He did not answer her right away, rather started with his own set of questions.

"Michaela, what do you remember the night of Thursday, February 7th, the night before…before you were taken to the hospital?"

"I was asleep when my husband, Eddy, Eduard", she corrected herself, "woke me up yelling at me."

"Why was he yelling at you?"

"He thought I was cheating on him." She went on explaining further. "He found this phone number on a napkin that a female friend gave me and thought it was a….." He interrupted her quickly before she went on with her long story.

"All I'm interested in Michaela is if he hit you or injured you in any other way?" He pointed to her bruised cheek that felt still tender although she had not seen herself in the mirror in several days. She touched her cheek gently with her bandaged hand as a reminder where Eddy had slapped her.

"Yes." She said simply.

"Mrs. Verner. How did you acquire the contusion that the doctor told us about?" When she was quiet looking down at her injured hand, tears, were falling down on the bandages. "Michaela. You have to tell me the truth if he did that to you."

"I don't want to get him into trouble."

"HE got himself into trouble. So how did it happen?"

"I hit my head on the wooden headboard when he slapped me….I fell backwards." The older man was writing down her statement, which made her anxious.

"Mr.....hmm, Constable, Meinrad, where is my husband? Is he alright?"

"He is currently in custody. We take domestic violence very seriously, Michaela and there are laws that protect abused women."

"How long will you keep him there?" He again did not answer her directly.

"When we found him, he was holding a knife and your hand was bleeding. Was he threatening you with the knife?"

"I told him I wanted to leave him and......and he got the knife and wanted to kill himself." Her voice broke down.

"An abused woman is at a highest risk when she tries to leave the abusive relationship. That doesn't mean that you should stay, but you have to be smart about it. So he did not threaten to hurt you with the knife?"

"No. The cut was just an accident. What will happen next?"

"He will be charged with misdemeanor of domestic violence and bodily harm. And with his criminal history, he is looking at least at six months to a year of jail time. But that will be determined by the judge." Michaela was upset.

"He is not a criminal. He doesn't need a jail, but he needs help."

"I agree. He needs help and the only way you can help him is to press charges. After he serves his time in jail, the judge usually mandates men like your husband to anger management or domestic violence therapy group for several weeks. Men like Eduard seldom seek therapy on their own. Trust me Michaela; I have been doing it for a long time." The older man talked to her with wisdom of experience.

"He promised he would get help." Michaela said naively.

"It is irrelevant what he promised you. Just think how many promises he probably had made to you before. Did he ever keep any of them?" Constable Meinrad knew what he was talking about and he had a good point and Michaela decided to press the charges in order to change what was happening in their relationship. This was Eddy's last chance, Michaela thought and a new wave of hope washed over her. This was the right thing to do even if that meant that Eddy would go to jail for some time, but they could not co-exists this way anymore. He needed help.

When she was released from the hospital, Michaela returned back to their lonely apartment. She knew that there would be nobody waiting for her. She stopped at the third floor to talk to Mrs. Ziegler. When she opened the door, she exclaimed.

"Michaela, sweetheart, you gave us quite a scare. Please come on in."

"No, I won't stay. I just wanted to thank you for….for calling the police."

"We heard so much yelling at one thirty at night and figured that something was very wrong. I was so worried about you when they took you to the hospital; you being pregnant and all. I hope we didn't cause too much trouble for your husband, but he can't treat you that way."

"Thank you, Mrs. Ziegler for looking out for me and for bringing some clothes for me to the hospital. If you excuse me, I'd like to get back home. The doctor ordered me to be off my feet as much as possible and I'd like to lie down."

"Of course darling; you get some rest and let us know if there is anything we can do for you." Mrs. Ziegler was a kind woman and her personality reminded her of her own mother who currently could not be with her.

The trial dragged on but when it was finished Eduard received six months of jail time and mandated group therapy for anger management skills with other men that had domestic violence charges before he would be able to return back home considering that by the time he was released, there would be a baby in the home.

When Michaela came to see Eduard in jail, he looked at her with sadness and regret in his eyes. She was not sure whether it was because of what he has done to her or because he was in jail.

"You're going to leave me, aren't you?" He said with hopelessness in his voice.

"I can't travel now, so I will not go back yet, but I plan to go back to see my mother and stay with her after the baby is born at least until you…… until you get out of here. Eddy, I want to give us a chance but only once you complete the therapy. We….I can't go on like that." He nodded to indicate that he understood.

"I never meant to hurt you, Michaela. I love you."

"I know Eddy. I'm sorry it had to be this way."

"I will not even see my baby being born. How could you have done this to me?" She could not believe her ears that even now, he was blaming her after all what he has put her through. On the other hand, she understood him; he was in jail and he was powerless to do anything about it until he was out.

"Eddy, you need help and this might be the best thing that happened to us as weird as it may seem."

"This is the best thing? Letting me rot in jail? This is your fault that I'm in here." His demeanor quickly changed to anger. "Thanks a lot." He said sardonically; then he stood up ready to go back to his cell. There was nothing else to say and it was pointless to argue with him. He was blaming her for telling the truth; for speaking out for herself.

If Michaela could travel, she would have been on the first train back home to her hometown, but the doctor said it was too risky and the trauma she had recently survived had a toll on her body and had placed her at a high risk pregnancy. She was told to stay in bed as much as possible and not to lift anything heavy.

She did not know how she would make it on her own. She still did not receive her Landed Immigrant status and was not sure whether she would be eligible to apply for social assistance with the new turn of events as she no longer had a husband to support her. She did not know how she would manage financially or physically as she was to stay in bed. She needed help. She needed someone to come help her at least until the baby was born. She was thirty-five weeks pregnant and to prevent to have the baby early, she knew she should not be walking around nor doing too many chores, but how else was she going to survive? There was nobody in Germany that could help her. She would have to tell her mom what was happening.

But every time she called her mother or her aunt there was no answer at either place. She stayed at home feeling depressed and miserable. Mrs. Ziegler was the one that brought her some bread and few other groceries considering that Michaela did not have anyone to take care of her. She wished her mother was here but every time she called her, nobody answered and there was no answering machine. She decided to try her at work only to find out that she was on a sick leave which surprised her. She kept calling Aunt Sylvie, until she got hold of her one late evening.

"Aunt Sylvie. It's Mika."

"Oh, darling, Mika. It's so good to hear from you. I was planning to call you."

"I've been trying to call mom and your place for about a week and I still did not speak with mom. When I called her at work they said she was on a sick leave. What's going on?"

"Oh, Mika, we did not want to worry you especially you being pregnant and so far away. Your mother asked me not to say anything to you now, but….."

"What Aunt Sylvie? Tell me!"

"I'm sorry, Michaela, but your mom has been recently diagnosed with breast cancer."

"Oh, my God! Is she going to be alright?"

"She started the chemotherapy and she is…..it makes her very ill, Mika. I don't want to scare you. She will stay with me when she comes back from the hospital. Hopefully she might not have to go through surgery, but they are not sure at this point. She started the treatment only recently. They'll try the treatment first to see if it works. Don't worry, Mika, I know my sister and she is a tough cookie. She will pull throw it and she's got me to take care of her so you don't have to worry about anything. You just take care of yourself and the little one that will come."

"I wish I could come back home, but I can't travel now….considering my advanced pregnancy."

"Is everything alright?"

"Yes, everything is just fine." She lied. "Don't worry about me and give my mom love. I hope she will be alright." She could not tell her the truth that she needed as much help as her mother, but she would have to manage on her own somehow. She did not want to trouble either her Aunt or especially not her mother who was seriously ill.

"I'm so sorry, Mika that we can't come to see you right now. At least you have Eddy there with you and he can help you, right?" She could not tell her; not after finding out what her mother was dealing with and she needed Sylvia to help her. They had enough to deal with and she did not want them to worry about her. She only wished she could go home. When Aunt Sylvie sensed Michaela's hesitation, she asked again perhaps sensing something was not quite right.

"Mika, are you sure everything is alright?"

"Yes, you don't have to worry about me. I will be fine. Aunt Sylvie, please call me when my mom is back from the hospital so I can talk to her and tell her that I love her." She quickly changed the topic before Aunt Sylvie's sixth sense kicked in and she became suspicious.

"I will sweetie. We love you too."

"Once the baby is born I'll come back. Ok?"

"Alright, Mika. Keep us posted."

"I will. You too."

Michaela felt completely alone. Her husband was in jail for at least six months and even after that he would not be allowed to come back home until he completed the sixteen weeks domestic violence program. She could not even think that far. And now she found out that her mother had breast cancer. She did not know what was worse; not being able to be there for her mother or the fact that nobody was there for her when she needed it the most. She did not know whom else to ask for help. Her family was so small, consisting of only her mom and Aunt Sylvie. Being an only child she did not even have any distant family. Then she remembered her little sister, Julia and her mother Svetlana. Without much thinking she found their number in her small phone booklet and dialed the number. When a woman on the other line answered, Michaela said with relief.

"Hi Svetlana. It's Michaela. I'm calling you from Germany."

"Hi. How are you?" Without really waiting for an honest answer she continued. "Thanks for all the letters and postcards you sent us. I meant to write to you but it's been so busy. Julia started first grade in September and the time just flies, day after a day."

"How is Julia doing?"

"She is a little chatterbox at school, but she loves school and brought home straight ones in the first term."

"That's great. I miss her a lot."

"How are you doing?" She never really told Svetlana that she was pregnant. It was always a great shame for a girl to be marrying 'because she had to'. But it did not matter at this point and she needed someone's help and Svetlana in some strange way was her family."

"I don't think I ever had a chance to tell you Svetlana but I am pregnant."

"Wow, congratulations." She pretended as if it was something new to her. "How far along are you?"

"Well, I am thirty-five weeks pregnant."

"Wow." She could almost sense Svetlana doing the math. "That's really close then to your due date, right?"

"Well, my due date is on April 24th but they say that it seldom is exactly on that day. I had some……complications, although nothing serious but I should stay off my feet. I need someone to help me." She hesitated before she even uttered the ridiculous question. "You would not be able to come to Germany to stay with me for a month or at least the last two weeks, would you?"

"Oh, wow, Michaela. I would love to help you, but….well, what about your husband? Can't he help you?" She wished she had a better lie prepared rather than thinking quickly on the spot. She was never a good liar but she was too ashamed to tell Svetlana the truth.

"Hmm, he got a job in Hamburg in the West Germany. It's a really good opportunity for him and he couldn't turn it down because we needed the money." She hoped that Svetlana would not suspect that it was not the truth.

"Well, what about your mom? Can't SHE come?"

"I just found out my mom is dealing with breast cancer. There is really nobody…."

"I'm so sorry, Michaela to hear that. I don't know what to say." There was a long pause and that was an answer in itself. She did not ask again. She knew it was a stupid idea to ask in the first place and Svetlana confirmed her thoughts. Embarrassed she quickly added.

"Don't worry Svetlana, I'll figure something out."

"Michaela, if it was just me, maybe, but I can't just drop everything here. Julia is in school and I have a job to go to. I'm sure you have some other friends there that can help you." Little did Svetlana know that there was really nobody that cared; nobody that would help her; nobody that she could ask for help; nobody that would be there when she was giving the birth to her first child in a foreign country. But that did not matter. The answer was clear and deep down she did not expect anything else. She barely knew Svetlana, why should she drop everything and come here for her deceased husband's long last daughter who never had any relationship with him in the first place.

"Of course, I'm sorry I asked. It was stupid of me. Don't worry, I'll be fine." Suddenly she was in a rush to end the conversation before self-pity set in and she would start crying again.

"Send hugs and kisses to Julia from me. I let you know once the baby comes and I'll send some pictures. I have to go. Bye." She quickly hung up the phone before her voice gave up and she curled up on the sofa crying herself to sleep. This was one of her lowest points in life where everyone that she knew just disappeared from her life and she was completely alone. It was worse than having Eddy around who was at times abusive. She was completely without any help and she was scared; not just for her but for her unborn child. This is certainly not how she pictured her life in Germany and she wished she could go back home; back to Czechoslovakia.

After the discouraging phone conversation with Svetlana and after talking to her aunt about her mother's breast cancer, she did not feel like talking to anyone or do anything. World suddenly seemed so unfair and so difficult.

For the next three days she lay in her bed. She did not feel like eating and she only went downstairs into the cold washroom out of bare necessity. She now knew how Mr. Ehrlichmann who had nobody to take care of him must have felt. She wanted to go to sleep and never wake up although she knew she would not do anything to harm herself on purpose. But she had no strength to go on; everything suddenly became so complex. When she was tired of feeling depressed, she needed to find new strength within herself to pull herself up and keep going. She could not give up. She was going to be a mother and her child will need her. She would have to manage on her own somehow. She bathed with difficulties after three days of neglecting to do so due to her depression, but she could no longer stand feeling sorry for herself. She had never given up in her life about anything and she would not give up now. This was perhaps one of her lowest times in life and yes, she was completely alone, but she would pull through that even though she did not know how she would do it yet.

She wished she could talk to her best friend Nikole, but in her last letter she wrote that she moved to Bratislava to a dormitory as she got accepted to a two year program to become a cosmetician. There was nowhere to call her, but she had her new address and decided to write to her. She wrote to her everything that has happened to her, including Eddy's abusive behaviours that got him into jail and how alone she felt. She asked not to tell her family about it but it felt so good to share it with someone she trusted; someone whom she knew since she was little. She was done with pretenses and she no longer wanted to lie to her best friend. It felt good to get it off her chest. She read through the letter several times before she decided to send it to her friend.

March 19, 1985

Dear Nikole,

I'm sorry I have not written to you for a long time, but my life has been upside down and I still have not figured out how to make some sense of it. I don't want to pretend anymore that everything between me and Eddy is great and how happy I'm because it could not be further from the truth. The truth is that I made the biggest mistake of my life for which I'm now paying a big price and I don't know how to change it. I don't expect you to do anything about it and I don't need any help other than a listening ear of a good old friend that I always found it you. I simply can't hold it inside of me and I have to share it with someone I trust.

I don't even know where to begin. I think it was on our honeymoon in Dresden when Eddy hit me for the first time and despite his promises it happened every so often. The last incident, don't be alarmed I'm fine now, but it landed me in a hospital with a concussion, bruise on my face and a cut on my hand that has almost healed by now, but the emotional pain does not want to go away. I pressed charges and Eddy is in jail for six months and even after that it is questionable whether he would be able to come back home right away considering that he has to get professional help first.

249

I used to be ashamed about it and always pretended that everything was fine. Even my own family does not know what I'm going through and I am asking you to keep it that way. I don't want to worry my mom and my aunt. You probably don't know that yet, but my mom is dealing with breast cancer which gives me a great concern. I wish I was back at home. I feel so alone. I have absolutely nobody here but myself to rely on.

I would come back home if I could but I'm bed ridden due to my advanced pregnancy and the stress and shock my body had endured. The doctors worry that I might deliver sooner than my due date and told me not to travel or go anywhere in my state. So I am stuck here at least until the baby is born. I want to go back as soon as the baby is born or shortly after that.

I don't know what I will do about Eddy. When I told him I wanted to leave him; he tried to kill himself. In a way a feel bad for him; he had a horrible childhood, but that's a story for another time. I think if I stay with him he would have to get some serious help and show that he is no longer physically abusive.

I live in a shabby apartment without even a toilet on the same floor or a bathtub. That's right, you're reading it correctly. It's hard to describe, you would have to see it for yourself. But somehow I learned to deal with it for now.

I know all that sounds like complaining and that's because that's exactly what it is. I can't hold it inside me anymore and there is no one else that I can share it with. I can't even describe how alone and scared I feel. I worry what will happen in a near future. I'm really scared Nikole.

I don't expect you to do anything other perhaps just write back to me soon. It's good to read your letters and try not to worry about me too much. You know me. I'll always find some way to get through tough times.

Write or call soon,

Love,
Your best friend, Mika

Michaela debated with herself for a long time before she placed that letter addressed to her friend. She did not know why she wanted her friend to know about her life or she just needed someone to hear her. She debated to send it because she did not want her friend to worry about her and she did mention it in the letter, but knew that Nikole would worry regardless and she did not like that part. But then the need to not feel so alone and isolated won over her as the letter slid into the red mailbox too late for Michaela to change her mind. The letter was symbolic to her; an end to the silence of domestic violence. From now on, she would start a new life. She did not know if it included Eduard in it or not, but that would depend how he behaved and whether he could really change. She decided that if he went to treatment after he returned from jail and stopped blaming her for the abuse, she might consider staying with him but as soon as she sees a glimmer of violence, she would be gone from his life forever. That was his last chance and he did not even know about it yet. For now, she would concentrate on her pregnancy, on her self-care. She was done starving herself and crying because of her unfortunate experiences. She chose this life although that was the least that she expected and now she needed to deal with that. Her baby deserved better and she would do everything she could to provide for the little one the best that she could. *'I can do it'*, she told herself with determination. *'I have to.'*

She stopped in the small store at the corner to buy some groceries to last her for at least few days. She did not want to buy too much because she did not want to carry overly heavy bags, but she needed healthy food for herself and for the baby inside her to survive. She checked the mailbox in the building for any new mail. There was only a bill that needed to be paid. Eddy always took care of all the bills. Now she will have to figure out how and where to pay and to make sure that she had enough money. She knew Eddy had some cash at home and she also had some saved up money from her previous small jobs that she has done for her neighbours that now would come handy. She would have to be very modest, but felt that she did not need much.

She prepared a large salad with a tuna fish for herself that gave her more energy. With all the commotion that has been happening for the past month with the latest incident and Eddy's arrest and trial, Michaela missed the prenatal classes. She remembered Juliane whom she met only once at the class and decided to give her a call.

"Can I please speak to Juliane?"

"Speaking."

"Hi Juliane. I don't know if you remember me. It's Michaela from the prenatal class. We only met once…."

"Of course, I remember you. I wanted to call you so many times when you did not come to the classes, but I didn't have your number. Is everything ok?" This was another person that Michaela for some unknown reason felt comfortable talking honestly about things the way they were. She did not need to pretend in front of Juliane, perhaps because, Juliane was quite blunt and open with her from the start sharing her own unfortunate experiences.

"Not so great at the moment, but I will be ok. I often thought about you what you said in the café. The same day when I talked to you, there was another incident with my husband and I ended up in the hospital and Eddy in jail." Michaela provided her with details when she heard Juliane's concerns.

"I wish you called me sooner. I could have helped you."

"It would be nice if you could come over sometimes."

"I'd love that." Juliane said honestly and Michaela provided her with her address and they agreed to meet the following day.

"Is there anything that I can do for you? Or bring you something?"

"Thanks, I'm fine for now, but I let you know."

"I hope so. You're not alone Michaela." She felt great after the conversation with Juliane and she was looking forward seeing her again.

When Juliane visited Michaela the following day and found out that she should be lying in bed, she said.

"That's it. You sit down and no more doing chores." Juliane stood up and went to the kitchen to prepare some snacks.

"It's not that easy around in my kitchen."

"I think I can manage, Michaela." She called to her from the kitchen. "Don't even think about getting up."

When she returned with two cups of tea and some plate of cheese and crackers, setting them on the coffee table, she concluded.

"Let me help you, Michaela. You should not be running around doing chores and stuff when the doctor ordered you to be in bed. Think of your baby."

"Well, you're pregnant too."

"Yes. But I only started my third trimester and I feel great. You on the other hand, have doctor's orders to stay off your feet. This is nothing to take lightly, Michaela."

"I can't ask you to do my shopping, laundry, go to the bank and stuff like that."

"You don't have to. I am happy to help you out with that. It's not such a big deal for me because I have a car. You would have to carry everything in your hands and that's not acceptable. No way will I let you do that now."

"How can I ever repay you?"

Juliane thought about it for a moment and then finally said.

"You could just be my friend and stop making it so difficult when I want to help you." They both smiled at each other.

"I'm very lucky to have found such a great friend, especially since I don't have anyone else here."

"Well, same here. I'm sure you would do the same for me if I needed it."

"You can bet on it."

Juliane came to see Michaela everyday for at least an hour a day. She brought her groceries and once a week took her laundry to the Laundromat. Michaela was grateful to have such a great friend and could not imagine what she would have done without her. Juliane tried to update her about what she missed in the prenatal classes. She brought her daughter with her on some of the visits and little Hannah started to call her aunt Michaela even though they were not related.

Even Mrs. Ziegler occasionally dropped by to see Michaela asking her whether she needed anything. There were good people in the world that wanted to genuinely help and she was grateful for that. She was filled with new strength and with new-found hope.

The one person she had never expected to see at her doorsteps in this small apartment in Germany was Nikolas. Yet, there he was, standing there at her doorsteps; looking at her with concern in his brown eyes. She could not believe he came to see her. She must be dreaming. But she knew it was real; he was real, standing there in front of her.

Chapter 22

As SOON AS SHE OPENED the door she gasped, placed her right hand on her large belly and the other hand on her left cheek looking at him in disbelief. She uttered his name but no sound came out, so she tried louder, but it was only a whisper.

"Nikolas!" Then she embraced him around his neck, resting her head on his shoulder for a moment. When she pulled away from him he spoke.

"It's so great to see you, Mika. Is it ok if I come in?" She nodded and automatically pushed the door wider for him to enter pointing to the love seat for him to sit down.

"Why? Why are you here?"

"I was worried about you."

"You could have just called."

He looked around locating her phone on the windowsill. He walked towards it and picked it up.

"I tried." He put it to his ear to check. "It's dead." He held the phone up to her to check for herself.

"Oh. I didn't realize. Eddy always paid the bills. The last time I used it was about two weeks ago."

"Let me help you, Mika. You can't stay here alone now."

"If Eddy finds out you're here, he'll kill you. You don't know how jealous he is."

"I know how jealous he is. I had the honour." He said sardonically touching his chin that was long healed from the time when Eddy hit him at the wedding.

"I know he is in jail and I know he hurt you. That's not alright."

"Oh, I see. Nikole told you about it." She felt a sense of betrayal from her friend.

"Yes, because she was worried about you and so am I. That's why I came." When she was quiet, he continued. "Mika, I'm here as your friend. I have my dad's van here, I can take you back home or I can wait here with you until you have your baby, but you should not be staying here alone now." He repeated watching her as she was evaluating her options.

"What about your military....duty? Don't you need to go back soon?"

"Yes. I asked for a time off due to 'family emergency' and I have five days off. If I don't return within five days they will likely put me in jail for disobeying once I'm back."

"Then you can't stay with me until I have my baby. I'm not due till next three weeks. I don't want you to get into trouble because of me."

"That doesn't matter. I'm not leaving you here alone." He said stubbornly.

Michaela did not want to stay in Germany by herself, especially now that she realized she did not even have a working phone, which could be taken care of easily although she did not have much money left to pay for it, and besides she did not want to be alone despite Juliane's daily help. She needed some time to think and talk to Nikolas about it. She could not believe that he came all this way just because of her to help her but she was glad he was here.

"Are you hungry?" She asked suddenly. "I'm starving. I haven't eaten anything yet and I don't have much food left in the fridge."

"What do you feel like?"

"Pizza."

"Alright, I saw a pizzeria at the corner. I'll be back soon."

She was reaching for her wallet trying to give him some money, but he refused to take it from her.

"I have some German Marks. Don't worry about it. What do you like on your pizza?"

When Nikolas returned with the pizza, they ate quietly until Michaela interrupted the silence.

"I still can't believe you're here."

"I told you before that I would be there for you whenever you needed."

"Nik, I feel like I messed up my whole life and I don't know what to do now. I'm scared and you're right, I don't want to stay here by myself. I don't want to stay in this cold apartment that doesn't even have a bathroom inside. I can't imagine staying here alone with the baby. This is not a place to raise a child."

"Then let me take you back home to your mom." Michaela nodded her agreement.

"That would be probably the best, but you know my mom has cancer."

"Yes. I'm sorry, Mika about your mom and about everything that you've been through." He placed his hand over hers as she was reaching for a drink. "Your mom will get through that and so will you. I'm sure she will be so happy to see you and her new grandchild once the baby is born." Michaela smiled at the thought of her mom becoming a grandma, holding a newborn baby in her arms. She wanted her mom nearby. She wanted to be home close to her and she needed her or her aunt's help with the baby.

"That would be nice. I am so scared, Nik, not just because of the childbirth but I have no idea how to take care of a baby." He looked at her lovingly holding both of her hands in his.

"You will be a great mom, Mika. I just know it." She smiled at him.

"Ok, Nikolas. I have decided. Take me home to my mom's."

"When do you want to leave?"

"The sooner the better, but I have to pack up and take care of few other things before we leave. I'm sure you must be tired from the long drive. So why don't you stay one night here and we go tomorrow morning. Also, my friend will drop by this evening to check on me so I need to tell her that I will be leaving."

"Are you sure I can stay here overnight?"

"Of course. Don't be silly. Where else would you go?"

"I could go to a hotel."

"Don't be ridiculous. Why would you pay for a hotel? And besides, I could use the company tonight. We can watch some movies or just talk.

"I like that. Alright, I'll sleep here on the sofa if that's ok with you and tomorrow we go back home."

"Sounds like a good plan." He took another bite of his pizza noticing his painting he gave Michaela as a wedding gift.

"You still have that?" He pointed to the picture with the pizza still in his hand.

"Of course I do. I love it. I don't want to leave it here." Remembering Eddy's reaction towards the painting and the fight it caused when she wanted to bring it with her. "Eddy never had an appreciation for art."

"Will you help me take the crib apart? I'd like to take it with me for the baby along with some other baby things."

"Sure thing."

When they were done eating, Michaela showed him around her modest apartment and explained to him that if he needed the washroom it was on the bottom floor and he needs to take a soap and towel with him. Nikolas just shook his head in disbelief.

"I can't believe he would bring you to a place like that especially when you're expecting. You're right; this is no place to raise a child."

"I know. I just don't know what will happen. I don't think I'm ready to divorce him, although I know I can't live like that anymore and I don't mean just the apartment."

"I know, Mika, but try not to worry about it now. You'll have time to figure things out later. Now you should just concentrate on yourself and on your baby. I'll get started on the crib." Then he stroked her cheek gently looking in her eyes affectionately. "Everything will be ok." She reached for his wrist, closed her eyes holding his hand on her cheek for a little while longer.

"Thank you for coming. You don't know how much that means to me."

Then she stood on her tiptoes trying to kiss him on his full lips. She was surprised when he stepped backwards away from her.

"Mika. Please." He exhaled his heart pounding faster.

"I'm sorry; I understand that I look hideous to you with my big belly."

"Mika! How can you say something like that!? That's not true. You were always beautiful pregnant or not. That's not why I pulled away and it's not because I don't want to kiss you. I dreamed so many times about holding you in my arms, kissing you, but.....we can't. You're married." He reminded her of the reality.

"You're right. I'm sorry." She said again. "I don't know what is happening with me. Maybe it's the pregnancy, the hormones. I've been so sensitive and emotional lately."

"You don't have to apologize. I do have strong feelings for you. The truth is I never stopped loving you, Mika but I'm afraid if I kissed you I would not be able to stop."

Michaela wished she could turn back in time and be back in Bulgaria. Why did she not see how much Nikolas has always loved her? She fantasized about reciprocating his love back last summer when they had a chance. Why was she so blind? She had love at her reach all along and did not see it. Why she was so easily swept off her feet by a foreigner; by a stranger that she did not know anything about and who has mistreated her so many times? But she did not see it until much later. Now it was too late for her and Nikolas. She was already married to someone else, expecting his child. She chose someone else; she chose Eddy and now she was painfully aware that she has made the greatest mistake of her life.

Nikolas was always a great friend and he has not disappointed her now. The fact that he did not take advantage while her husband was in jail despite his feelings spoke volumes to her and she had a great respect for him. She was glad he was the way he was; honorable and gracious. She was the one that would have succumbed to his gentle touch perhaps because she felt vulnerable and lonely but she was glad that Nikolas had his common sense with him since hers has left her ever since she fell in love with the wrong man.

Nikolas was here when she needed him the most. He was the one person she knew she could always count on. She just wished he was more than a friend; she longed things were different. She wished that he was the one; that he was the father of her unborn child. She wished she had started a relationship with him back in Bulgaria; not with Eddy. But that was all that she could do; *wish* for something that could not be. She made a mess out of her life and now she had to deal with harsh reality that she did not like.

She still cared about her husband and although she had strong feelings for him, her love was diminishing each time he laid a hand on her in anger.

"Can you hold me, just as a friend?" Nikolas embraced her and they were standing there together for a very long time while Michaela quietly wept, her head buried in his chest. He stroked her hair, comforting her and letting her cry it out. Nikolas had no idea how much she needed him now; and she just realized that.

Nikolas could not have come at a better time. She was sure that she was making the right decision of going back home despite her advanced pregnancy. She would go to her mom for a while. She could not wait to see her family and she also needed to be there for her mom who was struggling with her health just as Michaela needed her mother at a turning point in her life. She did not know what would happen later on once Eddy came out of jail and she did not want to think about it now. She just wanted to feel Nikolas' arms around her pretending for a moment longer that things were different.

When Juliane came to see her that evening as she did every night for the past two weeks, Michaela explained to her she was going back to Czechoslovakia to be with her family and did not know when or if she would be back.

"I think it's for the best."

"What about the baby? You shouldn't be travelling."

"Nikolas will be driving the whole way and whether I sit at home or in the car for a day, I don't think it will make such a big difference. You've been great; helping me so much. I don't know how I would have done it without you." She told Juliane.

"Take care of yourself and call me once you have the baby."

"I will; I promise." Michaela gave Juliane her address and phone number at her mother's to keep in touch. The friends hugged as Juliane was leaving the apartment.

"I hope to see you again soon with your little one."

"Me too."

"It was nice to meet you Nikolas." She waved to him. "Have a safe trip back."

Michaela spoke to Mr. Ziegler who was the landlord about her leaving while her husband was away in jail as she could not afford to pay the rent without any income. Mrs. Ziegler tried to reassure her saying that she did not have to worry about their things as long as they can rent it out to a student the way it was at least until Mr. Verner returned and resumed the payments. Michaela said it was fine with her but they should also speak to her husband and that she would let him know about it. Once Michaela packed up her personal belongings, the baby things and wrapped up Nikolas' painting, she decided to write a short letter to Eddy.

April 4, 1985

Dear Eddy,

I'm sorry things turned out for us the way they did. I never wanted you to end up in jail, but you cannot keep hitting me whenever you feel angry. I can't live like that anymore and I will not put up with that any longer. The only way we could possibly stay together is if you went for some anger management classes or therapy and really changed.

Meantime, I am going back to Czechoslovakia to stay with my mom. I just found out she has breast cancer and she needs me as much as I need her. I don't want to stay in Germany by myself with the baby, especially not in the apartment that does not have a bathroom and it's too cold for a newborn. I can't imagine raising a child here.

I don't know what will happen in the near future or if we can get through this together, but for now that's what I have decided to do. I will write to you and I'll send you pictures once the baby is born. I spoke with the landlord, Mr. Ziegler and explained the situation and gave him my key. I am not planning to come back to this apartment even if we stay together. I left everything there as it was except my personal things and the baby things that I will need. Mr. Ziegler wants to rent the apartment out to some students the way it is, along with the furniture, dishes and everything else that's left in the apartment at least while you're away if you give your permission. When you have a chance, please give him a call, otherwise he expects a monthly rent and I can't afford to pay it as I have no income. That is another reason why I have to leave.

You know where I'll be. You can write to me to my mom's address if you want. I don't want bad feelings between us. I still care about you.

Michaela

She wrote her mother's address and phone number where he could get into touch with her. The following morning when she was ready to leave, she looked back at the apartment before she locked it up and brought the key to Mr. Ziegler. She was quite certain she would not see this place again. She said her goodbyes and thanked them for all their help. She stopped to say goodbye to Mr. Ehrlichmann before she left. He was very sad to see her go as he got attached to her and lost the only visitor that he had in a long time. Somehow she knew she would not see these people again.

Verena was on the hallway getting some water into her bucket when Michaela was passing by. She looked at Nikolas checking him out, obviously liking what she saw. Michaela had déjà vu from the time when she and Eddy first met her. This time instead of greeting Michaela, who had no interest to interact with her since the closet incident with her husband, Verena addressed Nikolas.

"Hello, I haven't seen you here before. What's your name?" She said provocatively right in front on Michaela who harrumphed looking back at Verena with chagrin on her face and without saying anything, she simply told Nikolas in their language to ignore her. Nikolas busy carrying Michaela's suitcase and the crib did just that, leaving Verena wondering who he was.

Verena uttered under her nose "Lucky slut, she always gets the handsome ones", but neither of them heard her as they were already at the bottom floor.

As she was sitting in the minivan looking out the window she was filled with hope of new beginning; with the longing of better future. Funny enough this was the same feeling she had when she first married Eddy and hoped she would have a better future with him in Germany. Now she could not wait to escape from the country that did not promise anything good for her and where she barely knew anyone. Although she still had feelings for Eduard and wished things were different, she made up her mind that she would no longer put up with the abuse. She deserved better and her baby definitely deserved a peaceful and loving home. She was excited that she would be with her mother and her aunt and could barely wait to see them. They would be probably quite surprised to see her though and she would have to tell them what happened once she was there and that was something she did not look forward to.

Although it was a long ride, she enjoyed the ride with Nikolas as he was always a great company. They listened to music, singing together in the car. She has forgotten how much she enjoyed singing. When they did not sing; they talked about everything and anything. It was great to finally speak in her language. Nikolas entertained her with his early experiences, from the first few months from the mandatory conscript, which was nothing to envy.

"So Captain Zlodinsky comes, spills a bucket of soapy water all over the floor, throws a toothbrush beside my feet to use as a 'brush' to scrub the floors and tells me 'it better be spotless and if you think what is wet is clean you're not going to bullshit me'. To help the matter of course", he said sarcastically, "there are these second year solders that feel privileged and entitled, because they're there a full year longer than me, so they can basically bully the younger guys. So there they are, walking with their muddy boots all over the floor while I'm on my fours scrubbing the floor with the tiny toothbrush and with my bloody knuckles, while they laugh and yell at me 'you missed the spot' smudging the clean spot with their boots. Of course I had to clean it all over again before the Captain came." Michaela laughed.

"I'm sorry, Nik. I know it's not funny. It's terrible what you were going through, but it's the way you tell the story that makes it funny."

"I'm glad you're laughing with me, not at me." He commented jokingly, winking at her. "Just like the time when I had to pretend to be the cuckoo clock; that was a 'funny' time too."

"A cuckoo clock?"

"Yes, you know, cuckoo, cuckoo." Nikolas made exaggerated sounds to make Michaela laugh even more. "Yes, you stick your head in and out of the closet and you do the cuckoo sound for the sheer entertainment of the older soldiers to avoid the beating." Michaela got suddenly serious.

"That's terrible. Why do they do that, Nik?"

"Because they can; because they want to have the power and control."

"I hope the conscript doesn't change you into someone like that."

"That's not who I'm, Mika. I think it comes inside out, not the other way around. I don't need to prove anything to myself or to anyone else. I don't need to impose my power over anyone to feel better about myself. I know who I am and wouldn't treat anyone in such a degrading manner because I know how it feels. Not all the older guys are like that. There are some really good men there."

Nikolas was a good story-teller and kept Michaela entertained although some of the stories were sad. He always managed to make her laugh or interested in whatever they talked about and it was never forced. After they crossed the German/Czech border the sun was setting down.

"We can sleep in a hotel somewhere Nik when you start to feel tired. Alright?"

"I'm ok for now, but you can nap if you're feeling tired."

"I just might, the pregnancy makes me tired. I feel like I will be pregnant forever. I honestly don't think this baby will ever come out." He smiled at her as she closed her eyes and soon dozed off.

Nikolas pulled over in front of Hesperia hotel in Olomouc before midnight.

"I'm sorry; I can barely keep my eyes open. I don't want to push it. I hope you're ok with staying here overnight." When he inquired about a vacancy, he was told that there were only couple's suites available.

"Do you want two separate rooms or are you alright if we share the room? I promise I'll be a gentleman."

"The couple's suite will be much cheaper Nik than getting two separate rooms. It's only for one night. And I know you're a gentleman; you always were."

"I knew that would come and bite me one day." He joked.

After they got few essential things from the car for the night they settled in.

Michaela woke up to some mild pain in her lower abdomen and shifted uncomfortably on her side of the bed. Nikolas was soundly sleeping beside her. She wanted to touch his face, but did not want to wake him. *Go back to sleep.* She told herself, but as soon as she started to doze off, the pain returned. Although the pain was bearable, when it returned every fifteen minutes, Michaela started to be concerned. Surely that could not be it. Surely that was not how labour felt like. It was like mild menstrual cramping. She remembered her mother telling her that once her contractions started when she was pregnant with her, it was like a terrible cramp and she could not even move due to the excruciating pain. Michaela wished she attended all the prenatal classes; she only remembered the movie that she saw and she expected something a lot worse. She could not be giving birth now; it's been only thirty seven weeks the doctor told her just four days ago. She tried to relax and go back to sleep but could not sleep as the pain kept returning. She checked the time on her small watch; it was only 3:23 in the morning. She did not know what to do and she was getting worried. What if something was wrong?

"Nik? Nik." She gently shook him by his arm.

"What is it, Mika?"

"I have some pain that keeps coming back about every ten or fifteen minutes." Nikolas woke up from daze of sleep.

"Are you in labour?"

"I'm not sure. It's probably just the Braxton Hicks contractions which should pass after a short while. It's probably just a false alarm."

"Are you sure about it or should we go to a hospital?"

"I can't be having this baby now. I'm not due yet and besides the doctor said that first time mothers usually go past their due date. I have almost three more weeks to go. See? It's fine now; no pain and even when it comes back it's quite mild. I'm sorry I woke you up. I am just a bit scared. But it's nothing. Just go back to sleep."

"Are you sure it's nothing?"

"Yeah, I'll see Dr. Novak tomorrow when we arrive in Kosice. She is a gynecologist I saw before I went to Germany."

Every time the pain stopped she tried to relax telling herself that there is no reason for her to be panicking. But the intensity of the pain increased alarming Nikolas who sat up on the bed and put a nightlight on as he noticed Michaela tensing up in pain. Her breathing got heavier and faster.

"Are you alright?" Ridiculous question he quickly thought as he clearly saw her being in pain.

"Scratch what I said. The pain is not mild anymore. It's getting intense and more frequent. I still don't know if that is the labour, but I want to see a doctor just to make sure everything is ok." Nikolas jumped to his feet.

"Ok, no need to panic, we'll do that later. I'm not going to be one of those guys that drives to the hospital forgetting the pregnant woman." He tried to joke to calm himself down making Michaela laugh for a moment before she felt intense pain again that made her wince. The truth was he was scared for Michaela. "Let me take you to the hospital now." Reluctantly, Michaela got dressed in between her contractions and with Nikolas' help. He checked at the reception where the nearest hospital was and told Michaela to wait for him in the lobby while he brought the van closer to the front entrance so she would not have to walk too far. By that point, Michaela's pain was severe returning every five minutes. Despite the intensity of the pain, she could not believe that this was it. She was going to have the baby soon; sooner than she had imagined.

Chapter 23

NIKOLAS WHEELED HER INTO THE Birthing and Maternity Department of the University Hospital in Olomouc. Michaela's contractions were occurring every two minutes with excruciating pain. This must have been what her mother talked about; this must be it. *I'm going to die from the pain. This is not happening.* Michaela thought as the pain was so intense she could barely move. Nikolas banged the nurse's desk for some assistance when nobody was paying any attention to Michaela.

"Excuse me. I have a new mom about to deliver a baby." While Nikolas was talking in panic with the nurse, Michaela stood up and walked to the bathroom in extreme pain, but she had to go. When Nikolas turned away, she was gone; emerging from the bathroom few meters away.

"Where did you disappear? You gave me a scare. Come sit down, the nurse will examine you shortly", he said, but Michaela was not feeling well. The pain was overwhelming her creating a great pressure and she returned to the bathroom, clutching the metal handle with each new contraction. When she came out, the nurse ushered her to a cod, scolding her when Michaela wanted to go back to the bathroom.

"No, I have to examine you. You don't want to have the baby in the toilet, do you?"

This was so embarrassing, especially in front of her friend, Nikolas who refused to leave her side although she tried to object, sending him away.

"But I have the feeling that I have to go...." She told the nurse in embarrassment while Nikolas was by her side.

"Don't worry about it. We've seen it all here. It's the contractions that put the pressure." After examining her, the nurse said.

"Eight centimeters dilated." Michaela suddenly felt wetness under her that she could not control.

"Your water just broke. Wheel her into the delivery room. This one will go next. She is at nine centimeters now." She yelled out to her co-worker who pushed Michaela's cod to another room; to a delivery room. Nikolas grabbed Michaela's bag and her shoes and her clothes that she had to take off replacing it with a hospital gown and followed her into the delivery room.

"No, you're not going." The nurse stopped him putting a hand in front of him.

"I'm not letting her go through this alone." He said stubbornly. The nurse made an understanding grimace.

"First time dad, hah? Alright. The doctors don't like people lingering in the delivery room, but.....alright, put at least this on." He did not correct her as she handed him a hospital scrubs with rubber buddies to slip on his feet.

"She is in so much pain. Is she going to be alright?"

"She will be just fine. You will have the baby in no time."

"What about epidural or something to ease up her pain? Did you even ask if she wanted an epidural?"

"It's too late for that. She will have the baby very soon. It would have just prolonged the delivery at this point. You brought her in just in time. Now go on." She pointed to the delivery room where Michaela has been taken.

As much as she felt embarrassed in front of Nikolas, seeing her all sweaty, in pain and with her legs spread out to deliver at any moment, she was glad he was there. Nobody else she knew was there with her and she needed someone with her; someone who cared about her. Nikolas out of respect, stayed close to Michaela's head, holding her hand the whole time. She quizzed his hand, nearly breaking it during the delivery. The pain was so excruciating Michaela thought she would surely not survive it. She did not even scream; only panted heavily with each strong contraction. She had to push; it eased her pain when she could just push.

267

"I don't think I can take it anymore. I just want to go home, Nik. Can I go…" She did not finish the silly question as the pain had overtaken her draining her of all the energy she had left and before she knew it she had to do it all over again and again until the baby was born.

"You can do it, Mika. It's almost behind you. I'm here for you." He wished he could ease her pain somehow, but felt completely powerless.

"Push." The doctor urged her and she did again and again, until she heard a small cry and an overwhelming relief came over her she felt the baby come out of her. Suddenly she was cold; she was so cold, her legs were visibly shivering.

"It's normal; it's just a shock to the body after the delivery. It will pass soon." One of the nurses explained as she placed a warm blanket over lower part of Michaela's body that felt good.

"Where is my baby?"

"She is fine; they're just cleaning her up." Michaela suddenly felt a great emptiness; as something was missing. She wanted to hold her baby; she wanted to see her.

"She?"

"Yes. It's a healthy baby girl. Congratulations." They handed her a little bundle in a pink blanket where a tiny little face was sticking out with dark eyes and surprising dark hair. The nurse stuck a little pink hat on the newborn's head. Michaela set up on the bed and took the baby into her arms talking to her daughter in a gentle voice for the first time.

"You can start nursing her."

"I have milk already?"

"Colostrum. It's very important for the baby. The milk will come in couple of days later, but you have to nurse to stimulate your breasts, to make sure you get the milk."

Without any shame, Michaela opened her night gown revealing right breast despite Nikolas still standing beside her. He was pale as the white hospital wall and one of the nurses was watching him to make sure he did not pass out during the delivery, but he stood his ground; stood tall and happy to see Michaela and her baby in her arms.

"The baby is 2, 530 grams. A little tiny peanut but healthy." The nurse smiled at Michaela. You must be a proud daddy." She looked at Nikolas whose handsome face was still pale. Neither Michaela nor Nikolas corrected the nurse that he was not the father of the baby.

"She is so beautiful, Mika. What a little miracle."

"I can't believe she is here."

"What are you going to name her?"

"I don't know yet. I want to talk to Eddy; to let him know his daughter was born."

Michaela stayed in the hospital for the next two days as 'little peanut' as the nurses called her little baby girl without a name had trouble nursing. The baby was so small that she did not have the strength to suck and fell asleep on her mother's breast shortly after. Nikolas went out and bought her a breast pump that was necessary for Michaela to pump and she finger fed her baby through a tiny little tube that she attached to her finger. The beginnings were difficult and she could not wait to leave the hospital. Her breasts were sore and so was her bottom as she had a fourth degree tear up despite the small baby that she delivered. She could barely sit comfortably. They provided her with some pain killers, but Michaela refused to take it because she did not want the baby getting any medication through her milk that was slow to arrive, but once it came, 'little peanut' and her mom became more proficient in nursing.

"It's a new skill for you and for the baby." One of the nurses told her at the beginning and she was right. Nikolas stayed with Michaela in Olomouc until she was released from the hospital and they got all ready for several hours ride back home to Kosice. Michaela was glad that she had purchased the stroller with the car seat attached which was necessary for her to take the baby home which Nikolas figured out how to attach in the van. She called her mom and her aunt to give them the great news about the healthy baby girl that was born on April 5, 1985 at 5:57 in the morning and let them know that Nikolas was bringing her home. Despite all the questions that her mother and aunt had for her, she did not want to explain everything to them over the phone and reassured them that she was fine and so was the baby and they will know everything soon enough. She was too tired and she had to braise herself for how she would reveal all the changes in her life.

"At least tell me my only grandchild's name, Michaela." Her mother insisted impatiently who was back from the hospital herself.

"A little peanut." Before more questions followed, Michaela hung up the phone trying to get the strength to call her husband at the jail. She did not know whether they would allow her to talk to him but she was ready to explain the circumstances that he is the father of a little girl. She had mixed feelings when she heard his voice. A big part of her still missed him and wanted him back the way he was when she first met him, although now looking back she was thinking of some of the warning signs even before she married him that she failed to see because she was blinded by love. The time when he stopped speaking with her when she wanted to enter the silly 'beauty contest' and he was so angry with her for that or the time when Nikolas warned her about his violent temper towards his brother whom he grabbed by the neck; or the time when he punched Nikolas because of his jealousy. She thought of how he reacted when she first told him about the pregnancy and then about the rape and his aggressive nature blaming her for what David did to her. She was not sorry he punched David in the face because he deserved it, but this was how Eddy solved problems and she only hoped he could change because she believed that deep down he was not an evil person; he was someone who endured a lot of abuse and trauma in his life when he was younger. He would have to change his ways if he wanted to be around their daughter. She feared how he would react once she told him about having a little baby girl earlier than the due date and in Czechoslovakia, but she had to tell him. The letter was on its way explaining why she was leaving.

"A girl?" He said with a disappointment in his voice. "I thought you were having my son."

"I didn't know what I was going to have. I found out once the baby was born. You don't sound very happy about it. I just been recently through excruciating pain delivering our child and this is your first reaction? I thought you would be happier."

"No, yes, I'm happy that the baby is healthy and that you're ok. You have to show her to me." Michaela took a deep breath. She had to tell him the truth. He would find out soon anyway and this was the best opportunity to tell him.

"I'm in Czechoslovakia, heading to Kosice."

"What the fuck, Michaela. You left Germany? You left me? Fuck, Michaela, I don't even know whether I should be angry with you first; because you left me or because you were not supposed to travel and the baby was born earlier than it was supposed to. You were lucky that something worse didn't happen to the baby."

"Eddy, please stop yelling at me and let me explain."

"What's there to explain, you left…."

"I can't do it alone and I can't live with you always….."

"Always what?" He yelled.

"Yelling at me like you do now and hitting me every time you get angry or drunk. You need help Eddy and that's the only way I would come back if you really changed. I'm going to stay with my mother for now. My letter I've sent you explains it more and I'll write to you soon again. I have to go now. The baby needs to be fed."

"Wait."

"What?"

"What did you name her?"

"I didn't yet. That's why I called you."

"I wish I could see her." He said it more calmly with a longing in his voice.

"She is beautiful. She has your dark eyes and surprisingly a lot of dark hair."

"Since you didn't give me a boy that I wanted so much and I can't even see my little girl now, let me at least pick her name, Michaela."

"What did you have in mind?"

"Orchid or Orquidea."

"Like the flower? I never even knew it was a girl's name."

"Well it is and it means love, beauty and sophistication and it represents eternity. It's more common name in Spain, but that's my way to try to connect with where I partly come from since I never really knew my real father." Michaela thought about the name for a little while still holding the receiver to her ear; she rolled each variation of the name on her tongue to get the feel for it. She finally said.

"I would have never thought about it and it is very unusual name, but I like it. Alright; Orchid it is."

"Thank you. It means a lot to me. I will do what it takes for you and Orchid to come back home to me. Please send me pictures; I want to see her. Maybe that will help me get through this."

"I will."

"I love you Michaela." She swallowed a lump that was forming in her throat.

"Me too." And she hung up the phone tears rolling down her face. Nikolas was watching her, rocking crying Orchid in his arms. She never told Eddy that Nikolas was with her during this difficult time because she feared his reaction.

"Are you alright?" She nodded wiping her tears away with the back of her hand.

"I will be." She held her arms out for him to pass her the baby for nursing.

"So, Orchid?" He asked her with interest as he was passing her the baby.

"Yes. Orchid because it represents the love, beauty and some history between me and Eddy." Michaela thought about the beautiful orchids that Eddy often bought her as a sign of his love. Nikolas bit his tongue thinking that he had longer history with Michaela than Eddy but he kept the comment for himself.

Shortly after Nikolas brought Michaela and her little daughter safely to her mother's home, he had to report to the military leaving back to Bratislava the same night. Michaela was grateful to him for all what he did for her and had hard time parting from him. She knew she could not do it without him and was glad to be back at home. Her mother recently finished the chemotherapy treatment and was on her way to recovery, filled with a new hope especially when she saw her daughter and her new granddaughter after such a long time. Her mother and Aunt Sylvie gathered around them with number of unanswered questions.

"What did you call this 'little peanut'?"

"Orchid."

"Orchid?" Klaudia and Sylvie said almost simultaneously surprise in both of their faces was quite evident.

"Now what kind of name is Orchid? It certainly isn't Slovak." Aunt Sylvie put her hands on her hips, lifting one of her eyebrows higher than the other. Michaela always wondered how she was able to do it to such an extreme.

"No. It's Spanish name from Orquidea, but we just simplified it to Orchid."

"Simplified it? It's nothing simple about that name. She will not even have a name's day to celebrate and kids will be teasing her." Aunt Sylvie continued to give Michaela hard time about the baby's name.

"In Germany they don't celebrate name's days anyway. Eduard is part Spanish after his father so he wanted to maintain part of that by giving the baby this exotic flower name that means love and beauty."

"I don't know Michaela why you guys couldn't pick a normal name." When Klaudia saw her daughter tearing up, she stepped in.

"Now that's enough, Sylvia. Stop pestering her about the name. I like it. It's beautiful and unique." She hugged her daughter stroking her hair in reassurance.

"I can just see how much she will hate her name when she is older."

"Oh, Sylvia, seriously, come on now! Everyone hates their name anyway. I remember the hard time you gave me about Michaela's name. *'They're gonna call her Miska - the little mouse'* you said and it could not be further from the truth." Then she turned to her daughter again and said. "It's a lovely name." Then she picked up her granddaughter admiring the little cutie.

"Now to more important questions; where is Eddy and why did you come so suddenly back with all your things?" These were the dreaded questions that were unavoidable. Michaela had to tell them the truth, even if it was upsetting to them.

"I knew he would hurt you." Aunt Sylvie who generally lacked emotional filter blurred it out despite best of her intensions. "I told you he was dangerous. You can't go back to him."

"He will go to treatment and I know he can change."

"Oh, please Mika, don't be so naive. Men like Eddy never change for the better. Do you think he will learn anything good in jail?" Before Michaela had a chance to respond, Aunt Sylvie answered her own question with agitation in her voice. "Of course he probably will learn how not to get caught again. I'm sure his inmates will give him some pointers."

"Stop being so stringent, Sylvia." Klaudia reprimanded her sister again.

"Well, if you were, she would not be in this situation in the first place, alone with a new born baby and abusive husband in jail across the border. That's really a great prospect for your only daughter." She told Klaudia still shaking her head in disbelief of what she had just learnt."

"Now look what you've done." Klaudia scolded Sylvia when she saw Michaela putting her head in her palms crying; she tried to comfort her daughter.

"Just stop arguing already about my stupid choices. I might have made some bad decisions but I have a beautiful baby girl and I don't regret that." The two older women looked at each other. It was Sylvia who spoke first again.

"I'm sorry, Mika. I'm just so upset because I predicted something like that would happen and I think it could have been avoided. We both love you so much and we'll help you in any way we can. Right, Klaudia?"

"Of course. You can stay here with the baby, as long as you need to and I help you with her."

Michaela looked up at them wiping her eyes and blowing her noise in not so lady like manner, but it did not matter. She nodded her head.

"Thank you." All three women hugged in a circle getting strength from each other.

Michaela picked up Orchid who started crying and put her to her breast for feeding.

"Now tell me how did Nikolas have gotten himself involved in all that?"

"He came to help me when I told Nicole what was happening."

"Now that's great." This time, her mother said sardonically. "You tell your friends but you don't say anything to your own family."

"I didn't want to worry you when I found out you're sick."

"Well, thank you for your concern, but I'm fine and you still should have told us." Her mother scolded her.

"Anyway, the two of you made a beautiful baby." Aunt Sylvie said when Orchid grabbed a hold of her finger tightly. Orchid was cute with her dark big eyes and a smile on her face whenever they talked to her, but most of the time she cried.

Dr. Novak whom Michaela went to see with the baby told her Orchid was colicky and that could be especially hard for a new mother.

"Try to rest with the baby when she is sleeping to get your rest, otherwise you will burn out quickly." The doctor advised.

It seemed little Orchid cried day and night, but especially at night when everyone wanted to sleep. Klaudia was a great help getting up to the baby when Michaela was exhausted and needed some sleep, but Michaela woke up anyway to nurse the baby or pump the milk. She did not like giving the baby bottle as she read that the baby would then not want to nurse. Michaela felt that was all that she did, nurse, changed diapers, burped the baby, pumped the milk, bathed her and it went on and on like that every day. Orchid woke her up usually every two or three hours and Michaela felt exhausted, emotional and irritable. She even forgot to write to her husband as she promised being reminded of him when she received his letter.

April 27, 1985

Dear Michaela,

> *I miss you so much. I can't wait to see you and the baby. Send me some pictures.*
>
> *I had a lot of time to think and I realized I have done many stupid things and I'm sorry that I hurt you. I know you heard it from me many times, but I really mean it. I want to make things right between us. I really hope that's not the end of us and that you'll come back to me. We have a child together. I think we owe it to Orchid to stay together and make it work.*
>
> *I never loved anyone as much as I love you, Michaela. Being in jail is horrible. It's only the thought of having you and little Orchid that keeps me going. Write to me soon.*
>
> *Forever yours,*
> *Eddy*

The letter was short but sweet and it reminded Michaela of the time when she and Eddy wrote to each other after they left Bulgaria. He was right, she thought. They had a child together and they had to make it work. She missed the old Eddy that she knew at the beginning before he ever laid a hand on her in anger. He had to know that she still loved him but that he could not be hurting her like he has and she decided to write it in her letter.

August 29, 1985

Dear Eddy,

> *I was happy when I got a letter from you. I would like to make it work between us too but I will not put up with you ever hitting me again. You can't treat me like that. You promised you will get help with your anger and I hope you keep your promise, not just for me but for your daughter.*
>
> *I miss you too although little Orchid keeps me occupied all day and night. I'm exhausted all the time and I wish you were with me. Orchid cries a lot but on the other hand she is a great joy. I wish you could see her. She is so cute with beautiful dark eyes, just like yours. I've included few pictures for you to see her.*
>
> *I hope we can get through that all but I don't want to return to that horrible apartment with the baby. You will have to find something more appropriate if you want me to come back to Germany.*

> *Sincerely yours,*
> *Michaela*

Eduard being one of the bigger guys in jail was seldom picked on due to his shear masculine body but the boss among the inmates, named Gandolf, did not care. He had his people standing behind him at all times and doing his dirty work. Eduard did not know whether Gandolf was his real name or whether it was just a name to portray a bad ass outlaw and fighter with a power within the jail and frankly he did not care, trying to keep to himself, until one day Gandolf tried to pick a fight with him surrounded with his bodies Gandolf's Gorilla, called GG as the other inmates called him for his little brain and big muscle and Armpit as he was called for his stench and his head locking abilities. Both GG and Armpit were the protective hands of Gandolf who himself was small in stature yet he was feared for his power and connections and he was highly respected because he awaited a trial for murdering a cop. Eddy was not popular among the inmates for the domestic violence crime he committed ranking just slightly above the child sexual perpetrators and rapists, but certainly behind the robbers, embezzlers and murderers like Gandolf who appeared to have most power.

"It came to my attention you haven't been paying your monthly fee." Gandolf said in a sweetly menacing voice.

"What are you talking about?" Eddy asked carelessly.

"You pay monthly fee to Gandolf for protection." Armpit explained to him with annoyance.

"I don't need your protection." Eddy retorted with chagrin on his face that made GG step closer to him snapping at him.

"You're mistaking, bitch. You certainly need protection." Armpit, whose nickname suited him well as he brought his stench whenever he walked by, lifted his fist to Eddy; which made him jump to his feet, looking as tall as Armpit and GG. He would not get so easily intimidated by bullies.

"I can punch him now, maybe he will understand." Armpit suggested looking to his boss for directions, but Gandolf lifted a hand in the air to stop Armpit from the punch for a moment.

"See, we don't like violence, just like we don't like wife beaters. If you gonna fight, fight with someone your own size or pay up for your protection." Eddy understood that he would pay for protection from Gandolf and his gorillas and tried to reason in futility as he was sizing up his opponents.

"I don't have any money, so I'm afraid I can't be much help to you."

"That's too bad." Gandolf shook his head and gave signal to Armpit who unexpectedly grabbed Eddy from behind holding him while GG started to punch Eddy in the stomach and couple of punches to his face for good measure, making him fall to his knees.

"Take his smokes." Gandolf ordered GG then he lowered himself close to Eddy's face.

"Next time you better have some dough for me or it will hurt even more." GG forcefully pushed Eduard backwards who was already on his knees, spitting blood.

"Hey, you're alright?" His cell buddy, a small but stoutly build man who called himself Billy asked him when he came back to the cell seeing Eddy beat up. Eddy wiped his bloody lip and sat on his bed. When he did not bother to answer, Billy continued talking.

"Let me guess. Gandolf with his Gorillas?" Eddy nodded.

"He's the king here and his gorillas will always have his back and start fights with you. I pay them two hundred Marks each month so they would leave me alone."

"I don't have any money to pay them and even if I had, I wouldn't give them anything." Eddy said with disgust on his face.

When GG and Armpit picked a fight with Eddy in the showers couple weeks later because he refused to pay anything, he was ready for a fight as now he knew who he was dealing with and learnt their methods of how to enforce their power. Although he got badly beaten too, as there were two against one, he held his own landing few punches of his own, braking GG's nose and braking Armpit's forefinger when he tried to put him in a head lock; a move he learned long time ago in a Juvenile detention for a second degree murder of his father.

The guards eventually separated them earning Eddy isolation for next three days without food and water to teach him a lesson. The isolation would not have been so bad for him if he was not hungry and especially thirsty. There was nothing for him to do; he only had a race with his own thoughts. That's what usually drove men in isolation crazy. Eddy on the other hand tried to occupy his thoughts, thinking about Michaela and his new baby girl. He tried to do some pushups to keep in shape but did not want to do too much exercise as he was already quite dehydrated.

However, when he returned from the isolation, he gained a new respect from the other inmates including GG and Armpit along with their boss did not demand any money from him. On the contrary, Gandolf tried to get Eddy on his side in vain as Eduard did not want anything to do with them; but at least his gorillas left him alone as did other inmates.

The only thing that kept Eddy going were Michaela's letters and the pictures of his baby girl that he placed above his bed. Michaela and Eduard kept writing to each other about every two or three weeks until he was released from jail. In his last letter he wrote her that he was recently released and is on probation starting soon the anger management group to deal with his issues as part of his probation and is not allowed to leave the country for another sixteen weeks until he completed the program and ended his probation. He reassured her that he will find a new apartment for them soon; having an idea what he needed to do to get his wife back.

Chapter 24

"**Y**OU'VE GOT TO HELP ME." Eddy said anxiously. "I have to get her back."

"If she left you; she probably had a good reason."

"She didn't leave me, but we couldn't stay in that old place."

"Well, what do I got to do with it? You just show up on my doorsteps after not hearing from you for months....."

"You know they just let me out three days ago. I told you what happened."

"Yes, I know and they had a good reason to put you in jail in the first place."

"Come on. Don't be an ass. I helped you when you needed money and I never asked back for it."

"Fine. How much do you want?"

"I don't want your money. I need a place to stay."

"You're kidding, right?"

"I got evicted while I was locked up."

"Why is it my problem?" Ritchie asked with reluctance in his face.

"Come on, bro. It's only temporary. I lost almost all the furniture. I was lucky the landlord kept some of my stuff considering I didn't pay the rent. They mainly did it as a favour to Michaela."

"You're not serious. You're not planning to move in here along with your family."

"That's exactly what I'm planning to do." Eddy pushed passed Ritchie who was still stunned standing with his hand on the outside door of his two bedroom apartment. He slammed the door following Eddy to the kitchen as his brother was helping himself to a cup of coffee that was already made as if he was already at home.

"You're not staying here." Richie said with determination, but knew that it did not mean anything when it came to his big brother.

"Got anything to eat?" Eddy changed the subject. Ritchie threw some bread, butter and ham on the table and set down across from Eddy glaring at him with disdain watching him eat greedily as if he has not eaten for days. He knew how irritable, even aggressive Eddy could get when he was hungry although that was often not the only reason. So, he let him eat and waited for him to speak again when he was ready, pouring a cup of coffee for himself as well.

"Look, Ritchie. I haven't asked you for anything before, but I'm broke and homeless. I had a baby girl and I don't even have a home to provide my family with. You got to help me until I get back on my feet."

"I'm sorry what you're going through, Eddy. I really am, but I don't think you moving in with your family will be a good idea."

"Come on, Ritchie. The place is big enough and I'll pay for half of everything, once I get a job. It will help you pay off the condo faster and we will move out as soon as we can. Besides, mother said that you go to West Germany for weeks on end to work and your girlfriend is a history." Ritchie made a grimace as his brother was right about both of those facts thinking briefly about that proposal, vehemently shaking his head in disagreement. Eddy purposefully ignored it and stood up from behind the table.

"You're the best brother I have, Ritchie." He placed his hand on his shoulder.

"I'm your only brother."

"The more reason we should help each other. I knew you would understand." And before Richie had a chance to object, Eddy headed towards the door calling back to him.

"I'll be right back. I have a rented truck full of stuff that I'm paying by the hour." Richie swore under his nose, realizing that his big brother has overpowered him once again in his life and he would not be able to turn him down. Eddy had a point, he thought, he did work in Berlin for weeks on end leaving the place empty. That way Eddy could look after it and perhaps even help him pay it off sooner. Besides, Eddy said it was only a temporary situation. Richie's girlfriend broke up with him soon after he decided to work out west, so that would not cause a conflict since she no longer lived with him.

Within relatively short time after he arrived, Eddy moved the things that were left from his old apartment in Halle to Richie's two bedroom condo, into the room adjacent to the kitchen that Ritchie cleared out for him. Eddy did not have many things, other than his personal belongings, some dishes, bedding and few essential appliances that the Ziegler family after conversation with Eddy who called them from jail, placed his things along with the new bed from the bedroom into a storage room that Eddy paid off in order to get it back. The Zieglers already went above and beyond for this family considering it as a favour to his lovely wife.

Richie not only stopped objecting about Eddy moving in but even helped him with the bed and mattress to the tenth floor as it would not fit into the elevator. Both exhausted after they were done, they collapsed on the sofa in the living room with couple of beers in their hands.

Eddy explained to Ritchie that he cannot leave Germany right now because he is still on probation and has to complete a sixteen week anger management program.

"It will be a drag, but I don't have a choice but to go to the group or back to jail, which I definitely don't want to do."

"Did you let your probation officer know that you moved to Dresden?"

"I'll give him a call tomorrow and they'll probably have such groups here too."

The brothers talked most of the night mainly about Eddy's life and how much he wanted to see Michaela and the baby.

"I appreciate, bro what you're doing for us." Eddy said sincerely finishing up his beer before he got two more from the fridge. "You've done so well for yourself, little brother. You were always more capable than me. You've always been the better son; the favourite one." Self-pity and jealousy was setting in for Eddy as the level of alcohol increased in his blood stream.

"Come on Eddy; don't start again with the favouritism."

"It's true; father never hit you as much as he hit me. Turns out, he wasn't my father after all." Eddy opened another beer bottle handing it to his brother explaining what he found out from his mother as Richie was not aware of that.

"Then you're lucky he wasn't your biological father." Richie concluded.

"I'll drink to that." Eddy took another sip of his beer. Richie let Eddy have the bigger room considering that Michaela and the baby would sleep there as well.

The following day, Eddy called Michaela at her mother's home to let her know that he was out of jail now for almost a week and had a new place for her and the baby.

"I thought you would come after me and Orchid." Michaela said with disappointment in her voice.

"You know I would have but I can't leave the country because of my probation. You have to come back soon because you will lose the opportunity to get your immigration papers. With you leaving Germany you might have delayed or complicated the process. Anyway, we'll figure it out once you're here, but you have to come now." Michaela did not even consider that she might have problems with the immigration and her status in Germany.

"So what do you expect me to do now?"

"I want you to come to Dresden with the baby to live here with me. You're my wife and we have a child together. You have to come back; you belong with me." He skillfully omitted telling her the apartment belongs to his brother. Instead he described the beauty of the cozy condominium and that everything was ready for her.

"Imagine; no more cold shared washrooms, there is always running warm water, a toilet right beside a large bathtub and the bedrooms are huge. The baby can sleep in the room with us in the crib. The kitchen and living room are also spacious with a large balcony leading from the kitchen with a beautiful view seeing the Dresden town from high above. You'll love it."

Michaela loved the idea of a nice condo although it was a mystery to her how he could afford it all after recently coming out of jail, but he reassured her that he always finds a way out of a tough situation.

"Eddy, do you remember what I wrote to you few times about.....you know.....being physical with me. That has to stop."

"Consider it done. I'm starting a group on Tuesday night once a week for sixteen weeks that is starting here in Dresden. They transferred my case to this jurisdiction after I spoke to my probation officer. So everything worked out well. I'm gonna get the help that you always wanted me to get and things will be better between us. Just come back to me, Michaela. I miss you, my love. You know I love you and can't live without you." This was what she missed hearing him say and she suddenly knew that no matter what, she would be coming back to him."

Michaela was trying to picture how all that could be done before she spoke again.

"It's not going to be that easy, Eddy. You know we don't have a car."

"I'm sure you find a way. Just take a train."

"How am I going to travel with the baby and all our stuff? She needs her crib, stroller and many other things that I can't possibly carry by myself."

"Well, I don't know. Ask someone to give you a ride then."

"Alright, I'll figure something out. I guess I can talk to Nikole's dad to see if he could take us in his van with all the things. Give me at least a week to make all the arrangements, Eddy."

"I wish you were already here. I miss you like crazy and I can't wait to see Orchid."

After the conversation with Eddy, Michaela talked to her mother and to her Aunt Sylvie who was opposed to her going back to her husband, but Michaela was so excited and filled with new hope that she did not want to hear any negative things.

"I can't stay here forever. He is my husband and besides, being away from Germany for nearly six months, I might lose a chance of getting the Landed Immigrant papers. I have to go back."

"You know he will treat you the same like before." Aunt Sylvie tried to warn her once again.

"No, he wouldn't. It's different this time. He is getting help." Michaela argued with her aunt who tried to persuade her in futility even more vehemently than the first time; however, all in vain as Michaela has made up her mind to go back.

As she predicted, Mr. Senko agreed to take Michaela and the baby to Dresden on the weekend. She offered him money at least for the gas but he absolutely refused to take anything from her.

"If I didn't want to help, I wouldn't drive you to Germany. You keep your money, dear, you will need it for the baby. I just hope you know what you're doing." That was the only comment Mr. Senko made about going back to Germany. Michaela was not sure how much he knew about her situation but she was glad he did not question why she had left in the first place and what was going on in her marriage. He probably had some information from Nikole who visited Michaela every other weekend when she was in Kosice, calling herself an Aunt to little Orchid.

When Michaela arrived with her daughter in Dresden at the new address that Eddy gave her she buzzed the apartment number downstairs. After a short moment she heard Eddy's deep voice.

"Hi. It's me. Come downstairs to help us with some things."

"I'll be right down." Excitedly, Eddy got down scooping Michaela in his arms who was standing by the open van beside the car seat where her daughter was napping. He kissed her passionately, not realizing that Mr. Senko was opening the trunk of the van standing close by. When he greeted his wife with a long passionate kiss making Mr. Senko uncomfortable standing nearby, Eddy finally acknowledged him.

"Sir." He handed him his hand. "Thank you for driving my family back home."

"No problem. Michaela is like a second daughter to me."

"Will you join us for supper? I have some roast beef in the oven."

"No, thank you. I want to be back by midnight."

Michaela took the baby with the car seat but Eddy rushed to help her.

"So this is my little princess." It was a statement rather than a question, but Michaela answered him anyway.

"Yes, this is your daughter, Orchid."

"She is so beautiful. And look at the curly dark hair."

"She has your hair and your brown eyes."

"But she is so beautiful." He repeated in owe.

After Mr. Senko helped them with the crib and other things they carried to the elevator, he said his goodbye and was on his way home.

When she walked into the apartment for the first time looking around, she asked surprised.

"So this is your new apartment?"

"Well, not exactly."

"Oh, you're renting it?"

"Ah, you can say that." He said evasively distracting her with the beautifully set up table with candles and the supper he had prepared for them which was unusual as Eddy seldom cooked, but it was a new start for them, a new beginning. She went to wash her hands and was glad that the place was nice and warm and she did not have to walk to the washroom few floors down to use the toilet in a cold place like she had to do in Halle. Orchid woke up from her nap, so Michaela picked her up and started nursing her. Eddy stopped for a moment what he was doing in the kitchen to look at them lovingly.

"Does it hurt?"

"No. It did at the very beginning because she was so small and both us had to learn it, but it doesn't hurt anymore. I want to nurse her at least for a year."

Michaela felt an overwhelming bliss of happiness when she later saw Eddy taking his daughter into his arms. She was glad to have her family back and believed that things would change for the better. They had to make it work; they had a child together now and Michaela did not have a doubt in her mind that Eddy cared about his baby girl who was cuing contently in his lap.

"I'm glad that you're both back at home."

"So am I."

"I hope you can forgive me everything I've done to you."

"I already have. I wouldn't be here otherwise."

"I'm getting help. I started my group last Tuesday." He said excitedly to please her despite the dislike of the group which he found annoying and unnecessary but he did not have another choice.

"That's great. I'm glad to hear that. How did it go?"

"I don't know. There are bunch of guys there and I don't think I'm anything like them, but I have to finish it." Michaela nodded her acknowledgement and pressed her head onto Eddy's large chest.

When Orchid went to sleep for the night, they have made love with passion as if it was the first time. Eddy was caring and considerate of Michaela and she believed that he had really changed. Things between them were really wonderful. Eddy did not drink since she came to Dresden and they did not even argue with one another. She could not believe that life could be so peaceful and amazing. They got into a new routine as a family and it appeared to work although little Orchid did still wake up throughout the night for feeding, but Michaela was quick on her feet tending to her needs and assuring that Eddy got a good night sleep. She was still on a maternity leave and was awaiting her immigration documents to arrive soon as she received a letter stating that it is being processed.

Michaela's life consisted of taking care of Orchid and Eddy as well as all the household chores. Eddy's point was that it was the woman's responsibility especially when she did not work and her husband was supporting her. Michaela could not argue with that as in retrospect it was the truth.

As she was getting Orchid ready for a daily walk in her stroller, getting her dressed, she heard a key in the door turning. She wondered how come Eddy came from work so early since it was only shortly after lunch. But when she walked to the outside door she saw Ritchie walking in.

"Oh. Hi Michaela. So you're here already. When did you arrive?" Michaela looked at him in confusion and instead of answering his puzzling question she queried.

"You have a key?"

"Of course."

"What are you doing here?"

"Excuse me? I live here." Astonished, Michaela looked at him with her big blue-green eyes.

"That's a joke, right?" Richie frowned and said.

"No, it's not a joke. I live here." He repeated. "This is my condo. Eddy didn't tell you that?"

"No. I thought he was renting it."

"Well, he still owes me money for the last month he's been here. He needed a place to stay so I helped him and agreed for you and your daughter to move in too, temporarily of course."

"I see. That was very generous of you. Thank you Richie." Michaela said uncomfortably as she suddenly realized she was a guest in this place which explained why the one room on the left was always locked up and they have never used it.

"That's not a big deal. I travel as an AZ driver out west for weeks on end so I wouldn't be here all the time."

When Eddy came home from work and they were alone in their bedroom, Michaela confronted her husband about their living situation.

"When were you going to tell me that this is not your apartment?"

"I never said it was."

"But you never said your brother lives here too and whenever I asked you about the spare room you lied to me saying that you had to fix it up making me think this was our place."

"What do you want from me Michaela? I do my best. I work my ass off and I come home tired from work to get an earful from you?"

"I understand that, but you could have at least told me. I looked like a complete idiot in front of your brother today when he showed up at the doors with a key in his hand."

"Well, you are what you feel." He retorted and turned on his side to go to sleep.

Their brief argument woke baby Orchid up who started crying in the crib that was in the same room.

"Shit. I told you Michaela; I'm tired and I just want to go to sleep, so make her be quiet." He said irritably.

Michaela picked Orchid up into her arms but the baby did not stop crying, so she walked to the living room that was separated by the kitchen, further away from the bedroom. She was rocking and then nursing her until she fell asleep again; placing her back into the crib. Eddy was fast asleep by the time she returned to bed. This was a pattern where Orchid would wake up once or twice a night and it was always Michaela that would take care of her. Eddy's argument was that he did not have milk to give to her anyway and he needed to wake up early for work while Michaela was home all day. They did not discuss the living situation again. Michaela was afraid to bring it up and ask how long they would live in his brother's apartment as she did not want to cause unnecessary arguments.

Richie was friendly and more than accommodating. In four days he went on the road again and the Verner family had the whole apartment just to themselves, although they have naturally not used Richie's bedroom. When she thought about it; their living situation was not so unusual to her as many young families in her country lived with relatives, usually parents or in-laws as there was a shortage of apartments or young couples could simply seldom afford it as the apartments were too expensive for a starting couple. If they lived in Czechoslovakia, Michaela was sure they would have lived at her mother's place at least at the beginning. She thought that Eddy did his best and was glad that at least they have moved away from the old and cold apartment in Halle, so she should not complain, but she was feeling upset that he withheld that information from her making her look stupid in front of his brother. But for the peace in the family, she did not confront him about it again and Eddy did not mention it either although she wondered how long they would live there.

She was glad that Eddy was able to find a new job so quickly. He worked as a helper at a road construction site mainly holding the stop sign to direct the traffic and although it was boring, it was a job that helped support his family. They needed every Mark they could save but Eddy was not the type to plan ahead and whenever he had the money he would spend it showering Michaela with flowers or gifts and Orchid with toys that she was too young to appreciate.

Michaela busied herself with daily chores of cooking, cleaning and doing laundry while at the same time taking care of their daughter. She liked doing it because Eddy liked warm meals when he came home from work hungry and tired and he was less irritable when everything was ready on time; nicely set up for dinner. Little Orchid was sitting every night with them in the kitchen in her highchair that Eddy recently bought and she was exploring new finger foods smearing and dropping things on the floor.

"Ah, man. Look at all that mess, Michaela." Eddy said with disgust in his face. "Can't you just feed her?"

"I do, but she also needs to explore and learn to feed herself." Orchid was stuffing in her mouth some peas from her little hand dropping more than half on herself and onto the floor that rolled under the table.

"She eats like a little piggy. I don't think she is even getting anything into her mouth and the mash potatoes are all over her mouth." Michaela wiped her daughter's face gently giving her another spoonful of mash potatoes.

"Eddy she is only seven months old. Don't worry; I'll clean it all up when we're done eating. You could help me sometimes, you know." She added in frustration. "I'm doing everything by myself."

"You don't expect me to clean that mess. Do you?"

"No, I said I'll clean it up. But you could take her out for a little walk in the stroller for about half an hour. She'll sleep better." Eddy signed with exaggeration as if spending time with his daughter was an inconvenience to him. She expected him to retort to her that he was too tired after work, but was pleasantly surprised when he agreed for a change.

"Fine, get her ready then."

Michaela finished feeding Orchid, cleaned her up and got her changed and dressed for the late October evening stroller ride. When she was ready she said.

"Here is a baby bottle with my breast milk just in case she cries, but she should be quite content now. She is fed and changed and she might even fall asleep for the night on the fresh air. You don't have to stay very long with her."

"Don't you take her outside during the day for fresh air?"

"I do, but like I said she sleeps better if she goes out in the evening as well."

"I hope you're right. I can't stand another sleepless night with her crying by my ear. Gosh, it's like having a puppy that you have to take out." When he saw little Orchid smiling at him with her little hat on, joyful as she already knew that she was going outside, Eddy could not help but smile at her.

"Alright, Kid. Let's go for a walk."

"Kid?"

"Yeah, short for Orchid." Michaela wrinkled her nose.

"I don't like that nick name." Eddy shrugged, looked at Orchid and told the baby.

"Mommy doesn't like it, Kid. But that's ok; wave to mommy." Michaela just shook her head but she was smiling at them as he was pushing the stroller towards the elevators. She actually did not believe that Eddy took the baby without much fuss for a walk which gave her some time to clean the floor, the highchair and do the dishes after dinner. She even had time to vacuum the whole apartment realizing that they have been gone for over an hour. When they did not come in other hour, Michaela started to worry that Orchid might be cold and wet and that she should be already in her crib sleeping. *Where have they been so long?*

She was pacing back and forth; she even called her mother-in-law if Eddy did not stop at her place now that they lived in the same town but she said she has not seen them. Michaela agreed to visit Eleonore with the baby soon; then anxiously hung up the phone looking out through the balcony hoping to see them coming any moment. Michaela was on the verge of hysteria nearly calling the police when Eddy showed up at nine fifty in the evening without the stroller.

Chapter 25

MICHAELA RAN TO THE HALLWAY all the way to the elevators looking for the stroller but it was not there.

"Jesus, Eddy, where is Orchid?"

"What Orchid?" Eddy slurred his words completely drunk; he stumbled inside, pushing her aside.

"Eddy, please, where did you leave Orchid?" She ran behind him as he collapsed on the sofa in the living room as it was the closest room from the front entrance.

"Eddy, Eddy. You took her with you for a walk. Where is she?" Michaela was shrieking in panic, shaking her husband who was still lying down and only mumbled something under his nose that she could no longer understand. She quickly realized that she would not get much out of him. She did not waste more time; she quickly put on her running shoes and jacket running out of the building in sheer panic. She saw a couple walking into the building and asked them if they have seen a brown-beige stroller but they have not. She was running around frantically, looking for her baby girl in the area. He did not go anywhere with the car as it was sitting on the parking lot in front of the building so he had gotten drunk beyond recognition somewhere close by. He must have gone to a nearby pub; but where would he have left the baby? She ran from one side of the street towards one pub she knew about asking around if anyone saw a man with a stroller but the half drunk man shook their heads. Michaela had tears running down her face in desperation asking anyone who walked by if they saw a stroller with a baby.

"Hey, lady. There is another pub three blocks down on the Bundestrasse."

Michaela thanked the old man in passing and ran towards the direction he pointed. She ran the whole way, tears streaking down her face imagining the unthinkable happening to Orchid. She was out of shape as she stopped running when she got pregnant and out of breath but if she died on the pavement, she would not stop until she found her daughter. *I should have called the police first.* She thought as she was running in desperation looking around if she would not see the brown-beige stroller. She was worried that the police would take too long with questioning her rather than taking immediate action of looking for her baby. Before she saw the stroller she heard the baby's crying from far away. She hurried until she saw a drunken man rocking the stroller in front of a pub.

"That's your baby, lady? She's been crying here for a long time."

"Oh, God. Thanks God." Michaela was whispering gratefully as she picked her baby up from the stroller. She was cold and wet and probably hungry too. *How could Eddy be so irresponsible and leave her in front of a pub like that. Anything could have happened. What if anyone had taken her?*

"Come here, darling. It's ok, it's ok. Mommy is here. Don't cry." She crunched down leaning by the wall of the pub holding her daughter toward her breast to feed her and to calm her down as she herself was still trembling in shock. She wrapped her jacket around her baby to warm her up. Men were walking in and out of the pub looking at her with curiosity but she did not care about that. Michaela could not believe what had just happened and how lucky she was she had found her quite quickly. She heard so many horror stories of stolen children for all kinds of sick purposes like for child pornography or for organ donations. She shook away those disturbing thoughts and held her daughter closely to her body never again wanting to let her go. She was shaking, not sure whether from the cooler night that set upon them or from the shock when her husband came home without their baby girl. When she calmed down and Orchid finished nursing, she placed her back into the stroller heading home with indescribable fury towards her husband. She realized that she would never trust Eddy alone with Orchid and she would never let him take her for a walk or anywhere unless she was there too. She thought he was a responsible father; she thought he stopped drinking, but she was wrong nearly paying by losing the most precious person in her life. She would not leave it like that; she would confront Eddy as soon as she saw him. How dare does he go to a pub and gets drunk when he has a child in his care? She would give him piece of her mind no matter what it cost her. She was still outraged when she arrived home finding Eddy snoring on the sofa still in his outside clothes. He just passed out the way he was; not bothering to even take his jacket and shoes off. She wanted to shake him; to slap him senseless for what he did, but she knew at this point it would be futile as he was completely out of it soaked up in hard liquor reeking from his breath and waking him up would be more disastrous.

She had to be smart about it. She knew from before that it was always better to let him sleep it off and talk to him in the morning because she was afraid he would become aggressive again like he did before when he was drunk. She would have a serious talk with him in the morning, she decided. She took his shoes off and threw a light blanket over him, placing a bucket beside the sofa in case he got sick throughout the night although he seldom did and often took a pride in how well he was able to hold his liquor without throwing up disregarding the fact that he often drank to a point of a black out, not remembering anything the next day. The truth was that Eddy should not drink at all because he became a different person when he drank; although the aggressive nature was there regardless of his state of mind and his impulsive behaviour could easily take over at anytime whether he was drunk or sober.

Michaela placed sleeping Orchid in her bed lying down next to her looking at her angelic face for a long time before she herself fell asleep with disturbing nightmares waking up throughout the night despite Orchid soundly sleeping nearby. She lay down again kissing her little hand and holding it for the rest of the night; not wanting to ever let her go.

The next morning Michaela and Orchid were way past breakfast time when Eddy finally woke up. His hair and clothes were a mess and he still smelled of alcohol that he has pickled himself in last night to oblivion. The whole living room smelled of alcohol too that Michaela tried to air out. He barely said good morning rubbing his head that felt like a volcano has exploded in his brain.

"Coffee." He said grumpily with a hoarse voice that she barely recognized.

"Go take a shower, change and I'll make you coffee and breakfast and after that we need to talk."

"No. Coffee first." He ordered her stubbornly sitting down on a kitchen chair placing his head in the palm of his hands not even acknowledging little Orchid who was cuing in the high chair. Michaela knew that she would not be able to have a decent conversation with him until he had his coffee and a cigarette and hoped that there was not much residue left from the remaining alcohol in his blood stream which was of course a distinct possibility. He was lucky it was his day off otherwise Michaela doubted he would be able to stand on his feet for very long.

"Do you want to eat something?"

"Not now. Just coffee." He repeated with annoyance.

He took his coffee with him outside to the balcony where he sat down on a white plastic chair, lit up a cigarette and leaned his head backwards blowing up the smoke above him. The cool late October mid-morning was helping him sober up from last night.

Michaela peeked out to see him, pulling away the curtains and asked him standing in the doorway of the balcony.

"Do you realize what you did last night?"

"Big deal. I got drunk."

"You don't remember?!"

"I remember meeting Otto and Ben and we got drunk. I haven't seen the guys in ages, so stop making such a big deal about it." He said with exasperation in his voice.

"You took Orchid for a walk in her stroller and when you came home drunk you didn't have her with you."

"What're you talking about?! I called you and you picked her up."

"NO, YOU DIDN'T CALL! I almost called the police when you came without her!" She was yelling at him in desperation trying to have him acknowledge what he did.

"Stop yelling at me. I have a horrible headache."

"How dare you get so drunk when you have your daughter with you?"

"Shut up and stop making such a big deal out of everything!" He raised his voice but Michaela would not be intimidated by him this time.

She needed to say what was on her mind and in her heart and his rude demeanor would not stop her.

"I can't believe that you drank to a point of forgetting your own child. I will never let you take Orchid anywhere by yourself because I can't trust you anymore. You have no idea that I was running around like crazy from pub to pub trying to find her and she was screaming, wet, cold and hungry because you just left her there. You drunken irresponsible piece of shit!" She said it with abhorrence in her voice because she was furious with him and did not care about his reaction. At that last statement Eddy jumped out of the plastic chair despite his headache ready to land a punch in her face with his fist as his fingers curled up for the blow that was so familiar to her.

"Go head. Hit me. I dare you. And I swear that will be the last time you see me or your daughter." Those words stopped Eddy surprising him of Michaela's lack of fear of his intimidation although his own fury was lingering above them.

"Is that a threat?"

"No, Eddy, it's a promise." She did not wait much longer for Eddy to change his mind and hit her; she closed the balcony door leaving him to his own rage. Then she dressed herself and Orchid quickly before he had a chance to finish his first cigarette and went out with her daughter to a park. She needed fresh air and she needed to be away from Eddy at least for a little while.

Although the sun was up high warming her up, she still had cold chills running down her back when she thought about what could have happened to Orchid if she did not find her in time last night. She replayed the event vividly in her mind over and over again coming to a conclusion that she should have called the police or even better she should not have let Orchid go anywhere with her father. But she did not know at the time that he was capable of doing something so stupid; something so irresponsible and negligent. It was her fault, she thought; she is the mother and she should have known better; she should have protected her daughter. They were all lucky that it did not end in catastrophe certainly a lesson she had learned the hard way being given another chance from God who must have heard her prayers when she was frantically looking for her child.

She heard so many horrible stories of children being simply abducted and used in unthinkable ways and her own husband would expose her to such a danger. It was bad enough that Orchid had now sniffles possibly from the cold night yesterday.

The fall weather was pleasant now though with a mild wind blowing up the colourful leaves under her feet as she pushed the stroller to the nearby park.

She loved autumn with all its beauty of multi-coloured world of orange, yellow, red and green that calmed her senses. Orchid appeared to be calm, dozing off for her early noon nap. Michaela sat down on a bench to admire the scenery in front of her taking deep breaths and thinking what happened last night and where she would go from here. She did not want to go home anytime soon and face her husband again.

She had hoped that Eddy had changed when she came back to Germany and the first month it seemed that he has. He did not drink; he was nice and attentive to her and she even felt happy again. That is until last night when her world was turned upside down once again. And this morning she thought about how close she came to being hit by him again; but she was surprised how little she cared about that.

There was something different about Eddy that morning though; he did not punch her although he had that inclination and the opportunity and certainly he would easily justify it, but he did not hit her. She knew in the past he would not have hesitated or controlled himself. That gave her a trickle of hope that perhaps the group that he was attending was somewhat helpful. Either way even if she stayed which she knew she would, she would never let him be alone with Orchid due to his irresponsible behaviour. She could no longer rely on him at least when it came to their daughter.

When she came back home she thought Eddy would complain or yell at her where she was and that she should have prepared lunch; instead she was pleasantly surprised that Eddy set up the table, prepared Saturday lunch for all of them. There was a little orchid in the middle of the table; his way of saying he was sorry.

"This will not happen again. I give you my word, Michaela. I've been thinking about it and I really thought I called you to come pick Orchid up shortly after I met up with Otto and Ben. It was Ben's birthday we were celebrating and they invited me to join them."

"I could care less about Ben's birthday. You had a responsibility. Do you get that someone could have just taken her? Or she could have gotten sick being outside for such a long time?"

"I sat by the window so I was watching the stroller and she was sleeping on a fresh air. I didn't want to bring her into a smoky pub. And really thought I called you."

"No, you didn't. I didn't even know where you were and I was beside myself when you came home without her."

"I don't know what happened. I don't remember much shortly after me and the guys went into the pub …. I'm so sorry. I'm sorry I got drunk when I had Orchid. It will never happen again." He walked towards Michaela giving her a hug that she only partly accepted still angry at him.

"That's for sure that it will never happen again because you will not be taking Orchid anywhere by yourself."

"Oh, come on, Michaela. Don't start again. I really don't want to fight. I already apologized. What else do you want me to say? Look, nothing bad happened. She is fine and I promised it will not happen again. So let's just drop it. Alright?" He was getting irritated but then he changed his demeanor and led her to the kitchen with Orchid in his arms.

"Look. I made us a nice lunch. So don't be so mad at me. Please." Michaela did not want to fight either and luckily nothing has happened to Orchid so there was no point of arguing more about what they could not change but she made a mental note of protecting Orchid as she could not trust Eddy anymore.

Although they have not talked about this serious incident again, Eddy was on his best behaviour, attending regularly his group, being attentive to Michaela and playing with his daughter and things at home started to normalize again. He did not go to a pub to drink although he had a beer or two each night at home; he was not getting drunk as he used to and Michaela believed that perhaps that was just a fluke incident and they could still function as a happy family. Orchid adored her daddy and they were ecstatic when just before her first birthday she took her first steps. Eddy was a proud father frequently spoiling Orchid with toys.

Eleonore who visited them once in a while and spent the Christmas holidays with them making it a living hell for Michaela, she took pride in being a grandmother to such an adorable little girl; her only grandchild. On another hand, Michaela was glad that Orchid adored her grandmother who was often quite critical of everything that Michaela did.

Eddy never told his mother off when she criticized Michaela for how she cleaned, how she cooked or how she has been taking care of Orchid creating tension between the young couple again. Michaela one evening told Eddy in frustration.

"Why you never take my side when your mother keeps nagging at me?"

"She is not nagging; she is just trying to help you be a better wife and a better mother. You must admit, she has more experience than you. You should be grateful for her help."

"She constantly criticizes me. I can't do anything right in her eyes and you always take her side. I can't believe you don't see that."

"Maybe if you kept the house cleaner and wasn't such a lousy cook she wouldn't have to say anything." These were often the comments that Michaela heard from Eddy who had never supported her whether it was about parenting or anything else and he often disregarded her point of view. No matter how hard she tried; how much she cleaned, ironed his clothes or how hard she tried to please him by cooking foods he enjoyed, it was never good enough. Instead of appreciation he always had something critical to say to her and often used hurtful words, degrading her and making her feel insignificant and incompetent.

"What the hell is this?" He said one day when she placed his supper in front of him.

"It's pork roast with sauerkraut and dumplings. You ate it once at my mom's, remember? It's a National Czech food. Just try it. Please." Although Eddy finished his plate, he did not stop complaining.

"The dumplings are too mushy and the sauerkraut is too salty. Seriously Michaela, we've been together for over three years now and you still haven't learned how to cook properly." When she had tears in her eyes, instead of comforting her he was lately quite annoyed by her sensitivity.

"Oh, Gosh, here we go again. You not gonna cry about it again, are you?" He wiped his month with the napkin, stood up grabbing a beer from the fridge as usual and went to watch TV. When Orchid who recently turned three years old ran to her daddy with excitement he picked her up swung her in the air few times, kissed her on her cheek and placed her on his lap pulling out a large doll from a plastic bag making her squeal with excitement.

"This doll can talk and sing too. Look." He turned a button in the dolls belly and the doll said 'hello'. "Do you like it?"

"I love it daddy." She said with a bright smile on her face.

"Ok, so now go and play in your room. Ok?" Eddy sent her off as he put his feet on the coffee table wanting to watch the news. Michaela smiled at her daughter who passed by her showing her the new doll and ran off to the bedroom.

"Eddy, you don't have to always buy her a new toy. She has so many toys already and you always say we don't have much money. The doll looked expensive." With annoyance he looked at her and retorted.

"I can do what I want with my money. I'm the only one who works so I say how it's spent. Is it clear?"

"I need some money for groceries, Eddy."

"I'll give it to you at the end of the week." He brushed her off.

"But your brother is coming home tomorrow and there is not much food left in the fridge for all of us. We don't even have milk or eggs. The least we can do for your brother is to provide enough food for all of us since we were not able to still move on our own."

"Stop bugging me."

"Well, what do I supposed to do? You don't let me work and I don't have any money left."

"You not gonna shut up, are you?" He jumped out suddenly startling her as she never knew what she could expect of him.

Chapter 26

S HE DID NOT LIKE ASKING him for money; she absolutely hated it. It was embarrassing and degrading but he did not let her have a credit card or debit card always telling her that she had no income and he provided her with everything she needed. He never volunteered to give her the money she needed for the household or for their daughter and she had to ask for every Mark that she needed having to tell him what it was for and he would decide whether it was necessary or not. On the other hand she often feared that he would spend most of their money with his friends drinking in a pub as he sometimes did.

When Eddy approached her she subconsciously expected a slap on a face although he has not done it for a long time but her past experiences with him have prepared her for the unexpected or so she thought. But he did not hit her; rather he went to the hallway, got the wallet from his jacket and slammed fifty Marks on the kitchen counter.

"Here! Happy?" He said sardonically as if the money was for her to spend foolishly; he then went back to watch the TV and drink his beer.

Michaela was careful not to cause a fight between them, but often felt quite helpless and frustrated. Although Eddy did not hit her for a long time and she believed the anger management group had really helped him as he had to acknowledge in writing what he did wrong, having to take responsibility for his physical abuse in order to complete the program, he would often tell her she was dependent on him even though she wanted to work to contribute financially, but Eddy was strictly against it despite Michaela having received her landed immigrant status along

301

with a working permit a year and half ago and Orchid was old enough to start a day care. Eddy refused to hear about it.

"I don't want a stranger raising my daughter while you work. Not to mention the childcare is expensive." He would argue as he believed that the woman's place was in the home taking care of the household and raising children just like his mother did and Eleonore has supported that notion. Michaela was bothered by that but at the same time she enjoyed her time at home with Orchid and wanted to spend more time with her, so she picked her battles with Eddy. She easily could have provoked the situation by retorting something sarcastic back to him but she knew it would end in a bigger fight and probably not getting any money from him for a while. So she acquiescently took the fifty Marks he just gave her for food and simply said.

"Thank you."

When she went to check on her daughter who was playing in the bedroom she walked on Orchid seeing her with the new doll. When she came closer she noticed that the doll's face was painted over with a black permanent marker.

"What are you doing Orchid Elizabeth Verner?" Michaela said sternly upset for ruining a new and expensive doll that she just got.

"I don't want her anymore."

"Why did you do that, Orchid?" She said it more calmly although she was still quite upset and afraid once Eddy found out about it what he would do.

"Cause I hate her; cause you and daddy always fight about money and it's my fault cause I always want dolls." She pushed the doll away and hugged her knees pouting.

"Sweetheart, it's not your fault. I'm sorry you heard me and daddy fighting. These are grown-up problems and it's not your fault or the doll's fault."

"I still don't want the doll or the other dolls from daddy. I hate them. I hate daddy."

"Don't say that Orchid. That's not nice." She reprimanded her daughter with a scorn on her face. "Daddy loves you; that's why he bought you those dolls." Orchid was sitting on the carpet across from her mother with a frown on her face looking at the doll as Michaela tried in futility to get rid of the marker but it would not wash off. She would have to hide it for now and then somehow save some money and buy the same one just so Eddy would not find out. But when she was looking for a spot to hide the doll for now out of his sight, he walked into the bedroom looking at the destroyed doll he just bought.

Immediate fury passed through him when he saw the damaged doll that he so lovingly gave to his daughter just moments ago.

"KID! Did you do that?" His loud and deep voice intimidated her and her big brown eyes quickly filled out with tears. Michaela hurriedly came to her rescue telling a white lie to calm the situation down.

"Eddy, it's not Orchid's fault. She is just a little girl and she was experimenting. You see, she saw this little black girl the other day on the playground with whom she played nicely and wanted the doll to look just like her."

"What kind of crap you're trying to tell me here. The doll is completely ruined. I buy her an expensive doll because I want to make her happy and she just destroys it within seconds." He was yelling making Orchid scared barely able to catch her breath.

"Eddy, please stop yelling. You're scaring her. The doll is not destroyed. She still will play with it." Michaela was worried what Eddy would do next as his expression was ominous and she knew that look very well, but she was prepared to do whatever she needed to do to protect her little girl. He would not lay his hands on her. He stepped closer to his daughter who looked so small by his feet and she curled up in a fetal position. Michaela quickly stood up in front of Orchid facing Eddy ready to take a punch instead. She was so much smaller and physically weaker than her husband, but the fearlessness she showed was larger than Eddy's rage.

"Don't you dare!" She warned him even though he never physically punished his daughter.

"You're not going to get anything from me anytime soon, Kid." He said instead sternly looking at his daughter over Michaela's shoulder. "And I'm taking away your other toys too because you don't appreciate anything. Spoiled brat!" He went to grab a large black garbage bag and started tossing her toys one after another into the bag.

"Just watch how quickly the gypsy kids will get your toys." He threatened, and then he left along with the bag of toys leaving the mother and daughter in each other's arms.

After few minutes, Michaela saw him walking towards the garbage cans tossing the whole bag into the large garbage container. Orchid was crying hysterically as she was peeking through the spaces in the railing while kneeling down on the balcony floor.

"Mommy, he took my teddy. He took my friend." She was watching Eddy through the balcony as she was trying to comfort Orchid who was in a lot of distress. Eddy did not go back home but took the car and went somewhere else.

"Don't cry sweetie. Mommy's going to get your teddy back. Ok?" Michaela knew that if Eddy found the toys he threw away back in the room, he would be furious and who knows what he would do, but she hoped that in that fury he neglected to notice Orchid's favourite teddy bear he grabbed that Orchid slept with every night and it was a gift from Michaela's mother. Orchid was attached to that toy and Michaela walked with her downstairs with determination to find the teddy bear before he came back. The smile on Orchid's face was priceless when Michaela retrieved it from the garbage bin disregarding the dubious and degrading stares of the passer-bys as she was pulling out the black garbage bags from the large garbage bin looking for the right one.

"I don't want the dolls anyway, mommy. I just want my teddy." Orchid said when she saw her mother's hesitation about what she wanted to do with the bag of toys.

"You're such a smart girl, Orchid. I'm sure some other little girls will find them and will get to play with them. Let's go hide your teddy under your pillow, ok?" Orchid nodded happy to have her favourite stuffed animal back.

Michaela was not bothered by the fact that Eddy wanted her to be always at home and she wasn't as much bothered by her mother-in-law who meddled in their business but she was bothered with Eddy's yelling and she was also getting quite frustrated with his frequent unjust accusations of her cheating on him and fits of jealous rages he displayed. She often tried in futility to persuade her husband that she did not go anywhere and has never cheated on him but he did not trust her. She saw the jealous tendencies from the beginning of their relationship but now that Eddy stopped his extreme drinking it was as if he found something else to replace his bad habits. One evening after Orchid was asleep; Michaela went to the balcony to get some fresh air looking at the clear sky in the spring night enjoying the breeze. As the wind blew her hair in her face, she scooped it up away from her face placing it backwards again as she often did when she did not wear her ponytail.

"Who are you waving to?" She turned to face him surprised to hear his deep voice behind her.

"What?" She did not understand his question at first.

"I saw you waving to someone just now. Who is he?"

"I wasn't waving to anyone."

"Don't lie to me! Just tell me the truth."

"I am telling you the truth!"

"Do you sleep with him?"

"With whom?"

"You tell me!"

"You're out of your mind." She shook her head in disbelief.

"Oh, so when I catch you in action, now you say I'm crazy?"

"You are behaving crazy. Have you been drinking again?" He ignored her question and continued with his set of queries.

"Which floor is he on?" He stepped to the balcony next to her looking intently over to the tall building across from them.

"Is it that guy on the balcony there?" He pointed with his index finger. Instead of following his finger, she was staring at him with incredulity. She did not need to look; she did not know anyone around here and his accusations were ridiculous.

"What's wrong with you, Eddy? I'm telling you there is nobody else. How many times do I have to tell you that? When are you going to stop accusing me of cheating?"

She tried to walk back inside shaking her head in disbelief. She did not want to listen to this nonsense, but he grabbed her arm pulling her back and pressing her cheeks with his thumb and forefinger to face the other building.

"Is it him? That guy that lit the cigarette on the...." He quickly counted the floors "....the 9th floor?"

"Eddy, I swear, I don't even know anyone around here. There is nobody, but you." She pulled away from him and wanted to go inside feeling agitated after his accusations that were unjust. She has never cheated on Eddy and had no idea why he would be so suspicious or jealous. She thought he knew her better than that. They have been together for three and half years and she could not believe that all this time he always made up ridiculous stories of her cheating that were untrue.

"I wish you just told me the truth. I could forgive you but not if you keep lying to me!"

"I'm not lying to you Eddy. I never cheated on you. I swear."

"Just like you didn't cheat on me with Nikolas when I was in jail?" He caught her off guard. She did not know he knew Nikolas was in Germany when Eddy was in jail but she did not cheat on him. She slowly and carefully chose her words.

"Just because Nikolas came to help when I didn't have anyone when you were locked up that doesn't mean I slept with him."

"Ah, so you admit he was there. He was in our old apartment, wasn't he?"

"How do you even know about that?" He laughed victoriously as if to prove his point but it was lacking in amusement.

"You think I'm stupid that I would never find out? I knew right after I was released. Verena told me and the description fits; you just confirmed it now." She should have known. She saw her on the hallway with her hateful expression the last day as she was leaving from Halle with Nikolas who was only helping her when nobody else had.

"Why didn't you say anything about it before? You accuse me of cheating all the time even though you don't have any reason to. Why didn't you ask about that earlier?"

"Because I wanted to know how far you would go in your lies." He retorted bitterly. "Where did you do it? On our bed? In our old apartment while your husband was safely away in jail?"

"Eddy, I swear, I never slept with Nik."

"Oh, it's Nik, now?"

"You're being completely irrational. I told you Nikolas was there only to help me. He drove me back home; that's all." But Eddy was not even listening to her anymore. He had his own truth that he has persuaded himself about and no matter what she said or how well she tried to explain to him he would still not believe her and every time she tried, Eddy was getting angrier.

"I'm being irrational? You cheating little whore!" He unexpectedly slapped her over her face, her hair flying over to the other side covering her face. She instinctively held a hand to her cheek where he hit her with chagrin in her expression, but she did not say anything to that; only went back to the bedroom to be with her daughter ignoring his ridiculous contention. But Eddy shortly followed her to the bedroom continuing in this senseless argument that did not have any basis of truth.

"Eddy. Please stop yelling." She whispered in desperation as Orchid was steering in her sleep. "You'll wake her up."

"This is not over. If I'll find out you cheated on me with Nikolas or anyone else.....I'll kill him." He was breathing heavily and was barely able to finish the sentence. He just hit the side of the wall with a palm of his hand making Michaela jump in fear and waking Orchid from her sleep. She was now sure that he started drinking again excessively.

When Eddy went to the living room getting another beer from the fridge, she was calming frightened Orchid.

"It's nothing, sweetie, just go back to sleep." She kissed the top of her head and laid down beside her daughter on her new bed that Eddy recently purchased for his girl as she was too big for a crib.

Eddy; however, did not give up his suspicions although Michaela had no idea what got into him. She knew from the beginning that Eddy was quite a jealous man but he was never that irrational. He would follow her whenever she went outside with Orchid whether it was to the store or to a park. He opened her mail that she received from back home looking for anything suspicious, especially when her friend, Nikole wrote to her.

Michaela often had to tiptoe around her husband making sure he did not have a reason for an argument. He always had clean clothes ready in his closet, his lunches were prepared for work and there was always warm dinner waiting for him whenever he came home in the evenings. She had never given him a reason to be jealous; she did not even look at another man although he would often accuse her of flirting even if another man just passed by them on the street looking at them briefly. He often demanded Michaela to be affectionate to him and to make love to him whenever he wanted it, making her feel used and unappreciated. She often felt like a piece of property that he could do with anything he wanted to. When she complained of having menstrual cramps or headaches, although he has not forced himself on her, she would hear about it often resulting again in jealous rages and accusations of having another lover rationalizing it especially when she was not in a mood for sex. The truth was that she was not only tired but she did not have any affection left in her to give him after being accused of cheating, being criticized and put down by him day after day which was becoming more frequent.

She often thought whether this was abusive when he was criticizing her, putting her down or when she had to beg him for money but she rationalized it that it was not so bad because he was not hitting her as he used to. She disregarded or dismissed the occasional rough touch, a slap on her face or pushing her out of his way when he was angry or the fact that she was alone with Orchid and did not have any friends around.

The only other person she had contact with in person was his mother-in-law who showed lack of support and Ritchie who was a great help to them but he spent a lot of time in West Germany more frequently as he had a new girlfriend there. She got used to the fact that she had minimal contact with her family who had visited her only few times in the past two years although they called her during the day usually when Eddy was at work. It was a bigger town and a bigger building where she did not know anyone and she was busy taking care of her daughter and the household that filled majority of her days. She came to accept that this was her life and persuaded herself that it was not that bad. She had a beautiful, healthy child which was a blessing in itself so what else could she want from life? She knew there were women being beaten by their husbands every day, ending up with black eyes, bruises and broken bones but that was not her case. She believed that Eddy had a good heart despite his jealousy and hot temper. She enjoyed watching him when he played with their daughter albeit it was seldom and usually only for brief periods of time.

Over the years, Michaela had learnt what worked with Eddy and what would create more arguments. She was smart not to pour more oil on the burning fire. When Eddy was raging for one reason or another, she would either agree with him to try to calm him or simply would stay quiet trying to please him. She even perfected hiding her own emotions and tears from him because she knew that he was irritated by it. She would hold it back and cry in the bathroom quietly where nobody would see her or when he was not at home; but little Orchid sometimes saw her mommy cry and would ask questions that were difficult to answer to a three year old child.

"Mommy, why you cry?"

"Well, you sometimes cry too, Orchid."

"I little, I cry. You're big. Why you cry?" She hugged her daughter lovingly more tears pouring down her face. How can she answer such a difficult question to a young brain that should not be burdened with adult issues?

"Mommy just feels sad sometimes. That's all, sweetie." Orchid whether consciously or subconsciously quickly learned that her father got easily irritated by her crying too and would sometimes yell at her for things she did not understand. Just like her mother, she started to learn to stifle her cries, whispering instead to her teddy bear when she was feeling sad or scared when her daddy was not watching.

Michaela was worried the most when on occasion Eddy would meet up with his drinking buddies, ending up in a pub and coming completely drunk and often blacking out again. Those were the times she feared the most, usually after his payday but not because he would drink away most of their money, although that was a big problem, but because of his level of aggression when he was drinking excessively. He seldom went to sleep right away and he would not remember next day what he did. He would often break things in their home that Michaela then tried to replace, especially when it was something that belonged to his brother. Luckily he did not do it every day; only once or twice a month and she learned to do whatever he wanted just to keep him happy and calm so he would not become aggressive. She was always careful not to let him go near Orchid who was soundly asleep when he came home drunk preparing a sofa bed for him in the living room so his daughter would not have to see him like that or smell the alcohol in the room.

One late November night, shortly after Richie went for another two weeks to work in Berlin, she was left alone with Orchid waiting for Eddy to come home soon. She got used to living in Richie's apartment as she noticed that Eddy was less likely to be abusive to her when Richie was around and she grew to like this young man who has provided a roof over their head and never complained about them living there. In fact he was a great uncle and Orchid adored him. Although this was to be a temporary accommodation for them as Eddy often told her, it stretched out to over two years and Eddy continued to say that they needed to save up more in order to buy their own home.

That night Michaela was pacing back and forth in the two bedroom apartment after she tucked her little girl into bed. She did not know when her husband, would be home or what she could expect from him each night. But she knew this waiting game way too well; this feeling of anticipation, unpredictability and fear. It was like walking on egg shells before another big blow up. Sometimes things were just fine and her husband was very loving and attentive to her. She did love that part of him so much and did not want to give up on their love. But when he was drinking, he became a different person. He became a monster that she feared. She knew that he often drank to a point that the next morning he would be oblivious to what he has done the previous night and blamed her for any damage, often denying that he played any role in it. She feared every pay day as that was the likely time that her husband went out drinking with his buddies and spent majority of their money. This would not be the first time that they would not have money for rent or for food. This would not be the first time that Michaela would have to ask her mother for financial help just to make it to the next pay day or promised his brother that he would get the money for rent.

Michaela's anxiety was building up even though she made sure that everything was perfect before Eddy came home. The supper was ready on the stove, the table was set, the apartment was neat and clean and Orchid was sound asleep for the night.

Michaela loved her daughter with all her heart and would do anything for her. Even when it meant putting up with Eddy's violent temper when he was drinking because she knew that he loved his daughter too and Orchid deserved a whole family. And little Orchid adored her daddy when he played with her and bought her toys. She wanted her to be happy, playful, untroubled little girl that she deserved to be. She has to make it work; she cannot give up on their love; on their marriage. That was the easy way out, she thought. Wasn't it? She did not want her daughter to come from a broken home like she lived in as a little girl.

Eddy did love his daughter, but at times he also made her feel scared and often made her cry, just like he made mommy cry. Little Orchid tried to stifle her cries the best that she could because even at a young age she already knew that daddy did not like when she cried and it made him very angry, but sometimes she could not help it. Nevertheless he would never hurt his little girl. She was his little flower; his little princess that he adored.

Michaela tried to distract herself by watching TV while waiting for her husband as she often did. This gave her some control to see him what state he was in when he came home. She tugged her legs under her, covering herself with a brown blanket that provided her with some warmth as she felt the chills go down her back when she thought of the worst possible situation. She was flipping channels mindlessly as nothing caught her attention; her mind wondering somewhere else. The long wait made her dose off waking up to a loud banging on the door and yelling. She quickly checked her watch; it was 12:37 a.m. and she immediately knew that it will be a tough night. She ran to open the door for Eddy before he woke little Orchid up as he was getting lauder, trying to get in. Michaela knew from being married to Eddy for four years that when he was drunk, it was best to be just quiet and hope she would not do anything to provoke him and that he would just go to bed to sleep it off and tomorrow would be a new day, a different Eddy. But she knew that Eddy never went to bed right away when he was drunk. In fact he would become aggressive, even violent and not remember anything the next day.

"Where the fuck are you?" Eddy yelled at her after she opened the door. He tumbled into the kitchen adjacent to Orchid's room and yelled at her.

"Woman, where is my fuckin' dinner?" Before Michaela had a chance to respond or give him a plate with his dinner, Eddy started pulling all the plates down from the cupboards starting with the bottom one, breaking everything he touched and making horrendous noise.

"No, not again. STOP, please, Eddy, stop, you'll wake Orchid up ....wait I'll give you your supper". It was too late; she quickly realized that mentioning their daughter's name at this point was a big mistake as he headed towards Orchid's room.

"Kid.....Kid!" He sometimes called his daughter 'Kid' for short as a derivative from her name, which Michaela despised but at the moment that was least of her worries.

"Where are you my little flower? Come to me. Daddy is home." Eddy was slurring his words and stumbling into his daughter's room. She needed to stop him before he opened the door and woke the little girl up. Although he never hurt Orchid, there was volatility of what he would do in his drunken state which he would normally not do when he was sober. Michaela instinctively and without lucidity grabbed an empty cooking pan that was sitting on the nearby stove and hit him over the head with it; not to hurt him but to stop him....she had to stop him for the sake of their daughter.

Much to her surprise, Eddy didn't fall to the ground after the impact. He shook his head briefly and turned his two hundred pounds body towards her physically unaffected by the impact but a lot angrier he lashed out for Michaela. She tried to run out of his way as he reached for her, but it was too late. He grabbed her by her long brown hair and dragged her towards the balcony. The cool November night sent chills down her spine as did Eddy's unpredictable reactions. Michaela was crying in pain, pleading for him to stop.

"I'm sorry, Eddy, please don't hurt me, please stop...." but Michaela's pleas were futile.

Instinctively she grabbed the curtain to hold on to as he dragged her over the threshold of the balcony grabbing her by her neck trying to push her over the fence. Luckily the metal curtain rod did not give in. Michaela's back was pressed against the railing. Half of her body was leaning over the balcony, her feet losing the ground from under her as Eddy was pressing her hard against the railing. She briefly looked down from the ten story building down to the concrete ground realizing her life hung on a thin line. Hanging with her head upside down she was sure if she fell there would be only a bloody mess left of her. She realized that the curtain that she was still clutching in her hands was her only chance of survival or maybe not. All of a sudden Michaela heard screams from her three year old daughter that distracted her father.

"Mommy………MOMMY!!!!! Orchid was screeching, terror in her face, big brown eyes staring in fear. Michaela was sure he would have throttled her to death if it was not for the sudden scream from the kitchen that quickly caught his attention. Eddy suddenly dropped Michaela down on the balcony floor like a little rag doll. Michaela holding her sore neck from the pressure of his fingers, trying to catch her breath and get to her feet, while Eddy turned his drunken awareness to their daughter walking back into the kitchen where Orchid was standing and crying uncontrollably. Wearing her pink pajamas with flowers in the middle of her top, she clutched her teddy bear to her chest, her little body shaking with fear. Even in her young age, she knew something was wrong. With her big brown eyes that she inherited after her father, she was watching his every move, mortified with fear as her father was fuming and walking towards her, bumping into the table and chairs. Eddy grabbed his daughter's small body with a force as she was screaming and in an instant Michaela realized that her worst nightmare has only begun.

The screaming ceased and for what seemed like an eternity there was a deafly silence. Orchid's lifeless body was lying on the floor after her father threw her against the wall. Eddy dropped to his knees beside his daughter and scooped her into his arms rocking her motionless body; he buried his face into her curly brown hair soaking them with his tears. Trickle of blood got on his shirt, but he could not see anything, he could not hear Michaela's loud screams when she realized what has happened. Everything seemed like in a slow motion. Nothing mattered anymore and everything ceased to exist. It was like in a nightmare except nobody could wake up from it.

The phone dropped to the ground from Michaela's hand with a loud thud on the kitchen floor after she called the police and ambulance giving her name and address not recognizing her own hoarse voice uttering what she never thought she would say, "Please hurry, I think he killed my daughter."

Chapter 27

"NO, NO. SHE IS NOT death. She can't be." Eddy yelled in desperation suddenly as if waking up from a drunken haze and at the realization what he has caused. "Oh, God what have I done? What have I done? My little Orchid. Wake up, princess, please wake up."

Michaela took Orchid's limp body from him as he was pulling at his hair in desperation now. She carefully looked for any wounds; she did not see any, but there was blood smeared up over her face. She checked for pulse on her neck realizing with relief that her daughter was still alive, but unconscious. Eddy disappeared from her sight shortly after she knelled down beside Orchid but it did not matter where he went or what he was doing. All her attention was on Orchid attempting CPR she had learned at school long time ago. During the pumps to her heart, she prayed and pleaded for the fragile life of her daughter alternating with mouth to mouth breathing.

"Stay with me, Orchid. Wake up baby. Mommy is here. It will be alright. Oh, please open your eyes." *Where is the ambulance when you need them?* She thought in desperation all the while she was attempting to safe her daughter's life. It seemed like an eternity before they arrived; although it only took about two and half minutes before she heard the sirens and another excruciating thirty seconds before they arrived bursting through the doors.

"She is alive. Please safe her, please help." Michaela pleaded with the paramedics who immediately set to work placing Orchid gently on the stretchers when she opened her lovely brown eyes.

"Mommy….." She stretched out her little hand when she saw her mommy standing nearby. Michaela grabbed the little hand as if she never wanted to let it go, grateful that Orchid woke up.

"I'm here, baby. I'm here." That's all she managed as her throat was closing down and she nearly passed out from her own injuries and from the overwhelming fear of nearly losing the most important person in her life, her daughter.

Michaela insisted going with her daughter in the ambulance and in fact she never let go of her hand, reassuring her she will be alright and that she will stay with her.

"Man trying to jump from the balcony." Someone called out, but it no longer mattered. Michaela did not stay to find out what was happening on the balcony; she followed the paramedics by her daughter's side and she made a promise to herself that she would never allow her daughter to get abused ever again. While Michaela was by Orchid's side in the hospital, Eddy was persuaded to climb back from the ledge of the balcony getting arrested for attempted murder.

Despite some reluctance and resistance at the hospital, Michaela eventually surrendered herself and her daughter to the medical professionals that insisted examining both of them. Michaela did not suffer serious injuries other than some redness on her neck that would likely develop into bruises from Eddy's fingers when he was chocking her. She had a large bruise forming on the lower part of her back where her husband pressed her hard against the balcony railing. Michaela tried to shake that memory away worrying about the well-being of her daughter instead whom she wanted to see as soon as possible. The nurse reassured her that the doctor will be with her soon with information about her child. Although Michaela was released from the hospital due to only minor injuries, she stayed at the hospital.

She was pacing the hospital hall of the second floor waiting for the news about Orchid's injuries. She could not stay still as if the senseless walking back and forth was easing her anxiety. She rapidly turned when she heard someone say her name. The man dressed in civil clothing did not look like a doctor and Michaela questioningly raised her eyebrows.

"Yes, that's me." She answered with hesitancy in her voice.

"I'm Detective Gottfried." He extended his hand to her which she accepted. She looked at him with expectancy in her eyes.

"I'd like you to come to the station with me to give your statement."

"I can't leave now, Detective Gott…"

"Gottfried." He reminded her.

"Look. As you may already know, my three year old daughter is in an intensive care suffering from some head trauma. You can't expect me to leave now. I'll be glad to come to the station to give my statement at a different time. Trust me; I would not miss that opportunity this time."

"I understand, Mrs. Verner. Do you mind if we sit down and I ask you few questions here, while you're waiting for the results?" He pulled out a small portable recorder looking up at her as he was already setting it up.

"Do you mind if I record it?"

"No. I have nothing to hide."

"Mrs. Verner, can you tell me what happened tonight?" Michaela gave him a detailed statement right at the hospital about the account of what has transpired in her home from the moment Eddy came home late at night.

"I understand that this was not the first domestic violence dispute." It was a statement rather than a question. "Mr. Verner has a previous charge. Correct?"

"Yes." He finished writing his notes then he stood up packing up his things.

"Thank you Mrs. Verner for you cooperation. I'll use this information you provided me with as your statement. Your husband is being charged with domestic assault against you and your daughter and bodily harm. If you remember anything else you can give me a call directly." He pulled out his business card from his shirt pocket and handed it to her.

"Wait." She suddenly thought of something. He turned back but did not sit down; he was looking at her with expectation.

"When I was leaving to the hospital with my daughter, I heard someone yelling 'man on the ledge on the balcony.' Can you tell me what happened?"

"It was a typical case of someone who is trying to avoid responsibility for his behavior, Mrs. Verner. Your husband tried to commit suicide although I don't think he would have jumped, but you never know. My men talked to him until he decided to come back over the railing. He knew he would be arrested."

When Detective Gottfried left, Michaela sat down trying to recapitulate all the events of the night unable to shake the thought that she nearly lost her only child because she failed to see an abusive relationship and she waited for the impact it had on her daughter, at least physically. She could not even imagine the psychological damage that it might have caused.

She jumped out of the seat startled when the doctor addressed her.

"We've completed a CT scan and MRI of the brain and luckily, she did not suffer any internal bleeding and there were no open wounds to the head or to the body; however, she suffered from a concussion."

"What does that mean? Will she be alright?"

"Concussion is a mild form of trauma to the brain. She suffers from severe headache so we have given her acetaminophen. She is currently sleeping but we will have to wake her up every two hours to assure she is alright by asking her simple questions such as her name. She may appear a little disoriented for a while. We certainly will keep her here for observation for few days."

"You said there were no open wounds to the head, but there was blood on her face."

"It was only a nose bleed which sometimes occurs during concussions as well as brief loss of consciousness. Mrs. Verner, you provided your daughter with CPR at a critical moment and you saved your daughter's life."

At that statement, Michaela collapsed to the seat behind her overwhelmed by the stress of the night and by the seriousness of the whole situation. 'You saved your daughter's life' was ringing in her ears.

"Are you alright?" The doctor asked her with concern on his face. She quickly regained her composure and stood up again.

"Yes, yes. I'm fine. Can I see her now?"

"Certainly, but she is sleeping now and you should get some rest too."

"I'd like to stay with her at least until she wakes up again." Michaela insisted and the doctor agreed and led her to Orchid's room.

It was four twenty in the morning and Orchid was sleeping on her back, her little body getting lost under the covers of the hospital bed. She was so small and fragile. Michaela could not believe that she nearly lost her today. At that moment she made a decision to leave her husband permanently and would fight for the sole custody of their daughter no matter what it took. He would not be allowed to stay alone with her again; she promised that to herself with determination. She decided to go back to Czechoslovakia as soon as Orchid was alright to travel and start all over again.

She pulled up a chair closer to the bed, holding Orchid's little hand in hers. Tiredness had overtaken her as she has not slept all night and she leaned her head beside Orchid's hand.

"Mommy……..mommy, where is my teddy bear?"

"Orchid, sweetheart. You're awake."

"Teddy."

"I'm sorry, it stayed at home, but I will bring it to you soon, ok?" Orchid nodded disappointed.

"How are you feeling?"

"My head hurts." She complained; Michaela gently stroked her cheek.

"I will tell the doctor. You will have to stay few days in the hospital, but you will be just fine." Michaela was not sure whether she tried to reassure her daughter or herself more. When the nurse walked in she asked.

"How is my little flower doing this early morning?" When Orchid just looked at her with confused look on her face, the nurse asked.

"What's your name, darling?" She looked at her mom who gave her a small nod.

"Orchid."

"Very well then, are you thirsty, Orchid?" She nodded.

"She still has a headache."

"I can give her another acetaminophen in another two hours." When Orchid fell asleep again, Michaela decided to go home for few hours to get her teddy bear and to catch few hours of sleep before she made her way back to the hospital for rest of the day.

Before she returned back to the hospital, she called her friend Juliane and summarized the accounts of the worst night of her life. With tears in her eyes, she was telling her friend.

"You were right; I shouldn't have come back to him. I don't know what I was thinking."

"You can't beat yourself up over this, Michaela. You did the best you could. I'm not surprised he sweet-talked you into staying as long as you did, but you are right; you have to look after your daughter."

"I need your advice, Juliane."

"Anything."

"You've been through divorce before. What's the next step of getting a divorce?"

"Are you sure about it?"

"I was never so sure in my life. I'm done with him; this time for good. I should have left long time ago. None of this would have happened." Juliane provided Michaela with some information and gave her a contact of her old divorce lawyer.

Week later just before Orchid was released from the hospital and Michaela signed the divorce papers submitting it to her lawyer to handle the rest who assured her that she will not have any problem getting sole custody of her daughter considering that her husband is in jail for domestic violence assault and bodily harm to her and of his daughter.

She packed up bare necessities and was ready to go back to her hometown once again just as she did once before, but this time with a new purpose and a new beginning that did not include Eddy in it. But before she left, she had one more thing to do. She took a deep breath, raised her chin high with clenched fists she entered the Dresden penitentiary to forever say goodbye to her soon to be ex-husband.

Chapter 28

S HE WAS STANDING IN FRONT of a see through non-breakable plexiglass when a guard walked Eddy to see his visitor. He was surprised
to see her there. He pointed to the black phone on her right. She sat down
while looking him straight in the eyes gaining back her power and control
of her life by coming here which gave her courage although her hand was
shaking as she picked up the receiver to speak to him.

"You're here…." He stated the obvious, feeling hopeful for a moment
which was quickly shattered for him when Michaela interrupted him with
new confidence and distant intonation in her voice.

"I'm leaving you Eddy; this time for good."

"NO, damn it. You can't leave me. I love you. Give me another chance,
Michaela."

"I gave you many chances, but what you did to Orchid is unforgivable.
I never thought you would hurt her but you did."

"I didn't mean to. I was drunk. I don't even remember hurting her.
You know I wouldn't hurt her on purpose."

"The fact that you don't even remember what you did is even more of
a reason I can't stay with you."

"Well, I'm her father, so what about my rights?"

"You violated your rights when you nearly killed her. But when you
get out and want to have any contact with your daughter, I'll make sure
it is only under supervision."

"You can't do that to me."

"It's not about you, Eddy. It is about what's best for Orchid." With
venom in his dark eyes that were so scary yet familiar, he curled up his
lips and uttered with hatred in his voice.

"Screw you and your daughter. I can have any other woman I want and have other kids. You think you were the only one?" He laughed but without any amusement. He wanted to hurt her. If he could not do it with his fists, he would do it with his words, but was surprised when Michaela showed lack of emotion about that new revelation.

"That doesn't matter anymore. I'm glad that both of us are in agreement to move on." She said sardonically although she did not expect the last blow of hurtful words from him, but was surprised she no longer had strong emotion about it. That just confirmed for her that she was ready to leave him. She simply no longer cared about that. "You will be hearing soon from my lawyer. I already signed the divorce papers."

She repositioned her purse on her left shoulder and was about to place the receiver back in its place standing up to leave, when Eddy hit the unbreakable plexiglass with his fist in fury yelling profanities at her. She jumped in a slit second from fear as she always did, but quickly recovered realizing he could not hurt her or Orchid anymore. She was no longer intimidated by his threats. She looked at him with confidence and determination in her face and in a calm voice yet irreverently said to him over the phone, her eyes never leaving his.

"By the way, your daughter suffered trauma to her brain, but she will be alright. Thank you for asking." That was more of a slap in his face than if she actually slapped him or said anything else because he never even asked about her. She then turned on her heel empowered and walked out of his life forever ignoring his pleas that turned into threats again as she walked away from him and couple of guards had to physically pull Eddy back to his cell.

Few days later, Michaela was sitting with Orchid in the Express train to Kosice. Looking out the window, Michaela replayed her last several years with Eddy ready to place a period behind all of that and start a new life with her daughter in her country. She knew it would be difficult not only as a single parent trying to create a new life for her and her daughter, but for Orchid to learn the Slovak language as Eddy did not want her speaking it at home because he did not understand it. Michaela was glad she had a mother where she could return to and she knew her mother would help her until she got back on her feet. She even considered going back to University to become a Psychologist. She has been through a lot and she wanted to help others and Psychology always appealed to her. Too bad that she could not help Eddy, but he never really wanted any help or took responsibility for his behavior. Despite the new challenges that awaited her, she felt she could finally breathe; she felt free and relieved. There was no tension, no fear, no anxiety about the unknown. Whatever awaited her now, she knew she could tackle with ease as the experiences with Eduard made her stronger.

"Mommy, where are we going?" Orchid interrupted her thoughts.

"We're going to see your grandma in Czechoslovakia. She has not seen you for a very, very long time."

"Oh. Is daddy there too?"

"No, honey, he is not." Orchid hugged her brown teddy bear closer to her body with a fear in her big brown eyes as she remembered what happened but did not say anything about it anymore. Michaela stroked her daughter's cheek gently sensing Orchid's unease.

"You don't have to be afraid ever again, Orchid. Mommy will keep you safe." The little girl looked up at her mom and gave her a slight smile and then she fell asleep to the rhythmic rocking of the train.

When Michaela arrived at her mother's apartment and rang the bell unannounced, her mother could not believe her eyes and exclaimed in excitement.

"Michaela, darling. What a wonderful surprise. And look at you Orchid! You are such a big girl already." She hugged the little girl who was looking at the older woman with her big brown eyes.

"You were this big when I last saw you." She lowered her hand beside Orchid to show how small she was when grandma last saw her, but the little girl did not remember that. Michaela was glad to be home with her mother; back in her country and mainly away from Eddy who caused so much heartache that it was beyond repair.

After all the excitement, greetings and hugs, Klaudia looked at her daughter's tired face and she suddenly knew.

"You're not here just visiting." It was more of a notice rather than a query.

"Orchid, sweetie, bathroom is that way, go and wash your hands with soap after the long trip." When she hopped away to the bathroom for a moment, Michaela said.

"I left him, mom, this time for good."

"What happened?"

"He hurt Orchid. He almost killed her. We'll talk later." Michaela stopped as her daughter ran back to her and she would not discuss it in front of her. She already had been through a lot and did not need to hear adult problems or be reminded of what happened, unless she brought it up. As she pulled two large suitcases behind her, all Michaela asked was.

"Can we stay here for a while?"

"Of course! You stay as long as you need to." Klaudia hugged her daughter and her granddaughter made her way into that embrace.

"Orchid, do you like cookies?" Grandma quickly changed the subject distracting the little girl. That was one of the few words that Orchid knew in Slovak but answered still in German language.

"How did you know that?" Orchid asked with surprise in her eyes. "I love cookies." Grandma quickly became her best friend whom Orchid grew to love. It did not matter that neither of them understood most of the things that were said, but somehow they found a way to communicate. Michaela was glad that her daughter would develop a positive relationship with her grandmother as she did not have much opportunity to do it before although Klaudia had visited them on three different occasions when they lived in Dresden, but certainly it was not enough for small Orchid to remember those times as she was very young.

When Orchid fell asleep for the night, Michaela sat down with her mother in the living room and told her everything that has happened. She told her not only the last crucial incident that made her decide to definitely leave her husband but she finally told her mother about the ongoing verbal, emotional and also physical abuse from Eddy from the beginning of their relationship. Her mother listened intently with horror in her eyes as she had no idea how difficult and abusive life her daughter had lived for the past four years.

"I should have seen the early signs." Michaela concluded with sadness and regret in her eyes.

"You couldn't have known, Mika."

"No, mom, there were signs but I was blinded by love. I ignored it or didn't take it seriously."

"It wasn't your fault." Klaudia tried to reassure her but Michaela thoughtfully continued in her scrutiny of her adult life.

"He was jealous from the beginning and he was isolating me from everyone even back in Bulgaria soon after I met him. It was so flattering back then that he wanted to spend his time only with me, but he actually did that to control me." She shook her head as she thought about it and continued in her scrutiny.

"Even Nikolas saw an aggressive side to him and tried to warn me but I ignored it or didn't want to believe it. Nikole didn't like him either although she couldn't say why. Aunt Sylvie, as much I hate to say it, was right and she warned me so many times. You don't even need a psychic to see that there were these red flags. Mom, how come I didn't see them?" Klaudia stroked her daughter's hair and said.

"I don't know, Mika. I didn't see them either. I wish I did. But then I don't have a good track record of good judgment in men either." Klaudia said with sadness in her voice.

"Anyway, it's over now. Eddy is in jail for quite some time and I have filed for divorce."

"You did the right thing. It's time to look forward and not cry over spilled milk. At least you have a beautiful little girl out of all that."

"Yes. That's the only positive thing that really came out of my marriage."

"And hopefully a life lesson."

"I hope so. I really hope so."

Michaela stayed at her mother's place even after she found a job at a doctor's office where she worked as a medical assistant. Meantime she applied to university to Psychology department.

Michaela started to get into a new routine and so did Orchid who started daycare and everyday learned in Slovak something new. Michaela was amazed how quickly she picked it up. Children always have a unique ability to communicate with one another even when they do not speak the same language.

Michaela also reconnected with her extended family and friends. Nikole in particular was excited to see her long last friend and going out to town shopping or for ice-cream felt just like the old times. Nikole moved back to town as she got a new job at a beauty salon and as they were walking through Kosice downtown, Michaela asked about her brother.

"How is Nikolas?"

"Why don't you ask him yourself? He lives in the same town again although he got a place on his own."

"He probably has someone and I don't want to disrupt his life." Nikole quickly volunteered the important information she believed her friend needed to know.

"He did, but I don't think he really loved her. He doesn't have anyone now and I don't think he ever got over you." Michaela looked at her friend with surprised expression on her face.

"How do you know that? Does he talk about me?"

"He doesn't have to. I know he still cares about you. He always gets this wishful look in his face whenever I talk about you. You should call him."

"I don't want to push myself on him. That's not my style."

"I think he would be very happy if he saw you again." But Michaela did not call Nikolas although she thought about him often, but did not want him to think that she called him only because she left Eddy. They have not been in touch since the birth of her daughter as she did not want Eddy to be even more jealous at that time but even though now she was free she did not want Nikolas to think that now he was good enough for her. So she decided to focus on her daughter and on getting her life back on track. She often hoped to meet him as he did not live far away from her now that she lived with her mother.

It would have been so easy to simply ask Nikole for his new number, that she would gladly give to her, but she resisted the temptation, although part of her was looking for him in every dark blond young man his size, but of course that was simply naïve. She told herself to just call him but her strong traditional upbringing and the belief that it was the man that had to make the first move was strongly ingrained in her. Michaela believed that Nikole would have mentioned to him that she had left Eddy and was back in town and rationalized it that he knew where to find her if he was interested. She did not even know what she was promising herself even if she saw him again. After so many years not seeing each other, he surely had moved on and found someone else. Michaela thought the feelings that he once had for her were long gone despite Nikole's encouragement to swallow her pride and meet up with him.

Nikole was getting frustrated with her friend and with her brother as both of them were stubborn and proud and both of them believed that the other would no longer be interested. Shortly before Christmas when Michaela was browsing stores in Kosice downtown hunting for the right presents for Orchid and when she least expected it, she heard her nickname from across the street. A bundled up man in a hat was waving to her and hurried towards her but in his clumsiness as he was crossing the road, he slipped on the old unused icy streetcar tracks that remained in the downtown even after the walking zone was put in place. She immediately recognized him and rushed over.

"Are you alright Nik?"

He fixed his winter hat that fell into his eyes trying get up as she passed him her hand, pulling her accidently down on the slippery road catching her in his arms while still sitting on the cold ground. Both of them laughed as Michaela knocked him backwards landing on top of him as he was already on the ground.

"It's good to see you, Mika although I didn't expect such a crushing welcome." He joked as Mika was trying to get up from his embrace unsuccessfully as the road was quite slippery and every time she tried to stand up she fell back on him. They both laughed which in the process did not help them get up any faster.

"I'm glad you're laughing with me, not at me."

"Hey, that's my line." Nik said with amusement in his voice.

"I just had a déjà vu. How are you Nik?"

"I think I'll be better once I get up." Nik finally scrambled to his feet, pulling Michaela up as well.

"It's really good to see you Nik." She handed him her hand so he could pull her up and they have embraced each other again as old friends that they were.

"I was hoping to bump into you." He said joyfully.

"You were? Why?"

"I wanted to see you."

"You knew I was back." It was a statement, not a question. "Why didn't you just call?"

"I should have, but I wasn't sure if you wanted to see me. I'm sorry about your marriage."

"I'm not. It should have ended long time ago. But at least I have Orchid."

"How is she? I haven't seen her since she was born. Little peanut", he remembered. "She must be so much bigger now."

"She is a beautiful little girl with big brown eyes and curly long hair. You have to visit us sometimes. You know that I'm at my mother's."

"I know and I'd love to. I thought about you and Orchid a lot. I'm glad you're back at home. Hey, let's go somewhere warmer for a cup of coffee where we can talk. There is a nice new restaurant with good coffee and wonderful crapes nearby."

"I like that. I like that very much." They walked arm in arm making sure they would not slip again and fall. The restaurant was only about a block away where they sat down and talked, laughed and remembered some good old times. They spent together several hours at the small restaurant getting some crapes with their coffee. Michaela gave up on the shopping idea that day; she wanted to spend it with Nikolas whom she has not seen for over three years. After she told him about her unsuccessful marriage with Eddy and how he recently hurt Orchid, Nikolas was angry not only at Eddy but he felt he should have done something to help her.

Michaela changed the conversation asking Nikolas about his life he had the last few years. He told her he finished the army conscript couple years ago and was studying Engineering at the Technical University in Kosice while also working part time on the weekends and some evenings to support himself as he moved out on his own.

"Being busy with school and work did not leave much time for a serious relationship." He concluded.

"That's quite impressive. I mean you studying and working at the same time. You were always such a hard worker and you have the smarts, so I'm not surprised that you got to go to University."

"Thanks. What about you? What are your plans now?"

"I don't know. I want to stay here because my family is here. I don't want to be far away from them anymore where I don't have anyone. I started to work at a doctor's office as a medical assistant, but I applied to the Paul Joseph Safarik University here in Kosice to the Psychology department for September."

"They'll be lucky to have you. I'm sure you'll get in."

"I hope so. Being through so much, psychology somehow intrigued me and I want to help others."

"You're intelligent and you have a good heart and I know you can do it."

"Thanks, Nik. That means a lot to me. You know, sometimes, I don't think I can do it, yet you always believed in me."

"I have and still do." He touched her hand gently with his warm hand and added. "I'm glad you're back."

"Me too." Their food arrived and they ate the sweet crapes in silence for a while when Michaela asked him.

"Tell me Nik. Did you know I would be in town today?"

"Well, maybe a little birdie told me."

"Nikole." She concluded without hesitation and he nodded confirming it.

"I was hoping it would not be so obvious that I really wanted to see you and I wanted to make it look like a coincidence. The truth is I really wanted to see you again."

"I'm glad. Well, do you want to bump into me tomorrow after work? We can go Christmas shopping together."

"I'll pick you up at five thirty and we can go out for dinner too." Nik said with a bright smile on his face showing his little dimples that Michaela barely noticed before.

From that day, they spent nearly every day together. Michaela wondered how he suddenly managed both school and work and still had time for her. When he had to work in the evening, he would still call her and talk to her at least over the phone.

Although they spent Christmas Eve with their own families, Nikolas dropped by her home in the afternoon and brought her a gold necklace with the initial 'M' and for little Orchid he brought a doll with long brown curly hair just like hers along with a fairy tale book. Michaela simply introduced him to Orchid as an old friend named Nikolas and Orchid instinctively warmed up to him from the beginning.

"Can I open the presents now?" She asked with curious and impatient expression on her face, clapping her little hands. Nikolas' German was a little rusty but he still remembered some basics from school which made it easier for Orchid to communicate with him. He looked at Michaela who gave him a small nod; then he turned again to Orchid and said.

"Yes, open it."

"Wow. The doll looks like me. I'll call her Orchid." She hugged the doll with excitement, then she tore up the gift wrap of the other present revealing the story book.

"I love stories. Will you read it to me, Nikolas?" And he did. Orchid sat beside him looking at the colourful pages hearing a story of the Red Riding Hood in the Slovak language. Nikolas spent the day with them, helping Michaela entertain Orchid and together they even ventured to make Christmas cookies by pressing the forms on the dough that Michaela was rolling making Orchid excited and happy that she could help with baking and decorating. They packed him some cookies and for his family whom he promised he would spend the Christmas Eve with. Michaela wished he could stay but she understood that his family also wanted to be with him on Christmas Eve and they would have other times to be together. She was happy that Orchid liked him from the beginning and they had a wonderful day together with a lot of laughter and fun. She could feel the real Christmas atmosphere after several years instead of feeling stress and tension.

The relationship between Nikolas and Michaela grew more serious and they naturally started dating. Shortly after Orchid's birthday, Michaela received the divorce papers and the sole custody of Orchid had been confirmed although she had to go to court in Germany on couple of occasions. For the first time, she finally felt free and happy.

By June she also received a letter of acceptance to the University and was very excited about it.

"I told you that you can do it." Nikolas told her sharing her excitement.

"It's only beginning. I haven't started yet."

"It will be a piece of cake for you. I know you can do it. The hardest part is to get in and you did it all on your own."

"I want to celebrate. I want to get away somewhere, Nik before I start school."

"Ok, where do you want to go?"

"I want to go hiking with you, just like we used to before, just the two of us. I miss that. You told me once about the Slovak Paradise you went to. I've never been there and I want to go."

"I've been hiking there before; it certainly is very beautiful. We can rent the cottage there, go hiking and at night we can make a camp fire and I can't wait to have you for myself for a weekend." He whispered to her the last part, but Orchid who overheard from the doorway part of their conversation and was intrigued and quickly asked.

"Can we really have a camp fire?" Nikolas turned to her with a bright smile.

"I promise we all go camping together this year at least once and we can make a camp fire and make smores."

"Wow, what's that?"

"It's roasted marshmallows."

"Mommy, please, please, can we go? I love smurfs, you know mommy, the marching mellows?" Orchid explained. They both laughed at Orchid's excitement and mispronunciation. She has been learning Slovak only for about seven months since they came to Czechoslovakia but she picked it up very quickly despite the difficult language and tongue twisters.

"How can you say 'no' to that?" Nikolas picked Orchid up in the air, making the little girl giggle and then he placed her onto his lap where she was quite comfortable giving him 'high fives' for their small conspiracy.

"Yeah, she can't say no, right Nikolas?"

"You two! You got me there. Alright, we'll go on an adventure."

"Let's go somewhere with Orchid first one weekend and the next we go hiking. She is too young for hikes at Slovak Paradise; not to mention dangerous."

"It's a deal."

Orchid jumped out from Nikolas' lap squealing with happiness she ran off to the other room returning in less than three minutes, interrupting the kiss between them.

"I have everything I need. We can go now." She exclaimed with enthusiasm which made them all laugh when her mother explored what Orchid had packed up.

"Let me see, teddy bear, your favourite story book and…..toilet paper? That must be Nik's school." She winked at him, remembering the old times. "Yes, yes I think that's everything." She smiled at her daughter, "but I will still have to pack up the 'less important things' we might need and we have to wait for the weekend."

Disappointed that she had to wait, Orchid dragged her little backpack behind her back to her room but quickly cheered up when Nikolas told her he would come soon to read from the story book he got for her for Christmas.

"You're spoiling us."

"Both of you deserve it and much more." He pulled her closer to him and kissed her again on her full lips. When she pulled away from him, she commented.

"I'm glad Orchid really likes you."

"Me too. She is like a daughter to me. Remember, I was there when she was born."

"Of course I remember. You were the only one who was there for me when I needed it the most."

"I only wish her mom liked me too." He winked at her smiling.

"She does." Michaela smiled back, sat down in Nikolas' lap just like Orchid did minutes before and returned his kisses.

Nikolas could not believe how their relationship was developing having all his dreams come true. He often thought that they never had a chance and that destiny was too cruel for them to be together. It took him a while to get over Michaela when she decided to marry Eduard and he wanted her to be happy even when it was not with him. But when he found out how badly Eddy abused her and her daughter; he was furious with him and with himself that he allowed it to happen. He hoped he would have the rest of his life to make it up to Michaela and to Orchid.

Chapter 29

AFTER A WONDERFUL WEEKEND THEY have spent under the tent at Alpinka after a magical children's train ride through the woods only fifteen kilometers out of town, roasting promised marshmallows, playing on the playground and going for small walks to admire the nature, Orchid was ecstatic and adored Nikolas who was often playing with her or carried her on his shoulders when her little legs got tired from walking. As they were sitting around the fire on Saturday night, Orchid asked her mom.

"Mommy, can Nikolas be my daddy now?" They both exchanged surprised looks over Orchid's head. Michaela picked up Orchid and sat her down on her lap to have a serious conversation with her four year old daughter.

"You like Nikolas a lot, don't you?" Orchid nodded her little head with excitement.

"Yes, he always plays with me and is nice to me and when he becomes my daddy then the old daddy can't hurt me or you anymore." Michaela was surprised how much her daughter remembered and how her little brain was trying to sort things out.

"Nobody will ever hurt you again, Orchid." She tried to reassure her daughter.

"But he will try to hurt you mommy; but if Nikolas saves you, he can't hurt us anymore." Michaela did not know what to say to that and she briefly looked at Nikolas for help. He stroked her curly hair gently and said.

"You don't have to worry, Orchid. Your mommy and I will make sure that you're safe." Supporting what Michaela just told her.

"But he is here."

"Who, sweetheart?"

"My daddy."

"No, Orchid. Daddy is far, far away." But Orchid got mad and jump off her mother's lap insisting.

"He is here!"

"No, sweetie, he is not."

"He is, he is, he is." She was yelling in frustration that the adults did not believe her. There was no point of arguing with a four year old and Michaela cradled her daughter in her arms calming her down with soothing words.

"Ok, sweetie, ok. Everything will be alright. Nobody will hurt you." When Orchid went to sleep, Michaela spoke to Nikolas almost in a whisper.

"Since her....accident, she is having quite a vivid imagination; seeing things that have not happened yet, but often they happen later. I worry, Nik....what if she is right?"

"You mean about Eddy being around? That's nonsense. Eddy is in jail in Germany, isn't he?"

"Yes, but....I don't know she sometimes says things that eventually happen. You know we have psychic abilities in the family and Aunt Sylvie told me once that sometimes trauma to the head can set off the psychic abilities even in young children if they have the gift in the first place, so I don't know what to think."

This time Nikolas pulled Michaela towards him reassuring her.

"I'm here for you and for Orchid and I be damned if I let anything happen to either of you." The camping weekend was uneventful leaving only a small uneasy residue of anxiety about Orchid's premonition. They all enjoyed the camping experience and Orchid did not mention her father again feeling happy and relaxed.

The following weekend just like they agreed, Michaela left her daughter at her mother's place to watch over her and she drove with Nikolas to south-east of Slovakia to the Slovak Paradise Friday afternoon to have a whole weekend to themselves for hiking and admiring the beauties of the Slovak mountain massif, mountain streams, caves and

Hornad River Canyon; one of the most amazing natural beauties of Slovakia.

They also planned to hike through the gorges in the picturesque site of Slovak Paradise National Park coming close to the waterfalls. Michaela has never been in Slovak Paradise; in fact she has not been anywhere for the past five years since Eddy has not taken her anywhere since her honeymoon in Dresden, so she was looking forward to seeing the natural beauty of her own country that she has only seen on the pictures.

Both of them loved hiking and were excited that they would get to do it again just like they did back in Romania years ago. Nikolas has hiked on different occasions through Slovak Paradise and was telling Michaela about what she could expect.

"It's not an ordinary hiking trail, Mika. River Hornad and many other streams have created deep gorges and valleys that we can hike through using wooden and metal ladders, bridges, metal footsteps and footbridges while we hold on to metal chains that are attached to the mountains at the wilder parts of the trails. The streams and valleys will be underneath us and the waterfalls will be so close that you will feel the mist of the water. I just hope you're not afraid of heights."

"I'll be fine, Nik as long as you're by my side." She smiled at him.

"I wouldn't want to be anywhere else, although I'll be mainly behind you looking at your buttocks when you climb the ladders, surely admiring the view." He laughed and she poked him into his arm for teasing her but she was in a good mood as Nikolas made her feel happy and safe.

"I'm really looking forward to it."

"So, we can start tomorrow morning that way we have whole day before it gets dark. Where would you like to go first?" Michaela was browsing through the tourist guide reading aloud about the Dry White Gorge, Big Falcon Gorge, Small Stoves Gorge and Monastery Gorge while Nikolas was driving. After careful review of each, she said.

"How about Dry White Gorge, Nik?"

"I think that sounds great. Whichever area you pick it will be amazing; not only because it's beautiful but because you're with me." She smiled at him for the compliment, then continued to explore the booklet.

"Well, it says it has the biggest waterfall and it is most frequently visited by tourists, so I think that would be a great start."

"So that's where we'll start tomorrow morning."

"Do you think I will manage the hike?"

"I don't doubt that."

"I haven't been hiking….well not since last time with you in Romania. Do you remember?"

"How could I forget? I thought about that time a lot and I was so mad at myself since then."

"Why?"

"I should have just kissed you then on the mountain before we got to the Bran Castle and I missed that opportunity. I should have told you how much I loved you before Eddy stole you from me." She could not argue that because it was the truth although she did not realize it at that time.

"And do you still….love me?" She asked with anticipation in her blue-green eyes that glittered in the sunset light when he briefly glanced at her then he looked back at the serpentine winding mountain road that led them up the hill around the mountain. He did not look at her as the serpentine was narrow and steep requiring the entire driver's attention, but he answered her question with gentleness in his voice.

"I never stopped loving you." He did not have to look at her again to know that she was smiling. She touched his hand; he took it and held it for a long time just as if he has done it all the time. They drove in silence for a while enjoying the moment when Michaela eventually interrupted it.

"When I can't move from the long hike tomorrow night, you'll give me massage." It was not a question; rather a request. The truth was she wanted to feel Nikolas' touch on her body that she up to this point has avoided and Nikolas did not pressure her. He respected her way too much to ruin it with his own desire before she was ready for it.

"It's a deal. You're lucky because I provide the best massages in the whole Slovak Paradise." He winked at her wiggling his fingers pretending to massage her.

"That sounds great. Can I get it tonight? I'm all broken up from the long ride." She tried to stretch up in the car.

"Anything you want."

"A bonfire too?"

"Bonfire too. You sound excited like little Orchid."

"I miss her. I wish she could come with us."

"We'll make it up to her. We can take her camping somewhere else again, but Slovak Paradise is really not for small children; it's just too dangerous. Promise me, Mika, that you will be very careful and no matter what, don't let go of the ladders or chains when we climb up and around the mountains. I don't want anything to happen to you. I would never forgive myself...."

"Don't worry, Nik, I will be careful. I'm not a little kid."

"I know that. I just remembered that I promised you long time ago that I would never let anything happen to you and I didn't keep my promise."

"What do you mean?"

"I didn't protect you from Eddy and let him hurt you and Orchid. That should have never happened."

"Nik, that was not your fault. You couldn't have known. If anything, you actually tried to warn me back in Bulgaria about Eddy's temper. You can't blame yourself for my mistakes. This was not your responsibility." She stroked his cheek lovingly. He caught her hand midair, brought it to his lips and kissed it. Michaela had no idea that Nikolas had blamed himself for her abusive relationship. She often regretted her decision and realized too late that she picked the wrong man back in Bulgaria; but perhaps now she got a second chance with Nikolas and their relationship looked very promising.

They arrived at the Cingov cottage in Slovak Paradise around seven o'clock in the evening. It was a cozy little wooden hut inside and out surrounded with charming forest nearby like from a fairytale. Outside of the cottage there was a wooden table and several benches where Nikolas started a bonfire as soon as they arrived just like he promised her. Inside the cottage was beautiful oak furniture, including the oak closet doors and even the top of the ceiling was matching the floor and rest of the furniture. The kitchen was small, but the living room had a wooden fireplace that would create romantic atmosphere or simply warm them up during chilly nights that were common in the mountain nights despite the summer.

There were several rooms in the cottage that were rented out to other tourists. Theirs was all the way on the second floor underneath a large triangular roof that gave the cozy little room a magical appeal.

When they went outside Nikolas found couple of wooden sticks that he perfected with his pocket knife and used it for the sausages he was preparing for supper. Michaela cut up some tomatoes and cubanelle peppers and took out the paper plates and bread along with mustard to go with the sausages that they have brought from home.

"This is nice." She said when she sat down beside him on a wooden bench that was close to the bonfire and snuggled her arm underneath Nikolas' to be closer to him.

"Are you cold?"

"No. You always keep me warm." He looked at her lovingly and pulled her closer to him and kissed her softly on her lips.

"Oh, watch out, you will burn it." The sausage caught on fire, but Nikolas skillfully blew it out quickly before it all burned.

When it got completely dark, suddenly it appeared to Michaela that the forest was full of creaking noises and sounds.

"What was that?"

"What was what?"

"That sound! Did you hear it?"

"It's just a fox or a bear, but don't worry, they're scared of fire."

"Are you serious?" Michaela got to her feet looking around with her big eyes.

"That they are scared of fire?"

"NO, that there are wild animals around."

"Of course there are wild animals around. We're in the middle of the forest." He said it with seriousness in his voice convincing Michaela of the natures' dangerous, but when he saw her spooked out face, he said.

"Sit down scary cat. I'm just teasing you. The wild life lives much deeper in the woods and they usually don't venture to the village or cottages."

"Oh. Usually?" Michaela sat down with hesitancy but Nikolas always liked teasing her since they were little kids and could not help doing it now.

"Of course, unless they're hungry, they might risk coming down here, but that's just in the winter months and even that is very rare." Nikolas was toasting marshmallows in a relaxed manner as he was explaining it to her when Michaela heard louder sounds behind them.

"Stop teasing me, Nik this is not funny." She said although she giggled when she saw Nikolas chuckling under his nose. She teasingly pushed him nearly knocking him off the bench; then she wrapped a blanket around her shoulders looking into the fire.

"Boo boo boo."

"Just keep teasing me Nik, but you're the one with the sausage in your hand, so I'm sure the bear or other wild animal will get you first." They both laughed.

"I think the wild life has plenty to eat in the deep woods during the summer rather than wanting my burnt sausages, so I'm sure we're safe here but if you are afraid of the squirrels and owls, we can go inside." They have heard another creaking of a branch that made Michaela turn quickly, her large eyes looking for the possible danger in the darkness despite the jokes. Another couple joined them by the bonfire although she thought she also heard a creaking sound of branches from another side closer to the woods.

The couple greeted them, but kept to themselves on the other side disrupting the playful atmosphere although she still could not shake away an uneasy feeling about the unknown predators. Nikolas sensing her restlessness whispered to her.

"If you want, we can go inside, although you do have a brave knight sitting beside you and willing to sacrifice his life for you." Even though he was joking in that moment, somehow she knew that with him she was safe as he would protect her giving up even his own life if he had to safe her. She smiled at him and did not object, still turning from left to right as she could not shake an unsettling feeling as they walked inside the cottage.

Michaela stood by the small window of their room looking into the darkness while only a small light was illuminating the room from a small night lamp. It was too dark to see anything outside only dark jumping shadows that appeared to play in front of her eyes, playing tricks on her in the outside moonlight. They could hear other tourists coming to the cottage at this hour. When Nikolas came out of the bathroom, not intending to frighten her but Michaela's mind was wondering somewhere else and she was easily startled when he appeared beside her.

"What are you doing? Looking for bears and other animals?"

"I don't know. I think my mind is playing tricks on me and I start to believe I saw some shadow of someone out there looking towards the cottage, but it's too dark and I'm probably just tired and frightened for no reason at all."

"You don't have to be scared. I'm here with you. And besides, it's probably the other visitors renting this cottage that just arrived that you have seen."

"You're probably right." She said although the window faced the forest where there was only darkness and the visitors would not likely wonder back near the woods at night. She shook those disturbing thoughts away and turned to Nikolas.

"I always feel so safe with you, Nik." She leaned against his chest as he wrapped his hands around her protectively.

"I'm sorry you've been through so much. Maybe we shouldn't have come here." He became suddenly serious. "I know I've been teasing you all evening but I don't want you to be scared. If you want, we can go back home right now or first thing in the morning if you don't like it here."

"NO, no. Don't be silly. I'm fine and the place is wonderful. I can barely wait for tomorrow's hike. I'm just a scary cat, like you said. I've been looking forward to spending the weekend alone with you. I don't want to spoil it." She kissed him passionately and he returned her kisses. They have made love that night for the first time in this small cozy room and Michaela realized that she has always loved him. Nikolas was gentle with her, not rushing her and letting her lead.

"I love you Mika, so much. I always have." He embraced her holding her in his arms.

"I love you too, Nik. And I think I always did, but I just realized it." She whispered in his ear quietly falling asleep in his arms.

After a hearty breakfast they started their hike towards the Dry White Gorge trail in Slovak Paradise which was really a paradise in its true sense. The fog was unusually thick that morning, but Nikolas believed that by the time they reached the trail it would lift up. One of the reasons why he picked out the Cingov cottage was that they could walk directly to the trail of Dry White Gorge or Hornad River Canyon.

They started on the trail quite early in the morning as Nikolas told her that during the summer there are often traffic jams at the metal and wooden ladders especially at the Dry White Gorge because it was so popular and frequently visited place by tourists and they wanted to avoid the crowds. The view on their path was breathtaking, unlike anything that Michaela has ever seen. Nikolas carried a larger backpack, while Michaela had the smaller one as he did not want her to be burdened with heavy things and just wanted her to enjoy the hike. They have climbed wooden ladders horizontally along the streams right under their feet, where they saw the white limestone pebbles. They were holding on to the metal chains attached to the cliffs and mountains in certain parts of the trail. The air was refreshing and invigorating. Nikolas was always behind couple of steps walking or climbing behind Michaela. Before they started their steep climb around the picturesque Dish Waterfalls Cascade alongside the biggest waterfall in Slovak Paradise on metal ladders, Nikolas warned her.

"No matter what, just hold on tight, keep climbing and don't look down." Michaela nodded, looked up what seemed to be an insurmountable climb but with the ladders it should be a breeze she thought and daringly started climbing up. Nikolas as always followed closely behind Michaela watching over her. Half way, Michaela stopped on the ladder and made the mistake to look below admiring the waterfall and the breathtaking view below her, catching her breath. Nikolas was right, the fog started slowly to dissipate in most parts shortly after they reached the trail. Her gaze fell on the lower section of the hike on some other tourist when her foot suddenly slid on the damp metal bar scaring both her and Nikolas who caught her leg and carefully placed her foot back on the nearest metal step.

"Are you alright?" He called to her through the deafening waterfall that was nearby. "I'm sorry; my foot slipped, but I'm fine."

"Please be careful, Mika."

Her heart was pounding hard in her chest and her breathing became heavy with overwhelming panic and fear although she was not sure whether it was because of the slight slip of her foot or what she thought she just saw.

Chapter 30

WHEN BOTH OF THEM FINISHED climbing that section of the mountain and sat down on the ground, safely away from the ladder, Nikolas again checked in with Michaela who was visibly shaking.

"I'm so sorry, Mika. I should not have brought you here. I should have known this climb might be too much for you. You gave me a scare."

"I got scared too, but it's not the climb that scared me, Nik."

"What is it then?" She took a deep breath and then went on.

"You'll think I'm crazy, Nik, but I think I saw Eddy."

"You said he was in jail in Dresden."

"I know. I told you it's crazy. Yes. He is in jail; as far as I know. Maybe I just keep seeing him in every tall, broad shouldered guy with dark curly hair. Or maybe I'm getting crazy because this is not the first time I thought I saw a glimpse of him." Nikolas was listening to her intently with concern on his face holding her hands in his as she spoke in a shaky voice.

"I thought I saw someone that looked like him in the Dobsina Ice Cave that we stopped at yesterday before we came to the Cottage. And last night, when I was spooked about the noises, I thought I saw a shadow near the woods, but it was too dark and it could have been anyone from the other tourists from the cottage. But then again this morning at the cottage, as we were leaving, I saw a big guy from behind that reminded me of Eddy's figure and the way he walked, but he wore a hoodie over his head so I don't actually know what he looked like. I keep seeing shadows or distant figures around that remind me of him, Nik. You must think I'm crazy." She finally concluded when Nikolas did not interrupt her. When he finally spoke, he said.

"No Mika, I don't think you're crazy at all, but I think you've been through a lot of trauma when it comes to Eddy and I'm not surprised that anything that reminds you of him would scare you or trigger you."

"You're probably right. Well, let's look at it logically; he is in jail for what he did to Orchid and even if he was out, how would he know where I'm. Right?" Nikolas nodded his agreement and commented.

"Look, we're somewhere in the middle of the trail. We can't climb down because it would be too dangerous, not only for us to do but for any other tourists that might be behind us on the ladders, climbing up. So we have to keep going now until we finish this trail. But after that, I understand if you want to go home earlier than planned. It's up to you."

"No, I told you yesterday; I don't want to ruin our weekend just because I carry a chip on my shoulder. There are still so many other places here that I want to see. I want to be here with you and I absolutely love it here. Look around; look at that gorgeous waterfall. Where else can we get so close to waterfalls? Let's go." She stood up with energy and pulled Nikolas by his hands to stand up to continue on their hike.

She started climbing on another vertical metal ladder with new determination; Nikolas was following her when suddenly she heard a painful sound below her. When she looked down she saw Nikolas hanging only by one hand holding onto the metal bar, fighting for his life trying to find his footing. With terror in her eyes she screamed.

"Nikolas, oh, God."

Still standing on the vertical ladder, she attempted to climb down to help him. When Nikolas saw her climbing downwards, he yelled up to her in Slovak.

"No, go up. HE is HERE." She did not need explanations about who was here or what he meant by it. She knew right away, Nik was talking about Eddy. When she leaned to the side she saw top of Eddy's curly head trying to grab Nikolas' legs and pull him down. Nikolas was able to grab with his other hand the side chain that was attached to the left side of the mountain and pulled himself up finding a metal bar under his feet, but Eddy did not give up and climbed up closer behind Nikolas grabbing him by his backpack that made Nikolas lose his balance again nearly sending him flying down. Eddy was still holding on to his backpack and the two struggled on the metal ladder. Nikolas was trying to regain his footing and balance and Eddy tried to pull him down to the rocky mountain side. Nikolas let go off the railing with his left hand briefly to free his left shoulder from the backpack that was pulling him down to the ground with Eddy's weight.

"Nik." Michaela screamed in panic when she saw Nikolas holding himself only by one hand again. As she looked down, her eyes met Eddy's dark stare that she knew so well. It was the look that he got just before he used to hit her; just before he used to hurt her; the look that he got in his cold and hard eyes that could end with a murder. She had to warn Nikolas; he did not know what Eddy was capable of doing and she yelled out to Nik in Slovak.

"Let go of the backpack or he'll kill you." Her words were getting lost in the noise of the waterfall but it was as if Eddy had heard and understood her. Still holding her gaze, he let go of the railing with his left hand, grabbing Nikolas' backpack now with both hands, yanking on it trying to have Nikolas fall. When he did not succeed, he mouthed something while still looking at terrified ex-wife who was frozen on the ladder and then he purposefully pushed himself off the ladder with his legs now dangling in the air putting all his weight on Nikolas whose hands started to slip from the damp bars. Nikolas' backpack was still hanging partly on his right shoulder sliding down his arm and putting a tremendous weight of his opponent whom he did not want to let fall into his death; albeit he deserved it for attempting to kill him. They struggled like that for few minutes. Nikolas yelled down to Eddy in German to grab on to the metal bars and find his footing otherwise they would both fall down. But Eddy ignored it as it was his intention to pull Nikolas down with him into their death. If Michaela did not want him anymore, she would not have Nikolas either and that would be Eddy's revenge. She should have known, Eddy thought; he told her often enough he could not live without her.

Nikolas' hands were slipping and he was not sure how long he would be able to hold on to the backpack with all its weight that was cutting into his right arm. His left hand was slipping on the wet bar and he quickly grabbed on to the ladder with both of his hands putting more pressure on his arm creating a bloody wound due to Eddy's two hundred pound body that was still hanging by the backpack when he heard a rip of the thin polyester material. Nikolas heard a loud scream and simultaneously the pressure along with his backpack disappeared below him swallowing Eddy up in the remaining fog below them. Nikolas regained his balance and a firm grip on the metal ladder preventing him from falling.

"Mika, get help; he fell down. I'm going to climb down to find him. He might be still alive." Nikolas called out to her.

"NO, Nik. Just climb up."

"Mika, please, just follow the green stripes along the way, they will get you to the forest path and then to the village."

"It's too dangerous. Please come up." She cried in desperation. "If he fell, he is probably dead and if he is alive, he will try to kill you again."

But he could no longer hear her as he was descending into the cloud of fog and her voice got lost in the rumble of the waterfall. Nikolas started his decline on the ladder which was dangerous because he could not see anything in the thick miasma and it was more physically challenging as he could not see where he was stepping.

"Eddy?" He called out when he descended one of the ladders looking through the mist of whiteness that surrounded him. He did not know if there were any tourists below him and he did not want to cause another accident, so he called out.

"Is anyone down there?" He called out several times but there was no response. The fog in the lower parts of the trail was still quite thick and overwhelming and despite his attempt to find him, Nikolas eventually gave up looking for Eddy who could have fallen anywhere in the rocky mountain or into the waterfall. He started to climb up and caught up with Michaela who was now sitting on the mountaintop by the ladder; she was crying in desperation. When she noticed him, she quickly stood up and embraced him; her heart pounding with relief that he was alive.

"I'm sorry, Mika, I couldn't find him. It's still too foggy in the lower parts and dangerous to keep going down. You can't see anything and he is not answering."

"I was so worried that something has happened to you."

"I'm fine, but I don't think Eddy was as lucky. I'm really sorry…."

"Nik, HE tried to kill YOU. I saw what he did. He tried to pull you down with him and he didn't care if he died. He just did not want you to have me or for me to be happy with someone else. He was always jealous, especially of you."

"How do you know that?"

"I know how he thinks. I've lived with him way too long."

"We better get someone to look for him. He might be still alive but hurt somewhere."

Michaela noticed a dark spot on his flannel shirt.

"You're bleeding, Nik."

"It's not as bad as it looks." He said in a husky voice that he barely recognized and pushed through the pain, but the climbing was becoming more difficult for him as he lost a lot of blood and was becoming weaker.

"Here, drink some water." She offered him from her backpack along with some food to give him strength.

They were glad when the gorge ended in the green forest with a winding path that was easier to walk on and they did not need to climb anymore ladders, but instead of admiring the beauty of this place, Michaela had to support Nik who was getting weak and needed to rest.

"Leave me here, Mika and get some help. I can't go on."

"You have to, Nik. I'm not leaving you here alone. You managed to climb up and down and up again on the slippery ladders; barely hanging on and now you can't walk on a straight forest path? Don't be a baby. Have some more water. We rest a little and then we continue together. You can lean on me with your other arm for support, but you're not staying here by yourself in this state."

"I didn't know you could be so bossy." He tried to joke revealing his small dimples that she came to love so much. She examined the wound and wrapped it with her tank top she had under her shirt to stop the blood flow above the wound preventing it from further bleeding. She noticed Nikolas' smirk when she took her shirt and the tank top off.

"You're an injured man, so don't get any ideas." She warned him jokingly although the situation was quite serious and Nikolas was in a lot of pain, he still enjoyed looking at Michaela's beautiful body that he explored last night. Joking was how both of them coped; they tried to make light of the situation to keep going. With her help, Nikolas stood up with the last of his strength that he had left and they walked on the forest path what seemed to be an insuperable task.

"According to the map we should arrive at the village soon and there we get help." Michaela reassured Nik who seemed very pale.

It took them another half an hour before they came to Cingov village and reported at the police station what has occurred.

As much as Michaela did not want their weekend to be ruined; it was due to the unexpected events of the accident, if that could even be called that way. Nikolas' wound also prevented him from going for more hikes as he had a lot of pain in his arm and even if he was not injured neither of them felt like hiking or celebrating their new relationship considering that the sheriff and his men have not found anything but repeatedly questioned them. Finally Sheriff Rubosky concluded.

"My men searched for the past two days and they haven't found anything. There is no body."

"But that's impossible." Michaela objected.

"I'm not disputing it completely. There are parts that have not been explored but they are not accessible and I'm not going to risk anyone's life looking for something that might not be there."

Eddy was declared missing and it was up to Michaela to notify his family which was not an easy task.

Eddy's mother blamed Michaela for whatever happened to her son.

"I knew you were bad news the first time I've met you. Now you killed my son."

"I didn't kill him. We don't even know if he is dead." Michaela tried a poor defense that did not faze her ex mother-in-law.

"All my son did was love you."

"No. Having power and control over me is not love. All he did was abuse me and eventually he seriously hurt Orchid too. You seemed to forget what he did to his daughter; your granddaughter who nearly died in the hospital because your son can't control his anger and his drinking." Michaela was outraged. On one hand she understood Eleonore as a mother who might have lost her son, but she could not stand her making excuses for his abusive behaviour.

"You suddenly have a big mouth on you, young lady. If you just listened to Eddy what he told you to do instead of leaving him; none of this would have happened. I don't have to listen to that." And she hung up the phone. Eleonore did not once ask about her granddaughter how she was doing and she did not show much interest of seeing her. There was so much blame and animosity that Michaela did not want to expose her daughter to that. Besides she was afraid in case Eddy was alive and well somewhere that he would kidnap Orchid. For the first time since Orchid was born she was able to shake her guilty feeling about not putting her father's name on her birth certificate.

Eleonore has not contacted Michaela once to even ask about her grandchild and Michaela withdrew all her contact with Eddy's family; not only because of the distance but because her determination to protect her daughter from further trauma. She did not want her daughter to be surrounded with negativity and hatred that Eddy's family was feeling towards her.

After several months have passed, Michaela started to relax and she genuinely felt happy again. Her relationship with Nikolas grew stronger and she started to learn what real love felt like. Love should not hurt like it did with Eddy. They have been through a lot and both deserved some peace and happiness and especially Orchid considering what she had been through. Michaela could not stand the thought of losing Nikolas and thought how close she came in the Slovak Paradise. Nikolas was good to them and her daughter started to call him 'daddy' and Michaela did not correct her. She confided in Nikolas that she did not put Eduard as her father on the birth certificate due to his abuse as she was not sure whether that would be a good idea even at that time. They talked even about Nikolas wanting to adopt Orchid who already considered him her father as he was there for her and loved her as his own daughter. Michaela moved in with Nikolas along with Orchid and they became a real family.

Michaela was getting Orchid ready for her fifth birthday party. Nikolas arranged a private magician to arrive at their home for Orchid's birthday. Orchid was excited to see a real magician especially since she knew about the big surprise that Nikolas was preparing. Towards the end of the Magic show, the magician picked Michaela as the volunteer for his next magic trick where she was to see inside a large hat which was initially empty or so it appeared. The magician covered the black hat with a handkerchief, waved his magic wand above it and when he uncovered it he asked Michaela to reach in. She pulled out a small box that had a beautiful diamond ring inside and simultaneously as she opened the box realizing what was inside, she heard Nikolas beside her say "Will you marry me?" Without much hesitation, Michaela turned to Nikolas with tears of happiness in her eyes and she whispered.

"Yes. Yes, I will." She hugged him and Orchid was clapping her little hands in excitement. After a moment of surprise, Michaela looked at her daughter who was jumping up and down still clapping her little hands in happiness, she asked Orchid.

"You knew about it?" Orchid nodded her curly head and ran towards both her mom and Nikolas to give them a big hug. Orchid was fond of Nikolas and wanted him to be with her and her mommy saying as Nikolas picked her up into his arms embracing both of them.

"This is the best birthday present ever." She said excitedly.

"And now for the finale...." The magician interrupted the special moment. "....Abraca Dabra.....an orchid for a little Orchid." The magician exclaimed and pulled out of his hat a purple Dendroc-Dy orchid just the kind Michaela wore in her hair on her wedding day with Eddy. The magician handed it to the little girl, who was smiling at him looking surprised at the sight of the beautiful flower in front of her. Michaela looked at Nikolas in confusion asking him in a whispered voice if it was from him but he shook his head with concern in his face letting her know that the orchid was not part of his plan.

1. Heise, L., Ellsberg, M. and M. Gottemoeller. _Ending Violence Against Women._ Population Reports, Series L, No. 11. Baltimore, Johns Hopkins University School of Public Health, Population Information Program, December 1999.
2. Gazmararian JA, Petersen R, Spitz AM, Goodwin MM, Saltzman LE, Marks JS. "Violence and reproductive health; current knowledge and future research directions." _Maternal and Child Health Journal_ 2000;4(2):79-84.
3. Murray A. Straus and Richard J. Gelles, _Physical Violence in American Families,_ 1990.

CPSIA information can be obtained at www.ICGtesting.com
Printed in the USA
BVOW03s0200160414

350745BV00001B/4/P